THE
GOOD GUY'S
GUIDE TO
GETTING
THE GIRL

Also by Peter Jones
How To Do Everything And Be Happy
Harper Collins / Audible

How To Eat Loads And Stay Slim
co-authored with Della Galton
soundhaven books / Audible

From Invisible To Irresistible
soundhaven books / Audible

How To Start Dating And Stop Waiting
soundhaven books / Audible

THE
GOOD GUY'S
GUIDE TO
GETTING
THE GIRL

PETER JONES

soundhaven books

Published 2015 in Great Britain,
by soundhaven books (soundhaven.com limited)
http://www.soundhaven.com

First published in 2014

Please visit
www.soundhaven.com
for contact details

ISBN: 978-0-9568856-7-8

British Cataloguing Publication data:
A catalogue record of this book is available from
the British Library

This book is also available as an ebook.
Please visit
www.soundhaven.com
for more details.

To Kate,
for giving me the impetus I needed
to start writing this book.

And to Della,
for giving me the courage to finish it.

Much love,

Peter

To Yvonne
Many thanks
Best wishes.
RC"
+

ABOUT THE AUTHOR

Peter Jones started professional life as a particularly rubbish graphic designer, followed by a stint as a mediocre petrol pump attendant. After that he got embroiled in the murky world of credit card banking. Fun times.

Now, Peter spends his days – most of them, anyway – writing. "The Good Guy's Guide to Getting The Girl" is his début novel. It wasn't a 'historical' romance when he started out. It just took that long to write. The sequel (snappily entitled "The Good Guy's Guide To *Keeping* The Girl") is currently sitting on his desk waiting to be edited. Occasionally it seems to wink.

He is also the author of three and a half popular self-help books on the subjects of happiness, staying slim and dating. If you're overweight, lonely, or unhappy – he's your guy.

Peter doesn't own a large departmental store and probably isn't the same guy you've seen on the TV show *Dragons' Den*. You can find out more about Peter Jones, his books, speaking engagements, and other author malarkey at: www.peterjonesauthor.com

CHAPTER ONE
BOXING DAY, 1997

Liz. Where do I start? I suppose the end is as good a place as any.

Despite that dreadful first date – sitting in a near-empty pub, trying to conjure sparks of conversation out of the void between us – I clung to the possibility that behind that cold, hard exterior was a warm heart, a sensitive soul, and someone whose yin was a close match to my less than melodic yang.

I was wrong, of course.

Liz was not the girl I'd hoped she would be. Any fantasies I'd had of 'romantic happy ever afters' soon gave way to a cast-iron certainty that I never, ever, wanted to see this girl again. And three years later I finally got around to telling her.

On Christmas Day.

Yesterday.

Right after she'd proposed marriage.

I hung my head in shame, and tried hard to blend into the background. But The Tulip, with its garish Christmas decorations, antler-wearing bar staff, and '*Now That's What I Call Christmas*' thumping out of the juke box, was really only adequate cover if you were a high-spirited festive drinker. Right now I was struggling to look like a drinker, let alone high-spirited or festive. I hadn't touched my pint. It was as lonely and dejected as me. Which made it all the more annoying when a chubby hand appeared and swept it away.

"This mine?" asked Alex. He drained two thirds, wiped his mouth with the back of his hand, let out a satisfied belch, then sat down next to me. "Where's yours?" he asked, after a moment or two. I stared at a fleck of melting snow caught in the stubble on his face and the pathetic strands of damp blond hair glued to a forehead that had once sported an impressive quiff.

"That was mine!" I said.

"You only bought your own?" asked Alex. "You selfish bastard."

"I didn't know how long you'd be, did I! Happy bloody Christmas."

"Yeah," said Alex, "you too." He glanced in the barmaid's direction and gave her a nod to indicate that one of us required another beer. "Look – can't stay long. Mum's serving lunch in half an hour. I only managed to sneak out by volunteering to walk her dog. Poor sod's tied up outside. Weren't you supposed to be spending the day with Liz's grandmother?"

I let out a long, tortured sigh.

Alex stared at the side of my head. "What? Did she die or something?"

"We broke up."

"You and Liz's grandmother?"

"Me and Liz!"

"Oh right," said Alex, nodding sagely. "Yeah, that can happen. Christmas gets them all worked up. Really brings out the bitch. Don't worry about it," he said. "By the time you get home she'll be standing on your doorstep, dressed in nothing but a raincoat, holding a four-pack of beers..."

He tailed off and stared into the distance, still holding the pint glass in front of him. I let out a single, humourless laugh as I massaged my eyes with my palms.

"Now you know that isn't Liz," I said. Alex frowned, then let out an exaggerated sigh.

"Ok," he said. "I give in. What the hell happened?"

We'd just left my parents. The first few flakes of snow had started to fall. As I drove, eyes fixed ahead, Liz broke the silence.

"Jason," she said. "I think we should get married." Then, when I didn't react in any way, she added: "Or break up."

Alex's frown deepened.

"So?" he asked. "What did you say?"

I blinked. "You know what I said."

"No I don't," said Alex.

"Well, you can probably guess!"

"Let's assume," said Alex, "that I can't."

I said nothing. Not immediately. Not until I realised that this was it. This was the moment I'd been waiting for, the past three years.

"Then we should break up," I said.

The rest of the journey felt like a bad dream. I clung to the steering wheel and stared forward, mesmerised by the way the flakes swarmed in huge silent clumps, before they rushed at the windscreen. Rushed at me. Occasionally I stole a glance at Liz, sitting there with a hand to her mouth, her sleek jet black hair shielding the side of her face. Every now and then her body jolted and shook as if someone in the waking world was using a defibrillator to bring her back from this nightmare.

And when we finally got to her place, I switched off the engine and we sat outside for what seemed like a lifetime.

"Want to come in?" she asked eventually. Just as she had done a million times before.

"No," I said. "No, I think I ought to make a move."

"Jason Smith!" said Liz, still facing forwards but raising a good inch and a half in her seat. "I believe you owe me an explanation!" I said nothing for a moment whilst I considered what to do next.

"Ok then," I said eventually.

"Fine!" said Liz, getting out of the car and slamming the passenger door behind her. I watched as she marched up to the communal entrance of her flat and started attacking the door with her key. Then I put my hands back on the wheel and took a dozen deep breaths.

"You didn't go in?" asked Alex. I waited for a moment or two whilst the barmaid put two fresh pints before us. Alex dug around in his pocket for some change, and whilst he did so I handed her a five pound note.

"Of course I went in," I said, once the barmaid had returned to the till.

"Are you mad?"

"What was I supposed to do?"

"Drive home!"

"She'd have only phoned!"

"Unplug it!"

"Or come over!"

"Change the locks!"

"In the middle of the night? On Christmas Day?"

Alex raised a finger, but when no further words of wisdom were forthcoming, he lowered it, picked up his pint, and brought it to his lips.

By the time I'd removed my coat and hung it on my allocated hook, Liz was in the kitchen. And for the first time in months, possibly years, I took a good look at my now ex-girlfriend.

She was wearing one of my sweaters. And though it was gigantic on her petite frame, it looked good on her. Certainly better than it did on me, although any hint of a bosom was lost within its deep woollen folds. Still, I liked the way her hair fell long and straight to the centre of her back, and though I'd long since given up on seeing her in some sort of skirt or dress, those skinny jeans were very flattering. I could almost fancy her if she wasn't – well, if she wasn't Liz.

In many ways she was a woman out of time. Forced to live in a century which required her to at least acknowledge some sort of feminine side. In another era she'd have been commanding armies of bloodthirsty, muscle-bound warriors. Crushing her enemies. Bending whole nations to her will. Expanding her empire. But here there were no nations to conquer. No empire. Only me.

I glanced into the lounge. If I went in and waited for her to come and find me I could put off the inevitable for at least another minute or so. Then I saw the two-seater sofa and thought better of it. Rock hard cushions stuffed to within breaking point, upholstered in the textile equivalent of sandpaper. If doilies had been in fashion there'd have been doilies.

"So, that's it then?" she asked, as I walked into the kitchen.

"What do you want me to say?" I asked. She stopped what she was doing and turned to face me, one hand perched high on her hip, the other gripping the edge of the kitchen worktop like she might break off a chunk and use it as a blunt instrument.

"I want to know why you want to break up!" It hadn't occurred to me that this was something I still 'wanted' – I'd assumed the deal was done.

"You gave me a choice," I said.

"But you didn't even have to think about it," spat Liz. "It was like your mind was already made up." I said nothing. "It was, wasn't it!" continued Liz, but all I could do was shuffle. "How long?" she asked.

"A while," I said.

"What – a week? A month? A year?" My mouth opened, but no words came out. Liz frowned. "Longer?" she asked. I took a deep breath, then blew it out through puffed out cheeks. "Jason! That doesn't make any sense! You can't have spent the whole of our relationship waiting to break up!"

"I wasn't," I said. "I was..."

"What?"

"Waiting. For things... to get... better."

"Better? What does 'better' mean? How can our relationship get any better? I love you, you love me – at least I thought you did. We get on with each other. We like the same things, sort of. I cook. I put up with your mess. We don't even argue that much! I don't see what I could do to make it 'better'! Other than magically transform into bloody Kylie Minogue, of course!"

"Don't be silly," I muttered, but the blood was already rushing to my cheeks. Liz stood there. Her jaw clamped shut, her lips thinned, her eyes flickering with rage. Then she pushed past me and marched out of the kitchen. A second or two later the bedroom door slammed with such force it shook the whole flat.

Alex shook his head.

"You should have dumped her months ago," he said.

"Probably. But I didn't want it to end that way. This way." Alex's face contorted into a mixture of confusion and disbelief.

"How did you expect it to end?" he asked.

"I dunno. I kinda hoped that she'd meet someone else."

"That was never gonna happen," said Alex, shaking his head again. "She'd pegged you for a keeper from the start."

I turned and gave Alex a long hard look.

"She didn't even like me at the start!"

"Probably not," said Alex, working on his drink, "but she saw potential. Thought she could change you. Women think like that. It's why they get so frustrated. We're a major disappointment when we stay as we are."

"That's just cynicism."

Alex shrugged. "It's true," he said, and drained his second pint. I looked at mine, still untouched. Then I picked it up and put it in front of my friend. Alex took it without question. "So?" he asked. "Then what?"

I sat in the hallway with my back against the bedroom door. I'd more or less given up trying to explain how I felt without *actually* explaining how I felt, and the various sounds of Liz punching pillows or sobbing into them had long since stopped. For all I knew, Liz had climbed out of her bedroom window and was slashing my car's tyres whilst I sat holding the watch she had given me for Christmas, watching the seconds tick by.

I opened my mouth to speak. "It's not you," I wanted to say, "it's me." But that would have been a lie. Of course it was her. Liz had been manipulative, devoid of humour, and at times cruel. She'd spent the first few months of our relationship calling me James because, and I quote, "I don't really like the name 'Jason'." She'd even tried to change my name. That was how controlling she really was!

Then why was I feeling guilty?

Because her real failing wasn't her faults, but the fact that she wasn't the person I'd hoped she would be. And once I'd realised that, I should have come clean, set her free, returned to my miserable single existence. Instead I started waiting. For a miracle.

Any miracle would have done. I'd have settled for a slight thaw in the Ice Queen's demeanour. Or an opportunity for us to part with a minimal amount of bloodshed. But in truth, the miracle I'd set my heart on was to be rescued – for someone specific to walk back into my life and give me the impetus I needed. That sounds ridiculous, I'm sure. But against all the odds it had actually happened. And when it had, Liz had done what Liz did best: She'd rallied her armies. And crushed the opposing nations.

From that moment on I no longer wanted to be a part of her empire.

"Are you still there?" she said eventually.

"Yes."

"Can I ask you something?"

"Of course," I said.

"If it's not me, just what is it that you do want, Jason Smith?"

I said nothing for a moment. "I don't know," I lied.

"I've been such a fool," she said after a pause. "You never loved me. I see that now. I too was waiting. Waiting for a moment – one that was never going to come."

I shivered. Partly at the coldness of her words, partly because I knew what it was like to spend your life waiting for 'a moment', but mostly because she was right; I'd never loved her.

"Jason," she said eventually, "just leave."

I left the watch on the side as I left, then crunched through the fresh snow to the car and somehow summoned the courage to glance up at her window, just in time to see her draw the curtains.

And that was it. In typical Liz fashion, she'd decided on a course of action. The three years of her life with me were over. Why then did I feel so wretched?

"Stupid," said Alex. I looked over my shoulder to see if he was talking to someone else.

"What's stupid?" I asked. Alex stared back at me for a moment, then shook his head.

"Mate, I know I'm your best friend, but when it comes to women, you don't have to be a genius to know what you want."

"How can you say that?" I asked. "I'm not even sure *I* know what I want!" Alex said nothing. Just frowned slightly and stared into the space in front of his nose like he was attempting long division in his head.

"Fifteen years," he said eventually.

"I'm sorry?"

"You've been hung up on the same girl for the past fifteen years."

"What girl?!" I asked. But Alex said nothing. He just turned his head slowly until he was looking right at me.

He was right, of course.

CHAPTER TWO
BOXING DAY, 1982

Were anyone else around at the time, they might assume that my slightly gaping mouth, my wide eyes and dilated pupils, the sheen on my forehead, and the blush in my otherwise gaunt cheeks was evidence that nothing that the world had to offer could possibly trump the images on the screen in front of me.

And yet, Alex seemed less interested.

He lay back against a pile of pillows at the other end of the bed, his shirt wide open to reveal his *Empire Strikes Back* t-shirt, his hands behind his head (though carefully avoiding the fragile construction of gel that passed as a hair style), oblivious to the high pitched wail of a siren and what sounded like a squeaky toy being repeatedly stamped on.

After a while he let out a long exaggerated yawn and watched as I clutched the chunky joystick in sweaty hands and jerked the controls up, down, left and right to manoeuvre a crudely animated slice of lemon round a maze of dots whilst being pursued by four multicoloured ghosts.

I was completely rubbish at this game – I'd already eaten all my power pills, and still had more than half the screen to complete, and now the ghosts had me cornered. It was only a matter of seconds before my lemon slice ran into one of them and shrivelled up to what sounded like an electronic penny whistle being deprived of puff.

Alex sniggered as I met my computerised demise, and bounced along the bed until he was sitting next to me. I thrust the control in his direction and, after he'd blown on his hands and pretended to push up the sleeves on a shirt that had never ever been unrolled past his forearms, he snatched the joystick from me.

I rested my bony elbows on my knees, cupped my chin in my hands, and watched the master at work. It was a stupid game. I could see the point of *Asteroids*, or *Space Invaders*, even some of the lame racing games, but *Pacman* was just ridiculous and when Mrs Cooke bellowed up the stairs, a small spiteful part of me delighted at what would happen next.

Alex continued to play. I gave him an enquiring sideways glance, which he met with an expression that said, "If she calls again, then I'll see what she wants."

She did.

"Bollocks," said Alex, launching himself off the bed, hitting the reset button on the games console as he did so. He tossed the control into my lap and stomped out of the room. I listened until I could hear the muted sounds of my friend and his mother shouting at each other. And then slowly I turned my head and looked up at the glossy addition to Alex's bedroom wall. Maybe there was time.

I took the calendar from its hook and sat on the edge of Alex's bed. Several 'stunners' adorned its pages. At least that's what the text on the cover promised. But by the time I'd got to August, 'Samantha' had made at least three appearances. There was nothing particularly unpleasant about Samantha; she had enormous breasts, and long blonde hair, and those things were very nice, but there wasn't anything … else. It was as if she was missing something. Not a limb. Not anything important or disfiguring.

Just, well … something. Whatever that was. And without the 'something', once you'd seen her breasts there wasn't any need to see them again. Like Mickey Mouse's ears, they looked pretty much the same from any angle.

I turned the page and, finally, there she was.

Linda.

Now she definitely had the 'something'.

Wearing only a pair of skimpy bikini bottoms under a see-through black lace sarong, she stood with one hand perched provocatively on a hip, whilst the other rested against her exposed thigh, long fingers and painted nails brushing against smooth curves. Her tanned skin, speckled lightly with beads of water. Her wild back-combed hair, lit from behind to create a halo effect. Her exaggerated pout. The heavy make-up around the eyes. The way she looked at me, as if she could see the contents of my head. And as she did so I wished, not for the first time, and certainly not the last, that I had been the man behind that camera, taking her picture, ignoring the beat of my heart, thumping louder and louder, like the rhythm of ancient drums –

"Oi," said Alex, snatching the calendar off me, "stop perving."

"I wasn't!" I protested, but it was too late; the calendar was out of my hands, and back on the wall.

"Best of three?" he asked, without turning to look at me. Of course! Who would want to spend Boxing Day looking at Linda Lusardi when the alternative was ritual humiliation in the form of stupid bloody *Pacman*!

"Yeah. Sure," I said. Alex's large bottom hit the bed, and a moment later he had that glazed look on his face like he was wired directly into the console.

I glanced up at the calendar. She was probably ten years my senior. Which meant that by the time I was twenty-five,

Linda could very well be the kind of woman I was going out with on a regular basis, and probably about to marry.

"Tell you what," said Alex, his eyes never leaving the television. "I'll do half – you see if you can complete it. Deal?"

"Ok," I said with a shrug.

Thing was though, none of the girls I knew at school seemed to have that Linda-potential. Even with ten years to go, it seemed like a transformation of evolutionary proportions if they were ever going to reach full Linda-ness.

Apart from Melanie Jackson, of course.

Even at fourteen, Melanie Jackson didn't just have the 'something', she was practically made of the stuff. Which is why there'd been an emergency meeting of the governors when Mr Thomas allowed Melanie Jackson to play the music department's one and only saxophone.

There are certain things in this world that, on the face of it, shouldn't be any more sexy than the next thing, but really, really are. Girls in men's shirts are one thing, and girls playing saxophones are another. Everybody knows this. Anybody who's ever seen those Robert Palmer or Rod Stewart videos knows this. Even the girls know this. That's why any girl who casually expressed an interest in learning the saxophone was given a stern look and promptly handed a clarinet. Or an oboe. Maybe a flute. But giving a girl a saxophone in a school full of raging adolescent male hormones, especially a girl like Melanie Jackson, would be a little like tossing a glowing cigarette end through the open window of a firework factory.

Practically overnight, membership to the school orchestra doubled and became almost fifty percent male. And whilst none of the newly formed brass section would admit to joining because of Melanie Jackson, it was most definitely the case. I should know. I was one of them. And Alex was another.

It also wasn't a coincidence that from my place in the orchestra I had a better view of Melanie Jackson than anyone else. The musicians sat in two rows that radiated in large arcs facing Mr Thomas. The brass section was to his right and arranged in order of instrument size. So the small spotty kids with their trumpets came first, then Nigel with his French horn, then Derek on the euphonium, followed by me on the trombone, and finally Alex on the tuba. Except that Alex and I would, accidentally on purpose, swap places, putting me on the end and giving me a clear view of the reed section in front of Old Thomas, and the object of my desire.

"Move up," growled Alex. I ignored him. "I can't see," he said. Alex elbowed me in the ribs, but I stayed rooted to the spot. If anyone was going to be leering at Melanie it had to be me and me alone. If we both started gawping that was only going to draw attention.

"If I move along any further, I'll be sitting amongst the bloody audience," I hissed.

"There isn't an audience, bonehead," said Alex. "It's why we call this 'a rehearsal'."

"Shut up," I said.

"Next time, you're sitting here," grumbled Alex, "like you're s'posed to." But I ignored him.

She was a good inch or two taller than the other girls, with a mass of permed chestnut hair that bobbed and bounced and fell in front of her stunning green eyes so that when she looked at you – if you were ever that lucky – it was like she was playing peek-a-boo. That alone got my insides in a tangle but if she smiled – revealing the whitest, most perfect set of teeth you were ever likely to see – well, suddenly I felt like I was sitting there in nothing but my vest and pants, skinny arms and legs on show to the whole world. And whilst I might feel self-conscious at first, everyone else just evaporated until the entire universe consisted only of Melanie and me.

Not that she looked in my direction that often. Most of the time, she sat there, staring at Old Thomas, wide-eyed and wonderful, waiting for her cue. Meanwhile I mentally catalogued every detail: the stud earrings she was wearing, the paleness of her lipstick, the thin gold chain round her neck, the number of buttons undone on her shirt, the V-neck of her school sweater, and the two small mounds just beneath it.

"Pervert!" said Alex, burying his outburst within a pretend cough. Mr Thomas glared in our direction for a second before turning his attention back to the violins. I put my right foot on Alex's left and began to press down, until he thumped me on the arm.

None of the other girls had breasts. Nothing to talk of anyway. I mean ok, some of them did, but Melanie had had them for ages – which meant that any other girl who'd recently acquired a bust was just imitating the original. A point that Alex insisted on making, albeit in far cruder terms, each night on the way home from school.

Alex's obsession with Melanie's breasts was beginning to get on my nerves. I swear if she had a head transplant Alex wouldn't notice – but the day she went from an A cup to a B he was telling anyone who cared to listen. One more reference to her bust as 'Mount Jackson' and I'd have stuffed my trombone in his great fat cake hole.

Truth was, Melanie could have been flat-chested for all I cared, because like Linda, she had grace. Though back then

I wouldn't have used that word. I wouldn't have used any words. Around Melanie I was reduced to a mute idiot, and any attempt at conversation was nothing more than a collection of squeaks and whistles like I was trying to conceal a set of bagpipes about my person. All I could do was watch from my place in the orchestra and wait for the moment when she lifted her saxophone to her lips.

The slice of lemon devoured a pixelated bunch of cherries, rounded a corner, gobbled up a power pill, then turned and chased after the four ghosts that were now blue with squiggly mouths, indicating that they too could be eaten.

"You done any band practice?" I asked Alex, hoping the question would put him off his game.

"Nah," he said.

"Aren't you worried about the New Year's concert?"

Alex shrugged.

"Not really," he said, completing half the screen. "I'll just mime. No one will notice. It's not like I'm the one with the big solo or anything!" He nudged me in the ribs, then handed me the control as promised. I took it and looked back at the screen.

"It's not a 'big solo'," I muttered. "It's just one note."

"That'll be why you cock it up every time then," smirked Alex. Seconds later I ran into a ghost, and died.

"Ready when you are, Mr Smith," said Mr Thomas, and as he did so the rest of the world rushed in to fill a space that had previously been occupied by just one person. The entire school orchestra was looking at me.

"Sorry," I said weakly. "I … lost my place."

"Really," said Old Thomas, a bushy grey eyebrow climbing his wrinkled forehead. "Because from where I'm standing, it looked like you knew exactly where you were. Sadly though, it didn't happen to be with the rest of us." I felt my cheeks flush whilst the orchestra rippled with the smirks of my fellow students. Mr Thomas tapped his baton against the side of his lectern. "Settle down people, let's take it from the top of the page. And one, and two, and..."

"You numbskull," said Alex, elbowing me. I said nothing. I just put my trombone to my lips and waited for my cue. Then I glanced over at Melanie again – only this time she was looking back.

And then she smiled.

CHAPTER THREE
MONDAY 29TH DECEMBER, 1997

Despite it being almost ten o'clock, only half the office appeared to be in. The missing contingent belonged to that strange group of people who routinely waste several days of valuable annual leave between Christmas and New Year. Sian was already engrossed in something. She supported her head on a bony arm that didn't seem capable of taking the weight, and massaged her forehead with long thin fingers. I hung my jacket on the back of my chair and, as I did so, noticed a small silver envelope with my name on it leaning against my computer monitor.

"What's this?" I asked, picking up the envelope.

"New Year's Eve party invite," said Sian, her hazel eyes flicking from the document on her desk to the screen before her without ever settling on me.

"Really? Thanks."

"You and Liz will come, right?" she asked.

"Erm, well... I, we, might have plans." I placed the invite on my desk. Sian stopped what she was doing and looked at me for the first time that morning.

"What plans?" she asked. I swallowed hard.

Four days earlier I'd known exactly how I was going to spend New Year's Eve; I'd be standing in a kitchen, along with other assorted boyfriends and husbands, listening to this guy called Cameron describe the highlights of his year to us – in real time – whilst Liz and his wife Rachel huddled in a corner and cackled like witches. I'd make my one and only beer last until midnight, after which point I'd gently start persuading my girlfriend that we should make our excuses and leave. Eventually Liz would relent and I'd drive us back to her place, where I'd spend the night, and probably make Miss Grumpy Pants breakfast the following morning as an apology for ending her evening prematurely. And at some point on New Year's Day I'd return home and breathe a huge sigh of relief. This was how I'd spent every New Year's Eve for the past three years. And whilst alternatives often presented themselves, they still involved standing in someone's kitchen, talking to people I didn't care for, and waiting for that magical midnight moment when the universe would shimmer slightly, and the dull old year would be replaced by an equally dull and totally identical new one.

But that was four days ago. And it hadn't occurred to me until this precise moment – nine forty-five on Monday morning, my first day back at work after the Christmas break – that not only would I never have to endure one more second of Cameron's deathly monologues, but for the first time in... well, ever... I'd finally be able to choose how I saw in the New Year. I could, for instance, ignore it completely.

"Not the same people you spent last year with?" asked Sian.

"Er... yeah," I said cautiously as I sat down. Confessions of how I dumped my girlfriend on Christmas Day might have to wait.

"But you hated that party!"

"It wasn't that bad," I said. Sian's eyes met mine, then she pushed her keyboard to one side, put both arms on the desk and leaned as far forward as it would allow. A lock of brown hair came loose and dared to slip in front of her eyes. She jerked her head sideways to remove it.

"And aren't these the people who live in Colchester or something?"

"Witham I think."

"But far enough away that you have to drive?"

"Yes."

"So you can't have a drink?"

"Well – I don't mind really..."

"Jason – come on!" said Sian, leaning back in her chair and opening her arms. "I'm a ten minute cab ride from you! I guarantee there will be no boring people, everything Sainsbury's has to offer in the way of alcohol and, best of all," she lowered her voice for a moment, "it's fancy dress!! Woohoo!!" Sian jigged around in her chair with as much energy as office etiquette would allow, her skinny arms going up and down like pistons, her head rolling from side to side to the sound of the music in her head, all in an effort to demonstrate what larks awaited me at her party.

I hate fancy dress.

"Well, I'll erm..."

"Charlotte will be there!" said Sian, still spinning in her chair.

"Really?" I said, trying not to convey too much interest.

"Apparently," said Sian, feigning disinterest whilst she pulled herself back to her desk, "she has this ridiculously short, very revealing French maid's outfit, and she's dying for an excuse to wear it." She fluttered her eyelashes at me, wriggled her freckled nose, then picked up a pencil and chewed the end provocatively.

"Yeah?" I said, forcing a laugh. "Well that's very... I mean... She probably won't wear it – if it's – you know, that, erm... And anyway, Liz wouldn't... I mean, if Liz was there then – which she would be – obviously – then I wouldn't – couldn't... could I?" Pathetic. I slumped back in my chair and let all the air escape from my lungs.

"So you'll come then?" asked Sian after a moment.

"Sure," I lied. "Sounds like fun."

I hate parties. I shouldn't do; parties usually consist of beer, music, people hell bent on enjoying themselves and girls in revealing clothing, and to a lesser or greater degree I enjoy all these elements – parties should be my kind of thing. But they're not. Beer is better enjoyed in a pub or at home in front of the TV. Music, contrary to popular belief, sounds better when it's played at a volume that your eardrums can cope with. 'People hell bent on enjoying themselves' are only enjoyed by other people of a similar disposition, and as for 'girls in revealing clothing'... well, in truth that's the only half decent reason I can think of to go to any party. There's something about a party that will make a high percentage of women consider wearing a scrap of fabric so flimsy it could easily be dislodged by a moderate breeze. And whilst a party that has been declared 'fancy dress' would strike terror into the hearts of most men, for some women it's a welcome opportunity to put on a French maid's outfit and show more leg and cleavage than would normally be considered decent.

Some women. But certainly not all women. And definitely not Liz.

To Liz, clothing was functional. Its primary purpose was to keep you warm. Its secondary role was to cover up anything that perverts might leer at. If it managed to carry out these tasks whilst simultaneously being 'pretty', in the sense that your mother or Queen Victoria might use the word, then that was a bonus. An acceptable alternative to pretty would be what Liz called 'chic' or 'classy'. Anything that wasn't chic, classy or pretty was usually 'tarty', and there was never an excuse for tartyness. Not even fancy dress.

The one and only time Liz and I had ever been to a fancy dress party it was of little surprise – to me – that she elected to hire a floor length, Cinderella-style ball gown, complete with shawl. And even then she complained that the plunging neckline was somehow lower than it had been when she'd tried it on in the shop, and proceeded to spend the entire evening glowering at anybody – including me – who dared glance at her chest. What a fun night that had been.

I might have been able to salvage some elements of enjoyment from the evening if I'd been allowed to pick my own costume and enjoy a beer or two, but no. Apparently Cinderella needs her Prince Charming, and I spent the evening dressed in bright yellow three-quarter-length trousers, a coat with far too many buttons, a pair of Liz's opaque tights, and – the ultimate humiliation – shoes *with buckles*. All whilst I nursed a single glass of wine from a goblet that wouldn't have so much as chipped if you'd taken a mallet to it.

Ever since that evening I've always thought of parties as miserably lonely places. And the only thing that has the power to make you feel more alone than standing in a room full of people you don't like, trying to give the impression that all is well with the world, is being stuck in a relationship with someone you don't like, doing pretty much the same thing.

I shook my head at the memory. Out of the corner of my eye I could see Sian's party invite lying on my desk. If it could have winked, it probably would have.

I stared at it for a moment.

I'd had it with Ball Gown women. I never wanted to spend another New Year's Eve wedged in the corner of someone's kitchen watching my life trickle away. But what was the alternative, now that I was single? Stay at home? On my own? Waiting for Kylie Minogue to knock on my door? That wasn't going to happen, was it? Once that door was closed there'd be bricks and mortar between me and every person on the planet for at least thirty six hours. Only the obligatory phone call from my mother at some ungodly hour on New Year's Day, and my daily phone call from Alex, would break the silence. I'd spend New Year's Eve as I spent most evenings, surfing the internet, working my way through four cans of cheap lager. Occasionally a noise from outside might draw me to the window, and I'd look down at party revellers in the street. All smiles and laughter and good spirits. United in their celebrations. Forming bonds that would see them into the New Year and beyond. Maybe one of them would look up at me and wave at the sad lonely person who hadn't the courage to grab life by the balls.

No. Not if I had anything to do with it.

The invite winked again.

I picked it up and stuffed it in my bag.

Chapter Four
New Year's Eve, 1997

The taxi pulled away and drove up the street. I took a deep breath, put the straw hat on my head, and raised my hand to ring the bell. But before my finger had even made contact with the buzzer the door opened, and there was a large man in a white tuxedo. And he didn't seem happy.

"Hi," I said, "Sian… in?" This was definitely the address on the invite. And the muted sounds of Blur thumping through the walls in time to the multi-coloured light show behind the lounge curtains, evidence – if you needed any – that a party was in full swing. But maybe I was wrong. Maybe there was another Boscombe Road in Southend-on-Sea, and I'd happened upon the home of a particularly grumpy man with a fondness for loud music. And garish lights. And tuxedos.

"Who's at the door, Clive?" said a familiar, albeit slurred voice.

"Another of your 'friends'," said Clive, as if 'friends' might be something you found on the bottom of your shoe. I peered round Clive's shoulder and there was Sian. Her already pale skin seemed even paler due to the dark lipstick, heavy eye makeup, and a dress made entirely of feathers. Black ones. She looked a lot like the weird one from Shakespeare's Sister.

"Jason! You came!" said Sian, and she half fell, half stumbled towards me, bursting into giggles as she grabbed Clive's arm for support. "Jason," she slurred, "this is Clive." I looked back at Clive and gave him a nod. Sian tipped her head back to look up his sleeve. "Oh what's wrong with little Clivey-wivey?" she said, sliding down his arm until she was sitting on the floor and hanging onto his fingertips.

"You're pissed!" said Clive.

"I am not *pished*!" said Sian, closing her eyes and shaking her head dramatically. I glanced at Clive, then back at Sian. But before I could suggest that maybe Clive had a point, he'd shrugged Sian off, pushed past me, and stormed off down the path and into the night.

"Don't mind Clive," said Sian, holding onto the door frame as she performed a complicated and somewhat inelegant manoeuvre back to her feet, "he's just a little..." she stopped for a brief fit of giggles, "e-mo-tion-al," she continued, pronouncing every syllable.

"Should we go after him?" I asked, genuinely afraid that the answer might be 'yes'. But Sian lunged forward and started dragging me into the house by my sleeve.

"Come, come, come, come, come, come, come..." she said.

"But the door..." I protested, as I tried in vain to close it.

"It's ok," said Sian. "We've got plenty more."

Sian didn't release her talons until she'd dragged me into the kitchen. Once free, I scanned the room for a familiar face, preferably Charlotte in her much-talked-about French maid's outfit, but anyone would do – just someone to rescue me from my feathered captor. To my left, by the fridge, was a tall man in an afro wig and bright pink shirt. He was in deep conversation with Danger Mouse, who occasionally removed his head to take a sip of his drink. Behind them, Count Dracula was fondling an androgynous blood-stained surgeon who was standing between two characters from the Wizard of Oz: a slightly shocked-looking Tin Man, and Dorothy, who at some point had acquired a beer belly and was in desperate need of a leg wax. Further into the kitchen a cave man and Sherlock Holmes were in discussion with a nun who kept glancing back at Dracula, whilst behind her Elvis was balancing twiglets on his upper lip, much to the appreciation of a small group of 1920s gangsters. But my eyes stopped when they reached the naughty schoolgirl. And a moment later I realised I knew who she was.

Sarah's a nice enough girl. A little serious. Sits on the same bank of desks as Sian and me, and certainly not the kind of girl I'd have expected to see in high heels, knee-length white socks, and a skirt so short it barely qualified as clothing. Not that it didn't suit her. Quite the reverse. And in the absence of Charlotte, I couldn't have asked for anyone better to talk to.

Just as that thought entered my head, Sian started to flap her arms wildly and scream at everybody to pay her some attention. I covered my ears until Sian seemed satisfied that no one else was talking.

"Everyone," bellowed Sian, "this is Jason. Smith. Jason, this is... everyone! Woo hoo!" I tried to dodge her flailing arms whilst Sian danced. And then she fell over.

"Hi," I said to the silent kitchen. And for the second time in as many minutes I thought about going home.

"Hi Jason," said Sarah, as I shuffled through the kitchen throng into her corner.

"Hi Sarah. You alright?"

"Yes – yes," she replied.

"That's a great costume," I said airily.

"Thanks," she said, and immediately turned her attention to the floor.

"Much better than mine," I continued. "Still, that's what you get for leaving things to the last minute, I suppose."

"Yes," said Sarah, as she examined the kitchen lino.

"Did you have to hire it?" I asked. "Or was it something you already had?" That didn't seem right. "You know – the, er, uniformy bits. I mean – it's not like you'd have a school uniform hanging in your cupboard, would you?" Sarah started to flush, first pink, then a deeper crimson. "Unless you go to a lot of – er, fancy dress... things," I said, "which you might! I mean – how would I know? How much do we really... know, about..." I took a deep breath, "each other?"

I suddenly became aware that an American footballer standing next to us was looking at me intently. I smiled, hoping it might provoke a reciprocal action. It didn't.

"Jason, this is Lee," said Sarah, wringing her hands. "My husband."

"Right!" I said, "Well... hi!" Lee was very tall. "You're really tall," I said.

"I know," growled Lee.

"Lee, let's go and dance," said Sarah, grabbing him by the hand. "Jason, we're going to go and dance."

"Oh, great – well, have fun. I was, you know, gonna get started on these babies," I said, indicating the four-pack of lager I was still holding, "and then I'll probably, you know, join you. Or something." Sarah nodded and then proceeded to drag her hulk of a husband out of the kitchen. I gave them a little wave as they got to the living room door and watched as Sarah pushed her husband inside. Then I let out a sigh and felt my shoulders slump.

This was a bad idea. I looked at my beers. Wouldn't they be better enjoyed in the privacy of my lounge? I straightened my posture, took a decisive lungful of smoke and cheap perfume, and headed for the front door.

I'd barely made it out of the kitchen when someone touched my arm. There, standing next to the coats under the stairs, wearing a faded *Star Wars* T-shirt, was someone I knew only as 'that guy from Debt Recovery'.

"Hi Jason."

"Oh, hi, erm..." I said, my voice trailing off where I would have inserted his name.

"You weren't leaving, were you?" he asked.

"No! Well, actually, I suddenly remembered..."

"Do you mind if I have one of those beers?" he asked, his eyes widening like a puppy that suddenly suspects it might have been a bad idea to chew up your shoes. I cracked one off and handed it to him, and watched as he took his first sip. And moments later I too was seeing the new year in, under Sian's stairs, amongst an assortment of coats and umbrellas, drinking warm beer.

No one ever meets the girl of their dreams at a New Year's Eve party. They should do, of course they should. It's a crowded environment, everyone's having a good time, the drink is flowing, the lights are down low – and then there's this delicious expectation that something magical should take place around midnight, and as that hour approaches every lonely person starts looking out of the corner of their eye for that special someone to grab as Big Ben strikes twelve. New Year should be a breeding ground for new relationships. But it's not. And why is this? Because there's always some boring idiot like Debt Recovery Guy ready to attach themselves to you like a giant leech and suck the party spirit right out of you!

As I stood talking... no, listening... no, just *standing* with Debt Recovery Guy, I estimated the number of women in the rooms around me, what percentage of those might be single and, finally, the chances that one would walk up to me, push Debt Recovery Guy to one side, grab me by the shoulders and plant a big tongue-filled kiss on my face. There were – if I'd done the maths correctly – roughly, if not precisely, *zero*.

Which is when a miracle happened.

The door to the lounge burst open and a girl in a home-made bubblewrap mini-dress, spray painted silver from head to toe and with a pair of antenna stuck on her head, fell into the hallway in a semi-drunken state of euphoria, closely followed by another girl in a matching costume and party-like demeanour. The second girl slammed the lounge door behind her, and for a split second they stood and stared at the two sad individuals before them: the idiot in the sandals, Hawaiian shirt and straw hat – and the other bloke in a *Star Wars* T-shirt. They laughed in that way that you do when you've had a few drinks and everything is funny, before they staggered past us and into the kitchen.

My eyes followed them and when I looked back at Debt Recovery Guy his mouth was hanging open as if he'd just seen an angel. Or two angels. Two angels cunningly disguised as space aliens from the planet Bubblewrap. Here was my opportunity to escape.

"Hey," I said, "I'm going into the lounge. To. Er. Dance." I swallowed. Debt Recovery Guy stared at me, his mouth still open. I handed him my empty beer can, which he took without question. "Right," I said. I swallowed again and walked towards the lounge, pausing for a moment as I put my hand on the door handle. Then I opened the door, and went in.

Sian's lounge ran the entire length of the house and, aside from a lava lamp, the odd tea light candle and assorted Christmas lights, the only illumination was an enormous bank of disco lights that could have been seen from space. As they pulsated in time to whatever it was being blasted out of the speakers at ten thousand decibels, giant silhouettes of grotesque and misshapen demons flickered against a wall of ever changing colours.

The last thing I wanted to do was join them but behind me, in the hallway, was the ghost of New Years Past. I had no choice. I had to take my chances with the demons. I sashayed into the throng, and hoped to God that I wouldn't crash into anyone. Not unless they were female. And gorgeous. And ten seconds later my prayers were answered.

As I manoeuvred further into the room I accidentally stepped on what turned out to be a tail. When the owner of the tail tried to move, and found she couldn't, she was propelled backwards into me. It wasn't much of a collision, but it was enough to make us turn round and face each other: her into the terrified eyes of a dancing buffoon, and me into the beautiful oriental-shaped eyes of Cat Woman.

"I'm sorry," I said. She screwed up her face somewhat, then leant forward, cupping a hand around one ear. I leant forward and brought my hand to my mouth to create an ineffective megaphone.

"I said, I'm sorry." She smiled, waved a hand to indicate there was no harm done, picked up her tail and tucked it into a loop on her sleeve. She was ridiculously slender. And tall. In her high heeled boots she must have been at least six foot four. Long dark hair cascaded from the back of her headpiece and down the back of a leather costume so fitted she must have been sewn into it.

"I'm Jason," I yelled.

"What?" she mouthed. I leaned forward.

"I'm Jason!" She nodded her head slightly to indicate that she'd heard me this time, then leaned forward herself.

"Nicola," she said.

I nodded and then, for some insane reason, gave her a 'thumbs up' – of all the stupid, idiotic, lame things to do – but she just smiled, and carried on dancing. And whilst she wasn't gazing lovingly into my eyes, there were glances. Normally accompanied with a smile. It was only when she did a snake-like 360 degree turn in front of me, her arms unfurling into the space above her head, that I finally realised – oh my God – we were dancing – *with each other!*

At that moment a gloved hand grabbed hold of my shoulder to steady its owner, but before I could turn to see who it belonged to Sian was already screeching something inaudible into my ear. Then she cackled to herself, and staggered off in the direction of the Christmas tree. I was still clutching my ringing ear when, moments later, the tree fell over, the music stopped, and all I could hear was Sian's slightly muffled hysterical laughter from under the foliage. I looked at Nicola.

"That's Sian," I said, gesturing in the direction of the laughter and felled tree.

"I know," replied Nicola, still smiling.

"So, that's the end of the dancing," I said hopefully.

"I'm sure they'll fix it in a moment."

"Yeah. Yeah." Bollocks. "Nice costume," I said before I could stop myself. I squeezed my eyes closed for a moment and waited for her reaction.

"Thanks," she said. "Nice hat."

"Hat? Oh, my hat! It's just, you know, a hat. Nothing special. Just something I had. Probably should have thrown it out years ago – but then I found it again. Tonight. And hey presto – key part of my costume! This is my costume, by the way. They're not, you know, 'real clothes'." I swallowed.

"Right," she said, her smile fading slightly.

"Get a grip!" I said.

"Sorry?" said Nicola.

"I said can I get you a drink?"

"That would be nice, sure," she said.

"Wine? Beer? Something else?"

"A Bacardi and Coke if you can find one," she said.

"Right you are!" I said, shooting at her with my fingers. "Back in a flash!" I fought my way through a line of Sian spectators and out of the living room, pausing only to beat my head against the door before I opened it. Gun fingers? 'Back in a flash'? Really!?

The kitchen was now full of pirates who were systematically removing items from Sian's fridge and replacing them with cans of lager. Tomorrow, when Sian sobered up, if she wanted anything to eat she'd find most of her food options rotting on top of the kitchen work top.

"You're back!" said Debt Recovery Guy, as I edged my way through the 'swashbuckle' – or whatever the collective noun for pirates is.

"Oh, hi," I said. "Look – can't stop – I'm in a bit of a rush."

"I got you another beer," he said, offering up an unopened can.

"Oh, thanks," I said, "actually I fancy something else." My eyes danced over the dizzying array of drinks. The Bacardi was eluding me.

"So, here's an interesting question for you; do you know where Han Solo actually got the Millennium Falcon from?" asked Debt Recovery Guy.

"Can you see any Bacardi?" I said out of sheer exasperation.

"Bacardi? That's a girl's drink, isn't it?" asked Debt Recovery Guy.

"Not any more," I said, moving the dozen or so enormous bottles of cheap lemonade to one side "From now on it's my drink of choice."

"Oh, well. Here it is." He opened a cupboard, took out a half full bottle of Bacardi, and offered it to me. "One of those girls – you know, the aliens? She put it in here earlier. I think she might have been hiding it." And then he winked at me. "You know – maybe I'll have one of those," he said, a big stupid grin breaking all over his face. "Can't do any harm, eh?"

"Smith!" said a voice from behind me. "Wasn't expecting to see you here. Isn't it past your bedtime?"

I turned around.

Though the Batman mask covered most of his face, I knew who it was from the sheer arrogance of his swagger. Whether he was walking to the photocopier, or jumping the queue in the staff canteen, Gary swaggered like he owned the very ground beneath his feet. And now he was swaggering in our direction.

Our eyes met.

"Nice costume," said Gary, with a sneer. My mind raced in a desperate effort to find something clever to say. Something cutting. Something sarcastic.

"Thanks," I replied.

"And Scud; what are you doing here? Were you invited?"

Scud? And then I remembered Debt Recovery Guy's name, or his nickname at least: Scud. As in the missile; you can see him coming, but there's bugger all you can do about it.

"Oh I get it," continued Gary, "you're here to make another attempt to steal Sian away from her husband. Hilarious!" He let out a snort, and as he did so the colour drained from Scud's face, and his bottom lip started to quiver.

"See you later, Jason," said Scud. He put down his can and walked out of the kitchen, stopping briefly to grab an old sailing jacket from under the stairs.

"Oi!" yelled Gary, "you just nicked my anorak!" Around me several pirates roared with fake-laughter, and as Scud closed the front door behind him I suddenly felt a pang of remorse. He couldn't help being dull – whereas Gary chose to be a complete and utter arsehole on a daily basis.

The familiar hiss of a beer can being opened brought me back to the room.

"Lads," said Gary, moving amongst his troops and passing out cans, "time to party!" His entourage cheered. "Follow your dick!" he declared, and then entered the lounge.

I put the bottle I was holding on the work surface.

A bottle of Bacardi.

I span round and started opening kitchen cupboards in a desperate bid to find two vaguely clean glasses.

Two things struck me as odd as I went in search of Nicola. Firstly the hot, stale party air had been replaced with a fresh, cool breeze, and secondly, an awful lot of people seem to have vanished – including my Cat Woman. It took me a moment to realise, as my eyes adjusted to the light, that the French doors at the far end of the room were now open, and half of Sian's guests had spilled out into the garden.

I took a deep breath and –

"Jashon!" said Sian, appearing from nowhere and grabbing my arm, then my shoulder, then my face, anything within arm's reach that offered support – "Jashon!"

"Oh, hi Sian, whoa! Careful of the drinks."

"Don't worry," she said, waving her arms about wildly, "we've got plenty more!" I stepped backwards to avoid her epileptic limbs.

"Ok, but, you know..." She stepped forwards and put both hands on my shoulders.

"What, Jashon? What do I know?"

"Sian – I really need..."

Suddenly the music went off, and the lights came on. "New Year's!" shouted a voice, "New Year's!"

"New Year?" said Sian. "New Year!" She let go of my shoulders and started doing her on-the-spot arms-in-the-air fancy-dress dance. She'd almost managed a complete revolution too before the wall got in the way and once again she fell over. I stood there, a drink in each hand.

"You ok? Sian?" I said, looking down. "Sian?" She wasn't moving. "You ok?" Nothing. "You're ok," I reassured myself, stepping over her motionless body and starting towards the garden.

By now people were flooding back into the lounge and I fought my way through human rapids, whilst trying to keep from spilling my drinks.

As I got to the French windows a group countdown from ten had started. I peered out into the garden. There were people out there... shadowy figures, mainly couples, in various corners. Was Nicola one of them? What if she wasn't alone? What if she was with someone?

Don't be daft.

Then why would she be in the garden? You wouldn't go into the garden on your own, would you? Not when someone was getting you a drink.

Not unless you wanted to be alone with that someone.

Yes. Yes – that must be it – she was waiting in the garden for me! She wanted to be alone with me!

A chorus of *Auld Lang Syne* started up behind me. I stepped outside, then – stopped.

I couldn't just start walking up to people!

I coughed, cleared my throat, and was about to call Nicola's name when, from the other side of the garden, a familiar male voice said: "Oi mate, fuck off, there are people out here trying to have a shag!" Somebody giggled. I took a step forward and as I did so I felt something underfoot. I looked down and saw a slightly crushed Batman mask next to a discarded can of lager. I squinted into the gloom, my face cool and clammy, and there, across the garden, in the shadows, were two people, one significantly taller than the other, locked in an awkward embrace. And as the taller one turned I saw what could only have been... a tail.

I was out of there in the time it took to empty two drinks on the ground, throw the plastic glasses into the bushes and walk from the garden to the front door with only the briefest of detours to grab the Bacardi bottle from the kitchen.

As I strode down the front path Scud was leaning against the garden wall, smoking a cigarette. I walked straight past him.

"Jason? Jason! Hey Jason – wait up," he yelled, surprised and delighted to see me leaving the party so soon. I heard his footsteps shuffle quickly to catch up with mine.

"Fuck off, Scud!" I spat, without bothering to look over my shoulder. "Go steal Sian from her husband!" The footsteps stopped abruptly, and a wave of guilt washed over me as I imagined Scud in a crumpled, wounded heap on the pavement behind me. But I kept moving, too afraid to let anyone see the tears that were beginning to form.

I walked the whole way home, swigging from the Bacardi bottle, yelling at street lamps when the disappointment inside me could be contained no longer. I don't remember how long the journey took. But I do have vague recollections of Southend sea front, of lurching across the sand, and of standing on the beach whilst I tossed my straw hat and an empty Bacardi bottle into the sea.

I hadn't intended to answer the phone, I just wanted the ringing to stop, so it was a little disconcerting when I heard a small tinny voice somewhere outside the duvet.

"Jason?" said the voice. I pulled the cordless handset under the covers.

"Hello? Yes?"

"Jason – are you alright?" A moment passed whilst my ears and my brain conferred. Neither seemed in the mood for work.

"Oh, Mum. Yes, I'm fine. Hi."

"You don't sound alright, you sound dreadful."

"No, really," I lied, "I'm just great."

"Are you drunk!?"

I snorted. "No – no, definitely not drunk."

"Hung over then. Were you drinking last night?"

"On New Year's Eve? Of course not!"

"There's no need for sarcasm, Jason," snapped my mother. "I just phoned up to wish you a Happy New Year!"

"Sorry," I said. "Happy New Year to you too."

"Thank you, Jason. A little late," and then with genuine warmth, "but appreciated none the less. Did you and Liz see the New Year in together?"

Now I was awake. I yanked the covers back – surprised to find that I was still wearing my sand-covered clothes from the night before – and gripped the handset with more urgency.

"Erm, yes," I lied. "Of course."

"Is she still there?"

"No?" I said. I hadn't meant to sound like a question, but I wasn't entirely sure what the correct answer should be.

"Oh," said my mother, a little disappointed. "Well, never mind, I'll call her later."

"What?! No – no, don't do that!" I said, sitting bolt upright.

"Why on earth not?" asked my mother. My mind raced.

"She's – ill."

"Ill?"

"Yes! Yes – flu, I think. Very poorly. She's probably sleeping."

"Oh," said my mother. "How awful."

"I know – she can, er, barely stay awake."

"Flu can be like that, Jason," said my mother.

"Uh huh."

"These days people call it flu when it's nothing more than a bad cold, but *real* flu – that knocks you off your feet."

"Well," I said, letting out a long sigh, "there you are then."

"I'm quite surprised you're not looking after her. Fancy leaving the poor girl on her own!" I froze again, my eyes widening like I was caught in the headlights of an oncoming juggernaut.

"What? Oh, well... I just got back."

"You didn't make her go out last night, did you? Because if she's got flu –"

"No! No, we just, you know, stayed in and – watched the TV. Jools Holland. On the TV. Did you see it?" I slapped my hand against my forehead and then ran it through my hair, digging the nails into my scalp.

"I'm a bit worried about her, Jason," continued my mother, ignoring the important question about Mr Holland. "Maybe I ought to pop over." I jumped out of bed and hopped around on the spot, performing the dance of the desperate to the god of deception.

"She's fine, Mum, honest. She's – just sleeping off the dregs. Look – why don't we…" I screwed my eyes shut and prayed hard that the deception god would give me something else to say other than the words in my head, but he didn't. "Why don't we come over, er… at the weekend. If she's feeling better. How's that?" There was a pause.

"The weekend," said my mother. "Well, ok. That would be nice. How about Sunday lunch?"

"Terrific," I said. "That would be – great. Let's hope she, you know, makes a full recovery." My legs gave way. Fortunately the bed was there to catch me.

"Ok, well – see you both Sunday!" said my mother, sounding quite buoyant at the prospect. "Give my love to Liz." And with that she was gone, leaving me feeling wretched, guilty, and very, very hung over.

What a fabulous, fabulous start to the year.

I walked across the hall and into my study, putting the phone back on the base unit before I ventured downstairs in search of food. I got as far as the lounge before I needed to rest.

I hadn't wanted to lie to my mother – I just wasn't ready to tell her that the future daughter-in-law she was hoping for wouldn't be the girl she'd always assumed it would be. But it was worse than that. In my mother's eyes Liz had become a permanent feature of the family landscape. Any unsanctioned changes to that vista would involve several long discussions, all of which would require a clear head.

I shuffled past the enormous bloody Christmas tree Liz had made me buy, and with one arm swept the pile of TV magazines and assorted sofa debris onto the floor so that I could lie down. Something square and glossy lay amongst the avalanche. I reached down and picked up a Kylie calendar – a stocking-filler from Liz, and another way for her to raise the whole you-and-your-unhealthy-interest-in-Kylie-Minogue debate.

Yes, I like Kylie. And yes, for all the obvious male reasons – she's cute, pretty, she occasionally doesn't wear very much – but there's more to her than that. Ok, I confess I'm not basing this on much – the odd interview, her cameo appearance in the Vicar of Dibley – but there's only so much a person can fake. Sooner or later the façade slips, and when it does, if you're paying attention, you get to glimpse the real person underneath. And from what I've seen, the real Kylie is an interesting, funny, caring, feeling, beautiful (on the inside) woman. She's this 'normal girl' who settles down in front of Frasier on a Friday night with a glass of Chardonnay, and croons to soppy love songs when she thinks nobody's listening. Who wouldn't be attracted to someone like that? And if there's any justice in the world then someday she'll walk into my life.

Of course, some might say my chances of meeting Kylie, let alone getting her into my life, are slim, non-existent even. But that's just negative thinking. In my head I have it all worked out: I'd be at home one Saturday or Sunday afternoon, dressed in my very smartest togs due to a washing backlog, when, quite by chance, the doorbell would ring and a distressed Kylie would be standing in the porch.

"I'm terribly sorry," she'd say. "I've just broken down and this piece of junk," (holding the latest mobile phone for me to see) "has chosen this precise moment to run out of juice. Could I use your phone?"

And, being the perfect gentleman, I'd wave her in with a heady mixture of sympathy about shoddy phone batteries, and absolutely no hint that I recognised her at all.

Then, while she sat on my sofa recovering from the shock of being told by whatever car recovery company rock stars use these days that they "couldn't possibly get anyone to her in under three hours", I'd breeze in from the kitchen with a chamomile tea, and she'd tell me how the whole celeb thing had just become too much, how soothing the tea was, and please, call her 'Minnie' and... oh, could I just hold her for a while because she really needed a hug right now.

I mentioned this to Liz once.

Not all of it.

Just bits.

It didn't go down well.

From that moment on, Kylie had a starring role in pretty much every argument we ever had. The average spat might start with a vigorous but none the less sensible exchange of views, but by the end we'd be going ten bells over whether or not this was the sort of behaviour Kylie would tolerate from her boyfriends – of which she probably has hundreds, several a night if the truth be known – and if I thought for one moment that someone like Kylie would even glance in my direction...

I shook the voice of my ex-girlfriend out of my head. Kylie smiled back at me from the cover of the calendar. Why couldn't I have met someone like her three years ago? I wouldn't be lying to my mother if I'd met Kylie. I probably wouldn't be feeling quite so hung over either! We'd have taken a morning stroll along the sea front, enjoyed brunch at the arches, and right about now we'd be returning home to have sex. Again. Why couldn't Kylie have been at the New Year's Eve party? She'd have seen Gary for what he was – an idiot behind a padded costume and a mask.

From nowhere a new resolve to sort out my life swept through me, blowing open the windows of my mind and letting the New Year in. I was going to find, if not Kylie, then someone just like her.

I ripped off the polythene packaging and climbed the stairs back to my study. So the hangover was still there, and after this expenditure of energy I was probably going to have another lie down, but I wouldn't let 1998 begin without taking at least one positive step.

I hunted around on my desk for a drawing pin and then, picking a part of the wall that had the thickest layer of wood-chip paper, hung Kylie above my computer.

New Year? I thought. Bring it on.

Chapter Five
Monday 5th January, 1998

"You still here?"

I sat bolt upright, startled by the sound of someone else in my flat.

"Err – yes. Hold on!" I yelled back, whilst I tried to manage the questions filling up my head: Who was I? Where was I? What time was it? What day was it? Who was the person downstairs? Why were they announcing their presence? Why did they seem surprised that I was here? And why did it feel like I'd only had four hours' sleep?

Answers started coming back, though not necessarily in the order that I'd asked them: Martin the builder. He had a key. I was at home. In bed. He expected me to be at work. Which meant that it was Monday, past nine in the morning, and I'd overslept, again, because I'd been surfing the internet until the small hours. Which meant I was Jason Smith, from Essex, England. I felt both better and worse all at the same time.

"Morning," droned Martin as I stumbled into the kitchen in my dressing gown. He was standing in front of the window, scratching the back of his head, then his beard, and as he did so specks of dust and plaster were freed from the unruly hair. "Late night, was it?" he asked without even looking over his shoulder.

"You want some tea?" I asked, shielding my eyes from the light.

"Got mine," said Martin, picking up a hammer and chisel from the work surface. "Yours is next to the kettle." I glanced over at the kettle. There was indeed another cup of tea. "Er thanks," I said, and scooped a wood chip out with my finger. "I'm going to – you know – go to work." Martin turned to face me, looked at me for the first time that morning, and nodded sagely, dislodging more debris in the process.

"I'd get dressed first," he said.

It's a fact of human existence that most new technology is invented by the military and then, after a significant number of people have been shot at, stabbed, crushed, blown up or spied upon, someone will figure out how to use the same technology to create pictures of naked people.

Take cavemen, for instance. Right after they'd finished throwing rocks at woolly mammoths and sabre toothed tigers, they realised that those same rocks could be used to mark stone. And whilst we're all familiar with those cave paintings of hunting scenes, the first cave art was undoubtedly a stick person with large breasts, a big willy, possibly both.

It's the same with the internet – originally created by the military, and now the single largest repository of porn on the planet. But only because we haven't figured out what else to use it for. Yet.

One day soon, you'll be able to do everything on the internet – access your bank account, order your groceries, pay your bills, listen to music, watch TV, catch up with old school friends, find a girlfriend – but not, it seems, in 1998.

I stared at my face in the mirror. My skin looked like it was too big for my face. It didn't quite fit around the eyes. I prodded it with my fingers, then rubbed my palms against my cheeks to try and stimulate some blood flow and restore some colour to my pale features. Nothing happened.

After I'd recovered from my two-day, post-New-Year's-Eve hangover, I'd spent Friday night scouring the internet for every dating website in the English-speaking universe.

There were six.

And whilst the number of websites was disappointing, my spirits were lifted when I discovered that between them they still had several hundred female members, perhaps thousands, many of them in my age range, and a fair proportion that sounded (well, read) really nice. Some even had photos. Some could even be described as pretty.

None, however, could be described as 'close'.

My definition of 'close' was fairly loose. Anywhere that didn't involve an eight hour flight was 'close'. And whilst I toyed with the idea of moving to America, it dawned on me that even in the land of the free (and single) my potential mates weren't wandering the plains like a herd of bison. They were dotted all over the place. I could spend the rest of my days hauling my computer from one American town to another like some sort of dating hobo. In years to come they'd make a seventies style TV show out of the idea. Have some burnt out movie star in a checked shirt playing my part. Give him a dog called Benson, and put his computer, all flashing lights and reel to reel tapes, in the back of his truck. The sad thing is, he'd probably have more luck than me.

And that's when I should have given up on the idea. Right then. On Friday evening. Slumped in front of the screen. Empty beer cans all over my desk. Echoes of a banjo theme tune in my head.

Instead, I spent the remainder of the weekend, until four A.M. this very morning, looking at every single profile just to make certain that there wasn't a London-based Kylie lookalike misfiled under North Dakota.

"You really are a first class idiot," I said to the reflection in the mirror. The reflection shrugged and started to brush his teeth.

"I'm off now, Martin." A stiff January breeze hit me as I entered the kitchen.

"Right you are," replied Martin from underneath the sink. I looked around the kitchen at the rubble, the debris, the partially assembled kitchen units, the paint splattered tools and toolboxes, the lunchbox, the pouch of tobacco, the small packet of cigarette papers, and the big hole where once there'd been a window.

"Martin?" There was the usual Martin-length pause.

"Yep?"

"Am I going to have a window in my kitchen when I get back this evening?"

"Tomorrow," said Martin.

"Tomorrow!?"

"Tomorrow."

"Martin! It's like a bloody..." I struggled to think of a sufficiently cold analogy.

"Ice box?" offered Martin after a moment.

"Yes! Ice box!"

"Put some more clothes on then," suggested Martin.

"Martin," I said, gathering all the assertiveness I could muster, "I'm going to need you to put the window back today." I waited for his reply, and just as I was going to repeat myself the sink popped up out of the worktop by an inch or two.

"Righto," said Martin.

"Right," I said, my assertiveness waning slightly. "Good. I'm, erm..."

"Off to work?" asked Martin.

I opened the car door, threw my bag onto the only other seat in my aging sports car, and got in. This was typical of me. I decide to find myself a girlfriend and where do I start? My back bedroom. On the computer. Is it any wonder that IT departments are largely made up of single men? I started the engine.

The internet wasn't the answer. That just allowed me to find single girls who had a computer. No wonder they'd been scattered across the globe. The truth was I'd probably driven past a dozen or so single women in the last thirty seconds and not even realised it. Finding a potential girlfriend was simply a case of meeting as many women as I could and establishing whether they were single.

Nightclubs. That was the answer. Girls in nightclubs are used to cheesy chat up lines. "Are you single?" on the other hand, had a refreshing sense of honesty about it. In some ways it didn't even sound like a chat up line, it was more of a casual enquiry, like "Is that your car parked outside?" or "Did you know the state of South Dakota has only three women who are computer literate?" I pictured myself leaning against a bar, posing the are-you-single question to a tall attractive redhead in a figure-hugging dress. She seemed unimpressed. Or bemused. Bored, even. Why wasn't it possible to imagine this scenario working out? Because it was utter nonsense. It simply isn't possible to have any kind of conversation in a nightclub that doesn't involve bellowing in the other person's ear at the top of your lungs. In my imagination I leant forward and perforated the redhead's eardrums with my question. She rolled her eyes, and turned her back on me.

Nightclubs weren't the answer. I pulled into the car park, parked, and walked into the offices of Conway Financial Services.

"Morning, Jason," said Janet on the security desk.

"Morning, Janet."

I didn't need nightclubs; I met countless women every day of my life. All I had to do was ask whether they were single. How hard could it be? "Hi, how are you? Are you single? You are? Me too! What were the chances? Can I buy you a coffee?"

I stood at the turnstiles and checked my pockets for my security pass. I didn't have it. I wandered back to Janet's desk.

"Forgot your pass again?" asked Janet, pushing the visitors' book towards me.

"Looks like it," I replied, signing the book.

"Maybe if you got out of bed a little earlier you'd have time to find it," she smirked.

"Yeah," I said, without really listening.

"There you are," she said, "number sixty-nine."

"Thanks," I said, taking the pass, looking up from the book, and seeing her properly for the first time that day. Janet, it had to be said, wasn't an unattractive woman. She was in her early forties, certainly, but those big pale blue eyes had a certain sparkle, and with the eyes came a smile as big and as warm as a mug of hot chocolate. Plus she had a great figure, in a busty, security guard kind of way. Perhaps it was the uniform. Or the way her blouse gaped a little too much. Either way, something about Janet pressed all the right buttons.

"Janet?" I said.

"Yes Jason?" she replied, the smile getting warmer and more chocolatey by the moment.

"Are you..." I paused, and took a deep breath. "Are you... If I asked... Do you... I..."

"Are you alright?" asked Janet, the smile fading slightly as those pale eyes looked deep into mine. But there it was again – the sparkle. What on earth was I worrying about? A man ten years her junior asking her if she was single – I'd probably make her day. And anyway, I was just asking a simple question. That was all. Just a question.

"Yes, yes. Fine. What I meant was, are you... are you..."

"Yes?" Godammit! I was going to get this out if it took all day! I glanced down to find some composure and as I did, I saw Janet's hands on the desk. Large soft hands, with plump fingers, glossy painted nails and big chunky rings, the most impressive of which was a plain gold band and, on the same finger, a slimmer band with a diamond the size of a small boulder set in the centre.

"Are you," I started again, "opposed to a charity box? Here on reception?"

"A charity box?"

"Yes. For guide dogs. Or something."

"Well, I don't know. I suppose it's a good idea," she answered, barely hiding the confusion in her voice.

"Good!" I said. "Excellent."

"Was that it then?" she asked.

"Yes," I said. "Just something I've been thinking about." I gave her a big smile and then used the temporary pass to get through the turnstiles.

Of course Janet was married. She was an attractive woman – why wouldn't she be married? Attractive women should be married – if they wanted to be – though not all of them, obviously; a few of them needed to remain single for a little longer, otherwise I'd have a serious problem on my hands.

I hung my jacket over the back of my chair. Thing was though, I genuinely couldn't think of a woman who wasn't married.

All those years with Liz, it hadn't registered that the girls I knew were getting on with their lives. Getting hitched. Sure, occasionally I'd receive an invite to the wedding of someone who, in my head, was destined to be the future Mrs Smith. I'd experience a piercing stab of regret, and renew my vow to stop trudging around after Liz, waiting for our relationship to blossom or die of natural causes, and just put the damn thing out of its misery. But the moment would pass, and I'd either tell myself that Liz wasn't so bad, or that it was only a matter of time before she'd dump me. I'd ignore the fact that the pool of Liz alternatives was diminishing, safe in the knowledge that there'd always be one or two left when the time came. Surely.

"Jason?" said Sian.

"Sorry, yes?" I answered, coming out of my trance.

"Are we going to get any work out of you today? Only you rocked up at ten thirty and since then you've been staring into space."

"Oh. Right. Yes. I was thinking."

"About what?" she asked.

"Erm, stuff," I answered.

"Stuff about the requirements document you have in front of you?" she ventured.

"No!" I said, laughing. Sian didn't laugh. "Sorry," I said, and started leafing through the pile of paper in front of me.

I had to be wrong. There must be some single girls left, surely. I glanced up at Sian, who was now engrossed in a phone conversation, and, trying not to draw attention to myself, performed a quick visual sweep of the office.

Sian. Married.

Sarah. Married. To a tall man with strong opinions on his wife's dress sense.

Caroline. Married.

Cathy. Married.

Avril. Married.

Shirley. Married. Somehow.

Joanne. Married.

Laura. Not married – engaged.

Isabella. Married.

Charlotte. I paused to catch my breath. If anyone ever doubted the existence of God, Charlotte was proof that he was alive and well. No one that beautiful could have come into existence without some kind of divine intervention. Tall, slender, elegant, and utterly sexual without even realizing it. Even her starkly conservative, prim and proper clothes became uncharacteristically erotic the longer they remained in contact with her.

Take, for instance, her plain grey cardigan. Having discovered proof of his existence, I bargained with God every night to be reincarnated as that cardigan. No item that plain, or that grey, could have hoped to spend so much time draped over shoulders that delicate, or wrapped round breasts that perfect. It must be the envy of cardigans everywhere.

And her hair. Though she nearly always wore it in a tight aggressive bun, stabbed into place with a large metal rod, a few rebellious locks found their way free, soft ash-blonde curls falling around her face, and suddenly the whole hair up thing was even sexier than the hair down thing. How was that possible? Charlotte made it possible.

Even the way she tucked her phone between her ear and her shoulder, playfully twisting the coiled cable round her finger, was a joy to behold. And whilst somebody, somewhere, was listening to that silky, breathy voice pronouncing each and every word with her careful, well-schooled precision, they were being denied the chance to watch her lips move as she formed each word. I loved that mouth. They couldn't see it widening into a smile. I loved that smile. They couldn't see her throw her head back and laugh. I loved that laugh – more than anything I loved that laugh, and –

A frown formed on Charlotte's face. "What?" she mouthed. Flustered, I gestured that it was nothing and swivelled round to face my desk.

So that was Charlotte. Was she married? No. Was she single? Possibly. Was she out of my league? Most definitely.

Moving on then.

Sally. Married.

That was it. I'd completed my sweep. In the whole of IT there were only two unmarried women! And neither of them were in the slightest way eligible! What the hell had happened in the last three years? How could the entire female population have got hitched? Who to? Where were all these married men? There were more blokes in IT than women and yet nearly all of us were, and possibly always had been, single! Mind you, this was IT – yes, that was it. Somewhere in the building there would be a department of a dozen or so married men, and thirty single Kylie clones. A Yin to IT's Yang.

Accounts, Acquisitions, Finance, Marketing, Credit, Admin, Fraud Prevention, Debt Recovery. Nothing! Every bloody woman in the entire building was, in some way, taken! Apart from the Call Centre of course; that was heaving with women, some of them fairly Kylie-esque, although most of them barely eighteen years of age. Far too young for a man fast approaching thirty. Probably. I chewed over the idea for a second or two, but it was a moot point – I never had any reason to venture into the Call Centre. It might as well be relocated to India for all the good it did me.

So there it was.

I was destined to remain a bachelor.

For the rest of my life.

"Jason!" said Sian. I looked up. "What are you doing now? No no, don't tell me – you're thinking."

"Sorry," I said, rubbing my face with my palms to stimulate a little wakefulness.

"What, for the love of God, has got you so distracted?"

"Oh, nothing," I said.

"No, come on, out with it. Just tell me, so that you can get it out of your system and I can tell you to finish that damn requirements document!"

"It's nothing important."

"Tell me."

"Don't worry about it, really."

"Jason!" she barked. Several of my colleagues stopped what they were doing and turned to face us.

"Ok..." I said, aware that the eyes of the world were on me. "Now I really can't tell you."

"Right," said Sian. She stood up and lifted her jacket off the back of her chair. "Come on."

"Where are you going?"

"We're going to lunch."

"It's eleven thirty!"

"When has that ever stopped you?"

She had a point.

"Out with it," said Sian.

We were sitting at a plastic table on plastic chairs, eating plastic food with plastic cutlery in Southend Victoria Plaza's plastic food court. It was grim, but Sian had insisted that we come here so that she could squeeze in ten minutes of bargain hunting before we went back to the office.

"Out with what?" I said, as I tucked into my chilli jacket.

"What's got you so distracted?" I glanced at the empty space immediately in front of Sian. I should have paid for lunch; I could have insisted that she have something and right now there'd be less talking, and more eating.

"I'm just tired."

"No, that's not it," said Sian.

"Really, I am."

"No, Jason, I understand that you're tired. But that's nothing unusual. You're tired every day."

"I'm not!" I protested.

"Name me one day when you've made it in before half past nine."

"There've been times," I said through a mouthful of potato. Sian raised an eyebrow and folded her scrawny arms across her chest. I chewed thoughtfully. "There was that day! A while back – October, was it?"

"You mean when you forgot to put your clocks back."

"There! See!"

"The point is, you're always tired – but despite this we still manage to get a day's work out of you. Just. Today, however –" I raised my hand to stop her talking.

"I've just got a lot on my mind!"

"Like what?"

"It's private!"

"Fair enough." Sian grabbed the polystyrene tray I was eating from, and stood up.

"Hey! That's my food!"

"No, it's mine. I paid for it!"

"Yes but – you gave it to me."

"And now I'm taking it back."

"You can't do that!"

"Really? Watch me," she turned, and headed towards the nearest bin.

"Sian! Ok, ok!" She returned to the table and sat back down, still holding my lunch.

"Spill."

I looked longingly at the half eaten potato. Then at Sian. Her eyebrows raised. Both, this time. I sighed, and shook my head. I couldn't even think of a convincing lie.

"Where have all the single women gone?" I blurted.

"Are you changing the subject?" asked Sian, her eyes narrowing.

"No! It's been bugging me all morning and until you give my food back I ain't saying another word." She pushed the chilli back across the table. "Thank you," I said, though more to the chilli than Sian.

"So that's it? You've been sitting at your desk trying to figure out who's single and who isn't?"

"More or less," I said, my mouth full of food. Sian said nothing for a moment or two.

"You're not thinking about dumping Liz again?" she asked. "You are, aren't you! That's what this is all about! Jason, how many times do we have to talk about this? If you're that unhappy just –"

"Already have," I said. Sian blinked.

"You and Liz?"

"Yep."

"When did this happen?"

"Couple of weeks ago," I said with a melancholy shrug.

"Weeks?" I could see Sian doing the maths in her head. "When, exactly?"

"Doesn't matter," I said

"Jason!"

"Christmas Day."

"You dumped your girlfriend on Christmas Day?" I stopped chewing for a moment and met her eyes.

"Ok," I said. "I admit the timing was a little off."

"You think?" asked Sian. "You –" she started.

"There's no need for name calling," I said.

"Heartless –"

"Yes, ok."

"Bastard!"

"Ok, I know. I feel bad about it. Can we move on now?"

"Well," said Sian. "I'm impressed."

I frowned.

"There was me thinking you hadn't got the balls. That you'd be with Liz for the rest of your life. Then you go and do it on –"

"Really, you can stop now!"

"So you're single," she said.

"Yes."

"And already you're trying to find someone else?" Her eyebrows climbed back up her forehead.

I shrugged.

"Why? What's wrong with you?" she asked, leaning forwards and putting her arms on the table. "Why so desperate? Why not enjoy being single? God knows I would if I were in your shoes!"

"I don't know what you mean," I said, genuinely confused.

"Go out! Do things! Travel! See the world! Have meaningless sex!"

"Yes, and I'd very much like to do all those things," I said, waving my fork in the air. "I'd just like to do them with someone else!" I stopped my fork waving. "All that time I spent with Liz, it felt like, I dunno, treading water or something. Waiting for life to begin. Except that it never would. Not whilst she was around. But it's over now," I said, pausing only briefly to feel a pang of guilt, and shovel more food into my mouth. "I'm not proud of how it happened, but now that it has I don't see any point in waiting. I want to find someone nice, then we can travel the world together, and do all those other things you said."

"Jason, haven't you heard the saying 'Love comes along when you least expect it'? You'll never find anyone whilst you're looking."

I shook my head. "That's such rubbish."

"Trust me," she said with a condescending smile, "this is the voice of experience talking."

I stopped eating and put down my fork. "Tell me how you met your husband?"

"We just – bumped into each other," said Sian with a shrug and a smile.

I leaned back in my chair, folding my arms high across my chest. "When?"

"One morning."

"Whilst he was walking his dog." I prompted.

"Yes. See, you do know."

"And you were walking your dog."

"I don't have a dog," said Sian, stiffening, her already long neck extending further still.

"No, you don't. But you did borrow one for a while." Sian paused.

"That's when I was thinking about getting a dog. I was finding out whether I was a dog person."

"I get that. What I don't understand is why you had to get up at five in the morning to shave your legs and tart yourself up in order to walk the dog."

"Who told you that?" asked Sian.

"Sarah," I said, with a shrug.

"That bitch," said Sian. "She's so dead."

"Actually," I said, picking up my fork again. "I admire your ingenuity."

"Yes, well, that was a long time ago."

"Not that long." Sian bit her lip, and looked over the balcony and down at the shoppers below.

"Let's get back to you!" she said eventually. "Aside from my New Year's Eve party, where else have you been looking for this extraordinary woman you can call your girlfriend?"

I shrugged again.

"Nowhere really," I replied. My weekend spent trawling the internet would remain a secret.

Sian's eyes narrowed. "So what's your plan?" she asked.

"I thought I wasn't supposed to be looking!"

"Well," said Sian with a flick of her head, "strictly speaking it's more important to give the impression that you're not looking. But if you're going to look anyway, you need a plan. So what is it?"

"I dunno. Meet someone when I'm out and about?"

"You mean, when you're up London drinking with Alex?"

"I suppose so, yes."

"And would you say that getting shit-faced in noisy smelly London pubs is a good way to meet girls?"

"Well, they're not that noisy and we don't –"

"Has it ever worked?"

"No, but I wasn't trying to –"

"Then let's scratch that off your list of potential pulling venues," she said matter-of-factly. "And whilst you're at it forget about using work as your local hunting ground."

"But if work and pubs are out of the question, where on earth am I going to find someone – and please," I said, raising a hand, "don't say nightclubs"

"Nightclubs?" said Sian. "Terrible idea."

"That's what I thought."

"You'd never pick up a woman in a nightclub! You need somewhere with less competition. Somewhere you'd be the only man – and where you won't embarrass yourself. At least, not in a bad way."

"Oh," I said. Suddenly I didn't feel quite so hungry. I pushed the remains of the potato to one side.

"How do you feel about cookery classes?" she asked.

The flat was an ice box.

Cold and empty. The same could have been said of my life.

I closed the door and considered whether it was worth removing my jacket.

"Evening," said a voice. I walked into what was once my kitchen.

"Haven't you got a home to go to?" I asked Martin, who was kneeling on the worktop.

"Just finishing this second coat," he replied. "Don't touch that," he said, waving his free arm in my general direction, "it's still wet."

"Oh, right," I said, moving away from anything and everything, whilst trying to locate the wet item. The fridge didn't look wet. I moved towards the fridge. "You want a beer?" I asked. I took one out for myself and waited for Martin's answer.

"No. Don't drink."

"Right," I said, closing the fridge door. "I remember: 'Alcohol is the government's way of controlling the working classes'."

Martin climbed down from the worktop. "Not just the working classes," he said.

I took a swig from the can, and then looked at it. "This beer's warm," I said, more to myself than Martin. Warm beer. Cold flat. Typical.

Martin eyed me thoughtfully, and then scratched his beard.

"Fridge ain't working," he said. "Had to disconnect the power in here. I'll fix it tomorrow. Something bothering you young Jason? It's written all over your face." Martin turned his back on me and wrapped his paint brushes in carrier bags. I sighed. So we were going to discuss me, were we, and casually ignore the issue of the unfinished kitchen? I went to lean against the wall. "Mind the radiator," said Martin without looking. "It's not attached to anything."

"Oh, right," I said, moving away from the wall.

"Girl problems, is it?"

"Well, yes. Sort of. But not really." I gave up trying to answer the question.

Martin reached inside his overalls and pulled out his packet of cigarette papers and a pouch of tobacco. "Soon as you know what the problem is, the answer's usually right in front of you." I watched as he rolled a cigarette. It was hypnotic.

"Right," I said. Conversations with Martin generally followed a similar theme. I tried not to encourage them but sometimes I couldn't help myself.

"Plus your aura's all off balance," said Martin, "has been for a while – the colours are all over the shop. Only way to fix it is to give your soul new purpose. Listen to what the Universe is telling you, young Jason, and act on it. That's all there is to it." Martin finished making his cigarette, then put it behind his ear. Despite the whiskers, the flecks of paint, the dust and the plaster, Martin's skin looked remarkably smooth, and his eyes were unusually blue, like the pilot light inside an old gas boiler.

"And you can see this in my aura?" I asked, snapping out of the trance.

"Yep," said Martin. He nodded slowly to emphasise the point, then turned and grabbed his jacket and a bunch of keys from the worktop. "Right then," he said. "Be back Wednesday."

"Hang on," I said suddenly, chasing him down the hall. "What about the radiator, and the fridge, and all the other things that you're fixing tomorrow?"

"Wednesday. I'll do it Wednesday. Listen to the Universe, Jason," he said as he plodded down the stairs to the front door, "then act on it." The door slammed behind him.

What the hell did Martin know? The man lived in some sort of alternate reality where the government controlled the nation through alcohol and people had 'auras'. It just so happened that his wacky reality and mine seemed to intersect at exactly the point where my maisonette stood, which was useful because I needed a new kitchen. Or so Liz had told me.

It was nice that he was concerned though. Because without Martin and his ability to see my shitty aura I might as well be utterly invisible. No one else in the entire world cared one iota about Jason Smith. I wandered back into the kitchen.

Alex probably did. Care, I mean. In his own Alex-kind-of-way. And Sian. The lunch thing had been kind of nice. Though her cookery class suggestion was bordering on lunacy. But other than Martin, and Alex, and Sian – there was no one.

I lifted the beer can to my mouth, only to find it was empty, hollow, and drained of anything worthwhile. And in that moment I was seven years old again, and in need of my mum.

Because mums always care.

It doesn't matter how stupid you've been, or what scrapes you've got yourself into, or whether you dumped your girlfriend – the one that you've been faking it with for three years – on Christmas Day – your mum always cares, no matter what.

And instead of brooding I should be calling her and, well, maybe not talking, not about everything, but at the very least coming clean about Liz and how that made me feel sad. And lonely. And a little bit scared. In short, I needed to let my mother care for me.

I walked purposefully into the lounge, fresh beer at the ready, and picked up the receiver. Which is when I noticed the flashing light on the answering machine. I had a message. Someone out there cared enough to leave me a message. I hit play.

"Jason? It's Mum. Are you there?" She paused. "Ok. Well. I thought you should know that I called Liz today. I'm sorry if you think that I've stepped over the line, but I was worried – the poor girl could have been at death's door for all I knew – you weren't telling me anything! And now I know why.

"She's not sick at all, is she? She's angry. Understandably so. And very, very disappointed." Mum's voice thinned, as though someone had her by the throat. "As am I," she added.

"Of course, I realise that it's all the rage for people to 'separate' or some such nonsense, but that, Jason, is just another word for 'being selfish', and if you don't mind me saying, you, Jason, are being very selfish indeed. How could you? On Christmas Day of all days! After sitting there at my dinner table, behaving like nothing was wrong, whilst all the time you were... plotting. It's so typical of you, Jason!

Did you not think how this was going to affect your father and me? Or your sister? Or your niece? No, as usual you thought about no one but yourself. And even though everyone was perfectly happy... you just took it upon yourself..." She paused for a moment, and I heard what might have been the faintest of stifled sobs, but before I could be sure she blurted, "Selfish!"

Then the machine went quiet.

I stood there, agog.

"Well, you're obviously not going to pick up the phone," continued my mother, regaining her composure but adding a fresh layer of iciness to her tone, "so I'm going now. Perhaps you could do me the courtesy of returning my call when you get this message. Lots of love." The machine beeped.

I slumped onto the arm of the sofa. Gone was my misery and self-loathing, replaced instead by the stinging shock of my mother's tirade. That and the shoulder-stiffening, mind-sobering realisation that, whilst two or three people might offer me the occasional gem of wisdom about auras, the universe or cookery classes, the hard truth of the matter was I really was on my own.

And not for the first time that day, or indeed any of the days in the previous couple of months, my thoughts went back to a cold, rain-filled January night, ten years earlier.

Chapter Six
Friday 8th January, 1988

"**P**assenger announcement: British Rail regrets to announce that due to adverse weather conditions, services in and out of Liverpool Street are currently subject to delay. Passengers are advised to continue watching the information boards for further details. We apologise for any inconvenience caused."

As I descended the stairs from the rainy streets, the station concourse was a heaving mass of suited bodies, most of whom were gawping at the words 'cancelled' or 'delayed', but each one silently – or not so silently – doing what they did every Friday evening: hating British Rail.

Why was it always a Friday? The reasons varied, of course – overhead line problems, incident at Bethnal Green, engine failure, leaves on the line, wrong type of snow – but it always happened, always, on a Friday night, when all that I wanted was to get back to Chelmsford and join Alex in the Tulip. In a few weeks I would be twenty. And how would I be celebrating that particular milestone? If British Rail had anything to do with it I'd be standing on the concourse of Liverpool Street Station with the rest of the goons.

I threw my bag over my shoulder and headed back up the steps and into the city.

I was the only one in the Wimpy. Other than the waitress. And the burger chef. I sat by the window and watched the rain streak down the glass to the sound of the strip lights fizzing and popping over my head.

"*Kingsize and chips,*" stated the waitress as she placed my food on the plastic table. I turned to look at her, but she'd gone.

Kingsize and chips. Normally I'd argue that this particular meal was a bite-sized portion of happiness on a plate. Right now, however, it was taking the place of several pints of Guinness, the company of my best friend, and the promise of a five minute stagger back to his mum's house for as much toast as we could eat.

I let out a long, miserable sigh, picked up the burger, and went to take a bite.

"Jason?" I looked up into two gorgeous emerald green eyes, and froze. Those were her eyes. My field of vision widened to take in her nose. Regal in nature. That was definitely her nose. Then there was the slightly coy, but nonetheless playful smile. And those beautiful white teeth. And that hair, tumbling out from under a cerise beret – even though she was now a blonde my heart wasn't fooled for a moment; it was still her. And all at once I was fourteen again, trombone in hand, looking across at her from my place in the brass section.

"I thought it was you," she said. "You don't recognise me, do you? It's –"

I swallowed.

"Melanie. Mel! Hi! Of course I... of course – Hi!"

"I was walking by and I thought, 'Is that Jason Smith?' And, well – here you are."

"Here I am!" I said. Nothing happened for a moment. And then she smiled.

"That looks nice," she said, glancing at the burger in my hands. "Do you come here often?"

"Here?" I asked. "No – I – there's a problem. With the trains." I jerked my head in the general direction of Liverpool Street Station.

"So you can't get home?"

"Oh, I'm sure they'll sort it out. At some point. They usually do." I nodded. Then smiled. Then nodded some more whilst I tried to think of something to plug the gap in the conversation. "Is that why you're here?" I asked eventually.

"No, I saw you as I was walking past –"

"No, I meant, are you stranded in London?"

"Me? No, I live here now," said Melanie.

"In the City?"

"No!" laughed Melanie. "North London. I work in the City. I've just left the office." I glanced at the clock on the wall – it was a quarter to seven. "I was walking to the tube," she added. I nodded. And smiled.

"Right," I said.

There it was again. A gap in the conversation. Only not so much a gap, more a bloody great rift. Something was supposed to be happening now, but I had absolutely no idea what.

"I suppose I've got time to join you for a bit," Melanie said, taking off her mittens and matching scarf.

"Oh – really? That would be – Would you like a cup of tea?" I asked.

"Mmm – a Diet Coke would be nice."

"Right!" I said, putting my burger down. "Let me get you one!" I stood up and started digging deep in my pockets for loose change but my fingers met nothing but tissues and screwed up receipts. I dug deeper, hoping for a miracle, but considering Melanie Jackson had just walked back into my life after a five year absence, two miracles in one night seemed highly unlikely.

"Here," said Melanie, reaching into her handbag, "let me." She produced a five pound note and passed it to me.

"Thanks," I said, barely managing to conceal my humiliation. "I'll be right back."

"So you didn't go to uni then?" asked Melanie. I shook my head.

"More studying?" I said, stuffing the last of the chips into my mouth, then washing them down with tea. "Give me a break."

"But you were one of the clever ones!"

"Not really."

"I always thought uni sounded like fun," said Melanie, playing with the straws that poked through the lid of her Coke. "All those parties..." She leant forward to take another sip, looking up at me as she did so, which made her eyes seem all the larger.

"Yeah," I said. Parties? Ugh. "Why didn't you go to uni then?"

"Oh please," said Melanie after a long noisy slurp of her drink. "And study what? Brain surgery?"

"Why not?"

"Nah, I needed a job. A girl needs shoes! They don't buy themselves. Well, not unless you have a boyfriend."

I'd barely registered what she'd said before I heard the words "You don't have a boyfriend!?" tumbling out of my mouth with all the subtlety of a rhinoceros at a village tea party. But Melanie didn't seem to notice.

"Not really," she said, before hoovering up the last of her Coke.

"Oh," I said, following it with a small nod to conceal my confusion. Not really? What did that mean? Either you do or you don't, don't you? 'Not really' sounded as if there was a bloke in Melanie's world who thought he was her boyfriend but would discover, possibly in the not too distant future, that he wasn't. Poor bastard.

"Nothing serious," said Melanie, reading my mind. "You know what it's like."

"Yeah, yeah." I said. No. I didn't understand that at all.

"What about you?" she asked

"What about me what?"

"Any girlfriends?"

I laughed. "Me? No," I said.

"Really?"

"Well," I said, feeling myself flush slightly. "Nothing serious. You know..."

"Footloose and fancy free, eh?" said Melanie.

"Yeah, I suppose so."

"I always wondered," said Melanie, idly playing with her straw again, "why you never asked me out." For a moment or two, time ground to a halt. Even the strip lights above us seemed to stop their manic flickering whilst they waited for me to respond.

"You did?" I asked, swallowing.

"Yeah."

"Well..." I puffed my cheeks out. "I guess, I erm..."

"Maybe you didn't fancy me?" said Melanie with a shrug.

"What? No! I mean, yes! Yes I did."

"Did?"

"Do!" I said, correcting myself, then almost as quickly: "Did! No – Do! I mean –" Melanie's smile broadened until it was a fully fledged grin and her eyes flashed like a card player who's holding all the aces. I felt my face flush again, and took a deep breath. "You're messing with me, aren't you?"

"A little bit," said Melanie, running her tongue along the edge of her lovely teeth. I could feel my face getting redder still. Other things were happening too: my heart was beating out a rumba, and a shy smile was sidling across my face. I looked down into my empty polystyrene cup to try and hide it. "Come on," she said, touching my arm. "Let's find a pub – I'll buy you a proper drink."

I staggered back to our table with another round. I was extremely drunk. Though not the usual blurry intoxication that followed a few pints. Instead everything, and everyone, sparkled with a magical sheen. The barman greeted me with a cheery wink. Fellow drinkers smiled at me as I passed by. Even my stagger was just a side effect of feet that were through with walking and wanted to dance.

Melanie grinned as I sat down next to her. It had been the only way I could hear what she was saying over the collective din of the Red Lion's clientele. Now, of course, most of the after work drinkers had left but moving to the other side of the table would have seemed rude. At least, that's what I was telling myself.

"So where were we?" I asked.

"You were telling me about computer games," said Melanie, "the ones you would make – and how amazing they would be."

"I was? Oh." I scratched my head. "And yet somehow you're still here? Enough about me – tell me what you're doing."

Melanie's shoulders slumped.

"Oh, I just work reception for Harris, Harris and Harris. It's a law firm."

"Right. And is it good?"

Melanie gave me a long, serious look.

"No Jason, it's crap. It's the world's most boring job."

"Oh," I said. "But is the money good?"

"Not really."

"Right," I said. "So what did you want to do?" Melanie sipped her Malibu and Coke, and stared into the distance.

"I guess that's the problem," she said after a while. "I didn't really know."

"Alex always thought you'd be in a band with Robert Palmer," I said, bringing my pint to my lips. "Like one of the girls in that video..."

"Oh did he now?"

"Yeah."

"Uh huh. And what about you?"

"What about me?"

"What did you imagine I'd be doing when I left school?" I felt myself blush again. Melanie saw it and raised an eyebrow.

"Erm, I thought you might be a model. Or something."

"Really?" she said, that familiar evil grin working its way across her face. "And what kind of modelling did you envisage?"

"Just modelling," I lied.

"Uh huh," she said again, leaning forward to stare into my eyes. "Thought about this a lot, did you?" I swallowed

"Not a lot," I lied again.

"Mmmm," she said, and smiled. She leaned back and picked up her glass again. "Sounds like I should have come to you and Alex for career advice, rather than taking the first crappy job that came along."

"You could always get a different job," I suggested.

"It's not... that simple."

"Sure it is," I said. But Melanie dropped her gaze to her lap and suddenly I could see that the crappy job situation was a conversational minefield that we'd wandered into, and only a miracle, or something similar, was going to rescue us from it. "Look," I said, placing my pint on the table in a determined manner, "how about this – I'll grant you three wishes."

"What?" said Melanie, looking up.

"Three wishes. Right now. One time offer only."

"You're going to grant me three wishes?"

"Sure. But you have to make them now."

"And I can have anything I want?"

"Well, I thought we were talking about your career but –"

"If you're going to start handing out wishes, Mr Genie of the Guinness Barrel, I'm not going to waste them on work!"

"Well ok," I said. "Three wishes, to do what you like with."

"Right," she said, repositioning herself and putting her hands in her lap. She looked past me and bit her lip whilst she considered her options and, not for the first time that evening, I suddenly wanted to kiss her. And it was more than a mere urge. I found myself having to exert considerable effort just to prevent myself from leaning forward and –

"Ok," said Melanie. "Wish number one: I wish I had a pair of Jimmy Choos."

"Jimmy what?" I asked.

"Only the best damn shoes on the planet!" said Melanie. I frowned.

"You're going to use your first wish on shoes?!"

"Not just 'a pair of shoes'!" said Melanie. "Jimmy Choos – they're in this month's *Vogue* and everything!"

"Yeah, but why didn't you wish for a million pounds or something – then you could buy all the bloomin' shoes you –"

"What? I can do that?" she asked.

"Well, of course you can do that!" I said, and I picked up my pint.

"Ok – I wish for a million pounds."

I put up my hand whilst I took a sip. "Too late now," I said, "you've made your wish."

"What? No! That's not fair."

"Too late," I said again.

"It's not too late!" protested Melanie.

"Judge's ruling, I'm afraid." She let out a long exasperated sigh, then resumed her thinking pose, though this time her face was fixed into a determined frown.

"Ok," she said after a moment. "Second wish – I wish I could have my first wish back!"

I shook my head.

"Sorry. No can do."

"That's not fair!" I held up both my hands. "Ok, ok," she relented, putting her hands in her hair and massaging her scalp. My eyes dropped to her chest and for a second or two I was back at school, sitting in the orchestra, peering at her from behind my music stand. "Ok," said Melanie, unaware of my leering, "wish number two: a million pounds."

I frowned.

"That's a bit boring."

"What? I can't have wishes if they're boring? Who makes these rules?"

"I didn't say you couldn't have your wish – just that it was a bit boring."

"But you suggested it!"

"Yeah, for wish number one – instead of shoes! I was expecting something a little more interesting for wish number two."

"Well, I'm sorry!" said Melanie, folding her arms across her chest.

"No, no, that's ok. You can have your million pounds."

"Thank you!"

"What are you going to do with it?" I asked.

"I've got to tell you that as well?"

"No, I just thought you might have something in mind."

"Jason," she said, putting a hand on my thigh, "I'm a woman – it'll be spent in no time." She took her hand away and I glanced down, fully expecting to see some sort of glowing sparkly hand print.

"Ok," I said, after taking a moment to compose myself. "Wish number three?" She sighed.

"That's easy," she said, turning in her seat to face forwards. Her shoulders slumped, and a chill swept through the room. "Somebody who doesn't run out the door twenty seconds after... you know." Her chest rose and fell as she took a melancholy breath. "Someone who will lie there, just for a little while and maybe talk to me for a bit?" A lump formed in my throat. I wanted to put my hand on her shoulder to comfort her, but – I couldn't. This was Melanie Jackson. And I'm Jason Smith. Instead I watched as she traced her finger round the rim of her glass, acutely aware that somehow the magic had stalled, and that our evening had begun to nosedive into a black sea of despair.

No. I wouldn't let it. Not this evening. Melanie Jackson had walked back into my life, lent me the money to buy her a Diet Coke, invited me out for a drink and spent the best part of two hours flirting with me. Either this was destiny or, more likely, destiny had her back turned! Either way, this was a once in a lifetime opportunity and I wasn't about to let it crash and burn.

"Would you be wearing... anything... at this particular moment?" I asked, with a cough.

"What?"

"After, you know... the sex?"

Melanie blinked.

"Probably not," she said

"Well, I can't see why any man in their right mind would want to run off." Melanie blinked again. "I mean – this one wouldn't. Not in a million years. So, erm," I took a decisive breath, "- wish granted." She smiled. Not the cheeky grin that I'd seen several times that evening, but the warm, coy smile of someone who recognises when a friend is trying to be nice.

"Thank you," she said, softly.

"You're very welcome," I said. A thought occurred to me. "Ok, look, I feel a bit bad about your first wish – I'm not saying that it was unfair or anything, but I think that in hindsight, maybe I could have explained the rules a little better –"

"Yeah!" said Melanie, poking me in the ribs with a finger.

"So in view of that, and on the strict understanding that this is a goodwill gesture from us in the wish-granting community –"

"I can have another wish?" she asked, clapping her hands together and bouncing up and down in her seat.

"I'm going to let you amend one of your wishes." The bouncing stopped.

"Amend?" she asked suspiciously.

"Yes. But," I said, as she opened her mouth to speak, "think about it first! Don't just blurt out 'I want another pair of Jimmy blahdy-blah shoes.'"

"There's nothing wrong with wishing for a pair of Jimmy Choos!" said Melanie. "I don't think you appreciate just how amazing they are!"

"Yeah, well, whatever," I said, waving away the comment. She assumed her thinking pose. Her top lip curled and wriggled around under her nose whilst she considered her response.

"Ok," she said.

"You're ready?" I asked.

"Yes."

"So which wish are you amending?"

"The third one," she said.

I moved backwards like I was trying to assist my eyes in focusing.

"The third one?"

"Yes."

"Wha- ok then. So what is it now?"

Melanie took a deep breath.

"I wish that one day I'll meet a guy. And he'll be... well, perfect – and by perfect I mean perfect for me. Not necessarily the kinda guy I would pick, because I always pick bastards, but the kinda guy that, I dunno, my mum would pick... if my mum had decent taste in men. Do you know what I mean? Anyway, I'd meet this guy and it'll be 'the moment'."

"The moment?" I asked.

"Yeah. The moment. I might not even realise it at first, but looking back later I'll realise that that was 'the moment' – when my life changed, and everything got better, and all because of him. There, that's my wish. I want the moment. Can I have that please? Jason?"

"Sorry," I said, shaking the entrancement out of my head. "I was distracted."

"What by?" she asked.

"Erm..."

"Tell me."

"Your lips," I said. "Moving." She smiled. Not the cheeky Melanie Jackson grin, or the coyness I'd seen a moment ago, but the new, bright, sensuous smile of someone who knows just how powerful smiles can be.

"Melanie –" I said.

"Oh my God," said Melanie, looking over my shoulder.

"What?" I said, swivelling round to try and see what she was looking at.

"Is that the time?" There was a clock on the opposite wall. I checked my wrist watch.

"Yeah. Why?"

"Oh Jason, I had no idea it was so late – excuse me." She shuffled down the seat and stood up.

"Are you – are you leaving?"

"'Fraid so. Sorry. I was supposed to be somewhere else half an hour ago," she said.

"Really? Where?"

"Oh, just this place."

"Well, is it important?" I asked.

"Erm, yeah," she said, checking for something in her purse and producing a travel card. "Look, I've really enjoyed this evening. Maybe we can do it again sometime?"

"Yeah, that would be –"

"Ok. Great," she said, leaning forward to kiss me on the cheek. "Well, take care,"

"Ok, but when?"

"I'll – I'll call you," she said as she squeezed past me.

"But you don't have my number!"

"I'll look you up."

"But – look me up where?"

"Sorry, gotta run," she said as she got to the door, and all but sprinted out of the pub and into the city streets. I stood there, rooted to the spot, my hand on my cheek where her lips had brushed, swaying slightly as if someone had just slugged me round the back of the head with something heavy. For a split second I wanted to run after her, grab her by the arm, and... something. What? What would I do? I felt my knees buckle and I slumped back into the chair. There was nothing I could do. Because she was Melanie Jackson. And I'm just Jason Smith.

My eyes settled on her wine glass, noticing for the first time the lipstick mark on the rim, and I thought about Melanie's last wish – her amended wish – and 'the moment' she craved so badly. I picked up the glass and examined it.

"Wish granted," I said.

CHAPTER SEVEN
TUESDAY 20TH JANUARY, 1998

"**R**ight, look – I'm just gonna start," said Rog, running a hand over his bald head. "And if anybody else turns up," he paused to squeeze a finger between his tree trunk of a neck and the collar of his shirt, "well, they'll wish they'd arrived on time." The twelve-strong class of heavily tattooed, muscle-bound men rippled with a mixture of smirks, huffs of impatience, and the occasional burning stare of barely-concealed aggression.

I shuffled in my seat, and wondered – again – how I'd ever let Alex talk me into this.

"What's this?" I asked, picking up the magazine that had been lying across my keyboard.

"And a good morning to you too, Jason," said Sian. "Did you have a nice weekend? I had a lovely weekend – thanks for asking. Oh, you didn't. Oh well. What's it look like?" I stood there for a moment whilst my bewildered brain separated her sentences and made sense of them all.

"Erm, a magazine? From Southend Borough Council."

"That's right. Very good. Now let's try the smaller words towards the bottom." I looked. This was too much for a Monday morning.

"Evening class prospectus."

"Excellent! Top marks, Mr Smith. Now, if you'd like to turn your attention to the page with the post-it note sticking out the side..." I opened the prospectus; on one page a large yellow sticky note with a big red arrow drawn on it pointed to a heading that Sian had ringed: Cookery Classes. I slumped into my chair.

"I am not going to cookery classes," I said.

"Please yourself."

"No, Sian – really! I'm not."

"Ok."

"Look, it's no good going on and on about it," I said as I span around in my chair.

"Alex phoned."

"For one thing I can't cook!"

"That's why they call them classes, Jason," said Sian. "Otherwise they'd be cookery..." she searched for the word, "clubs."

"Alex called this morning?" I asked.

"Yes. He thought my cookery classes idea was a stroke of genius and you should stop being such an idiot."

"Really?" Sian rolled her eyes, then shook her head in pity.

"No," she said slowly. "He said something about meeting up for a beer tonight. There's a surprise; Monday morning and already your mate Alex is trying to arrange a trip to the pub."

"Look! I don't want to go to cookery classes!"

"Fine," said Sian.

"I won't know anyone!" I whined. "I'll probably be the only bloke in a room full of women!"

Sian stopped what she was doing and looked at me in that Sian-like way that she reserved for moments when my stupidity had reached new depths.

"Oh," I said. "I see."

"Barmy," said Alex. I sighed and brought the pint glass to my lips. "Women don't attend cookery classes to find a bloke."

"I realise that," I said patiently. "They are, however, full of women!"

"Yeah, old women."

"I like the older woman."

"Mate, these women won't be older," said Alex. "They'll be old – with granddaughters."

"Well, maybe they'll try and – I dunno – set me up with one of their granddaughters, or something!"

"That's the most stupid thing I ever heard," said Alex.

"Well, Einstein, if you have a better idea –"

"Actually, I do," he interrupted.

"You do?" I was taken aback. Alex never had ideas. His job was to shoot mine down in flames. "Ok" I said, my curiosity piqued. "I'm listening."

"Beer first," said Alex, getting out of his chair.

"In a minute – it's my round. Sit back down and tell me your big idea." We stared at each other across the table.

"Ok, ok," said Alex, after a standoff of three whole seconds. "Motor mechanic classes."

"Sorry?"

"Car mechanic basics," he continued. "Home car maintenance..."

"I don't understand."

"Jesus mate, it's not difficult. Most evening class places have them: car tinkering for..."

"No, I get that part," I said. "I just don't see how that can possibly be a good place to meet women."

"It's obvious," said Alex.

"Is it?"

Alex threw his head back and stared at the ceiling as if willing a grand piano in the room above to fall through the floor and bring the conversation to an abrupt end.

"Ok," he said, leaning forwards again. "Imagine you're a woman."

"Ok."

"And you want to meet a man. Right?"

"Ok."

"So you decide an evening class might be a good place to do that, right?"

"Yes..." I said slowly.

"So there you are!" He stopped, both palms flat on the table, leaning forward, his eyes pleading with me to buy him a beer.

"An evening class for car mechanics," I said.

"Not for car mechanics," said Alex through gritted teeth. "A class where you go to learn the things that car mechanics know!"

"That's where I would find women?"

"Yes!" said Alex urgently. If beer wasn't forthcoming in the next few moments, The Phoenix Bar & Tavern would become the final resting place of one Jason Smith.

"Because that's where women, looking for men, would go?" I asked, following his logic.

"Yes! Yes!"

"Ok," I said brightly. "Beer?"

"Finally!" said Alex.

I stood at the bar, mulling it over. It was intriguing. Sian had suggested cookery classes because logically cookery classes would attract women. Some of whom might be single. But Alex's idea was altogether more sophisticated; out there, right now, was a lonely, desperate, but none the less beautiful woman thinking along similar lines to myself. She'd be wondering what evening class she should attend to meet lots of men, and unless she had a genius friend with the same twisted logic as Alex, she wasn't going to come up with cookery. She was going to come up with 'car mechanic basics'. Or something similar. All I had to do was ensure that I was at that class when she turned up.

I returned to the table and found Alex thumbing through a magazine. I put his pint in front of him, pulled a magazine of my own from my back pocket, and sat down.

"What you reading?" I asked.

"*FHM*," said Alex without looking up. "There's this barbers where the hairdressers are all babes and work in just their underwear."

"Where?" I asked.

"Vegas," said Alex. He picked up his beer. "What's that?" he asked, after satisfying his thirst.

"Evening class prospectus," I mumbled as I flicked through the pages.

"What you looking for?"

"This!" I said, turning the page round and stabbing part of it with my index finger. "*Understanding The Car*. Starts next week." Alex pushed his copy of *FHM* across the table.

"And if it doesn't work out," he said, "get us a pair of tickets to Vegas. I could do with a trim."

Sandwiched between the man with a spider-web tattoo where most people would have had hair, and the man with more metal in his face than the contents of the average car mechanic's toolbox, I glanced over at the door again. It would be an extremely brave woman who'd have the nerve to walk in and join this particular evening class. And any woman who wasn't phased by – if we're being diplomatic

– thirteen strapping specimens of 'rugged manliness', was, I suspected, unlikely to be the kind of woman who would find me quite so alluring.

"Actually, Rog," I said, my heart in my mouth, "before you start, I think I'm going to make a move." Rog stared at me like his eyes were going to pop out of their sockets. "If you don't mind," I added.

"You what? Why!?" Rog asked, his eyes narrowing. I grabbed my jacket and felt the blood rush to my cheeks as all eyes turned to me.

"It's just – not what I was expecting," I said, edging towards the door.

"What were you expecting?" asked Rog, his voice getting more shrill with each passing word. "A fucking cookery class!?"

I relaxed. And smiled.

"Actually, yes," I said, and I closed the door behind me.

I'd had surprisingly little difficulty persuading the lady on the phone that 'car mechanics' wasn't for me, and that I'd like to switch class, but as I struggled to skin a pair of chicken thighs I started to wonder whether this had been a wise idea.

"Why don't you let me help you with that?" offered the short, silver-haired lady.

"Erm, well yes, thanks, that would be..."

"I'm Mary," she said, beaming up at me.

"Oh, right, I'm Jason. I..."

"You peel those garlic cloves," suggested Mary, nudging me out of the way.

"Right," I said. "Ok. Garlic." I picked up a clove and tried removing the skin. Mary looked up at me and smiled.

"Irene," she said over her shoulder.

"Yes dear?" replied Irene from the bank of worktops behind us.

"Could you help young Jason?"

"Of course, dear," said Irene, and a moment later a slightly taller, silver-haired woman was standing on the other side of me. "Oh, not like that, dear," she said, taking the clove from me. "I find it easier if you chop the tops and the bottoms off first, then crush them ever so slightly under the blade of a knife. The skins just come straight off. See?" She peeled a second clove in the same manner. "Would you like me to chop that onion up a little more?" she asked, nodding towards my pile of partially disassembled onion.

"Oh – do you think it needs it?" I asked as she reached across for my onion, re-slicing it before I'd finished my sentence.

"That's your chicken done," said Mary. "Now, is your pan ready?"

"Pan?" I said. "Oh, I hadn't..." I opened a cupboard and desperately started looking for a frying pan.

"Not a problem," said Doris, the large lady from across the worktop.

"Thank you, dear," said Mary, taking Doris's pan and placing it on my stove.

"Right," I said, with as much assertiveness as I could muster. "I've got some oil." I pulled a plastic bottle of sunflower oil from my carrier bag. Irene glanced at the bottle in my hand and raised an eyebrow.

"That's alright, dear," she said, crossing back to her workspace and returning with a sleek glass bottle, "use some of mine."

"But," I said, "I bought it specially."

"Yes, but this is olive oil," said Irene reassuringly. "Save that for another time. Don't you agree, Mary?"

"Oh absolutely, dear. Extra virgin every time."

"Extra virgin?" I said. "I'm really not that fussy." I sniggered at the sharpness of my wit – which was met with a resounding silence. Then Mary smirked and elbowed me in the ribs.

"I see," said Irene, tossing my chicken into the pan, "and are you in the market for a lady friend?"

I swallowed hard. "Well, I..."

"What about your niece, Irene?" asked Mary, rooting through my carrier bags for whatever we needed next. "She's available, isn't she?"

"What, Anna?"

"Oh yes," said Doris in approval. "Anna and Jason – they'd make a lovely couple."

"Do you think so?" asked Irene. Nobody seemed the slightest bit interested in my opinions on the matter.

"Oh, Anna is a lovely girl," agreed Mary. "Ever so pretty." She nudged me again.

"Well, she's certainly pretty," said Irene, emptying the onions into the pan. "But I'm not sure I'd go as far as 'lovely' – for one thing, she's such a terrible cook."

"Jason doesn't need a girlfriend who can cook," said Mary, taking my arm in hers and looking up at me with a warm smile. "We'll soon teach him!" I felt a little uncomfortable at this display of affection. I was also dimly aware that Doris had passed something else to Irene and that this too had been added to the meal I could no longer claim any credit for.

"Well, that's true, I suppose," said Irene. "Although I wouldn't like to cook for her – she's a terribly fussy eater. Only the other day I met her and her mother for lunch, and she complained that there was no vegetarian option on the menu. 'Anna,' I said, 'this is a pub! You can't expect to dish up half a dozen baby carrots and an asparagus to beer drinkers. These people need proper food.' She turned to me and said that if she had her way pubs wouldn't be allowed to serve food, and restaurants wouldn't be allowed to sell alcohol. I mean, how ridiculous."

"Oh Irene," said Mary, still crushing my arm in hers, "you are being beastly. Anna's a charming girl. I'm sure Jason will think so. Look, you can see that he's interested." I felt my cheeks start to glow.

"I just don't want to put poor Jason in an awkward situation, dear. She can be very difficult. I put it down to working with computers all day long. I'm not sure they'll have anything in common."

"What is it that you do, Jason?" asked Mary.

Exactly a week after the cookery class, and two weeks after my ill-fated car maintenance class, I was standing in front of my wardrobe, staring at its contents, trying to choose something suitable for a first date.

My first date, that is, with Anna.

Anna, niece of Irene. Anna, topic of much discussion amongst the attendees of certain cookery classes in the Southend area. Anna, occasionally difficult, terrible cook, but ever-so-pretty. Apparently. It was vital I made a good impression. And already I was out of my depth.

Like most men, the contents of my wardrobe consisted of bits and pieces that I'd acquired over, say, a ten year period. Trying to put together what could loosely be referred to as 'an outfit', especially one that 'made a good impression', was the clothing equivalent of trying to build a particle accelerator from a box of old pinball machine parts when I had only the vaguest notion of what a particle accelerator should look like or how it works.

I checked the time. Ten past six. She'd be here in twenty minutes. Probably earlier. I sighed, reached into the wardrobe and pulled out the shirt and trousers that Liz bought me a couple of birthdays back. Whilst Liz had never torn them from my body in a moment of unbridled passion, she knew more about clothes than I did. She'd told me so on numerous occasions.

I hunted around in a drawer for matching socks. Already I had a strong feeling that this was a colossal waste of time. Aside from the cookery class revelations, everything else I knew about Anna had been derived from a telephone conversation that had lasted all of three minutes – and it hadn't gone well.

"Is that Anna?" I'd asked.

"Who is this?" said a voice.

"My name's Jason –"

"The boy from my aunt's cookery class?"

"Yes," I said. "That's right."

"My aunt said you'd call over the weekend."

"She did? Oh, sorry, I was a bit –"

"I can't make tonight," interrupted Anna. For a moment I didn't know what to say. I'd been hoping for a bit of a chat before arranging anything.

"Oh. Well, that's –"

"I could make tomorrow, I suppose," she said. "If we kept it brief. I don't like to be out too late."

"Tomorrow? Yes, tomorrow would be –"

"Where are we going?" she asked.

"Well," I said. "Why don't we go for a drink?"

"I don't drink." I floundered for a second.

"Oh. Erm..."

"I don't like pubs," she continued.

"Right," I said. "Well. We could... do you like Indian food?" It was the only thing that came to mind.

"I don't know," said Anna. She paused. "Indians are vegetarian, aren't they? I knew this Indian girl once, and she was a vegan."

"Well, I'm sure they do vegetarian dishes..."

"Ok then," said Anna. "Six thirty."

"Oh, right," I said. "Well, that's... Shall I erm, pick you up?"

"No. I'll come to you," said Anna. Then she asked me for my address, and once I'd given it to her she put the phone down on me. And that was it. Not the most promising start to our relationship.

And here I was, worrying about socks.

I sat on the edge of the bed and waited for the doorbell to ring. 'Toll' would have been a better word. Then something caught my eye. Stuffed in the side pocket of my work bag was the copy of *FHM* Alex had given me, still folded open at the article about the semi-dressed hairdressers in Vegas. If anything was going to lighten my mood, 'Barbers in the Buff' ought to do it. I pulled it from the pocket, turned to the front cover, and there, in a slinky little black dress, was Kylie.

My Kylie.

I flicked through the magazine and found the feature. Nine pages, as I'd never seen her before. Gone was the girly pop princess. Suddenly she was all grown up – all choppy shoulder length red hair, all bust, all legs, all heels, all crystal blue eyes and smiles, all – woman. And though each of her outfits barely covered much more than was absolutely necessary, she still had such class, such dignity, such grace. Had I been the man behind the camera it would have been rude to address her as anything other than Miss Minogue. And oh, to be the man behind the camera.

And then the doorbell rang.

As Anna and I sat down at the table I snuck a glance at my watch.

"Am I boring you?"

"No, no!" I said, smiling. "No – I was just checking. The date. Can't believe it's February. Already." I smiled some more.

"Oh," said Anna, placing her hands in her lap.

"What can I get you to drink?" I asked

"Water please," she said, without looking up.

"Sparkling?" Her elfin face flushed.

"Oh no! No bubbles. And room temperature too – I don't like drinks that are too cold."

"Right," I said, and smiled again.

From the moment Anna arrived the evening started to nosedive. All we'd done was walk to the restaurant and ask for a table, yet in that short space of time her mood had gone from 'cool' to 'frosty', forcing me to compensate by beaming like a has-been comedian. My cheeks felt as if I'd spent the night with a coat hanger in my mouth.

I watched as Anna arranged the serviette in her lap. Maybe she was nervous. Maybe she didn't enjoy first dates. I mean, who does? Really? And Mary had been right, she was extremely pretty. Though she would be a whole lot prettier if she held her head up and smiled once in a while. Brighter clothes might flatter her too. Or darker. Something other than the assortment of beige jumpers and cardigans she'd chosen to wear over that brown smock. I forced another smile and tried not to feel bitter about the amount of time I'd put into matching socks.

"But that's not the kind of work I want to be associated with, do you see?" I nodded in agreement, although I'd stopped listening a while back. In the dim and distant past, sometime after the arrival of my starter – she hadn't ordered one; no vegetarian option. At least not the specific vegetarian option she'd had in mind – I'd foolishly asked Anna to tell me more about what she did for a living. The short answer to this question would have been "I'm a freelance desktop publisher for select clients." An even shorter, and somewhat more honest answer would have been "Nothing." But I was getting the long answer, the very long answer, complete with a detailed history of all the BTEC courses Anna had started but never finished, and how, having finally completed an evening course in desktop publishing, she had set herself up in business and was waiting for a client who had been certified as one hundred percent ethical, environmentally friendly, politically correct, and against the drinking of anything other than water. Still water. At room temperature.

"That's very interesting," I said, when she paused for breath.

"Yes, it is, isn't it!" she said with a surprising amount of passion that woke me up slightly. Clearly nobody had ever said those words to her before.

"And do you have any hobbies?" I asked, in an attempt to regain control of the conversation.

"What d'you mean?" she asked.

"What do you do for fun?" I said, spelling it out as clearly as I could.

"Fun?"

"Recreation."

"Nothing really," she said. I believed her. It explained a lot. "Why? What do you do?" she asked bitterly. I was a little taken aback. This was the first time all evening she'd asked me anything.

"Me? Oh I erm..." I faltered slightly whilst possible answers queued up in my mind. I sorted them quickly into true answers (drinking beer, surfing the net, drinking beer with Alex, dreaming up stupid ways to meet the girl of my dreams) and the completely fictitious answers that everyone gives to these sort of questions. I opted for the latter. "The usual stuff, I guess: listening to music, going to the movies, reading."

"Oh yeah. What sort of things do you read?"

"Science fiction mainly," I answered. I racked my mind trying to think of science fiction novels that had been made into films in order to anticipate her next question.

"Oh," she said. And then silence.

"Do you read much?" I asked.

"Not really," she answered. I let out a scream of desperation, although only in my head. I wanted to reach across the table, grab Anna by the shoulders and shake her until something interesting fell out. But instead I picked up my glass of water.

"What about the internet?" I chirped.

"The internet?"

"Yes. Do you read much... on the internet?" I wasn't even sure there was anything to read on the internet.

"Read?"

"Well, surf"

"Surf?" she asked.

"Surf the internet." Jesus. "I think the internet's great," I continued.

"Great?" she said.

"Well, good. Lots of... interesting websites. You can while away hours just, you know, surfing." I bunched my toes in my shoes and did my very best not to look like I was about to explode.

"Yes. I'm sure you can," she said, without raising her eyes. Something wasn't right.

"You're not into the internet much?" I asked.

"Not really," she said, looking up. "I mean, no. I don't have an internet connection."

"Oh," I said. "Why's that?"

"I don't agree with it."

"The internet?"

"It's full of pornography and perverts." I said nothing. "Sorry," she added. "It's just I have strong views on the portrayal of women as sex objects. It shouldn't be allowed. And in my opinion men that look at women in that way should be castrated." I looked at her for a couple of seconds. "No offence," she said after a moment.

"None taken," I said, with a smile. "Everyone's entitled to their opinion." I ran my finger around the rim of my glass as my thoughts wandered back to Kylie and her photo spread in *FHM*. Was I guilty of being a pervert – of seeing Kylie as nothing more than a sex object? Had I seen only the body, a pleasing figure – flesh moulded into exciting curves – and not the woman they embodied?

Had I?

No.

Of that I was certain.

And had it been Kylie – Miss Minogue – sitting opposite, I'd have had no problem looking her in the eye. My conscience was clear.

But would I ever be able to convince Anna of that? Were I to invite her back to my place, and she happened upon the copy of *FHM* magazine, would she see Kylie being portrayed as a confident, fun, sexy, 21st-century woman?

Not in a million years.

"Shall we get the bill?" I said.

It was never going to happen. Kylie was never going to break down just outside my house. And even if she did the chances of her being alone, needing to borrow a phone, and picking my door of the dozen or so around her, were infinitesimal. Strange though it may seem, in the light of my disastrous date with Anna, that seemed hideously unfair.

I wasn't even asking for a guaranteed romance, just a chance. An opportunity. A moment. Blimey, if the truth be known I wasn't even asking for Kylie – just someone like her. Someone nice. Fun. Friendly. Someone who didn't think all men were perverts for finding those qualities appealing.

Here she was. Frozen in time between the pages of *FHM*, smiling, laughing, and enjoying herself. And someone had taken those pictures. Made her laugh. Had that opportunity that I wanted so badly.

I wanted to be that someone.

That man.

The man behind the camera.

CHAPTER EIGHT
THURSDAY 28TH MAY, 1998

"**P**ick a team."

I turned, half a doughnut in my hand, the other half in my mouth, and looked up into the smiling face of Charlotte – and all at once my world was slightly brighter. She hooked a stray lock of hair with a long slender finger, gently pushing it back behind one ear, then shook the waste paper basket held in front of her. I blinked, swallowed the mouthful of doughnut, and peered in. There, at the bottom, were a dozen or so tiny balls of paper.

"What am I picking a team for?" I asked.

"The World Cup," said Charlotte.

Really? I mused. I'm picking teams for the World Cup out of a near empty waste paper basket? I had no idea that FIFA had become so desperate. Actually, if the truth be known, I had no idea who FIFA were.

"You need to pay a pound too," she said.

"Oh, right," I said, fumbling around in a pocket for some spare change, "and then what happens?" Charlotte shrugged.

"If your team wins," she said, "you get everything."

My eyes accidentally strayed to the buttons on her shirt. The idea of 'everything' was too enormous to contemplate. I'd settle for 'something'. Those buttons, for instance. They seemed to be straining unnecessarily. I wanted to help those buttons. Free them. Relieve them of their burden and–

"What did you draw?" asked Charlotte.

"Oh, erm..." I uncrumpled the paper. "Italy," I said. She handed me the waste paper basket, took out the pen and folded sheet of paper that had been tucked into the waistband of her skirt, and leant forward to use my desk.

"Italy," repeated Charlotte, as she wrote. "That's not going to go down well with Isabella!" She may have said something else too, but I was mesmerised by a small amount of bosom, nestled within a lacy white bra. From across the desk Sian coughed loudly and glared at me.

"Right," said Charlotte, standing upright. As she did so, I was drawn to the curve of her thighs under the sleek grey pencil skirt. She held out her hand, and smiled.

It took me a moment to realise that she wanted her bin back. I handed it to her.

"Don't go," I said, as she turned to leave.

"Sorry?" said Charlotte.

"Would you like some cake? Or a biscuit? Or – something?" I waved my hand at the remains of the bakery products scattered across my desk, and as I did so I saw Sian roll her eyes and shake her head.

"Oh," said Charlotte. "Is it your birthday?"

"Here ya go," said Alex, returning to our table – the same table we'd sat at back in January when evening classes had seemed like the answer to all my problems. "Happy birthday."

"A pint of Guinness!" I said, "How did you know?"

"I didn't have time to wrap it," said Alex, taking his seat.

"It's the thought that counts," I said, and brought the pint to my lips. "Even if it is a week late."

"So what presents did you get?" he asked. I paused for a moment whilst I considered my reply.

"Digital camera," I said eventually.

"Yeah? Who from?"

"Me," I replied. Alex frowned. I could almost hear the cogs creaking and squeaking as they reluctantly started to turn inside his head. He lubricated them with a mouthful of Guinness.

"You still not talking to your mother?" he asked.

"I'm not not-talking to her, I just don't want to... talk to her. Yet."

"You can't ignore your mother on your birthday," said Alex.

"It's my birthday."

"Yeah, but it was kind of a big event for her too."

"I got her card. I put it on the mantelpiece. And at some point I might send her a thank you note."

"For a birthday card? Call her!"

"She wants to beat me up about Liz!"

Alex shrugged. "So let her," he said.

"I don't think you understand what that involves – I might not survive!"

"You can't kill someone from the other end of the phone," said Alex.

"We're talking about my mother here! She's very resourceful. Whilst I'm sitting there listening to her rant there'll be a sniper on the roof of the building opposite. Thirty years she's been waiting for her son to get married! Granted, most of that time I was a kid, but when Liz came along she could see light at the end of the tunnel. I've spent the last three years being told what a lovely girl Liz is. How much she likes her. How I shouldn't let her slip away. I've watched my mother's face light up whenever I've said something like, 'Oh, I've got some news' – and then fall again when it turned out that all I'd had was a promotion or something equally 'unimportant'." Alex opened his mouth to speak, but I cut him off. "Never mind the fact that Liz was a controlling bitch, or that I wasn't happy – that's just me being selfish. What's important is that my mother gets to put on a big hat, wear more pearls than there could conceivably be at the bottom of the ocean, and shed a heartfelt tear or two whilst a white limousine carries me off in shackles. And now that I've stamped all over that fantasy she's probably ringing her pals at the W.I. to see if they know of a hitman, and whether he'll accept Clubcard vouchers!"

Alex sat opposite me, his eyes as big as dinner plates. "So – you're not calling your mum then." He looked around the pub as if hoping to see someone who might join us. His eyes stopped for a second or two on the TV that hung in the corner. "You gonna watch any of the World Cup?" he asked.

I hate football. Always have. So as such I'd pretty much forgotten about the office sweepstake. When someone did mention it I couldn't even remember what team I'd drawn, and when they reminded me, I had no idea whether the Italian football team was any good, and whether, as a consequence, I stood any chance of winning the loot. But I didn't particularly care either. At least, not at first.

"Jason, you must give to me Italy, and in return I will give to you France." I minimised everything on my computer desktop as quickly as I could, then swivelled in my chair to look Isabella in the eye.

"I'm sorry?" I said. Even though I was seated we were more or less the same height. "Why?"

"Because I am Italian." I frowned.

"It's a sweepstake," I said. "You get what you draw. That's how it works. It's like a raffle. Should I get England just because I'm English?"

"No," said Isabella. "Because I do not have England to trade with you." I took a deep breath.

"So let me see if I've understood this correctly: You should have Italy because you're Italian, and I should have France because that's all you have to trade with?"

"Yes."

"But I don't want France. I'm happy with Italy." Isabella shifted her weight from one leg to the other, tossed her head to move her jet black fringe out of her eyes, perched a hand on her hip and gave a hugely dramatic sigh. "O'kaye," she said, "if I can trade someone France for England, would you trade with me England for Italy?"

"No," I said.

"Why not?!" she asked, throwing her arms in the air, her accent thickening by the moment.

"Because I like Italy. I want to keep it."

For a second her dark eyes flashed with rage, then she tossed her head again, turned sharply and headed back to her desk. I glanced over at Sian, who was engrossed in a document, then turned to admire Isabella's rather lovely bottom in her sleek black trousers.

"I saw that," said Sian as she turned a page.

Though her temper meant that most of my colleagues preferred to keep Isabella at arm's length, for me her quintessential Italian traits gave her an almost magical charm. The most tedious, dreary, work-related conversations could suddenly become infused with colour and passion if Isabella were involved, making them as interesting as her figure-hugging roll neck sweaters, and as infuriating as her blatant disregard for the company dress code.

I could quite fancy her.

If she wasn't married.

Still, married wasn't a reason to stop enjoying our little chats and verbal sparring – and now that I had something she wanted I was assured several daily visits for entertaining conversations that included anything from threats to begging. Sometimes in the same sentence.

"Please, Jason, give to me Italy or I will never ever speak with you ever again!"

"Oh-my-God Jason, I am begging you – give to me Italy or I will nag you and nag you and never stop even when Italy have won the World Cup and you have my money!"

"Please, Jason. Please. I will do anything. Anything at all. And if you don't give to me Italy, then – I won't. So you see, you must give to me Italy!"

"Anything?" I asked.

"I do not understand?" said Isabella, thrown by an answer which wasn't my usual "no".

"Anything. You said you'd do anything."

"Yes! That is right," she said, becoming more animated. "Anything, if you will just give to me Italy. And I will give to you France." I mused this over for a second. "What?" she asked, seeing an opportunity. "What are you thinking? You have something in your mind – tell me, Jason. I must know!"

"No, it's nothing," I said, losing my nerve.

"No! You must tell me," she said, grabbing my shoulders, spinning me round to face her and fighting to regain eye contact. "I must know this thing that you think. Tell me now – I will do anything!"

It had seemed like an epiphany at the time. That night, four months previously, thumbing through *FHM*'s Kylie photo spread after my ill-fated date with Anna. If I wanted to be the kind of man who meets fun, exciting girls who pose for magazine photos, I needed to be the kind of man who takes photos for magazines.

The man behind the camera.

Then the morning came and with it the realisation that you can't just become 'the man behind the camera'. At the very least you need a camera, a job that provides you with a constant stream of women expecting to be photographed, and the skills to combine the two. And I had none of these things. Which is when the whole notion should have shrivelled up and died. But it just wouldn't.

Instead, I found myself handing over a considerable wad of my hard earned cash for a *Nikon CoolPix995* digital camera. Aside from my flat and my car, it was easily the most expensive thing I'd ever bought. And suddenly I was one step closer towards turning this crazy, stupid idea into a reality.

From that moment on I became acutely aware of every image I laid my eyes on. Daytimes were filled with a continuous stream of women looking back at me from the pages of glossy magazines, websites I'd happen across, billboard advertising I drove past. They winked at me, or ignored me, or snubbed me, but always they goaded me. Daring me to go further.

I went back to my evening class brochure. Read it from cover to cover, looking for the elusive course on photographing women – or something similar – but there was nothing. Just one measly course on the art of still life photography.

So I turned to the internet, and spent my evenings trawling through search engine results. Then my lunchtimes. Then any moment when I was pretty sure I wouldn't be caught. Just searching for any kind of glamour photography course, or workshop, or weekend away, where I could learn how to point my camera at girls. But I found nothing.

Absolutely nothing.

Anna had been right: the internet was nothing more than a vast electronic library of pornography. Even the most innocent of search terms – 'photography courses' or 'photographers Essex' – led me straight to pictures of naked and near-naked ladies. Pictures that some lucky bastard, somewhere, had taken, and I had not. And never would – short of a miracle – short of someone pretty walking up to my desk and offering me anything I wanted.

"Let me get this straight," said Alex, returning from the bar with two more pints. "This French bird –"

"Italian."

"Whatever – offered you anything?"

"Yes."

"And you asked if you could take her picture?"

"No, I asked if she'd model for me!"

"Like a glamour model?"

"Yes. Sort of."

"What – naked?"

"No! Not naked!" I said. "Just – you know – in a bikini, or something."

"A bikini!?" said Alex, spraying me with a mouthful of Guinness. "She's French!"

"Italian..."

"Either way - she's probably got piles of frilly... lingerie... or whatever, stuffed in every drawer! And you ask to photograph her in a swimming costume!"

"After all," I said, "back in Italy you probably wore a bikini on the beach? And that would have been in full view of God knows how many, er, people." I felt a trickle of sweat form under my hairline as I watched Isabella consider my argument and come to the conclusion that yes, that was indeed the case. I swallowed hard.

"O'kaye," she said.

"Ok?"

"Yes." I looked around the office to see who was listening. There didn't appear to be anyone.

"You'll do it?"

"Yes," she said.

"You'll pose for me in your bikini?" I hissed.

"Yes," she said again. And then she added, "When?"

"Well – how about Friday evening?"

"Friday? No. I cannot do Friday. Tomorrow."

"Tomorrow?"

"Yes. Tomorrow. Thursday. And then you will trade with me France for Italy?"

"Absolutely," I said.

"O'kaye."

"Hang on," said Alex, choking on his pint. "She said yes?"

I frowned. "I thought that was obvious," I said.

"No, you said you asked her. You didn't say she agreed."

"Well she did."

"And when did this happen?" asked Alex.

"Lunchtime."

"And you're only telling me now!?"

"When was I supposed to tell you?" Alex gripped the side of the table and looked out of the window for a moment whilst he sucked his top lip, then turned back to me.

"How long have we been sitting here?" he asked.

"About twenty minutes, I think."

"Listening to you talking about being 'the man behind the camera' and all that crap..."

"Thank you."

"You never thought to phone me?"

"When? Before or after I'd asked her?"

"Both!" spat Alex.

"Why?"

"Never mind," said Alex, brushing the point aside with his hand. "When's she coming over?"

"Tomorrow evening. Don't you listen to anything I tell you?"

"Not really, no. Tell me you're planning to do more than take a few mucky pictures."

"Like what?"

"Like her!"

"Alex – when a girl agrees to let you photograph her in her bikini, it means she's happy to let you photograph her in her bikini! It doesn't mean 'something else'!" I said, making air quotes. Alex stared at me as if he was considering snapping my fingers off one by one, and making me eat them.

"Let's find another pub," he said, getting out of his chair.

"Why?" I asked. But Alex was already walking away.

"Hi," I said, panting slightly as I opened the door.

"Hello, Jason," she said. "Have you been doing the exercise?"

"No, no, I just had to run down the stairs," I said. Isabella looked at the steps, and then at me. "I haven't been to the gym for a while. Used to go a lot. Do a bit of running. Swimming. Maybe some weights." I did a set of arm curls with imaginary weights, complete with sound effects to illustrate the point. Isabella stood there patiently. "Anyway, come in, come in."

"Thank you," she said, and she walked past me. I closed the door, then turned to follow her up.

"So I was thinking maybe we could – hello?" Isabella had vanished. When I found her she was upstairs in my bedroom, sitting on the edge of my bed, bouncing up and down slightly as if testing the mattress.

"Oh, hey – there you are. Would you, er, like a cup of tea? Or coffee? First?" I said.

"No. I am good," said Isabella casually. She was so cool about it! "So. What now?" asked Isabella.

"Well..." I said, "do you need to... change?"

"Change?"

"Into... your er, bikini?" I said nervously.

"I am already wearing it. Underneath."

"Oh, right. Ok. Good!" Focus Jason, focus.

"So - do you want me now to undress?" asked Isabella, standing up. "Or do you want something like, what is the word..." She paused whilst she searched for the vocabulary she needed. "The striptease," she said. My jaw dropped open.

"The striptease?" I asked.

"Yes. The striptease." I looked her up and down. She was dressed in a v-neck short sleeved black top and a pair of jeans. There wasn't a lot to strip out of – not if we were stopping at her bikini – but even so, this was more than I could have ever wished for. Finally my brain started to catch up, and my stomach filled with butterflies.

"Erm," I said. I swallowed. "Yes. Why not. That's a very, er, good idea."

"O'kaye," said Isabella, visibly pleased with my compliment. "Maybe I should kneel on the bed, and do the striptease?"

"Ok. Yes. Let's do that then."

"O'kaye," said Isabella, smiling at me broadly.

"Ok," I said. Then we both just stood there, and I could feel myself breaking into a cold sweat as the seconds ticked by.

"And you are going to take pictures?" Isabella asked.

"If that's alright?" I said tentatively. Isabella bit her lip, then glanced at my arms folded tight across my chest. I frowned, then realised what was missing. "I'll just get my camera!" I said.

Isabella relaxed.

"What's bugging you?" I said, as I chased my friend down Throgmorton Street.

"Nothing," said Alex.

"It doesn't seem like nothing."

"Do you know how many times I've had sex in the last year?"

"No."

"Neither do I," he continued. "I can't remember."

"What has your love life got to do with anything?"

"Sex, mate. We're talking about sex."

"No – you're talking about sex. I'm talking about taking some photos. It's got nothing to do with sex."

"It's got everything to do with sex! This French bird wants to shag you. How can you not see that?"

"First of all, she's Italian. Second of all, no – she doesn't. Third, fourth and possibly fifth – it doesn't matter anyway because she's married!"

"So what!"

Isabella knelt with her hands on her hips, whilst I stood at the foot of the bed, and fumbled with the camera.

"Are you ready now?" asked Isabella.

"Yes, yes. Absolutely. Hang on. Ok. Yes, fine."

"So – what to begin with?" she asked.

"Erm... to begin with?"

"Yes. What clothing to begin with?"

"Oh, I see... well." The blood ran hot to my cheeks. "How about," I said, taking a deep breath, "we just take a couple of you like that. Just to warm up."

"Oh," said Isabella. "O'kaye. Yes. I see."

"Great," I said, and I lifted the camera. This was the first time I'd ever used it. I framed Isabella inside the small screen on the back and pressed the shutter. There was no click; just an egg timer that appeared for a second or two, before it was replaced with an image of Isabella kneeling on my bed, one hand on her hip, the other playing with her hair. "Ok, excellent," I said. "Let's take another."

"Again with clothes on?" asked Isabella.

"For the moment," I said, and took another picture. It was identical to the first, but somewhere deep inside, the single-cell organism that was my confidence doubled in size.

"Now, the striptease!" declared Isabella.

"Erm, ok," I said. "If you're ready." Her hands moved to the buckle on her belt. "Why don't you start with your top," I said, wiping the sweat from my brow with the back of my hand.

"O'kaye," said Isabella. She crossed her arms and grabbed the hem of her top, and my heart faltered slightly as I realised what was going to happen next.

"Hang on!" I said. She cocked her head on one side and gave me a look that said 'Oh for God's sake' in any language. "I just... just take it off slowly, ok?" She smiled.

"O'kaye," she said, "slowly. Yes." She moved her hips from side to side as she inched the top over her midriff, and upwards. I took a picture. Then another. Then another. I snapped off as many frames as the camera would allow, which wasn't that many. By the time she was kneeling there in her jeans and bikini top I'd only managed to take half a dozen pictures.

"Ok," I said with a dry mouth, my heart pounding in my chest. "That was – good!"

"Jeans now?" asked Isabella.

"Ok," I said, "but..."

"Yes, yes," she said. "You want it slowly." And her smile grew bigger. I couldn't help myself – I smiled back.

Isabella looked down at the bed as she unbuckled her belt, then slowly lifted her eyes to peer at me through her fringe, and as she did so I could feel the pulse in my neck. I could hear the blood rushing past my ears. And whilst this was, without a doubt, the sexiest moment of my entire life, I just hoped that my heart would hold out long enough so it wouldn't be my last.

"I happen to believe that being married is a big deal!"

"You would," said Alex. "You're single."

"Just because you're in a miserable marriage doesn't mean there's something fundamentally wrong with the concept."

"Oh yeah?"

"Yeah."

"Ok, well – if marriage is so great, why is this married French bird coming round to shag you?"

"She's not – she isn't – she's –" I stopped walking. "You know what," I said, "forget it! There's no talking to you. I'm going home." Alex turned to me and shrugged. "Right," I said. "Catch ya later."

"I'm right," said Alex. "You'll realise that."

Isabella pouted and preened, turning one way, then the other. Occasionally she broke into a smile, and when she tried – and failed – to pull down her jeans beyond her knees whilst still in a kneeling position, she burst into peals of laughter, and so did I. It was the most exciting five minutes of my life, the last sixty seconds of which I was only pretending to take photographs as the camera had long since presented me with a 'card full' message.

"That's it, I'm afraid."

"Finished?" said Isabella.

"Yep – camera's full."

"But maybe you have another film?" she asked.

"No," I said. "There isn't any film. It's all held on a card. And I only have the one. Sorry." I bit my lip.

"Is that a camera digital?" asked Isabella.

"Oh, yes, actually it is," I said proudly.

"So we can see the pictures now?" she said brightly.

"Well, I suppose we can. Yes."

"O'kaye."

We sat in my study, sharing my office chair, Isabella still in her bikini, whilst I tried hard to retain my composure and connect the camera to my computer at the same time. A part of me, the gentleman, kept nudging me in the ribs and telling me to let Isabella know it was ok to get dressed – but the rest of me was ignoring the gentleman and wondering whether, once I'd got the images off the camera, I could persuade her to get back on the bed and do some more pictures.

We sat in silence and watched the egg timer on the screen.

"Is anything happening?" asked Isabella, her smile still broad and sexy.

"Erm, yeah yeah," I said, intentionally keeping my eyes to the front. "It's just – slow." I swallowed hard. "Ah! See!" I said, with way too much enthusiasm as the images started to appear on the screen.

We cocked our heads to look at the images.

They were a little dark.

And perhaps a little samey.

But I'd taken them.

I'd taken them!

I – Jason Smith – had taken them!

"Oh, they're not bad, are they?" I said, casually. "That's quite a nice one, isn't it? I like the way you're erm, bending forwards. Slightly." I felt myself blush, intensely aware of the warmth of Isabella's bare thigh through my jeans.

"They are hot!" said Isabella, her eyes glued to the screen.

"Really?" I said, turning to face her. "You think so?"

"Jason Smith! I think you make me look very sexy! No?"

"Erm, well erm, I'm not sure about that," I said, our eyes still locked. "I think you did that all by yourself." Isabella's smile grew by an inch or two.

"Thank you," she said, her eyes dropping slightly to look at my mouth. Then, despite being only inches away from me, she somehow edged even closer. I went to say something, but before I could utter a word her mouth was on mine.

In the seconds that followed I experienced shock, then pleasure, before panic kicked in.

"Isabella," I said, my hands on her shoulders as I pushed her away from me, "you're married!"

"Yes, but," said Isabella, taking a moment to brush her hair out of her face before grabbing my arms and forcing them down by my sides, "this does not matter." In an instant she was sitting astride my lap, pressing herself against me, leaning forwards to take a bite out of my neck.

"Isabella! – No!" I said, arms flailing. "I don't – no – stop!" I kicked out, my foot making contact with the desk, propelling the chair backwards before the shifting weight of its passengers caused the whole thing to topple over and crash to the floor.

I lay for a moment amongst the wreckage, then turned to look at Isabella, who was sitting up, cupping an eye with her hand.

"Isabella –" I said as I started to extract myself from the carcass of the chair, but she raised the other hand to cut me off.

"I think, Jason, maybe this was not a good plan."

"No," I said, "maybe it wasn't."

She nodded. "But," she said, locking eyes with me, "I have an important question."

"Oh?" I said, gripping the chair for protection. She looked at me through her long dark fringe.

"Jason," she said, "now will you trade with me France for Italy?"

I breathed a sigh of relief.

It had been my intention to remain cool and ever so slightly dismissive of the previous evening's events in the hope that Isabella would do the same, but before I'd managed to put my jacket on the back of my chair she was standing at my desk, dressed in her usual roll neck sweater and black trouser combo, hair as slick and sleek as ever, but sporting a rather nasty bruise above one eye.

"Hello, Jason."

"Hey," I said, trying not to notice the bruise. "Hi, er hi. Hi! How are you? This morning?" I glanced around nervously. Sian was nowhere to be seen.

"I'm well," said Isabella.

"Good. Excellent. So –"

"Italy!" said Isabella, cutting me off and fixing me with an intense stare.

"Oh. Right. Of course." I opened my desk drawer and started fishing around for the small piece of paper.

"Jason – please tell me. You are going to be talking to Sian?" she asked, lowering her voice so that it was barely audible against the usual office hubbub.

"About?" I countered.

"The photographs we have made, and... the other thing," said Isabella. I looked up.

"Absolutely not!" I said. "God, no – it's 'our secret'."

"Our secret. Good. Yes. It must be our secret." She gave a short sharp nod.

"Ok then," I said, forcing a reassuring smile as best I could. I went back to rooting through the drawer. "Italy!" I said eventually, holding out a tiny scrap of paper.

"Thank you," said Isabella, taking it from me. "And for you, France." She handed me a similar scrap. I took it and threw it into the drawer. "I will tell Charlotte we have exchanged. Ciao." She turned and marched back to her desk.

"Yeah, erm, see you later," I said to the space she'd occupied a second before, and slumped into my chair. Which is when the phone rang.

"CFS Jason speaking how may I help you," I said with my usual lack of sincerity.

"Mate."

"Alex! Thank God."

"So?" he asked.

"What?"

"Was I right?"

My mind quickly replayed our last meeting until I'd figured out what he was referring to. "Yes," I said eventually.

"I knew it," said Alex. "And?"

"What!?"

"Did you?"

"Did I what?"

"Do her?"

"No!"

"Ok."

"Is that it then?" I asked after a moment's silence.

"Yes," admitted Alex.

"Amazing." I shook my head, then rested it on my free hand.

"You want to come over this weekend?" asked Alex.

"What? Your place?" This hardly ever happened.

"Yeah," said Alex. "Tina's away. Thought you could stay over." I considered it for a second or two, and glanced in Isabella's direction. Maybe it wasn't such a bad idea to be away this weekend.

Just in case.

CHAPTER NINE
SUNDAY 7TH JUNE, 1998

As if waking up in a strange bed wasn't disconcerting enough, it was made worse by the pinkness of the duvet, and curtains so thin that I could barely open my eyes without squinting. For the second night running I'd spent the entire night clinging to the edge of a sofa bed that refused to lie flat, trying to prevent myself from sliding onto the floor. A feat that was all the more impressive given the amount of alcohol I'd consumed during the many hours spent slumped in front of Alex's TV, getting beaten at Mario Kart.

Still, it had been worth it. Alex had even dug out an old girly calendar and hung it on the wall. It was like old times. Simpler times.

I crawled out of the 'bed' and plodded downstairs in search of my friend and something to soak up the contents of my stomach. I stuck my head in the lounge, but Alex wasn't there. Neither were the numerous cans from the previous two evenings. Or the umpteen empty crisp packets. Even the games console had been tidied away. And where the girly calendar had hung was now a large picture of Alex and Tina on their wedding day.

A frown formed on my face as I scratched the stubble on my chin. Then I shrugged, and thought nothing more of it.

The kitchen was equally tidy. Gone were the takeaway cartons. Gone was the empty pizza box from Friday night. And where once had stood an impressive pile of dirty mugs and plates, a testament to the amount of mess two grown men can generate in a thirty-six-hour period, there was now a bottle of bleach and a blue cloth. Beneath it the dish-washer rumbled. My frown returned.

I wandered over to the kettle, filled it, and took two mugs from the cupboard. If Alex had done all this cleaning, where was he now? Back in bed? I wandered to the foot of the stairs.

"Oi! Lazy bones! You wanna cuppa?"

No reply.

I walked back into the kitchen. A short dumpy woman with frizzy brown hair screamed and dropped the plastic laundry basket she'd been holding.

"Jason!" she barked.

"Tina!" I wheezed as I held onto the door frame with one hand and my thumping chest with the other.

"What on earth are you wearing?!" she asked. That wasn't the question I'd been expecting. I glanced down.

"Boxer shorts?" I offered, still not entirely sure that this was the answer she was looking for.

"Where are your trousers?" she demanded.

"Upstairs."

"Why?"

"Well, I... I didn't know you'd be here!"

"Of course I'm here! It's my house!"

"Yes, but... erm..."

"Have you been here the whole time?"

"Of course!"

"Where?"

"In bed."

"But it's two o'clock."

"Really?" I asked. Tina said nothing, just bit her lip, then knelt on the floor and started putting the spilt items of clothing back into her basket. I watched for a moment, then squatted down to help, but Tina raised a hand.

"Leave it!" she snapped, turning her head away slightly. "Just go and put some trousers on." I got to my feet. "I wish Alex had told me you were still in the house!"

"Where is he?" I asked.

"God knows! Said he needed a part to fix the garage door, so he's probably in a pub somewhere." I turned to leave. "Don't be getting any ideas about joining him – it's bad enough having one drunk man in my house. I don't need two. And I certainly don't need any more mess." I turned back and watched as Tina stuffed the last of her spilt laundry items back into her basket.

"Erm yeah," I said. "Sorry about that. I would have cleared up. A little. Before I left."

"Yeah, well, it's done now," said Tina, getting to her feet. "Just hurry up and get another girlfriend. Then you can spend your weekends messing up her place."

"I'll erm, get right on it," I said, and turned to leave again.

"Jason," said Tina.

"Yes?"

"Can you dance?"

"Sorry?" I asked, turning back.

"Have you got any rhythm?"

"Erm... well," I scratched my head. "Why do you ask?"

"I go salsa dancing every Thursday evening," she said.

"Right," I said. "Ok. Well that sounds..." Like a proposition! But I kept that thought to myself. "Have you asked Alex?"

"Alex?" exclaimed Tina. "Give me a break. He couldn't hold a rhythm if it came in a pint glass. Besides, I'd probably spend the entire evening having to apologise for my husband's wandering hands. No – you're a big boy now, you're old enough to come on your own."

I shook my pickled head, but it didn't help. I was utterly confused. "Right. Well. Thanks for the offer, but I'm not sure it's my kind of thing."

"Typical," said Tina, putting the basket on the side and looking even more annoyed than usual.

"Sorry about that."

"Yeah, yeah – whatever." I gave her a quick nod and turned to leave. "I just don't get you men," she continued. "Alex told me you took a cookery class with a bunch of old women to try and find a girlfriend! But I tell you there's a room full of young, salsa dancing ladies and suddenly 'it's not your kinda thing'! I dunno. It's a wonder the human race hasn't died out!"

I turned back slowly. "Thursday, you say?"

A sensible person would have found out what Thursday evening salsa dancing involved before committing themselves. But I'm not a sensible person. Which is why, as I crept into the back of the room and watched three rows of thirty or so women wiggle in perfect synchronicity to a frantic Latin rhythm, I realised I'd made a mistake.

In my head I'd imagined something akin to a disco – a kind of 'salsa club'; a darkened room where people were free to mingle, dance and, perhaps more importantly, not-dance, as the mood took them. But this – this well-lit white room of gyrating female bodies stamping out a rhythm on beech flooring – appeared to be a full-on dance class.

Just as that thought entered my head a female voice from the front bellowed: "And step, and step, and step, and step – don't forget those hips, people." That was the moment I should have slid back out of the door and made my retreat, but instead I craned my head to see the owner of the voice, and saw the confident, swaying, curvaceous rear of a slender woman in tight three-quarter length trousers and strappy heels that flirted with the floor just long enough to keep her upright. Hands with long fingers drew small circles at the end of beautiful bare arms, whilst freckled shoulders supported a head that rolled and flicked a punky mop of the most vivid, poppy-red, bobbed hair I'd ever seen.

"And turning on the count of three – ready? And one, and two, and pivot..." Thirty students simultaneously drew one leg behind the other and, on the very next beat, turned, en masse, through one hundred and eighty degrees, only to discover a slightly shocked man standing in front of them. Instinctively I backed against the wall, flattening myself against the plasterboard as though I were trapped between two panes of glass. Some of the dancers exchanged looks whilst others stopped dancing altogether, until the red-haired lady took back control.

"Come on, people, it's only a man! I know they're rare, but stay focused – turning on the count of three..." She gave me a wink and a grin before counting her minions into the next manoeuvre.

I'd always thought of dance instructors as grumpy elderly ladies with flowing silvery locks, armed with canes that they beat against the floor, but perhaps they only end up that way. Perhaps they always start out young and sassy. And beautiful.

Out of the corner of my eye I noticed Tina trying to get my attention. I raised my hand in a half wave, but she glared at me angrily, stabbing her wrist with a finger as the music came to an end.

"Ok – get your breath back, people," said the instructor, "then find yourself a partner. Meanwhile I'm going to make sure security doesn't let our interloper escape." The class rippled with laughter.

"Jason! Where have you been?" said Tina as she came over. "You were supposed to be here half an hour ago!"

"Er yeah, sorry about that – I didn't realise..."

"Didn't realise what?"

"Well, I thought it was more of, er –"

"Hi," said the instructor, sliding into our conversation and blasting me with a smile so warm and wide it could fill a room. "You must be Jason. I'm Ria." She extended a hand.

"Oh, hi," I said, taking Ria's hand and noticing how warm and soft it felt within my own. It was the first time I'd ever caught myself wondering exactly how long a handshake should last before it becomes inappropriate. "Sorry I'm late," I said, releasing my grasp with more than a degree of reluctance.

"Oh – no problem," she said, waving away my apology. "Nice that you could come at all. Have you ever done salsa before?"

"Er, no. Never."

"Well, you're in for a treat! Why don't you partner with Tina –"

"Me?!" Tina looked appalled.

"Or not," said Ria, recovering gracefully. "How about..." She turned to scan the class, and I caught myself hoping that despite a roomful of women I'd be 'forced' to pair up with the instructor.

"I'd be happy to be Jason's partner," said a shorter woman with hair so blonde it was virtually white. "If that's ok with you, Jason?" My mouth opened and closed. I looked at Ria.

"Well ok then," said Ria. "Jason, meet Viv. Viv, meet Jason. Viv – be gentle with him. If he doesn't come back I'm holding you responsible!" Ria gave me another wink, then turned and clapped her hands to get the room's attention.

"You'll be safe with me," said Viv, taking my arm. Tina looked at us both. She still seemed vaguely annoyed, though I could tell from the look on her face that she wasn't sure why. I gave her a nod, and she turned and walked away.

Viv turned out to be almost as new to salsa as me, and much of the remaining half hour was spent stepping on each other's toes or crashing into each other, due in part to Viv's complete lack of rhythm and her total inability to lead or be led. But it didn't matter. Each time a foot was stood on, or bodies collided, Viv giggled or laughed and blue eyes sparkled under her choppy bleached fringe, her grin widening to reveal slightly crooked but perfectly white teeth, and I started to realise that Viv was a girl who had perfected the art of being imperfect.

"You're rubbish!" said Viv, beaming and poking me in the chest with a pink fingernail as Ria announced the end of class.

"Why thank you," I countered, with a smile as genuine, if not as broad. "So are you." I poked her back.

"So do you live local?" asked Viv as we wandered to the edge of the room to collect our things.

"Not really. Southend." I pulled on my jacket.

"Southend? That's miles!"

"Yeah, I –"

"I've never been there," interrupted Viv.

"It's –"

"We should go out some time!"

"Really?" I glanced around me to see if she was talking to someone else. She wasn't. "Well, that would –"

"You could show me the sights. How about Saturday night?" asked Viv.

"What? This Saturday?" I asked. "Ok then. How –"

"Great," said Viv, diving into her bag and retrieving a small address book and pen. "Here – write down your number." I did as I was told, then handed the items back. "Saturday then," said Viv, throwing her bag over one shoulder. "I'll give you a call."

"Right," I said. "Shall I –"

"I've gotta run," said Viv. "Do you think you could do me a favour and pay for me?" She thrust a five pound note into my hand and jerked her head in the direction of the queue forming around Ria. "Thanks," she said.

"See you Saturday," I replied as she darted out of the door.

"Ah! There you are," said Ria as I reached the front of the queue. "And how was it for you?" She batted her eyelids playfully, causing my heart to flutter in time.

"Oh, yeah. Good," I said. Ria raised an eyebrow.

"Good?" she asked.

"Fun," I reiterated. She mulled this over.

"I was kinda hoping for 'excellent'," said Ria, "but I guess I can settle for 'fun'."

"Oh, it was," I said. "Excellent, I mean. In its own way." Ria's warmth returned. Eyes bright and sparkling.

"Well that's far more reassuring," she said. "And a bargain at only five pounds."

I handed over two fives. "There's one for Viv too," I said, feeling a pang of guilt at the mention of Viv's name, and the thought of our hastily arranged meeting.

"Much obliged," said Ria, taking the notes and stuffing them into an envelope with many others. "So will you be coming again?" I paused, just long enough to lose myself in those eyes, that smile, the poppy red hair. Just long enough to marvel at how sometimes in the time it takes to hand over two five pound notes it can suddenly feel both as if you've known someone your whole life, and also that you'd like to spend your whole life getting to know someone. It was also just long enough to realise that arranging to see Viv might have been a huge mistake, and that depending on how Saturday went, returning to this class and seeing Ria again, might be hugely awkward and complicated. "Before you answer," said Ria, misinterpreting the frown on my face, "I think I should lie and tell you that you wouldn't be the only man in the group. We have lots. And they all enjoy going for a beer and a curry after class."

I narrowed my eyes. "So where are these men?" I asked.

"Man flu," said Ria. "Dreadfully contagious. Trust me – I'm a medical professional."

"Uh huh," I said.

"Look! There's one now!" she said, looking over my shoulder. I turned and, standing by the door, was the type of man who anyone with half an ounce of imagination would instantly assume was a rugby player, possibly by profession, and probably called Roger. "Be with you in a moment, darling," said Ria. Roger gave a half wave, pulling a crumpled tissue from his pocket as he did so, before blowing his nose with such force it was a wonder the building didn't shake.

"Poor love," said Ria with an exaggerated pout, before turning her attention back to me. "Anyway," she said, brushing a lock of vibrant red hair to one side and extending a hand, "I do hope I see you again." I took her hand, and this time it seemed... at least I could have sworn... that it was her who didn't want to let go – but then the handshake was over, and she cantered across the room, into the arms of her rugby player. My world was uncomplicated once more. All I had now was Saturday.

Once again I was sitting on my bed, staring at the contents of the wardrobe, agonising over what combination of clothes would constitute suitable first date attire. It was further complicated because I wasn't entirely certain that this was an actual date. I'd replayed those few seconds in my head over and over, from the moment when Viv had suggested we should 'go out sometime' to when she'd bolted for the door, and I was still none the wiser. Worse still, given that it was just past eight on Saturday evening I was seriously beginning to wonder whether our 'could-be-a-date' was going to happen at all, or whether I should call the restaurant, and cancel our reservation.

I walked into my study, picked up the phone, and was just about to press last number redial when the thing went off in my hand.

"Jason!" yelled a voice at the other end of the phone.

"Viv?"

"Yes, Viv! I'm here!"

"Where's here?"

"Some hotel place."

"You're in a hotel?"

"Of course I'm in a hotel. I need somewhere to crash tonight! I can't stay at your place – you might try and take advantage of me, you cheeky boy!"

"Right, yeah. Ok." I forced a laugh. She sounded different. "So what's the name of your hotel?"

"Dunno," said Viv. "It was the first place I found."

"Ok, but maybe there's something in the room with the hotel name on it?"

"Hold on," said Viv, before I heard what sounded like someone throwing furniture around a room. "You're right!" she said eventually. "I'm in the Grand."

"The Grand? You mean the Grand pub? That's just up the road."

"Great!" said Viv. "Well get your arse over here, young man, and I'll meet you in the bar!" And with that she hung up.

The Grand was not the most salubrious of drinking venues, and it certainly wasn't somewhere I'd have described as 'a hotel' – but it did mean my 'first date outfit' could be resolved with a pair of jeans and a vaguely ironed shirt. But as I walked into the pub, Viv was standing at the bar and dressed for an altogether different evening – black snake-skin leather trousers and a pair of silver strappy heels competed for attention with a backless vest top that was so silver it was almost mirrored, and so clingy it barely functioned as clothing. I swallowed hard.

"There you are!" said Viv. "Where have you been? I'm already on my second – you've got some catching up to do!" She nodded towards a pint of lager and a shot glass sitting next to it, before she necked something from a shot glass of her own. For a moment I was speechless – not at the outfit, or what it failed to conceal, nor at the queue of drinks that apparently represented a second round, but at her bloodshot eyes. She looked as if she'd been crying for a week, and no amount of makeup or false lashes would ever have been able to hide the fact. But as I opened my mouth to say something another thought occurred to me. These weren't the eyes of someone who'd been crying. They were wild, bouncing around in her sockets as if she'd swallowed a car battery.

"Erm – are these for me?" I asked, indicating the pint and its companion.

"Of course. I guessed you were a lager boy."

"Well actually," I said, "I'm more of a Guinness man – but this is fine." I forced a smile.

"Guinness!" said Viv, making a wretching noise. "Don't ever drink that around me! Smells like Brussels sprouts! Tonight you're drinking lager!"

"And the shot?"

"Vodka," said Viv. "Just to get things going." She picked up her wine glass and when she put it back down it was empty. "Come on then," she said with a manic grin, "buy me another!"

I didn't drink the shot. That had been a smart move. Electing to keep our dinner reservation, on the other hand, hadn't. Though Viv had turned her nose up at the suggestion, I foolishly thought she might calm down a little if she were amongst moderately refined surroundings and she had something to soak up the alcohol.

Instead, whilst I perused the menu, Viv treated me to her impression of a walrus by stuffing a breadstick up each nostril. And when she'd exhausted her repertoire of hilarious breadstick impressions, she turned her attention to our fellow diners and offered me her opinion on their choice of clothes, choice of food, choice of partner, all with a breathtaking inability to notice that we weren't sitting in a soundproof bubble. And then when our food finally arrived she pushed it to one side, declaring that it wasn't what she thought it would be, and instead helped herself to my ravioli. And a forkful of chicken from the man on the next table.

Not that Viv's buffet approach to dining got in the way of her drinking. Each time a waiter passed our table she ordered more alcohol. Mainly for herself. Despite the fact we had wine. Or did, until she poured most of it down her front – during an attempt to drink directly from the bottle.

As she staggered to the ladies' to clean herself up and, I'm guessing, snort something from a convenient flat surface, I hung my head in shame, and tried to ignore the glares from those around me.

"Hey, this place looks alright!" declared Viv as we passed the glitzy exterior of a bar on the way back from the restaurant. "Shall we?" she asked, and without waiting for me to answer she walked straight past the imposing suited gentleman standing at the entrance. I stood my ground for a second or two. All I'd wanted to do for the last two hours was get Viv back to the Grand, make my excuses and leave. It had been difficult to see how the evening could get much worse, but I hadn't factored in the hellhole that was 'Club Viva'. And despite my natural instinct to turn and run as fast as I could in the opposite direction, a small part of me knew that I couldn't leave her. Not in her current inebriated state. Not wearing that 'top'. I took a deep breath, let it out slowly and then followed her in.

There wasn't anything particularly wrong with Viva, at least nothing that couldn't be solved by closing the place down and reopening it as a trendy bistro – something that thankfully happened several years later – but in 1998 it was brash, loud, garish and, wherever the décor allowed, mirrored. Much like my companion. It was like she'd found the mothership. And there she was. At the bar. Chatting to some towering chisel-jawed beefcake with mirrored sunglasses hanging from the pocket of a black leather jacket. I stopped in my tracks. Watched as Viv roared with laughter and grabbed his jacket for support. And as the laughter subsided her hand lingered on his chest, and then gently slid down his front.

I fought my way through the people waiting to be served and sidled up to her.

"Hi!" I shouted over the booming noise of the music. Viv turned to look at me, her manic grin faltering just slightly. I glanced at Mr Beefcake and gave him a nod. He raised an eyebrow, gave me a nod in return, and then without a word turned and walked off into the crowd.

It was then that I noticed four more drinks being lined up on the counter. Before I could protest Viv was handing the bar-tender a ten pound note.

"They only do bottles," yelled Viv, nodding at the *Budweiser.*

"That's ok," I said.

"Let's go over there!" she said, jerking a thumb in the direction of the window – and, far more significantly, Mr Beefcake. I glanced at Viv, then back at Mr Beefcake, and for a millisecond felt the tiniest stab of rejection, followed by a flash of anger that the fun girl I'd spent a pleasant half hour dancing with two days earlier was clearly looking for her next date before ours had officially ended – but neither emotion lasted longer than an instant, my need for self preservation being far stronger. And perhaps this was my one and only opportunity to not only ditch my date, but hand her over to a male equivalent.

I grabbed my beer and followed her through the crowd, and for a brief flickering moment salvation seemed in sight for both of us. But as we neared our mark, a heavily fake-tanned brunette came into view, an orange arm wrapped tightly round Mr Beefcake's waist. Viv snorted her annoyance, and the two of us skulked in silence by the window, her surveying the crowd for an alternative quarry whilst I stared at the floor and prayed for a miracle.

Something brushed my arm. I raised my head and Viv held out her empty glass. I sighed, took it without question, and headed back to the bar.

"What time do you close, mate?" I asked the barman as he put Viv's drink in front of me. I hadn't ordered one for myself – no point, I had hardly touched the last one. The barman frowned.

"Last orders are at eleven," he said. Eleven? I blinked. Normal pub opening hours? I glanced at my watch. It was ten to now. Twenty, maybe thirty minutes, and this whole ordeal could be over.

I handed the barman a fiver. "Keep the change," I said with a renewed passion for life. Thirty minutes. That was all.

"That's ridiculous," said Viv as Club Viva spat its patrons onto the streets. "It's not even midnight!"

I stuffed my hands in my pockets and breathed in the cool night air. "Yeah, I know."

"Hey! Let's find a proper club!" said Viv. "I'll hail us a cab." She staggered towards the road. I grabbed her arm.

"Viv – wait."

"What's wrong?" she asked, brushing away my hand.

"I don't want to go to a club."

"Sure you do!"

"No, really. I don't. I've had enough for one evening."

"Enough?" Viv's mad vibrating eyes rolled in their sockets.

"Yeah, look – it's been..." I searched for the right adjective, "fun. But I'm going to turn in. Maybe we can do this another time. Maybe."

"You're going home?" asked Viv, losing her balance and swinging her arms wildly to stay upright.

"I'm afraid so. But you know – thanks for inviting me." She lurched forward and put a hand on each shoulder.

"Where do you live, Jason?" she asked.

"Erm, just round the corner."

Viv nodded sagely. "Got any alcohol?" she purred.

Gently I unclasped her hands. "No," I lied, before following it quickly with another untruth. "Viv. It was nice to have met you. But let's get you back to your hotel."

It was eight o'clock when the phone rang. I ignored it. It rang again. I pulled a pillow over my head. When it rang a third time I threw the covers off and walked across the hall to my study.

"Hello?"

"Jason!"

My stomach lurched. "Viv?"

"Of course Viv!"

"You're awake?" I wanted to add, "How?"

"Just wanted to thank you for a fun evening," said Viv. "It was great, wasn't it?"

I slumped into my office chair. "Erm... yeah," I said. "Yeah. Great."

"In fact, I was thinking, what are you doing tonight?"

"But it's Sunday," I said. "I've got work tomorrow."

"Come on, Jason," said Viv. "Live a little. I was thinking maybe I could check out and stay at yours. If you promise to be good." She giggled. She actually giggled.

"Mine?" I asked, my stomach lurching again to register its unhappiness at the prospect.

"Well, you were a perfect gentleman."

"I was?"

"Hey!" said Viv. "Better still – why don't we get breakfast? I can be ready in just a few minutes. You can come and get me. I'm starving."

My head started to swim. Breakfast? And a second date? How on earth...? I slapped my forehead gently with my fist, connecting random thoughts and forming a picture of the inevitable chain of events. We'd go on a second date which, in its own special way, would be just as hideous as the first. Later this evening I'd find myself standing in the gents' toilet of some ghastly club, staring into a mirror and making a sacred vow to never ever see this woman again. Meanwhile, back at our table, Viv will have tried on my surname for size and decided it was a perfect fit. And then approximately three years from now, probably on her birthday or some other significant family occasion, and at the precise moment she'd be expecting me to 'pop the question', I'd finally pluck up the courage to tell her that it had all been a huge mistake, that she'd wasted her time on me, and that we should never have seen each other again after that first awful date.

"No Viv," I said. "I'm sorry."

"No?"

"I appreciate the offer, but..." I searched for the words. "It's just... The thing is, you see..." There was no easy way to tell her. No words that could convey the hideous future laid out before us.

"You've got a girlfriend?!" barked Viv. "Is that it?" I was stunned. Where on earth had that come from? But then a moment passed, just long enough for me to see an opportunity to end this once and for all, and spare us both three years of disappointment.

"Erm, yes," I said. "Sort of."

"Sort of?"

"Well, you know. It's complicated."

"Complicated? How can it be complicated?" asked Viv, her voice sounding more like the screech reserved for fingernails against blackboards. "Either you're seeing someone or you aren't. And if you are then you shouldn't have led me on like that! What is it with you men? You're all utter bastards! And you, Jason, are the biggest fucking bastard I've met so far! Fuck you, arsehole! I hope you rot in hell!" She didn't even pause for breath. Instead the tirade of abuse continued until her words - echoing inside my throbbing head - blended together into an angry persistent drone. It was several moments before I realised I was listening to the hum of the dialling tone. Slowly, I put the phone back on its base unit.

I hadn't meant to upset her – but would the truth have been any better? That I was dismissing the possibility of a relationship with an otherwise attractive woman based on one high-spirited evening? How would that have sounded? Because right now it seemed idiotic. First dates weren't a regular occurrence in my life. How could I, Jason Smith, afford to be so picky?

I sat back in my chair, my gaze unintentionally falling on Kylie, smiling at me from the confines of her calendar. Behind her a Caribbean sun was setting, whilst a warm summer breeze played with her hair and tugged at the thin material of her summer dress. I could hear the waves in the background, the clink of a bottle being returned to an ice bucket, and the murmur of other diners. It was hard to imagine Kylie stuffing breadsticks up her nose, or pouring half a bottle of wine over her face and down her front. Almost as hard as it was to picture any woman that perfect ever entering my life. Instead I was doomed to chart my days through grey, solitary waters, carefully avoiding any Viv, Isabella or Liz that crossed my path.

And with nothing but that lonely thought to keep me company, I returned to the bedroom and crawled back into bed.

Chapter Ten
Tuesday 14th July, 1998

"I said, good morning."

I dragged my eyes away from the document in front of me, and looked up into the angelic, smiling face of...

Charlotte.

"Oh, hi," I replied, spinning round to face her, and in the process sweeping all the pages onto the floor, along with a plastic cup of water.

"So how are you this fine day?" she asked, dragging over a chair from the spare desk whilst I dumped the soggy sheets in front of my keyboard.

"Erm, fine, fine," I said, nodding madly and trying not to notice how her skirt rode up her lightly tanned thighs as she sat down.

"Did you have a good weekend?" she asked.

"Er, yeah. Yeah. Fantastic."

"I suppose you were glued to the TV?"

"No! I er, I went out. With friends. Can't remember much of it to be honest," I said with a wink, hinting at a fabulous evening of drunken debauchery. It was all nonsense, of course. She was right. I hadn't been out of the house all weekend and much of it had been spent in front of the telly. "You?" I asked, stepping out of the spotlight.

"Went clubbin' on Friday," she said casually. "Not much the rest of the weekend. Just shopping."

"Did you, erm... buy anything nice?" I asked, hoping this would lead to something we could actually talk about.

"I got this top," said Charlotte. Without thinking I glanced at her chest, and a millisecond later, once my brain had registered that I'd shamelessly stared at her bust, I snapped my eyes back above her neck line. Charlotte raised an eyebrow.

"Looks good," I said quickly. "Your top. That top. The top you bought. Makes you look good – I mean – it looks good on you. You know what I mean. Did you get anything else?"

"Not really," said Charlotte, spinning round in the chair. "Just some underwear."

"Really," I said, choking. "That's nice." Images of Charlotte in her underwear ran riot in my mind.

"So what are you going to do with your winnings?" asked Charlotte. The underwear images stopped rioting just long enough for me to herd them up and store them for later. Winnings?

"I, erm..." I said. "Well I –"

"Sorry it's taken so long, but there were a few people – mentioning no names," Charlotte paused to give me a sideways nod in the direction of the rest of the office, "who'd given me an IOU all those weeks ago and seemed to think they no longer needed to pay up! I mean!"

"Really?" I said. "That's... shocking?" I had absolutely no idea what she was going on about.

"I know!" said Charlotte. "Anyway, here it is." She handed me an envelope. I took it.

Inside was about fifty quid in cash. Maybe more. I stared at the notes.

I was missing something.

"You ok?" asked Charlotte.

"Yeah sure," I said. "So what's this for exactly?" Charlotte laughed and then, seeing the expression on my face, laughed again.

"You don't know?"

"Er, no. Sorry." She span in the chair again, allowing her shoes to dangle from her toes as she stretched her legs out.

"Jason Smith," she said, "what are you like!"

"Are you sure you've got the right person?" I asked.

"Perhaps not," said Charlotte, smiling from ear to ear. "Here, give it back." She leant forward, affording me a very brief, guilty glimpse down the front of her new top, and took back the envelope. Then she sat back in the chair, idly curling her blonde locks round one finger and giving me a long playful look. I started to feel awkward. "Jason! Have you been living on Mars for the past few weeks?"

"I've been right here," I squeaked. She shook her head.

"You must be the only fella I know who isn't..." Her voice tailed off.

"Isn't?" I prompted.

"Tell you what," she said, standing up and pulling the hem of her skirt down slightly, "when you figure it out, you come and find me." She chuckled, then went back to her desk, looking over her shoulder as she went.

I felt ever so slightly annoyed. I was clearly being teased and I didn't like that. Much. On the other hand, I had that familiar butterflies-in-the-stomach feeling that I had with every Charlotte encounter, and my heart was beating like a drum. That familiar tribal beat. Getting louder and louder.

The mysterious wad of cash and the invitation to "come and find me" gnawed at me for the rest of the morning until I was forced to broach the subject with the one person who would have the answers I needed. I glanced over at Sian, who was even more grumpy than usual and had spent the morning snarling at anyone who came within a few feet of her.

"I've finished reviewing this brief," I said.

"About time," said Sian without looking up.

"It's quite an interesting proposal," I said, undeterred by her abruptness.

"It's a waste of fucking time is what it is," said Sian.

"Yeah," I said, "it's that too." Sian looked at me over the top of imaginary horn-rimmed spectacles, then turned away to indicate that she was too busy and important for conversations like this, or perhaps me in general. I looked round the office for inspiration. Perhaps a more direct approach was the answer.

"So er, Sian – do you know why Charlotte tried giving me money earlier?"

"Jason!" said Sian, slamming her pen on the desk.

"What?" I said defensively.

"Is that why you've been working so hard this morning? So that you could ask me about that damn money!?"

"No!" I lied.

"It bloody is!" insisted Sian.

"Ok, maybe a little, but I haven't got a clue, and I thought, maybe, you'd..." Sian let out a long, exasperated sigh.

"Look in your top drawer," she said. I frowned, but did as I was told.

"What am I looking for?" I asked.

"You don't see anything familiar?" asked Sian.

"I see lots of familiar things. Is there anything specific I should be looking for?"

Sian shook her head. "Tell me what you see."

"Couple of biros, half a dozen floppy disks, the world's missing supply of paper-clips..." I looked up.

"Anything else?" she asked.

"Nothing. Just rubbish."

"Rubbish?"

"Yeah, some crumbs, a crumpled piece of paper..."

"Bingo," said Sian, and turned back to her computer. I shook my head in frustration. Had all the women become even more inexplicable overnight? I took the small ball of paper out of the drawer and uncrumpled it. It had one word written on it: France.

I'd won the World Cup!

To: Charlotte. Subject: Money. Text: Give me back my loot!
I hit send.

Email flirting is one of the great inventions of the twentieth century. It was also one of the few things I actually considered myself good at. It was how I'd landed Liz all those years ago, back when she'd been a secretary and I'd been a lowly grunt. In a moment of madness I sent her a playful email asking why she always wore the same skirt – the one with a split in the side – on Wednesdays. Several days later we went for a drink, and I spent the subsequent three years living with the consequences. Such is the awesome power of email flirting.

My computer bleeped. I had new email.

How do you know it's yours? came Charlotte's reply.

I have proof, I typed. Brevity is the key to good email flirting. I hit send again, and moments later another bleep signalled her response:

Really?

I smiled. This was too easy. *Yes,* I typed. I hit send, and waited all of twenty seconds.

No proof. No money.

I interlocked my hands, stretched my arms out in front of me and cracked my fingers. *Come over here and take a look.* I took a deep breath, and prayed that she'd do the complete opposite. Send.

I have the money, replied Charlotte. *You come over here.* Predictable. Totally predictable.

Why don't we meet on neutral territory? I shivered. This was it. This was the moment. I'd dangled the bait. Now to see whether she'd bite. The computer beeped again. Sian gave me a look that said if my computer chirped one more time there'd be hell to pay. It didn't matter, I'd done it.

Ok, said Charlotte. *Where?*

I've never understood why anyone works through their lunch break. Lunch is an incredibly important part of the day. It takes place approximately two hours after you arrive (ok, two hours after I arrive) and two hours of work can be a real shock to the system. If you're going to stand any chance of making it through the afternoon you need a lunch break.

I returned to our table with two drinks in hand, having just ordered our pub grub, and shared these thoughts with bucket-loads of enthusiasm, hoping to appear as entertaining as possible. Charlotte listened politely and laughed in all the right places. And each laugh made my insides jolt and tingle like someone had just goosed me from behind.

"But if I work my lunch then I can go home an hour early," said Charlotte.

"Yes, but you'll only use that hour making something to eat on account of the fact that you're so hungry from skipping lunch!"

"If you say so," said Charlotte, smiling. She lit a cigarette.

"Of course, I haven't actually got any money to settle the bill," I said casually.

"Sorry?"

"It's ok. As soon as you give me my winnings..."

"Oh! So that's your game. If I don't hand over the cash I end up paying for lunch? Well, I'll just pay for our meals out of the winnings! So there."

"Isn't that a bit unfair on the person whose money it is?" I reasoned.

"No one's yet managed to convince me that they're the rightful owner," said Charlotte, blowing a cloud of smoke over my head. "I'm thinking I might just keep it." I put my hand in my pocket, took out the screwed up piece of paper, and flattened it on the table.

"I believe this is your handwriting." Charlotte reached into her handbag, took out the now familiar envelope, and offered it to me with a smile.

"Congratulations," she said. "You're a winner."

What happened next was a delightful blur. Food arrived, empty plates went away. I chatted. Charlotte laughed. She quizzed me as to why Isabella and I had swapped teams in the first place, and clapped her hands with delight when I regaled her with embellished stories of how Isabella had begged me day after day to "trade with her France for Italy". I skipped the bit about our photo-shoot, and the nature of our trade, but Charlotte was more than content that Isabella had missed out on the sweepstake money due to misplaced national pride. By the time we returned to the office the World Cup Sweepstake Angel didn't seem quite so out of my league, and I had a new friend in the making.

I drove Sian mad for the rest of the week batting emails back and forth with Charlotte – every time the computer beeped Sian flinched, tutted, shook her head, or gave me the headmistress look. Once she even tried to tell me that she had the authority to review my email, and that she was considering raising the subject of inter-office relationships with Ralph – head of IT – but I knew she was bluffing.

By the end of the following week Charlotte and I had been to lunch a couple more times – the second of which lasted well over an hour. Sian wasn't happy, but I couldn't care less. One hour in the company of Charlotte was worth any price.

That said, it was only lunch. And with each lunch date, the "only" part became more and more apparent. Nothing was ever going to happen between us. Not without a minor miracle or divine intervention.

"You're finished?"

Martin said nothing. Just gathered up tools from the kitchen worktop – the *brand new* kitchen worktop – and put them into a large leather bag on the floor.

"I can't believe you're finished," I said again, trying to spot the one thing that 'isn't working right now' and would be dealt with 'tomorrow'.

"If something's worth doing, Jason, it's worth doing properly."

"Yeah, yeah," I said, "of course. It's just that, well, you know, I guess I thought fitting a kitchen wouldn't take so... I guess I thought it would be..." Slowly and deliberately, Martin fastened the buckles on his leather bag. "But then I suppose a kitchen – that's quite a big job – deceptively so, probably..." I swallowed. "It looks great, by the way," I added.

"I'm glad you like it."

"So how much do I owe you?" I asked.

"We'll sort something out," said Martin after a moment.

"Right," I said. "Ok. You'll let me know then?"

"Yes," said Martin, "I'll let you know." I shuffled uncomfortably.

"You fancy a cuppa?" I asked brightly.

"Not for me thanks," he said, standing up. He leaned against the wall, took the pouch of tobacco from his breast pocket and started rolling a cigarette. "How's the world of computer programming?" he asked eventually.

"Oh, ok. I guess." I picked up the kettle and filled it. "I don't enjoy it that much anymore if I'm honest," I said.

"No. I didn't think so," said Martin. "A little on the dull side I expect," he observed.

"Yeah," I said. "A little."

"I see you more as a photographer." I bristled at the memory of my brief foray into the world of glamour photography. How on earth could Martin know about that?

"Yeah?" I said, forcing a laugh. I opened a cupboard and took out two mugs.

"Or something," he added. "Either way you'll never be satisfied in that job of yours. Anyone can see that."

"They can?" I asked.

"It's there," he said, "written in your aura."

"Ah," I said. We were having one of those conversations. Martin pushed the handmade cigarette behind his ear and started rolling a second one.

"You patched it up with your mother?" he asked. I shook my head. The only thing that prevented me from telling Martin to mind his own damn business was the shock that he knew any of this stuff in the first place.

"Not really, no," I said, opening the fridge and taking out the milk.

"You ought to," said Martin. "No one will ever love you like your mother. When everyone else has deserted you, your mother will always be there for you."

"Hmmm," I said, squeezing a tea bag and then tossing it into the bin. Where was my mother when Liz and I split?

Hurling abuse at me from the other end of the phone, that's where.

"You don't think so?" asked Martin.

"Maybe," I said.

"Give her another chance," he said. I handed him his tea and then realised what I'd done.

"Oh. Sorry – you didn't want a tea, did you?"

"That's ok," he said. "I quite fancy one now – you obviously had a premonition."

"Yeah," I said. But premonitions weren't a laughing matter when Martin was about.

Charlotte laughed.

"So you're saying that your builder is a psychic?"

"Why shouldn't there be psychic builders?" I asked. "You never know, there might be psychic business analysts."

"All business analysts are psychic!" said Charlotte, lighting her cigarette. "Impossible to do the job otherwise."

"Is that why you became an analyst? Because of your 'psychic powers'?" She laughed again. But it was a sad laugh.

"Being a BA is about a million miles away from what I wanted to be!"

"So what did little Charlotte want to be?" I asked.

She sat back in her chair and took a hard drag on her cigarette before blowing a cloud of smoke into the air above her. "I always wanted to be a ballerina!" she said after a moment.

"Really?"

"Or a princess!" she added.

"Aren't they a little different?"

"Not at all – both get to wear nice dresses!"

"Ah!" I said, seeing the female logic at work.

"Or a model." My interest was piqued.

"A model?"

"That was my teenage fantasy. I did it for a while too. You know, catalogues and things."

"Why did you stop?"

"Oh, it wasn't quite what I expected. I guess I thought it would be more about me and less about the clothes," she said with a laugh. "That makes me sound a little self-centred, doesn't it?"

"No," I lied. "Not at all."

"And what about you?" asked Charlotte. "What did you want to be?" I felt my skin goosebump. So here I was again. Sitting in a pub, with a beautiful girl, reminiscing about unrealised ambitions. I could tell her about my dreams of writing computer games or-

"I always wanted to be a photographer," I said.

"Yeah? What kind of photography?" asked Charlotte, taking another drag of her cigarette.

"Well, er, glamour. Actually." I said. Charlotte coughed.

"You wanted to be," she lowered her voice, "a glamour photographer – when you were a kid?" I flushed.

"No! Well, not really, I mean – when I was fourteen. Ish." I pictured myself sitting on Alex's bed, staring up at Linda on the wall. "It was more of an interest in creating exciting images." I swallowed. "Working with exciting, er, people. You know."

"I see!" she said. "And do you still want to..." She nodded sideways. My cheeks were positively glowing.

"Erm, well – yes. Yes actually. I think it would be fun." Charlotte's eyes widened. "Nothing seedy," I said. "Just, you know, stuff that you might see in *FHM*, or something."

"Right. A little different from what you do now!"

"I guess so," I said.

"You should do it!" said Charlotte, after a moment's silence.

"Really? You think so?"

"Oh yeah! What have you got to lose?" she enthused. "I mean, it's a million times more interesting than working for these thieving bastards – and it's not like you'd have to chuck your job in. You could do it on the side. See whether or not you were successful!"

"Yeah," I said. "I suppose I could." I smiled, then took a deep breath. "Thing is though, it's a bit difficult to do glamour photography without a glamour model."

Charlotte shrugged. "You'll find someone," she said. "Loads of girls want to be models."

"Really?" I said. She nodded, and I watched as she exhaled another plume of smoke, wondering briefly if that was why the air felt so hot, and why my heart was trying to break through my chest. "Hey..." I said. "How about... I mean... how about you?"

"What about me?" asked Charlotte.

"Modelling."

Charlotte wrinkled her nose. "Nah," she said. "I'm through with catalogues."

"No, I don't... not catalogues," I said. "I mean, you know, how about modelling –" I swallowed "– for me?" Charlotte's mouth fell open. Her face flushed as she looked down at the cigarette in her hands, and immediately I felt the urge to apologise. I fought it.

"Only if you want to..." I muttered, in an effort to fill the silence. I held off for a few more seconds, until the silence was a deafening roar. "Look..." I started.

"Ok," said Charlotte. I blinked.

"Ok?"

"I'll do it," she said, making eye contact.

"You'll model... for me?"

"Why not!" she said. "But nothing too... you know."

"No, no," I said quickly. "I was thinking bikini, swim-suit... maybe the old classic soft-focus picture of you sitting at a dressing table in some, er, nice, er, lingerie. Maybe." Charlotte shot a quick look around the pub to see whether any of the other diners had heard me.

"Ok," she said, leaning forwards and lowering her voice. "But let's talk about it later."

"Oh, sure, sure. Fancy another drink?" I asked.

"Well I shouldn't really," said Charlotte, looking at her watch. I gave her my 'come on, to hell with those thieving bastards' look. "Oh, ok then." She smiled.

I walked up to the bar, still reeling at the enormity of what had just happened but feeling a good ten inches taller than I had thirty minutes earlier.

"Same again?" asked the barman.

"Oh no," I replied. "This time's going to be much better."

Chapter Eleven
Monday 27th July, 1998

"Afternoon," said Sian, as I dumped my bag on my desk and took off my jacket.

"Morning," I replied, ignoring Sian's sarcasm. Nothing was going to ruin my sunny mood. "Good weekend?" I asked. Sian grumbled something in reply but I wasn't listening.

My weekend had been spent kicking myself – wondering why, having asked Charlotte to model for me, I hadn't thought to arrange it for the following day! Still, this had left me plenty of time to stare into space, and plan a photoshoot in my head. And when I could no longer keep track of the ideas floating around between my ears, I'd written them down. By Sunday evening I'd filled several sheets of paper.

I reached into my bag, pulled out the envelope containing my shoot ideas, and slid it into my desk drawer.

"Jason," said a female voice. I turned around, and there was Charlotte.

"Oh – hi," I said, and I smiled my broadest, friendliest smile. She didn't smile back. She stood with her hands in front of her, her shoulders rolled forward.

"I need to talk to you," she said.

"Oh. Ok. What's up?"

"Not here," she hissed. "Privately." Sian looked up, raising her eyebrows higher than one would have thought was possible. "Let's meet for lunch. If you're free?"

"Sure," I said. "Absolutely."

As Charlotte returned to her desk Sian looked up again. "What!?" I said. But she didn't say anything, and turned her attention to her email. Of course Charlotte wanted to talk privately; she probably wanted to discuss our photo-shoot. What other reason could there be?

"So how are you?" asked Charlotte as I returned from the bar, our usual drinks in hand.

"Fine," I said cheerfully. "How are you?"

"Oh, ok." she said. Then she burst into tears. Ok, so maybe she didn't want to talk about the photo session.

"Hey," I said, offering her a serviette, "what's wrong?"

"I'm sorry, Jason!" she said.

"For what? There's nothing to be sorry about – come on now, tell me what's wrong – what are mates for?"

"I don't know what to do. I'm so confused. I don't understand men at all!" she said. I smiled.

"We're not that complicated!" I said. She snorted. "D'you want to talk about it?"

"Oh Jason, it doesn't seem fair to burden you with my problems."

"Hey! Burden away – that's what I'm here for!" I said, puffing out my chest like I might rip my shirt open to reveal a big S-shaped logo. She sniffed and wiped her nose again. I took another serviette and wiped away a tear from the corner of her eye. She smiled and all at once my insides rattled and jumped about like I'd just hit top score on a pinball machine. She was so, so beautiful.

"Ok," she said, regaining her composure. "Well, I was down TOTS on Friday."

"Ok," I said. What had TOTS nightclub got to do with anything?

"It's a good night," she said. "You should come along."

"Yeah," I said, "I should." I made a mental note never to do that.

"Anyway, Gary was down there with some of his mates." My heart stopped briefly.

"Gary?" I asked, and suddenly I was back in Sian's kitchen, on New Year's Eve, a stupid hat on my head, a bottle of Bacardi in my hand, and my world starting to unravel.

"Yeah, from the helpdesk."

"Ok," I said, shaking the memories out of my head.

"Anyway, we've always got on quite well... he's a nice guy, don't you think?"

"Oh yeah," I said, "he's..." but words failed me.

"Anyway, we got talking... and you know, we were getting on really well." She looked me straight in the eye. My stomach lurched as my mind ran through a series of mental images illustrating just how well that might be. "Anyway..." Charlotte continued, taking a short breath and looking like she might cry again. "One thing sort of led to another."

"You mean you and Gary..." I waved my hand in an effort to suggest something that probably required at least another hand.

"Yeah. You know!" No. I didn't know. I really didn't. She went out to a night club on Friday night, started chatting to a guy from work and 'one thing led to another' resulting in 'you know' – how does that work? 'He asked me out on a date.' That I could understand. 'He seemed ok and I ended up giving him my number.' That too would be a possibility. But 'one thing led to another'?

"What exactly does that mean?" I asked, the sympathy draining from my voice.

"Well, we went back to his place and I kinda spent the night. Well, until 4am."

"What happened at 4am?" I asked.

"Oh, I had to go home. His girlfriend was coming round first thing Saturday, and anyway, I didn't want my mum to know I'd been out all night, so."

"Right," I said. "Of course." I felt sick.

"Anyway," said Charlotte for about the millionth time, her voice cracking as the tears started to come back, "now I don't know what to do."

"About what?" I asked, reeling slightly.

"Well, what does it mean?" she asked, her eyes pleading. "Does this mean he likes me?"

"Like you...?"

"I mean, do you think he'll leave his girlfriend? I waited in all weekend to see if he'd call, but he didn't. And then this morning I thought he might walk over... I just don't know what to do. I've thought about nothing else since Friday – and I'm so confused." And with that she let out two or three deep sobs. I handed her the last of the serviettes, leant back in the chair and watched as her heart broke.

I knew exactly how that felt.

And had there been a Superman logo hiding under my shirt Charlotte wasn't going to see it. Not today. Probably not ever. She was more of a Batman kinda girl. And I was nothing but a fool.

"You know," I said eventually, "maybe it would be best if we went back to work. I'm not that hungry."

"Oh," she said through her snuffles. "Oh. Ok."

And with that, we left.

"You're back early," said Sian. I grunted. "I mean, really early." She checked the clock on the wall. "How on earth did you get there, order, eat and return in under half an hour? And more to the point, why?" I ignored the question.

"Lovers' tiff?" she joked. I looked at her. "Oh," said Sian, and promptly went back to what she was doing.

"Jason, you're back." I turned to see Ralph, Head of IT, standing above me. "I thought you were at lunch."

"I was."

"Quick lunch."

"Yes."

"Well – I'm glad you're back. There's something I need to chat to you about."

"Ok," I said.

"In my office."

I got up.

"No no, it's erm... I'm not quite ready yet. Why don't you get a coffee or something? Come into my office at one o'clock, will you?"

"Right," I said. "Sure." I sat back down again.

"Great," said Ralph, and he marched back across the room. Something wasn't right. I looked over at Sian, who was watching Ralph.

"D'you know what he wants to see me about?" I said, gesturing in Ralph's direction.

"Haven't a clue," said Sian. "Maybe you're being put on Y2K. They've even got me looking at some stuff."

"Oh God, I hope not," I whined, dropping my head into my hands. "That would just about finish me off. It's difficult to see how this day could get any worse."

I was sitting on the floor in the lounge, leaning against the wall, when the phone rang. I reached up and took it from its cradle.

"Hello?" I said. A hysterical voice at the other end of the phone started wailing and shouting. "Sian, for God's sake – I can't hear what you're saying."

"I can't believe it Jason! I just... can't believe it! Oh my God!" I didn't say anything. I checked my watch. Four thirty. That would be about right. Sian must have left the office at four and was now at home. "Hello??" she said.

"I'm still here," I said.

"Are you alright? Do you want me to come over? I'll come over. Just give me ten minutes. Well, probably more like twenty, or thirty, but don't worry. Just tell me where you live."

"Sian! For goodness' sake, calm down!"

"Calm? Calm?" squeaked Sian hysterically. "How can I be calm at a moment like this? The bastards won't tell me what happened. I asked but they told me some bullshit about you being made redundant."

I sighed. "Yes. That's right," I said, rubbing my eyes. "I've been made redundant."

"Bullshit!" said Sian again. "That's crap and you know it. This is constructive dismissal! They fired you, Jason – God knows why, but they can't do it! You've got to take it to the union."

"The union rep was in the meeting," I said.

"He was? What did he say?"

"Nothing."

"Nothing? What do you mean, nothing? He must have said something! Jason – you have rights! They can't just get rid of you!"

"Yes," I said. "It seems they can."

"But why?" said Sian. "They have to give you a reason."

"'Surplus to requirements,'" I said, paraphrasing Ralph.

"Bullshit!" screamed Sian.

I let her rage on for a while, badmouth Ralph, the company, personnel, the union, then Ralph again. But I knew that Ralph wasn't to blame. Head office had told him to reduce the head count, and though it didn't make it any easier, there were logical reasons why I was the only one being booted out the door.

In an ideal world I'd have delivered some clever acerbic remark before slamming Ralph's office door behind me. Or some melancholy but insightful comment on the soulless nature of business today. Or a cool, cryptic exit line that hinted at a bright and exciting future ahead of me now that CFS were no longer holding me back. But this isn't an ideal world. If it were then my job would have meant more to me than a pay cheque, I wouldn't be out on my ear, and Charlotte wouldn't be obsessing over Gary.

Of all those things, the last seemed particularly unfair – proof, if you need it, that we live in a godless universe because what kind of god would create a world where beautiful, intelligent girls like Charlotte fall for utter slime balls? All I'd wanted was a chance for us to get to know each other better. A little time together, away from the office and other distractions. Just long enough to figure out whether she was the one. Just long enough to reach that 'moment'. But then Gary had come along. Again. And though I tried to take solace in the fact that I might be finally rid of him, somehow it wasn't enough.

Sian calmed down once I'd convinced her that I wasn't go to throw myself off the roof, that there was something edible in the fridge, and that I would look into appealing against the redundancy thing. The last bit was a complete lie. As was the bit about there being anything edible in the fridge. I was undecided about the roof.

As I put the receiver down I found myself wiping tears out of my eyes with the palm of my hand. If you could have torn me open – and it wouldn't have been difficult – where once I'd had organs there was now a whirling black hole of despair. How it got there I couldn't have told you. But it had been there a while.

I picked up the receiver again and pressed 'memory one'.

"Hello?"

"Mum."

"Jason! Well, this is a surprise," she said. She sounded a little bitter. Who could blame her?

"I've lost my job."

"Oh Jason," she said, her tone changing instantly. "I'm so sorry. When?"

"Today," I answered, biting back the tears. "They made me redundant."

"Have you eaten?"

"No," I said.

"Then come over, and I'll cook you something nice."

If ever you're unfortunate enough to be trapped inside a public building during a Zombie Apocalypse, you'll be in safe hands if it's a Wednesday morning and you happen to be in the Chelmsford branch of Tesco's.

You'll witness a harmless-looking, but immaculately well-dressed lady in her mid to late fifties effortlessly take charge of the situation: Tasks would be identified, jobs would be delegated, and everyone would ultimately be looked after, reassured, and generally kept in line with cups of tea and biscuits that Tesco would later find they had donated to my mother's survival efforts.

So it was with me in my moment of crisis.

My mother bustled around, produced a hot meal, endless cups of tea, and showered me with pearls of wisdom, most of which amounted to the same thing: Forget CFS.

Pick yourself up. Dust yourself down. View it as an opportunity. A fresh start. A new beginning.

And she was right. Of course. Just as Martin had been right when he said nobody would ever love me like my mother. For although she was my harshest critic, she was also my strongest supporter.

There was, however, the small matter of Liz.

And our breakup.

"It's your life, Jason," said my mother, standing over the sink, washing dinner plates by hand despite having a perfectly good dishwasher. "I'm sorry that you and Liz never worked out – I was very fond of her – and she was good for you, Jason – but you're old enough and ugly enough to make your own decisions." I nodded sagely. My own mother may have thought I was ugly, but she'd also just told me I was old enough to think for myself – and this was a major breakthrough! I waited for her to continue, but she didn't. And for the first time in thirty years, I felt like a grown up.

Chapter Twelve
Monday 7th September, 1998

The summer sun started its slow majestic descent, and for the third evening in a row the sky was a fantastic mixture of burnt oranges, reds and deep velvety blues. I sipped my pint, leant against the railings, and admired the scene across the river. Boats full of tourists. Commuters bustling across Blackfriars Bridge. St Paul's Cathedral overlooking it all. Had I been in the company of someone who might appreciate the poetry, I might have voiced these thoughts – but I was more than content to bask in the embers of another summer's day, the warm, fuzzy feeling brought on by three pints of Guinness, the hustle and bustle of The Doggett's Coat and Badge pub, and the companionship of my best friend.

"Oh shitting hell!" said Alex, stepping back from the railings and waving a hand at a bird perched on the wall next to him. "Fuckin' pigeons! Bastard thing almost crapped in my pint!"

"Fancy doing this again Friday?" I asked, when Alex had finished glaring at anything with wings.

Alex thought about this for a moment. "Can't think of a good reason not to. Other than the fact I'll spend half the weekend with a stinking hangover." Another tourist boat chugged past, its passengers waving at anyone who might wave back. I raised a hand.

"You need to get a job," said Alex after a moment or two.

"It can wait," I said.

"You won the lottery?" asked Alex.

I shook my head. "'Course not. But I'm not exactly a man of expensive tastes! Put a few cans of cheap lager in my fridge, give me an internet connection, my train fare to London – and I'm happy. Sort of. What else do I spend my money on?"

"Clothes?" ventured Alex.

"Do I look like I spend a lot on clothes?"

"Food?" he asked.

"Would interfere with my diet of beer."

"Ok, but your mortgage must be –"

"Two hundred and fifty a month."

"You lucky bastard," said Alex. "So, what... you're going to live on savings?"

"For a while." Alex shook his head as he tried to make sense of something.

"How come you have savings!?" he asked eventually.

"Just have," I said with a shrug. Though they weren't really savings. More the natural consequence of cheap living and a half decent job.

"But I earn more than you," said Alex. "How come I'm not rolling in money?" I looked at my friend.

"You have a 'Tina'." Alex did nothing for a moment, then went back to looking across the river.

"Ain't that the truth," he said, "I tried to sell that stupid exercise bike." He took a long swig at his pint.

"And?"

"Won't let me. Apparently 'it's useful'."

"I thought she never used it."

"She hangs clothes on it. Her exercise bike, the one I fuckin' paid for, is now an expensive clothes horse." A deep, grumpy frown passed across his face like the shadow cast by a lone cloud on a summer's day. He shook his head and drained his pint. "My advice to you, mate, is get another job and keep hold of those savings. If you ever get married you'll soon discover that women bleed you dry. You want another?"

"Why not."

He handed me his empty pint glass.

"Right, well... you're buyin', money bags, because I'm skint." I took the glass and headed back inside to the bar.

Married?

A familiar knot formed in my stomach and gnawed at my insides. There seemed very little chance of me ever being married. Losing my job had deprived me of something much more serious than a source of income. Despite Sian's warning about dating girls you work with, CFS had been my only consistent source of female contact.

What I needed was a new job that would both earn me a living, and enable me to meet new people. Specifically women. Attractive women. But at the same time, nice women. And fun. And single. Definitely single. Attractive, nice, fun, single women.

"Same again?" asked the barmaid.

Such a vocation would not only increase my odds of finding my perfect woman, but given enough time, make it inevitable. And to my considerable astonishment I knew of a career choice that fitted the requirements perfectly. I'd thought of very little else for several weeks.

But I could never pull it off.

Could I?

"Erm, yes please," I said to the barmaid, rooting around in my pockets for a fiver whilst noticing how the round neck of her lycra top scooped low enough to reveal the lace edging of her black bra, a bra that was doing a terrific job of gathering her comparatively small breasts together and shoving them skywards to produce an appealing valley between two delicious mounds of soft flesh. I lifted my eyes, and was met by hers. She raised an eyebrow as if to say "Don't think I don't know what you were looking at, you dirty dog," and her warm smile told me no harm was done.

Friendly. Nice. Fun.

And she was standing right in front of me.

I hadn't had to join a class, work in the same office, embark on a career change or some other hair-brained scheme, she was right here. All I had to do was talk to her.

"Five pounds exactly," said the barmaid. I looked at the crumpled fiver in my hands, then handed her the money. She took it, and opened the cash register.

Ask her something. Just think of a question. Anything would do, just–

She topped up our pints, throwing me a smile as she did so. I opened my mouth. When no words came out she raised her eyebrow again. This was ridiculous. How hard could it be to–

She put the drinks in front of me. Finally I summoned up the courage to say something.

"Thanks," I squeaked.

She smiled, turned, and walked to the other side of the bar. My shoulders slumped like someone had opened a valve at the base of my neck and let out my enthusiasm for life.

"She's lovely, ain't she?" said the fella next to me, folding his paper and placing it on the bar.

"Eh? Oh, yes. Yes she is."

"Becky," he said.

"Sorry?"

"Her name."

"Right," I said. "Thanks." The man drained his pint, got down from his barstool, picked up a briefcase from the floor and turned to head out of the door.

"Oh, excuse me," I said, calling him back. He turned. "You forgot your paper."

"Keep it," he said, "it's yesterday's." I put the paper back on the bar, and noticed that it wasn't a London paper, but the Evening *Gazette*. My local paper.

And in that moment an idea was born.

The following morning, as I sat in my dressing gown, head throbbing slightly in a half-hearted attempt to complain about the previous night's drinking, I flicked through my second-hand copy of the *Gazette* – past the numerous pictures of kids handing oversized cheques to local dignitaries adorned with medallions, past middle-aged couples pointing solemnly at the space where their wheelie bin had stood before it had been taken by wheelie bin thieves – and on to the classified ads.

Cars, cars, cars, more cars, caravans, carpentry, carpets, carpet cleaning, electrical, heating, plumbing, property, more property, even more property, yet more property, self storage, and finally – situations vacant. I ran my finger down the ads, ignoring them all, and eventually found what I was looking for. A phone number.

"Classifieds," answered the female voice.

"Oh hello," I said, my throat drying. "I'd like to place an advertisement please."

"Why do I want to meet this guy again?" I asked, as we entered The Sutton Arms and shuffled to the bar through the throng of suited city drinkers celebrating the end of another week.

"Because you need a job," said Alex.

"And this Wilson has one?" I asked.

"Yes," said Alex flatly. "He's desperate for anyone with half a brain. Guinness?"

"Look, Alex, I appreciate the thought but –"

"I'm not thinking of you," said Alex as he caught the eye of the barman. "I'm thinking of me. Specifically, my liver. Two pints of Guinness, mate."

"Your liver?"

"I can't keep getting trollied with you two or three times a week. I get it in the ear from Tina when I get home, and I feel like shit the following day. You might not want to get a job, but I need you to." I sighed. Sometimes Alex's selfishness knew no depths.

"So who is this Wilson guy?"

"Client. Top bloke. Head of strategic development and... some other crap."

"Right! Interesting job title. Which company?" But before Alex could answer he froze, a startled look on his face as if something cold or hairy had crawled up his leg. Confirming my prognosis, he slapped his thigh repeatedly before pulling a vibrating mobile phone from his trouser pocket. He glanced at it briefly, pulled up the aerial, then snapped it open.

"Wilson!" he said. "Right. Right. Right. What now? Ok." And with that, Alex walked past me and out of the pub.

"So if you'd like to dictate your wording," said the voice.

I cleared my throat. A bead of perspiration rolled down my forehead.

"Ready when you are."

"Right. Ok then. Well – here goes." I dabbed my forehead with the sleeve of my robe.

"Write down your number," said Alex as he fought his way back through the crowd.

"What? Why? I haven't got a pen," I said, checking my pockets.

"Here!" Alex produced a pen from his bag. I took it and held it for a moment before we both realised I needed something to write on. "Bollocks! Haven't you any paper?"

"I don't think so," I said, checking my pockets again.

"Use a beer mat or something."

"Hang on!" I said. "I've found something."

"Hurry up!" said Alex.

"Yeah alright, keep your hair on. What the hell do you –" But as I finished the last digit he snatched the paper from me and disappeared into the crowd. I stood there, bewildered, until the barman tapped me on the shoulder and handed me my change.

"Oh, thank God," said Alex, returning to the bar and claiming one of the pints.

"What was all that about?"

He held up a hand and continued to quench his thirst.

"Wilson needed it," he said eventually.

"Wilson? Wilson-with-the-job Wilson? Where is he?"

"Outside."

"Why doesn't he come in?"

"He was in a car. He's gone now."

"So he's not joining us?"

"No. I gave him your number. He'll call you."

"Right," I said, picking up my pint. I wasn't disappointed in the slightest. "Two more pints please, mate," I said to the barman.

"I haven't finished this one yet," said Alex.

"No, but you're not far off, and if this evening is to mark the end of my life of leisure I intend to make the most of it."

Alex drained his pint. "So who's Mandy?" he asked.

As I climbed the stairs from the front door, a red light winked at me from the lounge. I dumped my grocery bags on the floor, walked up to the machine and pressed the button marked play.

"Yeah 'ello?" said a female voice. "I'm phoning about the advert in last night's *Gazette*? For glamour models?"

"Mandy?" I said. "Oh – just, this... girl."

"What, someone from work?"

"No, no," I said, scratching my neck. "She's a... she's a model. Actually."

"What do you mean, model?" asked Alex.

"You know. A... er, glamour model."

"What? Like... a naked model?"

"No, not naked!"

"How comes you've never mentioned this Mandy bird before?"

"Well, she only contacted me the other day."

"Why?"

"Anyway," continued the voice, "I might be interested, although it depends, you know, on what's involved an' stuff. I dunna bit o' modelling before, and sum'times my boyfriend takes pictures of me, you know, in stockings or whatever..." The woman rambled on, but I was still struggling to comprehend the enormity of the situation.

The advert – had worked?!

"My number is..." continued the woman. I scrabbled amongst the pile of junk next to the phone, found a pen and wrote down her number on the back of an envelope.

"You placed an ad for glamour models!?" I shuffled on the spot for a moment, then looked around the bar for any way out of this conversation. There wasn't any. "I swear you're losing it!"

"You're probably right," I replied, trying to ignore how red my face looked in the mirror behind the bar.

"But – you're not a photographer!"

"I know, I know!"

"That's like... pretending to be a doctor so you can meet nurses."

"Yes, I suppose it is! Could we –"

"So why say you're a photographer?"

"Charlotte said I should give the glamour photography a shot, so I thought, you know – after the pictures I took of Isabella – why not?"

"But you only mentioned the photography thing to get into Charlotte's knickers."

"You have such a way with words," I said.

"It's true!"

"No! It's not! I liked her – and she seemed to like me! And that started me thinking. If Charlotte – possibly the most beautiful, sexy girl I've known in the past, whatever – was prepared to model for me then maybe, just maybe, others would too."

Alex said nothing. He just looked at me in that dumb-struck way of his, when he's marvelling at my new levels of idiocy.

"But you're not a photographer! You can't just –"

"Ok!" I said, my shoulders dropping. "I know! It's total madness! But I didn't stop to think about any of that until after I'd arranged the shoot." I took a deep melancholy breath, then picked up one of the fresh pints and put it in his hand.

"The shoot?" asked Alex.

"We arranged a photo shoot for Saturday."

"Tomorrow?"

"Yes."

"Where?"

"My place."

"Your flat?"

"Yes."

"But you're not a photogr –"

"I know that, Alex! I know! And first thing tomorrow morning I intend to phone Mandy and spin her some tale about how my best friend was involved in a hideous bar fight and has been rushed to hospital! I'll probably leave out the part about how I put him there!"

"You haven't cancelled it?"

"No."

"She's still coming?"

"Yes."

"But –"

"How about another drink?" I asked.

Alex blinked. "Ok," he said, glancing at the fresh pint in his hand.

"Good!" I said, turning quickly under the pretence of catching the barman's eye.

"Another two pints please, mate," The barman raised an eyebrow. I took a deep breath and tried to think of something harmless to talk about. There was our standard list of pub topics – movies, women, gadgets, time travel, the internet, women, music, ants (obscure, I know, but it's amazing how many times ants feature heavily in pub conversations), women...

A thought struck me, followed quickly by another, and then another, until my head was one huge thought pile up.

"Alex," I said, turning to face him. "I need that envelope."

"What envelope?"

"The envelope I wrote my number on."

"What are you talking about?"

"The envelope you gave to your mate, two minutes ago. Hinton. Hilton. Bilton – "

"Wilson?"

"Yes, him! I need that envelope."

"Why?"

"It has Mandy's details on it!"

"So?"

"If I don't have her details I can't cancel the photo shoot!"

"Bugger," said Alex, bringing his pint to his mouth. "I guess you'll have to go through with it." The vaguest hint of a smile passed across his face.

"I can't! As you have quite rightly pointed out, I am not a photographer! I don't have the knowledge, the training, the experience. I have nothing, in fact. Just a very expensive digital camera that I intend to sell to anyone who shows a passing interest."

"Really? How much d'you want for it?"

"Oh, for heaven's sake, will you focus! Tomorrow morning at eleven-ish, Mandy from Canvey Island is going to rock up at my place expecting to see an array of lights, umbrellas, big rolls of paper, possibly a photographer's assistant, with a light-measuring-thingy in one hand and a *Hasselblad* in the other. Whereas in fact it'll just be me, my meagre little camera and a weak smile."

"What's a hassle blad?"

"Sorry?"

"You said hassle blad."

"Oh – a really big camera, I think. I dunno. You see? I have no idea what I'm talking about! I need that number!"

"Fine," said Alex with a sigh, and he reached into his pocket for his mobile phone.

It took a gut-wrenching forty minutes to raise Wilson, and another thirty for him to find somewhere he could pull over and dictate Mandy's details back to me. Alex insisted that I talk to Wilson. His way of teaching me a lesson, I guess. But thankfully Wilson never asked who Mandy was. Just as he didn't mention the employment opportunities I was supposedly perfect for. After all, who wants to employ an idiot who writes important telephone numbers on the backs of envelopes and hands them to strangers without thinking about it?

And in the scrum to find yet another piece of paper to write down Mandy's number, I successfully knocked one of the many pints of Guinness down the front of my jeans.

I wish I was one of those people who could find incidents like this funny, but I'm not. I stayed for one more drink, then made my excuses and headed home, trying to ignore the whiff of my beer-soaked clothes and the strange looks from fellow passengers.

If I'd owned a mobile, this would have been a good moment to call Mandy and postpone the shoot. But in 1998, phones weren't the appendage that they are today. Calling her as soon as I got home would have been the next best thing. The smart thing. But it wasn't an evening for smart decisions, it was an evening for stupidity. Such as when I decided to take off my stinky brown clothes and put them through the washing machine. It was probably about half past midnight when I wondered where I'd put the second piece of paper with Mandy's telephone number on it, and only a moment or two later when I realised it was in the back pocket of my jeans. But as I pulled the trousers from the wash Mandy's telephone number, and the piece of paper it had been written on, had been pulped.

Alex was right. I had no choice. I had to go through with the shoot.

Chapter Thirteen
Saturday 12th September, 1998

I'd never been in a photographic studio but I was pretty sure that they were large, airy rooms, with cables running across the floor, lights on poles, silver umbrellas on poles, and big rolls of paper. On poles. There had to be good reasons for all this pole-related activity, but with barely an hour before Mandy was due to arrive I hadn't the time to find out what they were. All I knew was that Mandy had everything she needed to be a model, whereas I was just a guy with a camera, who'd taken a few saucy pictures of a work colleague. To describe myself as anything else was basically fraud.

And I was about to be found out.

The only way out of this was to come clean.

Mandy was a little taller than I'd expected. Five foot six, maybe? Not a classic beauty by any means, but reasonably attractive in her own gum-chewing way. Her bleached blonde hair was pulled back tightly over her scalp into a short stubby ponytail. Her baggy t-shirt failed to cover her midriff due to a hefty bust hogging the material. And her jogging bottoms were struggling to hang onto her hips or conceal the waist band of her thong.

"Alright?" said Mandy.

And she wasn't a patch on Charlotte.

"I'm Mandy," said Mandy.

"Right," I said.

"You Jason, yeah?"

"Erm. That's right." She nodded and chewed her gum some more.

"So shall I come in?" she asked, picking up the rucksack and throwing it over her shoulder.

"Erm, yes. Please do." I stood to one side, and gestured for her to go on up the stairs. Then I closed the door behind us.

"Would you like some tea?" I asked, as we entered the lounge.

"No fanks," she said.

"Right. Ok." I shuffled on the spot for a moment, then picked up the folder I'd left on the fireplace. "I thought you might like to see some of my, erm, pictures," I said. "I've only got a handful, I'm afraid." I slid half a dozen sheets of paper from the folder and handed them to her. "As you can see, they're not that good." Mandy frowned. "I'm, quite new to this actually – as I'm sure you can tell. You're probably used to working with, well, a more experienced – photographer."

"So is this your girlfriend or sum'fin'?" asked Mandy as she flicked through the pictures of Isabella.

"No," I said, and then, bending the truth somewhat, "she's... another model."

"But this is the sorta thing we'll be doin, yeah?" she asked.

"It's not what you had in mind, is it?" I said with a melancholy nod, an overly dramatic sigh. I held out my hand to take back my pictures. Mandy held onto them.

"Spose so," said Mandy. "I guess I fought you'd want somefing a bit more sexy like." My mouth opened and closed a few times as confused thoughts jostled for position in my head.

"Er, well," I said, "like what, exactly?"

"Well," said Mandy, "I've got this long see frough dress. It's kind of a black lacy thing."

"Right," I said. "Sounds... nice."

"Shall I go put it on?" she asked.

"What... now?"

"Yeah."

"Well, I... suppose...." Mandy nodded.

"Shall I wear something under it?" she asked.

"Under it?"

"Yeah well, it's see frough.."

"Oh right, well, I guess – some underwear? Or something."

"Black?" I nodded. "Yeah, I fought so." She handed back the pictures. "So where do I change?"

I cleared my throat, "Well, there's a bathroom next door – or there's the bedroom?"

"Ok. Where's that?"

"Just upstairs."

"Right. Back in a mo," said Mandy, as she walked out of the lounge.

I was dumbfounded.

So we were going to do this after all.

The dress, ball-gown in length, hung from Mandy's shoulders with bootlace straps, the neckline plunging low enough to reveal a cleavage of chasm-like proportions.

"Well?" she said, still chewing. "S'alright?" My eyes ran back up her body and I noticed her hair. No longer tied back, it was free to bob playfully above her shoulders and the sides of her face. She was lovely.

"Yeah," I said. "Yeah." And then again, "Yeah."

"So where do you want me?" she asked. I closed my mouth.

"I thought maybe you could sit here." I indicated a table and chair I'd set up by the window. Mandy sat herself down, instinctively resting her chin on her palm as she looked out at the view. She looked bored rigid.

"Right. Good. Ok," I said, switching on the camera. "Hold that pose." I pressed the shutter release.

"You sure you want me gawping out the winda?" asked Mandy, staying exactly where she was.

"Yeah, that's... well actually – why don't you look up at me?" Mandy shifted her gaze from the window to the camera – and suddenly she was all eyes, framed with long, dark, luscious lashes. I pressed the shutter release again, and waited for the image to appear on the back of the camera. "Oh, now, that's good," I said.

"Really?" said Mandy, and she smiled. It was the first time I'd seen her smile, and it seemed to make her entire face radiate. I pressed the shutter release again.

"That was even better!" I said.

"What if I lean forward a bit, cross my arms like this and squeeze me tits together?" said Mandy, putting both arms on the table and creating more cleavage than would normally be considered decent.

"Oh, yeah," I said. "That's, er, that's really good." I crouched down, took a couple of pictures, moved to the left, took a couple more, went to the other side of the table, and took a couple more. And all the time Mandy's eyes followed me, competing with her breasts for my attention. And with every "great," every "fantastic," each "oh that's good,"

Mandy's smile got broader and broader. "Fabulous," I said, "love it."

I stood up and took a breath.

"That was great," I said, running a hand through my sweaty hair.

"Good," said Mandy, chewing her gum again.

"Shall we try something else?" I asked.

"Sure," said Mandy, standing up. "A diff'rent outfit? I got stockings and suspenders wiv me, if you want. That's always guaranteed to turn me fella into a gibbering idiot – mind you, it don't take a lot."

"Right," I said, wondering how she'd managed to miss my own gibbering idiocy when she'd arrived.

"I got this sorta basque top fing I could wear wiv 'em."

"Ok," I said.

"And my black thong, yeah?" asked Mandy, leaving the room.

"Er, yeah. Yeah, that all sounds good," I said, letting out a long, deep sigh, and realising that I felt considerably better than I had twenty minutes earlier. In fact, there was a distinct possibility that I was actually beginning to enjoy myself. And when Mandy reappeared in the doorway, her ample bosom thrust skywards by a crimson basque, her thighs framed by lace stocking tops and suspender straps, I realised that it wasn't just a possibility.

"Right then," said Mandy, returning to the room in her regular clothes, her rucksack back over her shoulder.

"Well, erm, thanks for coming," I said, thumbing through my wallet, looking for two tens and a five. "Look, why don't we just call it thirty quid?" I said, handing over the money, "as we ran over a little."

"Yeah alright," said Mandy, taking the notes. "So will you want to use me again?"

Again? It hadn't occurred to me that there would an 'again'. An hour earlier I'd been hell-bent on wriggling out of the whole ordeal. But things were different now. Everything was different. Something inside had been switched on.

"Well," I said, "would you like to?"

"Don't see why not," said Mandy with a shrug. "It was kinda fun."

"Yes," I said. "Yes it was."

It took several minutes to transfer the pictures from the camera to the computer. The wait was excruciating. But when they finally appeared my eyes nearly popped out of their sockets.

They were fantastic.

Or at least, they were better than I thought they would be. Much better. Easily as good as anything I'd seen on the internet, or in a magazine. True, they weren't the raciest photos in the world – but in those brief moments between "y'know", "somefing", and her gum chewing, Mandy was nothing short of beautiful.

And I'd captured those moments.

"Blimey," I whispered. "I am a photographer after all."

Chapter Fourteen
Monday 14th September, 1998

"You're not a photographer," said Alex as we sat in a smoky corner of the Dirty Dick's, opposite Liverpool Street Station.

"Ok, so that one isn't one of the best," I said, handing Alex a sheet of paper from the folder on the table, "but what about this?"

"Let me put it another way," said Alex. "All these pictures are crap." I paused for a second to see if my friend was joking. He wasn't.

"No they're not!"

"Mate – they're shit!" He handed back the half dozen sheets I'd printed off earlier that afternoon.

"That's a bit harsh. Ok, they're not up to *FHM*'s standards, I grant you –"

"They're a bag of bollocks."

"Why?" I asked. "Explain to me why they're bollocks." Alex sighed and took back the sheets.

"Well," he said, leafing through the pictures, "they're all fuzzy."

"I told you, that's the printer. They look better on the screen."

"So why didn't you email them to me?"

"I tried. It took ages. I got a message telling me your mailbox was full. What else is wrong with them?"

Alex puffed out his cheeks. "They're just..." He cocked his head on one side and squinted.

"Yeah?"

"Rubbish!"

"Reasons! I need reasons!"

"I dunno... look... I mean – this one: It's a bird sitting at a table looking bored."

"Ok, but how about this one?"

"Same bored bird but now I'm looking down her top."

"But it's not a bad picture though."

"It would be better if she had her tits out – I thought that was the point of glamour photography!"

"What about this one?"

"It's alright, I s'pose.."

"But?"

"What's that stuff in the background?"

"Forget about the background –"

"Mate, *FHM* don't print 'forget about the background' under their pictures."

"Yeah, but they have proper studios."

"No, they have people who know what they're doing. You don't!"

"Oh come on – it's my first attempt."

"What about that French bird?"

"You mean Isabella?"

"Was she the French bird?"

"She was Italian."

"Whatever. That was your first attempt. And they were about a million times better. Mate, seriously – knock this photography lark on the head. You're getting worse." His words punctured my ego like bullets. Not that he noticed. Not that he ever noticed. He just fired off comments like a-

"Hang on," I said. "So the pictures of Isabella are better?"

"That's what I said," said Alex, bringing his pint to his lips and draining the contents.

"Better than these?" I asked.

"For the hundredth time – yes!" said Alex.

"Why exactly?"

"Oh, for fuck's sake," said Alex, getting up. "I'm getting another pint. Want one?"

"Hang on a sec, this is important –"

"Mate!" said Alex, slapping his palms on the table. "That's the one thing it ain't! It's not important at all!" I recoiled, my mouth snapping shut. Alex stood upright, threw his head back and took a deep breath. "Look," he continued, "you should be getting a fuckin' job, not poncing around with stupid ideas! It's time to grow up, and be – responsible." He sat back down again and leaned across the table. "We're thirty!" he continued. "Thirty! And what did we do with our twenties? Fucked if I know. Probably pissed them away in places like this. But those days are gone! We've got responsibilities now."

"I haven't," I said. It was true. I didn't.

"No? Well you fuckin' should have," said Alex, picking up his empty pint glass and looking inside it for our lost years.

I said nothing, just crossed my arms and looked at my friend. "Everything alright at home?" I asked.

"Just dandy."

"Tina ok?"

"Swell," he said.

"Really?"

"More than you realise."

Alex turned the empty glass idly in his hands. I could see the torment inside him, thrashing about like a lunatic in a straitjacket screaming at its own shadow and throwing itself at the walls. Alex wasn't capable of dealing with that amount of emotion. Not for extended periods of time. To Alex, emotions were something you felt, and then they were over. Like a good belch or another bodily function.

"So what is it then?" I asked. Alex's shoulders rose and fell. His usually cold steely eyes seemed bigger than usual as he stared at the glass in his hands. Then he blinked and wiped his nose with his sleeve.

"Tina's pregnant," he said. "I'm going to be a dad."

It's different for blokes. Obviously girls don't like getting older any more than we do – Liz spent most of her thirtieth birthday in tears – but the passing years and the responsibilities they bring with them seem to take us men by surprise. They sneak up on us in much the same way that we're astonished when a favourite item of clothing disintegrates. It's as shocking as the first time a work colleague says, "She's too young for you," because up until that very moment we're exactly the same person we've always been and we've never grown up. It's true what girls say: mentally we always remain boys. Then one day something comes along, like impending fatherhood, and forces us to take stock, look at what our life has become, and question our role within it. I understood my friend's pain. Reality had slapped him in the face, shown him a mirror and said, "See this bloke that looks like your dad? That's you, that is!"

"So it was an accident then?" asked Mandy.

"What was?" I put one foot either side of the taps.

"Getting his wife up the duff?"

"Oh, I see," I said. "No, apparently they've been trying for a while." I checked my balance before taking my hand off the wall.

"Then why's he surprised? That don't make no sense. Ain't he pleased to know he ain't a jaffa?"

"Well, probably," I said, switching the camera on "but that's not my point."

"Oh," said Mandy, frowning.

"What I'm trying to say is that now that his wife is, you know, up the duff, it's a bit of a shock to the system. Life isn't as simple as it used to be, and he's only just noticed. Just move that knee to the left slightly. That's it. Perfect."

"Oh, right. You mean a bit like the time I got measured for a bra in Deb'nams and they told me that I weren't a firty-four double D, like what I fought, but a firty-two F!" She grabbed her bikini-clad bosoms and thrust them up at me to make the point. "I mean, I knew me tits were big an' all but an effing F! Can you b'lieve it? I was well shocked, I can tell ya." I stopped for a moment and looked down at her. "Oh, sorry, I moved," Mandy said, and she put her arms back on the sides of the bath.

"That's ok. You can move if you want to. Why don't we try that pose?"

"What? Squishing me boobs together?" she said, doing exactly that. I raised my camera and took a picture. And then another.

"Fantastic!" I said. "That's really good."

"Can I have anuver sip of me beer?"

"Of course you can," I said, "you don't have to ask." She picked up the beer can from between her legs and took a slurp. I took another picture.

"Oi! I wasn't ready," protested Mandy.

"That's ok," I said with a smile, "you look better when you're doing something natural." Mandy raised an eyebrow.

"Jason," she said, "there ain't nuffin' nat'ral 'bout sitting in an empty barf, in a bikini and knee high boots, drinkin' beer!"

"Oh, that's wonderful news," said my mother.

"Yes, yes it is," I said, taking a nervous sip of my tea. I hadn't meant to tell my mother about Alex's impending fatherhood, but when she asked what I'd been up to, Alex seemed like a safer topic than photographing busty women in my bath.

"I bet they're thrilled."

"Erm, yes, they are," I lied. I couldn't speak for Tina, of course, but I thought it was best to keep Alex's near-suicidal thoughts to myself.

"When's it due?" asked my mother.

"I don't – I'm not entirely sure," I said.

"You don't know?"

"Erm, no," I admitted.

"Well, do they know whether it's a boy or a girl? They can tell you that these days."

"Erm," I said thoughtfully. My mother frowned.

"Has she had a scan?" she continued.

"Er," I said, then stopped. I hadn't asked Alex any of these questions. Somehow they hadn't seemed important. My mother shook her head.

"Honestly, Jason, you don't know much, do you! I wish you'd pay more attention!"

I fought my way back to our corner table with two fresh pints of Guinness. Alex was staring at the table, still reeling from the baby confession he'd made moments earlier.

"We've been trying for months," he continued as I sat down.

"Really?" I asked. It seemed odd that between all the pints we'd consumed over the summer Alex hadn't seen fit to drop that into the conversation.

"When she didn't get pregnant I just assumed that maybe... she couldn't." Alex looked at me with pleading eyes, then slumped back in his chair as the realisation that Tina most definitely could get pregnant swept through him yet again.

"Right," I said. "So what now?"

"What else is there?" shrugged Alex. "Act happy. Try and get my head around it. The little fucker's on its way," he said. "I just never thought it would happen. Not to us." And for a moment I thought he was talking about me and him, and maybe he was. I reached forward, grabbed my friend's arm, and gave it a matey shake. Alex frowned and gave me a look that told me matey shakes weren't necessary. Or wanted.

I looked away. At the folder still lying on the table. And made a mental note to get Mandy round for a follow-up shoot.

Of course Isabella's pictures were better! I'd shot her in the bedroom! The perfect setting for an attractive woman in various states of undress, and as Mandy knelt on the bed, I noticed the difference immediately.

After that there was no stopping us. I photographed her on the stairs, leaning her against the wall in the hallway, sitting on the kitchen worktop, and finally, when I found the silver bikini and knee high boots amongst the clothes she'd brought with her, lying in the bath. With a beer.

An hour later, after Mandy had left, I leapt up my stairs two at a time to the study. I had to get the pictures off the camera as quickly as possible to confirm what I already knew in my heart – those were the best damn pictures I'd taken so far.

"But Alex didn't tell me any of that stuff," I protested. Which wasn't true in the slightest but the details of my best friend's sex life weren't any of my mother's business.

"Well, you should ask," said my mother. "More tea?"

"No, no I'm fine," I said, finishing my second cup.

"I remember when your mum was born," said my grand-mother, wiping crumbs from the corner of her mouth. "Terrible, it was. Longest night of my life. I remember it like it were yesterday. Especially the midwife. Terrible woman. Cold hands. Beryl, her name was. That's my name, you know."

"Yes," I said. "I know."

"Course, things were different in those days."

"How so?" I asked, curious as to how bearing children had changed.

"Well," enthused my grandmother, "we didn't have the drugs. Not like they do now. Nowadays you can be admitted to hospital just after lunch and be back in time for the six o'clock news."

"Really?" I said, genuinely surprised.

"No," said my mother flatly, "not really. More tea, Mum?"

"Oh," said my grandmother, nervously playing with the buttons of her moth-eaten cardigan, "I don't really know. Have I had my second cup?" She looked to me for assistance, but my mother ignored the question and began pouring.

"How's the job hunt going, Jason?" asked my mother.

"Oh, yeah, good."

"Had many interviews?"

"Yeah," I lied.

"Really?" asked my mother.

"Well, erm, just the one." Just the none would have been more accurate.

"Oh good. Anyone we've heard of?"

"No, I don't think so," I said, desperately trying to think of a company name in case she called my bluff.

"It's a good job, though?"

"Oh, yeah. As far as I could tell. From the interview."

"Do you think you'll get it?" she asked.

"I don't… I don't think so."

"Honestly, you don't seem very enthusiastic. Mark my words Jason, most employers out there were brought up in a world where enthusiasm counted for more than qualifications. Show a little enthusiasm, Jason, and you'll at least have a foot in the door."

"Hmm," I said, "I suppose so." I glanced over at my grandmother, hoping to promote another fascinating segue into the world of wartime childbirth. Anything, rather than discuss my fictitious interviews. But she just smiled back, her crystal blue eyes twinkling like lights that had been left on in an unoccupied house.

"Honestly, Jason, don't you want another job?" I looked at her, dumbstruck. Oh yes, why wouldn't I? Why wouldn't I want to return to the world of the office? Back to clocking in and clocking out. Back to staying late to make up your flexi-time shortfall! Back to the world of project briefs, and deadlines, and managers, and meetings, and assessments, and grades, and colleagues, and female colleagues, and Garys, and female colleagues who fall for the Garys, and getting your ego stamped all over. Absolutely. *Abso-bloody-lutely*. Who wouldn't want to spend five sevenths of their waking hours like that? Alex wanted to know what we did with our twenties – where the time went. Work – that's where! We spent it at work! And when we weren't working, we were chucking pints of beer down our necks to forget the fact that nothing but a lifetime of work lay ahead of us. More. Fucking. Work. So, do I, Jason Smith, want another job?

"Not really," I said. "No."

My mother stopped what she was doing and looked at me. Then she carried on cleaning away plates and cutlery. "Now that's just silly talk," she said. "We'd all like to sit at home doing nothing but unfortunately we live in the real world, Jason, and there are bills to be paid and food to put on the table. Sooner or later your money's going to run out and don't start thinking you can move back in here because –"

"Mum, trust me, I'm not planning on moving back here." She looked at me as if considering whether to ask what was wrong with moving back in with her, then dismissed it.

"Well then, let's have no more of this talk about not getting another job. You can't go letting a little thing like redundancy put you off. Lots of people are made redundant these days, Jason. It's not very nice, I grant you, but it's the way of the world. You'll feel better when you've got yourself a new job, made some new friends, and you're writing computer programs again." I shook my head. She made it sound like some sort of crèche, where she could drop off her grown-up son to sit at a brightly-coloured Fisher Price terminal and bash out computer programs with my fists. "What?" asked my mother. "What was that look for?"

"Nothing," I said.

"Jason –"

"It's just... I don't enjoy writing computer programs."

"You used to."

"Yes, well, that was a long time ago – it's not the same any more." I folded my arms. "In fact," I said, becoming more defiant, "it was never that interesting. I mean, there's only so much pleasure you can get from coding interest calculations."

"Well, someone's got to do it," said my mother, with very little conviction.

"Absolutely," I said. "I'm just not sure I want it to be me!" I picked up the salt cellar, turning it in my fingers. "When I left school I wanted to write computer games, or do something cool with computer animation, not spec' out multi currency parameter enhancements. I mean, who gives a stuff about that? Not me!" My mother took the salt cellar from me.

"Well, that's all very interesting, Jason, but I suspect those sort of jobs are few and far between. Maybe once you have a normal job you can start looking for–"

"Maybe it's time for a complete career change!" I said.

"Really?" said my mother, as she sat at the kitchen table. "And do what precisely?"

"I dunno," I said. "Something else! Something – interesting."

"Your uncle did that once," interjected my grandmother. "Gave up his job as a bus driver and became a television repair man." Her wrinkled face beamed. I'd heard the story of how Uncle Jim had become a television repair man many, many times. My mother glanced heavenwards and took a deep breath.

"Yes, after about three years' worth of evening classes James did eventually become a television repair man. And maybe if Jason did the same –"

"I was thinking about photography," I said.

"Sorry?"

"Photography. I was thinking about becoming a photographer."

"But you don't know anything about photography."

"I know a bit," I said.

"I think you need to know more than a bit," said my mother.

"Well, I can learn at evening classes," I said, nodding in the direction of my grandmother, who smiled proudly.

"And become a wedding photographer, or something like that?" asked my mother suspiciously.

"Yes. Something like that."

"No, I don't think so. I don't think that's a very good idea."

"Why... not!?" I asked, editing out the swear words just before they left my lips. She always did this: I was thirty years of age and my mother was still telling me what I could do with my life. It drove me crazy!

"It just doesn't sound very secure. Weddings are very seasonal."

"There's more to photography than weddings!"

"Not much though, really," she said, shaking her head slightly. "No, Jason, I don't think photography's a very good idea at all. Best stick to computers."

I could feel my cheeks glowing. I glared at her for a moment, then turned away before I was tempted to say anything I'd regret.

"Apart from pornography," said my grandmother. "Plenty of money in porn."

Chapter Fifteen
Saturday 7th November, 1998

Mandy mouthed the words silently as her eyes moved along three, maybe four lines, before they jumped straight to the bottom.

"And what do I get out of it?" she asked.

"Well," I said, "you get paid."

"What, again?"

"No, not again."

"Oh." She frowned. "So why do I have to sign this thing?" I looked to Mandy's boyfriend, but he just smiled.

"Look, the thing is – I should have got you to sign it when we took the pictures, but I... forgot."

"Oh. Right," said Mandy.

"It's a permissions thing."

"Right. But I wouldn't have turned up if I didn't want to give you permission."

"No, yes – I know that, but this is permission for me to sell the pictures."

"And you need my permission?"

"Yes," I said with a sigh. "Yes, I do." I wasn't surprised that this was news to Mandy. I'd only discovered it myself the day before – if I wanted to sell my pictures of Mandy, by law I needed her written consent to do so. Fortunately, I'd also come across a template for a standard 'model release form'. All I needed to do was fill in the blanks and have Mandy sign it. That's all. Just a tiny little signature on the bottom of a piece of paper to be able to sell what anyone would assume was mine anyway.

"And how much do I get when you sell the pictures?" asked Mandy.

"Well... nothing."

"Nothing?"

"No."

"Why?"

"Because," I tried not to sound patronising, "you've already been paid."

Mandy thought about this for a second.

"Nah," she said, "that was so you could take the pictures. But I fink if you sell the pictures I should still get something. Like one of those royal fings."

"You mean a royalty?"

"Yeah. One of those. You might sell the pictures and make a bleedin' fortune and what would I have got? Fifty bleedin' quid."

"Mandy, I doubt I'm going to 'make a bleedin' fortune'."

"But what if I become famous or somefing?"

"Are you planning on becoming famous?"

"I might! I ain't decided yet!" she said, her eyes narrowing. "Trevor?"

"Whatever you think, babes," said her boyfriend.

"Oh, for chrissakes Trevor, grow a flippin' pair, will ya. Don't ya think I should get somefing if Jason sells the pictures?"

"Yes babes."

"Look, Mandy, as a model you get paid a fee for modelling. And how much you charge is down to you. But once you get paid, that's it! I, on the other hand, get paid once I've sold the pictures. Again, how much I sell the pictures for is down to me. But once they're sold I don't expect to get a cut from *FHM*, or whoever, every time some Joe buys a copy of their magazine. That's not how it works."

"So you're going to sell them to *FHM?*" asked Mandy.

"No! Maybe... I don't know. The point is –"

"If I'm gonna appear in the pages of effin' *FHM* I want more than fifty effin' quid!"

"But I haven't sold the pictures to –"

"What happens if I don't sign this?" Mandy waved the sheet of paper in front of me.

"Nothing," I said with a sigh.

"You can't sell the pictures?"

"No."

"To anyone?"

"No."

"Then I ain't signin' it!" said Mandy.

"Look Mandy, I –"

"No, Jason – it ain't fair. If I'm gonna appear in *FHM* I should get more. How's it gonna look if sum girl walks up to me and says 'I saw you in *FHM* – 'ow much did they pay ya?' And I turn round and say fifty bleedin' quid –"

"Alright, alright," I said, palms outstretched. "What if I paid you another fifty? Will you sign it then?"

"One hundred notes? For appearing in *FHM!*? You're 'avin' a laugh!"

"Mandy –" but before I could finish my sentence she'd torn the release into a dozen little pieces.

"Have it back!" she bellowed, showering me in model-release confetti before she stormed out of her lounge. Down the corridor I heard a door slam. I looked at the pieces on the floor and then at Trevor, who shrugged. And smiled.

It wasn't a good start to my new career.

As I let myself in I could hear the now familiar sounds of a bathroom being disassembled, and the low drone of a man muttering to himself.

"How's it going?" I asked, as I walked into what used to be a bathroom. Having to trudge downstairs for my morning ablutions had always been a pain. Then I'd met Liz and she'd persuaded me that converting one of the smaller bedrooms into an ensuite would enhance my life considerably. And whilst it was certainly convenient, it also meant that for almost four years now I'd had two bathrooms, one which I never ever used. Just how many bathrooms did a single man need?

"We're getting there," said Martin, as he crouched on all fours and peered into the hole in the floor. The shower had gone, and the basin, the radiator, the window and much of the floor, but the bath was still there, and for a moment I wondered exactly where Martin felt we were getting. "So what you going to do with this room?" he asked, coming up for air.

"Oh, I dunno," I lied. "I'll think of something."

"Too small for a dining room," said Martin. "And you've got your study upstairs."

"Yeah."

"I suppose it could be a spare bedroom." He scratched his beard.

"Mmm."

"Is it a secret?" asked Martin.

"No – of course not. I was er, toying with the idea of perhaps turning it into a small studio. Like, you know, a photographic studio." Martin nodded as if that would have been his next guess.

"I see," he said. "What sort of photography?"

"Oh well, you know," I said.

"Not really," said Martin.

"Portrait," I said flatly. "Mainly portrait. And erm, maybe a bit of glamour."

"Glamour?"

"Yeah, you know – girls and stuff."

"And stuff?"

"Well, just girls really."

"Sounds like fun," said Martin eventually.

"Yeah," I said, "it is. Sometimes."

"There lots of girls who want to do that?"

"Oh, yeah. Loads," I said, with zero conviction.

"No?" asked Martin.

"Well if there are, they obviously don't read the *Gazette*!"

Martin pulled a face, then scratched his beard some more. "Can't see many glamour models being that interested in the boring old *Gazette*," he said. "In fact, I'm not sure the kind of girls you're interested in are big on reading."

"That's nonsense," I said, defending the honour of glamour models everywhere.

"Oh. Well. You'd know best, I'm sure," said Martin, picking up a large hammer.

"Ok, well, even if that is true, what else can I do? Stand in the middle of the high street and stop any girl that takes my fancy?"

"Why not?" asked Martin

"You can't be serious? 'Hello, I'm Jason, I'm a glamour photographer and I'd love to take some pictures of you.'"

"Sounds like you've got your patter all worked out," said Martin. My mouth opened and closed.

"I can't just start walking up to random women in the street!"

"Why not?"

"I might get arrested!"

"For introducing yourself?" asked Martin.

"They might call me a pervert and slap me round the face!" Martin considered this for a moment.

"I don't think so," he said. "You strike me as a polite chap." And with that he reached inside the hole and started to pound one of the few remaining floorboards from underneath.

"They might say no!" I yelled over the racket.

"Ah. Yes. That's true – they might," said Martin, continuing to strike the floorboard until it started to move.

"So what's the point?" The floorboard came loose. Martin pulled it up and tossed it to one side.

"Well," he said, rubbing his forehead with the back of his hand, "they might say yes."

"Ok, but even if they did, how would I take their details?"

"Give them yours," he said. "Hand them your card."

"I don't have a card."

And for the first time in the whole exchange Martin looked directly at me.

"Can't that computer of yours print business cards?" he said.

"Well, it might be able to, I suppose."

"Well then," said Martin.

"So how long can you continue living on your savings?" asked Alex. It was never going to end, this preoccupation with my lack of employment.

"I don't know. A few months, maybe." That was a lie. I knew precisely how much money I had in the bank, exactly how much my mortgage was, exactly, more or less, how much Martin was going to charge to convert my bathroom into something useful, and exactly how much I'd allocated for food, beer, studio lights, modelling fees and other essentials.

And according to my calculations I had six point five nine months from the date of my last salary cheque before the money ran out and I'd be forced to do the unthinkable and get myself a job. But by then, hopefully, I'd be a full-time glamour photographer.

"Right," said Alex. He wasn't satisfied with my answer, but I didn't care. He turned and looked out of the window and I did the same. The rain was still pounding against the glass. "Why did you want to come here again?" asked Alex.

"I like it. It was good the last time we came."

"Yeah, but it was summer when we could stand outside."

I lifted my pint to my lips, and drained it.

"Ok. Let's have another in here and then move on," I said, and I got up from our table. Alex looked at his half full pint and then at me.

"You're knocking them back a bit."

"Dutch courage," I said.

"What for?" asked Alex.

She was the only one serving. I forced a smile when she looked over but already I could feel my heart beating faster than seemed healthy, and I prayed that it wasn't showing in my face.

"Same again?" she asked.

"Er, yeah. Thanks." I started to repeat my lines over and over in my head, but as I did so I became distracted by the man sitting on the bar stool next to me, and the folded copy of the *Evening Gazette* in front of him. And though it was the same man I'd met in here before – the one who'd told me the barmaid's name, and given me his paper – the dishevelled neck tie and rolling eyes suggested that he may have been here some considerable length of time, and that recognition might be a one way thing.

"Hi," I said. He stared at me for a moment, then nodded.

"Sheee's lovely, ain't she?" he slurred.

"Yes," I agreed. "Yes she is." I felt my confidence begin to wilt. Could I do this with some pissed barfly listening in on every word?

"Five pounds fifty," said the barmaid, putting two pints in front of me.

"Right," I said. I started digging around in my back pockets for change, knowing full well that the exact money was in my front right pocket. I needed time to get my head round what I was about to do. I 'found' a ten pound note and handed it to her just as my mouth went dry. As she opened her till for change I ran over my lines one more time. She closed the till.

"Look," I said. She passed me my change.

"Yes?" she prompted.

"Erm, tell me if this is a bad idea," I started, "but I just wondered, well, I was just… I wondered whether you'd, you've, whether you've ever considered being a, doing – glamour. Modelling. Have you?"

"Sorry?" she said, the beginnings of a smile forming.

"No, seriously," I said, "this isn't a 'line' or anything. I'm a photographer – really – hang on..." I rooted around in my pockets and cursed myself for not having it ready, then I found the card and handed it to her.

"Oh," she said, her eyes taking in the words. "Right."

"So anyway, I'm looking for models, to work with, and I think you'd be fantastic." She blushed, but somehow that didn't deter me. Instead I felt a surge of adrenaline and confidence.

"Well, that's very..." she said, glancing sideways to see who was listening. "But I've never done anything like that before."

"That's ok," I said, putting both palms on the bar. "Really! That's not a problem at all! I'm used to working with beginners." It was true. If I included myself. I swallowed hard. "Anyway, if you're interested, give me a call." I forced a smile. "Or something."

"Ok." She looked at the card. "Jason," she added. I felt my insides jump.

"Sorry, what was your name?" I asked, though I already knew. She looked up, her striking hazel-coloured eyes meeting mine.

"Becky," she said.

"Nice to meet you, Becky."

"You too," she said with a smile.

I grabbed the drinks and turned, and as I did so I caught the eye of barfly guy, staring at me in utter disbelief. I nodded, then walked back to Alex.

"You took your time," said Alex. "What were you talking to the barmaid about?"

"Oh," I said cheerfully, "nothing."

But it wasn't nothing. It wasn't nothing at all.

Chapter Sixteen
Saturday 5th December,
1998

"I didn't know what to bring," said the girl, as she opened her pink suitcase, "so I just, you know, brought a bunch of stuff. I hope it's ok." She delved in and pulled out something black and sparkly. "There's this dress," she said, holding it against her front. "It's kinda short – but I like it. Still wear it out sometimes – if I go clubbin'." She laid the dress on the bed and returned to the case. "Then this skirt's quite cute. And this one – I thought it might be good if you wanted to do a, you know, school uniform thing, or something? I brought a shirt to go with it somewhere." The girl fumbled around in the bag and found a short sleeved white shirt and lay it on the bed next to the other items. "Then there's this little top. Quite sexy. And the same, but in blue. Oh, and I brought my gym top because, well, I like the colour – and it makes my tits look bigger." She laughed. "Then I brought my fab boots, my killer heels, me strappy sandals..." My eyes flicked from one item to the next whilst I played around with photo ideas inside my head. The girl curled a lock of blonde hair around a finger.

"Did you bring any, erm, underwear?" I asked.

"Well, yeah," she said, biting her bottom lip, "but none of it's very, you know – exotic or anything. I don't wear a bra, well, for obvious reasons really." She thrust her chest forward and looked down at two tiny bumps where a fuller bosom should have been. "But I brought these," she said. "And these – they show off my bum really well. And these are quite sexy." She dangled a purple thong with Japanese writing on it in front of me. "And obviously there's what I'm wearing." Without warning, she unbuttoned her jeans and dropped them down an inch or two to reveal the pink knickers she had on.

"Oh! Well, yes. Very, erm – nice." I grasped my composure with metaphorical hands, took a deep breath, and concentrated on the clothes laid out on the bed. "Ok then," I said. "Why don't we put you in the little black dress? And... maybe these boots."

"Ok," said the girl, crossing her arms in front of her, and grasping the bottom of her sweater.

"I'll be downstairs – arranging the studio," I said, as I exited the bedroom. "Come down when you're – you know – ready." There wasn't any need for coyness. At least, that's what I was telling myself. Not when this girl seemed so carefree and open. But even if God had given her very little in the bosom department, it still didn't seem right that I got to see for myself without at least dinner and a movie first.

There wasn't an awful lot of arranging to do. The studio was completely empty except for my studio lights. Tall metal tubes on tripods with a light on top and a big reflective silver umbrella. I bought them cheap from a camera shop that was having a closing down sale, and to this day I'm still not convinced that they're meant for photography. They look the part though. And when I erected them in the freshly decorated room, with its matt white walls and laminate flooring, it completed the transformation to portrait studio. I felt 'professional'.

There are, I was beginning to realise, two ways to become a glamour photographer. One involves very expensive equipment, years of study and probably a diploma from the London School of Portrait Photography – should such a place exist – and the other involves gutting a bathroom, a set of cheap lights, and a big second-hand flash gun that transforms your camera from a fairly unimpressive digital compact to a photographic monster that wouldn't look out of place amongst the paparazzi.

Other essentials, for those students wishing to attend the Jason Smith School of Glamour Photography, include a wad of business cards, big smiles, and plenty of bravado.

"You ready to go?" asked Alex, returning from the gents and grabbing his jacket from the back of his chair.

"Almost," I said, "just give me a second." I fumbled around in my wallet, removed a card and tucked it into my back pocket. "Back in a tick."

"Where you going?"

"Nowhere," I mumbled. "Just wait here." I made my way through the pub throng to a group of people sitting on the other side of the bar. I glanced over my shoulder at my impatient and confused friend, and took a deep breath. Big smiles, I thought. Big smiles. "Hi," I said to the group, then focused my attention on the blonde sitting amongst them.

"OK – what just happened?" asked Alex as he followed me out of The Pride of Spitalfields and into the cold.

"What d'you mean?"

"In there. A moment ago."

"Oh, nothing," I said. "Which way d'you want to walk? Liverpool Street or Aldgate?"

"Liverpool Street."

"Right then," I said, starting off in that direction.

"Are you going to tell me or what?" asked Alex, chasing after me.

"There's not much to tell." I adjusted my collar and zipped up my jacket as high as it would go.

"But there's something," said Alex, "and I want to know what it is."

"Mind the vomit."

"Oh jeez – filthy bastards!"

"You know, I heard they were going to call this Bangla Town or something."

"Amazing," said Alex. "Stop changing the subject."

"Kind of an Indian version of China Town."

"Mate!" Alex stopped and put his hands on his hips. I turned to face him.

"I just asked a girl if she would model for me, that's all." Alex frowned.

"Who? What girl!?"

"Just a girl. Sitting at that table."

"The one with all those students?"

"Yes."

"You asked a girl sitting at that table if she would model for you?"

"Yes! Look, do you mind if we keep moving," I said, plunging my hands deep into my pockets. "It's bloody freezing out here."

"You mean the blonde?"

"Yes!" Alex shook his head and started walking. I caught him up, blowing into my hands to prevent the blood from freezing in my fingertips, whilst I tried to interpret the frown on his face.

"Are we talking about the same thing?" asked Alex eventually.

"Probably not."

"When you say modelling, you mean your glamour photography thing?"

"Yes."

"You just asked a complete stranger – in front of her friends – if you could snap a few pictures of her in the buff?"

"Well, those aren't the words I used, and I've never actually photographed anyone naked, but yes, I suppose I did." Alex said nothing. I sneaked a sideways look to see if his mouth was hanging open in amazement. It wasn't. He just shook his head. Again.

"Jeez, mate. You can't just walk up to women in pubs and ask them to model for you."

"Why not?"

"One of them blokes might have been her boyfriend!"

"One of them was," I said.

"What?"

"The guy sitting next to her. Her boyfriend."

"You're lucky he didn't deck you!"

"For what?"

"Making a play for his woman, dumb arse!" Now it was my turn for head shaking.

"I wasn't making a play for his woman. I told her that I was a glamour photographer and that I thought she'd make a good model. When he made it clear he was her boyfriend I told him he was quite welcome to come along and watch."

"You said that?"

"Of course."

"Then what?"

"Then nothing. I handed her my card."

"You... have a card?" Even if we'd been on Bishopsgate, with buses and taxis thundering past, rather than a deserted side street, I'd still have been able to hear the turning of rusty cogs as Alex's brain generated another thought. Presently they were all concerned with why I would have business cards, and how long I may have had them. "Have you done this before?" he asked.

"Done what?"

"Hand out cards?"

"Just the once."

"When?"

"Couple of weeks ago. In The Doggett's."

"Doggett's?" asked Alex. Another thought emerged from the tarnished machinery inside his head. "Where was I?"

"Sitting at the table."

"Then who... the barmaid?"

"Becky."

"You got her name?"

"Yes."

"And did she?"

"What?"

"Phone you? Model for you?" I paused for a moment.

"No," I admitted. Alex's shoulders relaxed, and his gait resumed its usual swagger.

"I'm not surprised," said Alex. "That was crazy."

"Maybe."

"Same goes for tonight."

"Whatever you say."

"You'll never hear from either of them," said Alex

"Ok."

Alex stopped walking.

"Why are you doing that?" he asked.

I turned to face him. "Doing what?"

"Agreeing with me."

"I dunno. Because you're right?"

"No," said Alex with a stiff shake of the head. "There's something you haven't told me." I rocked backwards and forwards on my heels whilst I blew great clouds of vapour into the night air.

Though I hadn't appreciated it until that precise moment, being a 'good guy' is an absolute essential for the would-be glamour photographer. Alex was right, at least in part – you can't walk up to a girl, particularly when she's sitting at a table surrounded by friends, one of whom is her boyfriend, announce that you'd like to photograph her near-naked, and hope to get away with it. Not unless you're a 'good guy'.

Emma had blushed a little but as I continued talking, and particularly after I'd invited her boyfriend along to the shoot, I could see it in her eyes, just as I'd seen it in Becky's, Mandy's, even Charlotte's. It was the realisation that I wasn't going to try anything on. Not because I didn't want to, or wouldn't think about it, but because I was a 'good guy' and good guys just... don't. Or can't. The one thing that had hindered me throughout all my fruitless years of trying to find a girlfriend – the very thing that had been responsible for all the girls I'd pursued over the years regarding me as a friend but nothing more – was turning out to be my strongest asset as a glamour photographer. If you're going to get girls to pose for your camera, particularly if they're going to be wearing very little, then those girls need to know that there'll always be a camera between you. And nothing guarantees that more than being a 'good guy'.

"Sure," said Emma, "I'd love to." Her friends looked horrified.

"Babe!" said her boyfriend.

"What? It's not like I'll be the first model girlfriend you've had. Have you got another business card? I'll write my number on the back."

"So I make that seventy five quid?" I said.

"Yippee," said Emma, taking the notes and stuffing them into her purse. In three hours we'd used every single outfit she'd brought with her, and every room in my two-floor flat, and though I could fill a lifetime with all the ways I wanted to photograph her, I'd only drawn a hundred out of the bank, and I was in danger of blowing the lot.

"So what happened to your boyfriend?" I asked, sitting on the bed. "I thought he was coming with you?"

"He was going to," said Emma, gathering up her clothes and stuffing them back into the pink suitcase, "but he had to work. Had a delivery or something. I dunno."

"Right. That's... a shame," I said.

"Not really," said Emma. "He's been getting on my nerves recently. He'd only annoy me if he was here. If he wants to see the pictures he can damn well go and buy the magazine." She picked up her sweater and pulled it over her head. "You will tell me when they're printed, won't you?"

"Of course."

"Good. It'll be nice to get one over on his ex." She grabbed her jeans from the bed.

"How d'you mean?"

"He used to go out with this girl," she said, stepping into her trousers. "Real bitch. She dumped him for a stockbroker or something. But anyway, he's always thinking about her. He tells me he isn't, but I know he is."

"Right," I said, half wishing I'd never asked.

"Anyway," said Emma, her chin on her chest whilst she zipped up her fly. "She appeared in *Razzle* a few months back." I felt the blood rush to my cheeks. Magazines like *Razzle* were the dirty little secret of men everywhere, and shops put them on the top shelf so that nice girls like Emma wouldn't accidentally pick them up or look at them or acknowledge their existence.

"And you know this how?" I asked.

"He told me," said Emma.

"Oh," I said. "And he knows this because..."

"She told him. At least that's what he told me."

"Right." I didn't believe that in the slightest. "You know *Razzle* is a top shelf magazine, right?"

"Of course! Stick of gum?"

"No thanks. So was she... naked... in *Razzle*? This ex-girlfriend?"

"I guess so," said Emma, idly stuffing knickers into her bag. "Do they print pictures of girls with their clothes on?"

"Not usually," I said.

"I'm all done here," said Emma, zipping up the bag. "I hope the pictures turn out alright. I think I was getting better towards the end there."

"I think you were great from the start," I said.

"Well thank you kindly," she said, putting on an accent and doing a courtesy with the hem of an imaginary dress.

"Would you like to do some more? Modelling? With me, I mean?"

"Really?" said Emma. "Cool! Yeah! Absolutely. I could use the money. When?"

"How about next weekend?" I asked.

"Yeah great – oh no. Hold on, Luke and I are going to Brighton for the weekend. Christmas shopping."

"Right, ok, well, what about during the week?"

"During the week's a bit tricky – I'm working in this tele-sales place –"

"Ok, well, what about the following weekend?"

"That's the day after our office Christmas party. I might be..." She pulled a face. "Then the following weekend is Christmas!"

"Ok, what about the weekend after?"

"New Year's?"

"How about between Christmas and New Year?"

"We're at Luke's parents. They live in Barnsley. Sorry."

"That's ok," I said, concealing my frustration as best I could.

"Look – Luke will have his laptop with him, why don't I email you?" said Emma, picking up her bag from the bed and slinging it over her shoulder. "Thanks again for asking me to model." She extended a hand for me to shake.

"You're very welcome," I said, taking her hand and trying to ignore how soft it felt.

And how much faster my heart was beating.

I fought my way through hordes of sour-faced Christmas shoppers; delinquent teenagers high on festive spirit, armed with cans of spray snow and silly string; the Round Table Association with their enormous fake sleigh, but very real megaphone; and a clutch of earnest volunteers shaking collection tins under my nose. A shifty-looking man next to a frame draped in cheap gift wrap waited until I was within a foot or two and then bellowed in my ear that he was selling, would you believe, cheap gift wrap. I marched past him and into a card shop, only to be greeted with "*I Wish It Could Be Christmas Every Day*" blaring out of the tannoy.

Christmas every day? Are they kidding? It was bad enough that it was every year! Why couldn't it be every other year, or every four years? Nobody suggests the Olympics or the World Cup should be forced upon us every twelve months! Or how about only when the year is a prime number? Or how about just not this year – not right now – not when I've embarked on the best career known to man, with the best model I'd had so far. Sodding bloody Christmas. I grabbed the first pack of Christmas cards I laid my eyes on, three rolls of the same gift wrap the idiot outside was selling and a calendar, and made my way to the till.

The annoying thing about Christmas, other than the fact that it couldn't have picked a worst moment to waltz into my life, was that I hadn't budgeted for it. When I'd sat down and worked out how long my savings would last I'd taken into account everything: exactly how many payslips I was due, my mortgage repayments – I'd even estimated how much I usually spent on train fares and beer – but I hadn't budgeted for Christmas. I knew that I had enough to see me through Christmas, sure, but the whole "It's Christmas, you might need to buy people presents" thing just hadn't registered.

Sodding bloody Christmas!

If I saw another reindeer, if I heard another carol, if I had to endure one more verse of "*I Wish It Could Be Christmas*"... My head was so busy trying to filter out all the Christmas-related nonsense that as I left the shop I collided head-on with a woman. I stepped back, started to apologise and –

"Jason!" barked Liz.

"Liz!" I blurted – though more to myself than to her. "Hi!"

"You great chump! Why don't you look where you're going?!"

"Sorry, I –"

"You almost had me over!" she said, thumping me in the chest.

"Yes, sorry – I was in a world of my own."

"No change there then!"

"No, I guess not." I shuffled on the spot for a moment or two, wondering whether there was anything else I should apologise for. I was about to launch into "Well, it's been great meeting you like this..." when Liz took control of the conversation.

"So. How have you been?" she asked.

"Er, good. Yeah. Fine."

"Excellent." She nodded, held eye contact and stayed exactly where she was. She was waiting for something.

"You?" I asked.

"Good," replied Liz. "Great, in fact. Thanks for asking." I nodded enthusiastically, tried forcing a smile, gave up, took a deep breath, and resumed my exit.

"Ok. Well –"

"Little late for Christmas cards," she said, eyeing the contents of my bag.

"I'm going to hand deliver them," I said, holding the bag behind my leg.

"Nice wrap though."

"Thanks."

"No ribbon?"

"Probably have some at home," I replied.

"And what's this?" she asked, bending down and using her fingers to peek inside my bag. "Oh! But of course! A Kylie calendar." She stood up and gave me a wide, conde-scending smile.

"It's for Alex," I said flatly.

"Of course it is." She batted her eyelashes. Only Liz could turn such a playful gesture into a sarcastic one. I waited until I was sure she'd had her fun.

"Ok. Well. Have a lovely –"

"How about a coffee?" asked Liz, grabbing my arm.

"I don't drink coffee."

"It's a turn of phrase, Jason. Oh, don't look so scared! I'm only offering to buy you a mug of something hot, for God's sake. We could go," she glanced over her shoulder, still holding onto my arm, "in that place over there. Come on!"

"Erm," I said, followed a moment later with "Ok then," as I felt my free will wither and die.

"Married?"

"Yes."

"When?"

"Five weeks ago."

I blinked.

"Really?"

"Yes – I was there!"

"But – married?"

"Well don't act like it's so hard to believe!" said Liz, sitting back, arms folded across her chest as she studied my reaction. I nodded, both hands wrapped around the mug of tea she'd bought me. She was right. It was only marriage. Not hard to believe at all. Someone had married Liz. My ex-girlfriend. Someone had married her. Actually married her – not just agreed to it...

"But –"

"What?"

"Married!"

"Oh, for goodness' sake, Jason. You're supposed to say 'congratulations'!"

"Oh, yes, of course, congratulations. But –"

"What!?" said Liz, slapping both hands on the table.

"It's just," I chose my words with care, "you're... I'm... we only just split up."

"No, we split up a year ago," she said, breaking eye contact only for a second or two to pick up her mug of Earl Grey. "Christmas Day, I believe." She sipped it slowly.

"Yes, but –"

"Why is it so incomprehensible to you that I might have met someone else and that I'm getting on with my life?" I looked into her eyes. Those decisive, determined eyes. And for a moment I was back standing in the snow outside her flat as she closed the curtain on our relationship and decided on an alternative course of action. And somewhere out there some poor sod had become part of that master plan.

"It just seems so," Liz's eyes narrowed. "Quick," I said. Liz shrugged.

"I suppose some people might see it that way," she said. "But when it's right, it's right. The problem with you, Jason Smith, is that you think life should be one long 'romantic comedy' – and it just doesn't work like that." She sipped her tea again as she continued to study me.

"Right," I said. "I mean... yes. I see." 'When it's right it's right'. Is that how it works? I could only think of one moment in my life when things had felt that 'right', and seconds later the girl in question had made a bolt for the door. 'Right' wasn't the word I'd use to describe it. "So was it a big wedding?" I asked.

"Quite big, yeah," said Liz.

"Right," I said, and looked into my tea. So how come things had turned out 'right' for Liz? How did she deserve someone more than me? How was that fair?

Liz raised an eyebrow.

"Sorry I never invited you," she said. "Dave would have been a bit miffed."

"Dave?"

"My husband."

"Oh yeah, no – I understand completely. Really."

"You're pissed off about that though, aren't you?"

"Well, I – no, not really. I mean – no, of course not. I'm just –"

"Good," said Liz, giving me another of her icy smiles. "Let's call it quits."

"Ok," I said. Quits for what?

"How's your mum?" asked Liz.

"Oh – good. Yeah."

"And your sister?"

"Fabulous. Very... fabulous."

"Your niece must be getting big now."

"Oh, yeah. So big. I mean, not huge, just – well, you know."

"And work? How's work?"

"Oh, I left."

"Left?" asked Liz.

"Er, yeah."

"So where are you now?"

A second passed. A second that should have been invested in some careful thought before I said anything else, but the words were out of my mouth before it occurred to me to think through the ramifications.

"I'm working for myself," I said.

"Yourself?"

"Yeah."

"Really? Doing what?"

I felt my cheeks begin to glow.

"Well – photography, actually."

"Photography?"

"Yeah."

"You're doing photography?"

"Yeah."

"Do you like photography?"

"Of course!"

"Since when?" asked Liz, her brow furrowing. "You never showed an interest in photography before. In all the years we were together I don't remember you even having a camera, let alone pointing one at a sunset, or landscape, or... me! The only times you ever seemed remotely interested in anything photographic were the times I caught you..." She clasped a hand to her mouth, her eyes widening. "Oh my God!"

"What?" I asked.

"You're not?"

"What?"

"You're not... making porn?"

"No," I said, rolling my eyes. I placed both hands on the table and leant my head back until I was looking at the ceiling.

"Then what?"

When was I going to learn to keep my mouth shut? I took a breath, then looked at my ex-girlfriend, my married ex-girlfriend. So she wasn't going to approve. So what? She was an ex. She'd moved on. So had I. And I was proud of my photography. I had nothing to be ashamed of.

"I'm a *glamour* photographer," I said.

"That's the same thing!" hissed Liz.

"No it isn't! And even if it is, you make it sound like a bad thing!"

"It *is* a bad thing!" she hissed again.

"No it's not." She looked over both shoulders and then leant forward as far as she could.

"Desperate girls having to pose naked for money? How is that not bad?!"

"They're not desperate! And they're not naked." Liz raised an eyebrow again.

"They're not?"

"No," I said. "I'm a glamour photographer. Totally different."

Liz considered this.

"So where are these 'glamourous' pictures appearing?"

"Oh, you know," I said, picking up my tea.

"No. I don't."

"*FHM* – places like that." I took a sip.

"Places like that?"

"Well, *FHM* mainly."

"Mainly?"

"Ok, just *FHM*."

"You've been published in *FHM*?"

"Well, not yet. But, you know – soon..."

"But surely they have their own photographers?" asked Liz. "And aren't all their pictures of celebrities? Like your precious Kylie?" She frowned. "Does your mother know you're doing this?" asked Liz, leaning across the table.

"No."

"I'm going to tell her!"

"And why," I said, looking over the top of imaginary glasses, "would you do that?" Liz's mouth opened, then closed again. She sat back in her chair.

"I don't believe it," she said, shaking her head.

"What?" I asked.

"That you're –" She opened her mouth and, whilst waiting for some suitably chastising words to make an appearance, waved a pointy finger at me, then put both elbows on the table and dropped her head into her hands. "Forget it," she said. "Just... forget it." She gave a deflated sigh, then rolled back into her chair. "I thought I'd knock your socks off with the whole marriage revelation."

I frowned.

"So you didn't get married?"

"Yes, of course I did, I just didn't think you'd be able to top it! I thought you'd sit there with your mouth hanging open, but instead that lasted all of twenty seconds, and I'm sitting here with my head spinning on my shoulders whilst I try and work you out." She folded her arms. "We didn't stand a chance, did we? We're poles apart. I don't know why I didn't see that earlier."

"I'm sorry," I said. It was a reflex action. Liz looked at me.

"For what?" she asked. "Being yourself? Don't be. Does it make you happy?"

"What?"

"Your porno photography thing?"

"Well, yes. I suppose so," I said.

"Then I'm pleased for you. I think it's perverted and a hideous affront to women everywhere... but what the hell do I know? Good for you."

"Thanks," I said. "And are you happy? With Dave and everything?" She smiled. A genuine one this time. She even managed a single laugh.

"Yes," she said.

"Excellent," I said, taking another sip of my tea. "Then let's call it quits."

It was over.

I'd survived Christmas. Two days of probing questions about what I was doing to find a job, what interviews I'd attended, and how on earth I was making ends meet in the absence of a career. And it didn't matter how many times I answered the questions, deflected them, or changed the subject, the only time my professional life was not in the spotlight was when my love life – or my lack of one – took centre stage.

This time the questions took on the form of thinly veiled statements of disappointment. "Don't you think it would be nice to settle down and get married?" "Do you ever wonder if breaking up with Liz was the right thing to do?" "Did you see that documentary on how long-term bachelorhood causes leprosy? It did make me worry."

"I knew a bachelor once," said my grandmother. "Terrible, he was."

I shook my head. I didn't want to be a bachelor. Of course I didn't. Obviously I wanted to meet someone nice. But at the same time I had very specific ideas of what 'nice' was, and if this past year had taught me anything it was that I'd been looking for someone nice in all the wrong places.

But I wasn't any more.

I finished answering Emma's email, and hit send. Nine days. That's all I'd have to wait until I could see her again. I smiled at the prospect, then turned in my chair to mark the date on the calendar, but the calendar had run out of pages. I glanced at the clock. Almost midnight. Almost a new day. And in this case, almost a new year. A new year full of exciting possibilities.

I got out of my chair, skipped down the stairs to the kitchen, got another beer from the fridge, and walked back to my study to see in the New Year with Kylie.

"Happy New Year," I said to the calendar as I took a slug of beer.

Kylie.

Something wasn't right. I was missing something. Something about Kylie. Something important.

It didn't help that the beer in my hand was my fourth – no, fifth – of the evening, and that I was trying to focus through an alcohol-induced haze. But there was something in the back of my mind. Buried. Just beneath the surface. Like an itch that was just out of reach.

And then it happened. Pieces in my mind shuffled into place and I could feel myself breaking into a cold, clammy sweat as the connections formed: Kylie – the calendar – the card shop – Liz – the coffee shop – our conversation...

I put my beer on the desk and rummaged through the pile by the side of my computer, trying not to notice that my hands were shaking, until finally I found the copy of *FHM* that Alex had given me all those months ago – the one with Kylie on the cover – the one that had started me on this glamour photography path in the first place. I laid it across the computer keyboard and as I flicked through it, aside from the adverts, the barbers in the buff, and a girl who'd won the monthly get-your-girlfriend-in-print competition...

Liz had been right.

Every woman featured was a celebrity.

Which meant that, unless Emma was planning on overnight stardom at some point in the not too distant future, *FHM* were unlikely to buy my pictures of her. Or any other model I found.

Ever.

I stood up, ran my fingers through my hair and dug my nails into my scalp. How could I have missed this? Something so obvious? Almost four months surrounding myself with all the things I thought I needed to be a glamour photographer and not once had I given a moment's thought to how, or where, I was going to sell my work.

My watch chimed the hour.
I glanced again at the calendar.
New Year.
And already there was nothing happy about it.

Chapter Seventeen
Saturday 9th January, 1999

The doorbell rang and continued to ring until I got to the bottom of the stairs to see what could be so damn important that one ring wasn't enough.

"Finally," said Alex, standing there with his finger on the bell and a large sports bag slung over his shoulder.

"What are you doing here?"

"Movin' in," he said, as he pushed past me and proceeded up the stairs.

"What!? Why?"

"Why not? Don't you want your ol' mate to move in with you?"

"Not really," I said, watching him disappear out of sight. I closed the door and followed him up the stairs.

"Come on, it'll be fun," said Alex. "Two young dudes like us."

"Yeah? And what about your wife?"

"Not much point in leaving the ol' ball and chain if she just comes with you," said Alex.

"You've left Tina?" I asked.

"Yep," said Alex. We stood facing each other for a second or two and when it became clear that no additional information was forthcoming I moved onto the next obvious question.

"Beer?"

"Finally!" replied Alex. I turned and walked down the hallway to the kitchen. Alex dumped his bag in the middle of the floor and followed me. I opened the fridge, took out two lagers, and handed one to my friend.

"Cheers," he said, pulling the ring on the can. I watched as he proceeded to pour the contents down his throat.

"So," I said, gearing up for a second attempt, "you've left Tina?"

"Didn't we cover this?" asked Alex during a brief pause, before continuing to drain the can. He belched, and handed the empty can back to me. "Man, I needed that," he said. I gave him the other beer. "Mind if I look around?" said Alex as he walked out of the kitchen.

"Why?" I asked, following him.

"I'm not allowed to look around?"

"Why have you left Tina?"

"Oh, well – you know," said Alex, reaching the portrait studio and peering in. "She hasn't got anything I want. What goes on in here then?"

"She's having your baby."

"Like I said, nothing I want. But you, me ol' mate," he slapped me on the shoulder, "you've got everything. Nice pad, plenty of space, a fridge full of beer..." He broke off and walked into the lounge.

"No – wait – hang on." I followed him. Alex turned, his face one of genuine shock.

"– and the biggest pile of wank mags I've ever seen," he said. "What the fuck?" I let out a sigh.

"Research," I said.

"I've never heard it called that before!" He looked at the pile of pornography in the middle of the floor. "Settling in for a long one I see – there must be thirty mags here!"

"Fourteen," I said, "and seriously, it's research."

"Mate – we're going to have to have rules about this stuff. I can't come home and find you spanking the monkey in the front room."

"Alex, we won't need rules because you're not moving in." He collapsed into the nearest armchair.

"Thanks, mate. Kick me whilst I'm down."

"No problem," I said, sitting in the chair opposite. Alex leant forward and picked up a magazine. "You and Tina had a row then?" I asked.

"I don't want to talk about it," he said, flicking through the pages.

"Fine. What do you want to talk about?"

"Nothing," said Alex.

"We could have talked about nothing over the phone, or in a pub. You didn't need to come all the way over here to do it."

"Research into what?" asked Alex, lowering the magazine.

"Potential markets," I said. Alex frowned. "I'm trying to work out where I can sell my work."

"What work?"

"My photography!"

"Oh, right," said Alex. "You still doing that?"

"Yes! No. I don't know." I looked out of the window, folded my arms, then shrugged. "I'm not sure. I'm supposed to have a shoot tomorrow."

"Really?" asked Alex, his eyebrows climbing his forehead. "Can I...?"

"No," I said. Alex huffed, threw the magazine to one side, popped his second can and took a long lug. After a while he picked the magazine up again and resumed his browsing. "So you think one of these magazines will print your stuff?"

"Fucked if I know," I said, and continued to look out of the window. Alex stopped leafing through the magazine, looked at me, and frowned. He opened his mouth to say something, then closed it again to do some more brow furrowing.

"So I can't move in then?" he asked eventually.

"You know that ain't going to happen."

"Just until I get my own place?"

"You can stay tonight."

"Gee thanks."

"But you've got to be gone by lunchtime."

"Why?"

"I told you, I'm doing a shoot."

"No – you said you were supposed to be doing a shoot."

"Yeah, well – I haven't cancelled it yet. So right now, I'm doing a shoot. And you can't be here."

"Why would you want to cancel it?" I turned to face my friend. His eyebrows were raised expectantly.

"Because..." I stopped to rub my eyes with my fingertips and pinch the bridge of my nose. "It doesn't matter," I said. "I want you gone by lunchtime."

"And where am I supposed to go?" he asked.

"Back home!" I said. "To your wife!"

"Home," said Alex. "That's a laugh."

The rhythmic growl of Alex's snoring was loud enough to permeate the floor between us. If I'd matched him drink for drink then maybe I too would be passed out in a drunken stupor – but it seemed I was in the mood for heavy thinking, rather than heavy drinking, and whilst Alex made sure that neither I nor my neighbours were going to get any sleep, I had plenty of time to do just that. Though in truth I'd moved past thinking, and progressed to wallowing.

I leafed through another copy of *Razzle* magazine, pausing briefly to look at Suzy from Southampton, and my mood blackened further still.

From the age of sixteen through to my mid twenties I'd purchased *Razzle* and similar magazines at regular intervals. Then the internet came along, and a world of porn – most of it free – was at my fingertips. My shopping trips to corner newsagents became unnecessary, and my relationship with girly magazines came to an end.

Until now.

After my New Year's Eve epiphany, and a few days beating myself up for being stupid, I finally got off my backside and wandered into my local newsagent to survey the shelves for magazines that might buy my pictures. And after I picked up a few *FHM*-style magazines, packed with semi-clad *celebrities*, my eyes inevitably wandered upwards. Three minutes later I left the shop with a carrier bag of everything they had on the top shelf.

There were perhaps a dozen mainstream publications – *Fiesta, Knave, Escort, Mayfair, Men's World, Club*, to name but a few. Each tried to have its own niche, its own flavour of female loveliness. Some specialised in glossy, hard-bodied girls with vacant pouts who looked as though they'd come off a production line and were yet to have a brain installed; others featured groups of five or six fun-loving lasses getting friendly in a paddling pool filled with custard. But every photo set, regardless of the publication, always followed the same basic principle: the girl, or girls, began clothed, and got progressively less so – until they were nude. *Completely* nude.

Take for instance Suzy from Southampton. Staring back at me from the pages with flaming intensity, every fibre of her being broadcasting the same wanton message: "I'm naked!"

Oh sure, Emma – my Emma – knocked Suzy from Southampton into a cocked hat so far as looks went. Emma was girly, and cute. She was effortlessly sexy, despite being clothed. She had class, and grace, albeit of her own making. Suzy, on the other hand, was just tarty. A bit craggy. And dirty, in the sense that you wouldn't want to be within flea-jumping distance of her. But in a contest between a set of Emma, lying on the beech laminate floor of the portrait studio dressed only in her purple Japanese knickers, gym top and knee high boots, and Suzy's raw in-your-face sexuality, it was obvious which pictures were going to be published for the entertainment of men everywhere. And it wouldn't be mine.

I was no more a glamour photographer today than I had been four months ago. I had been deluding myself. And all those times Alex had made some sort of derogatory remark, that's what he'd been trying to tell me – albeit in an Alex kind of way. But he was right. And I hated him for being right.

I also hated *Razzle* magazine for doing the bleedin' obvious, just as I hated every red-blooded male on the planet, for being so stupidly red-blooded and male. I particularly hated Suzy from Southampton for being Suzy from Southampton, but most of all I hated myself and my stupid idiotic ideas.

"Bollocks!" I said, and threw the magazine across the room. It hit the wall opposite and flopped to the floor. Arms folded, I sat listening to the snores of my friend downstairs.

For the third time that morning Emma's phone went straight to voicemail.

"What time's this girl turning up?" asked Alex.

"Later," I said. "After you've gone." I hung up without leaving a message.

"But I don't know what time I'm leaving."

"You're leaving as soon as you've finished that cup of tea – or as soon as I deem it finished."

"Why can't I stick around?"

"Because you can't."

"You planning to get your leg over? Is that it?"

"No."

"Then why?"

"Because I don't want to work with you watching us, and I doubt Emma will either."

"I could hold a light or something," offered Alex.

"I have stands that do that really well, and they do it without leering."

"I won't leer," he grumbled.

"Of course you'll leer!"

"Why are you being such a grumpy git?"

"No reason."

"Is it because you're *not* going to get your leg over?"

"How's that tea coming along?" I asked.

"Finished. Can I have another?"

"No."

"Fine," said Alex, dragging himself out of his chair. "I know when I'm not wanted."

"Hiya," said Emma as I opened the door.

"Hi," I said, "hi." And again, "Hi."

"You alright?" asked Emma, cocking her head to one side.

"Fine. Yep. Just fine," I said.

"Cool. Can I come in then?"

"Yeah, sure," I said, stepping to one side and watching as she proceeded up the stairs. "So you didn't get my message then?"

"What message?" asked Emma. I closed the door and followed her up.

"I left you a voicemail."

"Oh, I ran out of credit," she said as I reached the top of the stairs. "As soon as you pay me I'll be able to get a new phone card. What did the message say?"

"Oh, nothing really, just –"

"I brought some new outfits with me," said Emma.

"Oh er, good."

"I borrowed this fab short dress from a friend of mine. It's strappy and completely backless."

"Sounds... great," I said.

"Don't be too enthusiastic!" said Emma, poking me in the chest with a finger. "Where are we going? Bedroom?"

"Emma, the thing is..."

"Yeah?"

"Fancy a cuppa?" I asked.

"Oh – ok," she said. I turned and walked towards the kitchen.

"So you been doing lots of photography then?" said Emma behind me.

"Not really," I said, flicking on the kettle and getting two cups from the cupboard. "Look, Emma –"

"I did some modelling last week."

My mind froze, like someone had upended a bucket of water over me.

"You did?" I asked.

"Yeah."

"Who for?"

"Couple of photographers."

"But... what... why?"

"Needed the money over Christmas," said Emma. "And after modelling for you I thought, why not?" I opened my mouth to say something else, but Emma was already answering my next question. "I went on this website. Kinda like this message board thing for photographers and models? These guys were offering work so I contacted them."

There were websites?

"Really?"

"Yeah. I emailed them. And sent some of the pictures we'd done. And they invited me along for a shoot."

"You emailed them my pictures?" I felt violated. Violated, betrayed, and... curious. "What did they think? Of them? My – our – pictures?"

"I think they thought they were ok," said Emma. "Mind you, they don't do the same kind of work as you."

"Oh?"

"Nope. They only had work for girls willing to do 'men's magazines'," said Emma, making air quotes with her fingers. "I thought they meant *FHM* and stuff, but then they showed me some examples and I realised they meant porno!"

"Porno?"

"Yeah – you know, like *Razzle* magazine? Most of their stuff appears in there. Turns out it's not anything dirty, just, you know, naked. Legs open. But that's ok. Pays a bit better!" She laughed.

"I bet," I said, opening the fridge and grabbing the milk. All this talk about other photographers was depressing me.

"Well, forty quid an hour. But that's ok. And they gave me Jaffa Cakes."

"Forty quid," I mused. It sounded a lot to me, though still nowhere near what Mandy had wanted all those months back.

"And Jaffa Cakes."

"Look – Emma, the thing is," I said, putting the milk back in the fridge "I'm having a little trouble selling my pictures."

"Really?" Emma looked surprised. "Why? Is it me?"

"No! No, no – not at all! It's just that..." I put my fingers in my hair and scratched at my scalp whilst I thought about how I was going to explain that I wasn't a photographer at all. And never would be. "The magazine I originally had in mind –"

"Yeah?"

"Well, they've – folded." I lied. "Gone bust."

"I know what folded means."

"Ok well – that's why I was trying to get hold of you."

"Oh." The kettle clicked. I turned and finished making tea.

"I've really enjoyed working with you and everything, but…"

"Oh. Good. Well, me too. You're fun. Those guys last week were kinda serious. I much prefer coming here." I felt myself flush.

"Oh," I said, "well that's... I appreciate that."

"You're blushing," said Emma with a smile. I squeezed out the teabags and handed her a mug. "Thanks," she said, taking it with both hands, her eyes not leaving mine as she blew on her tea.

"Anyway..." I continued.

"Can't you just do the same work as them then?" asked Emma.

"God no! I mean... no."

"Why not?" My brain stalled.

"Well... Actually... I've never..."

"I mean it's not *that* different from what we already do is it? And I'm up for it if you are."

I coughed. "You mean… what *now*? Today?"

"Why not?" She gave me another smile, then sipped her tea. I swallowed hard. I could feel my heart beating. But it was in my stomach for some reason.

"Do you have any Jaffa Cakes?" asked Emma.

I was at a cross roads.

Well actually I was sitting on the beach, in January, having just walked Emma to the station. She'd seemed disappointed, having arrived less than thirty minutes earlier, but I made up some nonsense about having to call *Razzle* first to see whether they would indeed be interested in working with me – then I'd paid her our agreed fee anyway.

My camera never left its bag.

There didn't seem to be any point in taking yet more pictures I'd never be able to sell.

I gave her a wave as she walked through the station barriers, then I crossed over the bridge, walked down onto the beach, sat on the sand, and looked out at the boats resting in the mud.

Did I want to be a glamour photographer?

Or did I want to find a girlfriend?

Prior to the weekend those two things had never seemed mutually exclusive; glamour photography was the perfect job. I'd spend my days doing something fun, meeting fun people, and in so doing increase my chances of meeting a Kylie, or a Kylie-in-the-making.

But now – faced with the realisation that there was no job – not unless I was willing to photograph women naked, and not just naked but, well, *really* naked – I couldn't see how that would work.

It was one thing to walk up to a woman in a pub and ask her if she'd considered glamour modelling, but the pictures in *Razzle* and the other top-shelf magazines stretched that definition to breaking point. My old fallback phrase, *you probably wear less on the beach,* wasn't going to cut it any more.

Even if I was wrong and the world was full of 'Emmas' – women for whom full-on nudity wasn't a big deal – eventually I'd meet someone who I really liked, and who liked me. But long before I'd managed to stammer the words "would you like to go out sometime?" I'd already have seen them rolling around on my bed without a stitch on – and somehow that still didn't seem right. Not in the sense that it was 'morally wrong' – just, well – wouldn't it steal something from the moment when we'd *both* be rolling around on the bed without a stitch on?

More than that, didn't it make everything a bit messy? Wouldn't there always be this '*did you just ask me out on a date because I took my clothes off*' thing, hanging over us?

And what about going forwards? Was the life of a Top Shelf Men's Magazine Photographer something you could continue to do whilst in a relationship? What sort of girlfriend would tolerate their boyfriend being alone with beautiful naked women day after day when his job was creating erotic images? And how would that sound when it came to meeting the in-laws? This is Jason, he's a professional pervert. Oh, and did I ever tell you how we met?

I tossed a pebble into the sea. Or where the sea would have been, had the tide been in. Even the Thames Estuary was refusing to co-operate with how I wanted the world to work.

Several things occurred to me. Firstly, my understanding of the female psyche was pretty much limited to my mother, my grandmother, my sister, and Liz – so any thoughts along the lines of 'what sort of woman…' were questions I could never hope to get to the bottom of.

But secondly, though my assumptions about womankind might be wildly inaccurate, it seemed to me that there was still a line. A line beyond which *I* would no longer feel comfortable, and could no longer, in my heart at least, claim to be a 'good guy'. And that line was the nudity.

So that was that then.

There was no way to make a living from taking and selling photographs that I could hand-on-heart refer to as 'glamour', and I couldn't pursue any kind of relationship with anyone were I to start taking the sort of pictures that many people consider pornography. My fledgling career, in photography, was over – and my chances of meeting someone as remote as ever.

"Jason Smith," I heard myself saying, "you really are a prize idiot."

If the Thames had been playing ball, I'd have stood up, walked purposely into the waves, and kept going. Anything rather than face the inevitability of the rest of my life. But instead I brushed the sand off my legs, gave the heaviest of sighs, and walked back to the flat.

Though I didn't realise it at the time, it had been one day short of an entire year since Alex and I had sat in The Phoenix, and discussed the pros and cons of Motor Mechanic verses Cookery Classes. And here we were again. I'd have given my right arm to be having that conversation, or any conversation, rather than the one we were about to embark upon.

"So I take it you went back to Tina?" I asked as Alex returned from the bar with our drinks.

"Don't want to talk about it," he said.

"Right," I murmured. I took one of the pints and stared into the black foamy liquid. I really wasn't in a drinking mood.

"How did your shoot go?" Alex asked.

"It didn't," I replied. *Ask me why Alex. Ask me why I didn't do it. Ask me and I'll tell you how my life's a mess, and nothing I do seems to make the slightest bloody difference to the outcome. Go on, ask me!*

Alex said nothing. Just looked at me for a moment, then shrugged before turning his attention to his beer. I let out a sigh and prepared to launch into my 'you were right all along – can you help find me a job' speech.

"I borrowed one your mags," said Alex before I'd managed to get the words out. I frowned. Was this a confession or an attempt at conversation?

"Well, you're very welcome to the rest," I said, and took a swig of my pint.

"Cheers," said Alex. "The one I took was shit." I frowned again.

"Which one was it?"

"Some magazine I'd never heard of. Curly writing on the front. I thought it said 'sleaze'. Turns out it was tease. With a 'z'."

Teaze? I was fairly sure that if you'd entered me into Mastermind and my chosen subject was 'UK Top Shelf Men's Magazines (1984 – 1997)' I could have confidently told you the names of every single title in circulation as well as who published them, but I'd never heard of *Teaze*.

"Are you sure it was called *Teaze?*"

"I'd happily stake Tina's life on it."

"What was wrong with it?" I asked.

"Pages and pages of fit looking women - not a single tit in sight!" Alex took another swig of his beer whilst my brain made sense of his remark.

"The models were clothed?" I asked eventually.

"Pretty much. What a waste of paper. It went straight in next door's bin."

"Next door's?"

"Well I couldn't put it ours – Tina might find it. Where are you going?"

"To find a newsagent," I said doing up my coat.

"What, now?"

"Yes now."

"What about your Guinness?"

"You finish it," I said. "I need to get a copy of that magazine before the shops close. I'll catch up with you later in the week. Maybe." And with that I hurried out the pub.

It took four attempts before I found a newsagent that had heard of, let alone stocked, *Teaze* magazine. But as I sat on the train – the front carriage where I might be guaranteed some privacy – and rifled through the pages, I quickly realised that *Teaze* was everything I hoped it would be: Pages and pages of beautiful girls – models, not celebrities – and as Alex had so eloquently observed, not a single bare breast in sight.

Sure, in each and every set the girl was undressing, and some actually ended up naked, or topless, but in each case a turned back, or carefully draped arm, hid anything that future parents-in-law might get upset about. It was glamour photography in the truest sense. Which meant that my camera and I had a place in this world after all.

I had to get home and phone Emma.

Three weeks later, and I don't think it would be too much of an exaggeration to say that I was, without a doubt, the coolest, luckiest man in the entire United Kingdom.

I spent my days photographing ludicrously sexy women – well, one of them anyway – in my spacious photographer's apartment with its inbuilt, multi-functional ex-bathroom studio. And, in a moment of decadent disregard for the savings that were supporting my rock-star lifestyle, I'd splashed out on a black leather jacket which, aside from her underwear and the dark glasses she was peeking over, was the only thing Emma was wearing as she perched on the bonnet of my *MX5*.

Another car drove past and, like the car before it, the occupants stared open-mouthed as they went by. Emma laughed and did her very best to cover up.

"That wasn't the same car, was it?" I asked.

"I don't think so," said Emma, her hands on her hips, "but maybe we should head back, or find a different spot, yeah?"

"I guess so," I said, barely concealing my disappointment. She ran round to the side and got in the passenger seat.

"God, I'm freezing," she said, pulling her jeans back on.

"Really?" I asked. "You should have said." I pulled the soft top back over the car and clipped it into place.

"Jason – it's February!" she said, zipping up my jacket. "You've got me standing half naked, in the middle of nowhere, in bloody winter!"

"Fair point," I said as I slid in behind the wheel and closed the door. "What say we get you home and put you in a nice hot shower?"

"Oh God – yes please," said Emma, squeezing my thigh. I smiled.

Three weeks. Three perfect weeks of photographing Emma in every location I could think of. My hard drive was filling up with set after set, each one about a zillion times better than anything I'd taken before or, more to the point, seen in *Teaze* magazine. They were more inventive, more intimate, and in their own non-nude way, just as erotic as Suzy from Southampton. And in about ten minutes I'd have a set of Emma in the shower to add to my stable.

I squatted on the floor opposite, trying not to get splashed, as Emma sat in the shower tray in a black bikini, water cascading onto her body, mascara running down her face. She closed her eyes and leant her head back into the spray.

I pressed my finger down on the shutter release, heard the pop of the flash gun, and felt my heart melt and spread throughout my body like liquid sunshine. I'd done it. I was the man behind the camera, and I couldn't imagine a more beautiful, more erotic woman to photograph. I'd have spent the rest of my days in that moment, given the choice.

Was I in love?

I'm not sure.

There was *lust*, there always was, lurking around in the shadows of my mind, but this was different. It felt deeper, hotter, harder, more intense. There was... a need.

God, the Universe, Fate – call it what you will – had delivered me the best model I'd ever worked with, but she *wasn't* modelling. I could see that now. Emma was just as sexy, just as charming, just as warm and sensual, just as beautiful, even when I put my camera down. And the longer I spent with her the more I realised there was a huge Emma-shaped hole in my life. I needed a woman like her. I needed her to stay and never leave. And I needed her to need me. Emma, I wanted to say, I need you. I want you. I think I might love you. But you can't say that. That wouldn't be the right thing to say. Saying that would severely fuck things up.

"My God, Emma, I want to kiss you so much."

I heard the words before I realised that I'd said them. If I could have snatched them out of the air before they reached her, then I would have done. But a second later Emma sat up, brushed water out of her face and looked around the shower cubicle as though she'd mislaid something.

"The water's cold," she said, without making eye contact.

"Ok," I said, jumping to my feet, "why don't we call it a day."

"Yes, I think so," said Emma, and she stepped out of the shower. I handed her a towel. She took it without a word.

"Right, I'll… I'll just go and upload these pictures to the computer. Would you like a cup of tea?"

"No thanks," said Emma, wrapping the towel around her tightly. "I'd like to get changed now." She waited.

"Right," I said. And I left her to it.

Chapter Eighteen
Saturday 6th February, 1999

I clutched the phone to my ear and tried to ignore the bead of sweat rolling over my cheekbone.

"Ok then," she said. Relief washed over me like a tidal wave, knocking me off my feet and onto my back. Fortunately the bed was there to catch me.

"Really?" I said. "That's great. I'm really... pleased! So pleased! So when's good for you?"

"Whenever," said Emma.

"How about tomorrow – or Friday?"

"Ok," she said.

"Yeah? Really? Great! Which one?" I asked.

"Friday."

"You're sure? I mean, normally you need to check to see what shifts you're working, or what lectures you have –"

"No, no," said Emma. "That'll be fine."

"Fantastic. I have some new ideas for shoots."

"Ok," she said again.

"Do you want to know what they are?" I asked.

"Email them to me."

"Oh," I said. "Ok."

"Bye then," said Emma.

"Wait. What time d'you think you'll be here?" I asked.

"Oh, normal time."

"What – ten? Eleven?"

"Yeah, something like that."

"Great," I said.

"Goodbye, Jason."

"Oh right, ok then. But I wondered if... Hello? Emma?" But she'd gone.

I lay on the bed for a while longer, basking in a medley of new emotions. I'd spent two days totally guilt ridden, wondering whether I'd destroyed the sacred bond of trust between photographer and model with my inappropriate declarations of desire. Whether there was any way Emma might see it for what it was – a slip of the tongue that would never happen again. There was only one way to know for sure. And so when the madness of 'not knowing' finally joined forces with the desperation to think about something else, and the courage to do something about it, I called her and asked her if she'd like to do another shoot.

And she'd said yes.

Two more days crawled by. Friday arrived. Ten o'clock came and went. Then eleven. Emma was nowhere to be seen. And she wasn't answering her phone. And this should have told me everything I needed to know, but like a five-year-old with a favourite blanket, I held onto that last remaining shred of hope.

She was running late.

She'd run out of credit on her phone.

Any moment now, she'd ring my doorbell and everything would go back to how it was before.

I set about getting everything ready, first by making the bed, then moving the studio lights into the bedroom. And when I was done with that I busied myself with household chores that I could drop the moment Emma arrived. But once I'd vacuumed every room in the house, cleaned out the kitchen cupboards and paired all my socks, the lure of the email became too hard to resist.

And late that evening, after sending three or four thousand where-are-you emails, I got a short reply:

Great Auntie Florence had died. Emma was very upset. She wouldn't be modelling for me any more.

My stomach lurched.

I'd never met Emma's great aunt. I knew she'd been ill, but it seemed more than a little coincidental that she'd chosen this very moment to die, and that the resulting grief had prompted Emma to reassess, and subsequently terminate, her short-lived career in glamour modelling. There were whole sentences missing from her email. Sentences that might explain the relationship between those two events. Was Great Auntie Florence the last of the suffragettes, her dying words a plea to her great niece to give up a life pandering to male fantasies? I needed more. My head demanded an explanation, something it could latch onto, something it could negotiate and reason with.

But my heart knew the truth. The whole Great Auntie Flo thing was a pile of hogwash. Invented specifically so that I couldn't negotiate, apologise, or atone for the real reason Emma had ducked out.

I dropped my reddening face into my hands as the gut wrenching continued. All the guilt that I'd felt two days earlier came rushing back, and the hopes I'd had that Emma might have forgiven me were replaced by embarrassment and self-loathing.

I lay on my front. Then my side. Then the other side. Then my back. I closed my eyes. Opened them again. Stared at the ceiling. The wall. The digital clock by the bed. I even prayed: squeezed my eyes closed and begged that the gods might let me sleep. Send me whatever hideous nightmares they reserved for idiots like me but please, just let me sleep. Anything rather than this guilt-ridden insomnia so massive it was filling the entire room, like some malevolent spectre. I opened my eyes and there, looming over me at the foot of the bed, was a shadowy figure, nine feet tall with an enormous silhouetted head. Instinctively I grabbed the covers and pulled them up to my chin

"I knew this would happen," said the figure in a soft, sinister whisper. "You can call it glamour photography, dress it up in fancy words, but at the end of the day you're nothing but a creepy, lecherous old –"

"I'm not!" I said, sinking under the duvet until only my eyes peeked above the covers. "Emma was ok," I reasoned. "Sure it was awkward, for a bit, but she never said anything, I thought..." I closed my eyes.

"What? Did you expect her to stick around? Have a big discussion? Over a nice cup of tea?" asked the figure, but sounding more and more like Liz with every accusing word. "You can hardly blame the girl for wanting to get out of here as quickly as possible – not after what you did!"

"But... I didn't... I really liked her. I –"

"How could you, Jason?" said my mother. "How could you force her to do those degrading, filthy things?"

"I never forced her to do anything! She was clothed!" I curled into a ball, pulled a pillow under the duvet and held it tightly over my head, pressing it against my ears. But the voices continued, as clear as before.

"It shouldn't be allowed," said Anna. "Men that look at women in that way should be castrated. No offence."

"I knew a glamour photographer once –" started my grandmother. "Terrible, he was."

"Shut up!" I shouted. "Shut up, all of you!"

"I told you to get a proper job," resumed my mother. "I warned you photography wasn't a good idea! And now a nice, sweet girl who trusted you doesn't want to be within five hundred miles of you." The menacing whisper of half a dozen female voices continued. "She's afraid of you, Jason. You did that. You!"

I threw the covers off, sat up, and switched on the bed-side light. The voices stopped. There was nobody there. Just one of my studio lights, with a shirt hung on a cable clip. But though I could feel my heart slowing to a normal rhythm it didn't make the voices any less right. And I felt tears prick the corners of my eyes.

"So? What!? What do you want me to do?" But the voices said nothing. And somehow that was worse.

I got out of bed and walked across the landing into my study. I would give them an admission of guilt. Or an explanation. Or something. Whatever the demons wanted.

I switched on the computer again and opened Emma's email. Then hit reply:

"Dear Emma," I wrote. "Thanks for your email. At this difficult time. You must be very upset. Death is always..." No.

"Hi Emma. Sorry for your loss. I can't help but wonder though if that's the real reason you..." No.

"Emma. This may seem unrelated, at this time of sadness, but I just want to apologise for being a lecherous old pervert and saying..." No.

"Emma. I'm so sorry. I know what I said was inappropriate. I only said what I did because... you see, what was going through my head was... what I was trying to say was I like you... have done for a while. Maybe the timing..." Definitely not.

There just wasn't a way to do it.

I went back to bed.

And failed to sleep.

The phone rang. The answering machine cut in.

The phone rang again, and again the answering machine got it.

Then again, the phone rang, and once more the answering machine saved me from getting out of bed to take the call.

When the phone rang a fourth time I began to get annoyed. I'd let the machine get it one last time and if it rang a fifth, I would give serious consideration to answering it.

It did.

"Hello?" I said.

"Jason?" asked a female voice.

"Yes?"

"So you are there!"

"Yes."

"Why didn't you answer the phone?"

"I was... sleeping." I rubbed my eyes.

"At one thirty in the afternoon? Never mind! Can you put Alex on please?"

Suddenly I realised who I was talking to.

"Tina?"

"Yes, it's Tina! Please put my husband on the phone."

"He's not here!"

"Well, where the hell is he?!" she asked.

"I... I don't know." Tina said nothing. It took me a few seconds to realise that she was crying. Nothing dramatic, just silence punctuated with the occasional gasp that she was unable to stifle.

"Tina?" I said eventually. "Is everything ok?"

Everything was not ok.

Here's what I now know about being twenty-eight weeks pregnant. Size is important. Both yours and the baby's, and if, as in this case, your baby isn't getting bigger, doctors get concerned. They start to question whether your placenta will be up to the job in hand. They talk about bed rest, hospital admittance – and whether they might have to perform a caesarean at some point in the future.

That was the abbreviated version of the significantly longer and more detailed catalogue of events that Tina was relaying to me at breakneck speed, pausing only to blow her nose or take long deep sobs. And in those brief moments of respite one thought dominated the space between my ears.

Where the fuck was Alex?!

"He's left me," blubbed Tina. "Moved out."

"But I sent him back to you!"

"When?" asked Tina.

"I dunno. Three, maybe four weeks ago?"

"Weeks?" Tina's tears dried up for a moment whilst she processed this new information. "You mean the Saturday night he spent at your place? That was just a tiff! He wasn't leaving me then."

That wasn't what he told me, I thought, but I decided to keep that to myself.

"Well there you are, maybe this is just a –"

"No, Jason! He left me a note. I found it this morning. Says I have 'nothing that he needs'." And with that she broke into great sobs of uncontrollable anguish. I rubbed my tired eyes, and silently cursed my best friend for being such an unbelievable arsehole.

"Is there anything I can do?" I asked.

"Yes!!" shouted Tina, before I'd had a chance to move the phone away from my ear. "Find my husband!"

I'd like to say that tracking Alex down had been harder than simply calling his mobile and asking where he was, but it wasn't. He answered immediately, and in surprisingly good spirits.

"Mate," he said.

"Where are you?" I asked.

"My hotel room."

"Your... hotel?"

"Yeah. Great place. Mini bar in the room. Porn on the TV. Ten minutes from work. Should have done this weeks ago."

"Alex –" I started.

"You wanna come over?" he asked. "Get a few beers?"

"Yes," I said, after a millisecond's thought. "I'm leaving now."

"Let's find a strip club!" suggested Alex many, many hours later. I glanced at my watch, and the half-drunk pint in front of me, and tried to figure out how many we'd had, as the room swayed around me. It was definitely bordering on 'a lot'. I was entering that stage where staying still and being mellow seemed like a much better idea than moving about.

"Really?" I asked.

"Why not? My treat."

"Look – maybe we should think about calling it a night."

"Nonsense," said Alex, downing his pint. "There's this place a guy at work was telling me about."

"Seriously, Alex, by the time we get home –"

"I live here now," said Alex, placing the empty glass on the bar. "Getting home isn't a problem." For the umpteenth time that afternoon I felt a knot form in my stomach, a reminder of why I'd made the journey into London in the first place. With each fresh round of drinks I'd attempted to raise the subject of Tina and the possible caesarean, only to have Alex change the subject, disappear to the gents, or stuff Twiglets in my mouth. He wasn't in a talkative mood, and to be honest, neither was I. "You can crash in my hotel room if you like."

I looked at my friend. "Yeah, look, about that –"

"Don't want to talk about it," said Alex.

I blinked. "You don't even know what I was going to say!"

"Was it something to do with Tina?"

"Well, yes, but –"

"I'm going to the strip club," said Alex. "I either go on my own, or I take you with me. Your choice."

A thousand excuses perched on the end of my tongue, each one waiting to be set free into the world, but the knot tightened in the pit of my stomach, and at the back of my head were Tina's distant echoey sobs. "Find my husband," she'd said. And whilst I could argue that technically I'd completed my mission, to leave now would only add to the guilt I was already carrying around with me. Another sleepless night of torment was all that I could look forward to.

"Let's go," I said.

It wasn't exactly art, but a lot of thought had gone into their routine. For starters, it would have been hard for two ladies to spin on a slightly greased pole without at least some agreement on the direction they would be spinning. But there was more to it than that. The two ladies wrapped themselves around the pole and each other, swapping places, pulling apart, coming back together again, removing the occasional item of clothing in snake-like movements, and all about four feet in front of our noses. You had to appreciate the skill, if not the art. And I would have, if it wasn't for the fact I found the whole experience excruciating.

I hate strip clubs. I shouldn't do – strip clubs consist of beer and naked women, and I enjoy both of these elements – they really should be my kind of thing. And yet somehow the whole experience is missing something crucial.

Each and every time I've ever been to a strip club I've stood or sat in silence, like some terrified schoolboy, whilst a towering, silicon-enhanced woman gyrates and wiggles her way out of a micro-bikini top and mini skirt, thrusting her breasts, bum and, well, everything, into my face at every opportunity. She gyrates, glides and slides, whilst I squirm, blush and grind. My teeth.

Liz used to say that pornography, strip clubs and the like were demeaning and dehumanising, reducing the women involved to mere objects. But every time I've ever been to one of these places I'm the one feeling dehumanised. My only purpose is to be part of an audience that isn't strictly necessary. I could step out of the room, or look away, and the stripper or strippers would carry on, robot-like, devoid of emotion. Like they're not really there.

They're not really there. I'm not strictly necessary. We're all just soulless shells.

I shuddered, and shot a sideways glance at Alex.

"Just watch the girls," he said, smiling, but not at me.

"I am."

"No – you're looking at me. I didn't pay twenty quid for you to look at me."

"I didn't want to come here in the first place, let alone have a private dance!" I said out of the corner of my mouth, and for the first time during the whole performance one of the dancers, the brunette, looked at me. "Sorry," I said. "No offence."

"What's wrong with you?" asked Alex, the irritation at odds with the fixed grin on his face. "You should be well into this."

"Why?" I snorted.

"You're not exactly a stranger to paying girls to take their clothes off." The blonde glanced at Alex and then at me.

"That's different."

"No it's not."

"Yes, it is."

"Look, I don't care whether you're enjoying it. Just shut up and let me." He beamed at the two ladies, who were hanging onto our every word, as well as the pole. It's amazing the way women can multi-task.

I folded my arms. The two girls went into another three hundred and sixty degree spin round the pole and as they did, the brunette removed her top, stretched out an arm and dangled the bikini top across my lap.

"Why're you being such a grumpy git?" asked Alex.

"I didn't get much sleep."

"Why not?"

"No reason."

"Did someone die or something?"

"Yes," I said, after a pause. The blonde faltered ever so slightly. I froze. So much for multi-tasking. Now I felt responsible – like she needed my attention after all and I wasn't providing it.

"Who?" asked Alex.

"Just... someone."

"Someone I know?" A pair of sequinned bikini briefs passed within an inch or two of my nose. This couldn't go on for much longer, surely; aside from shoes, both ladies had now removed the only two items they'd been wearing!

"No," I answered.

"Someone I know of?"

"A friend's aunt. Great aunt. It doesn't matter."

"A friend's great aunt died?"

"Yes," I replied.

"And this kept you up all night?"

"Yes."

"Why?"

Oh, for God's sake! "Because she's very upset and I'm worried about her. Ok?"

"This friend is a woman?"

"Yes." The music stopped and the dance came to an end. Every muscle in my body relaxed.

"That's it," said the blonde, whilst her friend picked up their costumes from the floor.

"Bollocks," said Alex, getting out of his chair. "Forty quid for that."

"Thanks very much," I said to the blonde. "That was really good. You must practise. A lot." She shrugged. "Sorry about – you know – all the talking."

"Don't matter," said the blonde. "You can go back into the bar now. Unless you want another dance?"

"Oh, I don't think we..." I looked over my shoulder to confer with Alex, but he was already walking through the beaded curtain that separated us from the rest of the club.

"Hope your friend is ok," said the blonde.

"Oh, he'll be fine."

"I mean the girl – who lost her aunt."

"Oh! Yeah. Thanks." A melancholy second or two drifted by whilst I thought about that, and then I noticed something profound: I was talking to a stripper. And she wasn't a soulless robot. And she'd said something nice. She was a nice person. I reached inside my jacket. "Look, before I go," I said, identifying the object I was looking for, "I wonder if I could leave you and your friend my card. Have you ever considered glamour modelling?"

"What were you doing?" asked Alex as I stepped through the beaded curtain. On the main stage a girl twirled round a pole to thumping music whilst a crowd of men stood silently, pints in hand, and watched her. "You just handed her one of your things, didn't you?"

"What things?"

"Cards. You just handed her a sodding business card!" He was angry. What I didn't understand was why.

"Yeah," I admitted. "So?"

"Fucking hell, mate," blasted Alex, "are you trying to get us beaten to a pulp?"

"For what?"

"You don't speak to the women, mate."

"Why?"

"The women are for looking at! Nothing else. You're not supposed to talk to them!" I stared into my friend's eyes. He was serious. I glanced over his shoulder to see if there were any large gentlemen who might be limbering up for a little pulp beating, but there weren't.

"That's bollocks," I said.

"No, mate. That's the way it is. And a good job too." I opened my mouth but words weren't forthcoming. "Come on," he growled, "before we're thrown out."

Out on the street Alex strode purposely, hands in pockets, in a direction of his choosing, and although my legs are longer I struggled to keep up.

"So where are we going?" I asked.

"Somewhere without women."

"What's your problem?" I asked. Alex stopped and turned to face me.

"It's not me with the problem, mate – I haven't got a problem. I'm not the one who has to hand a business card to anyone with tits!"

"Ok," I said.

"They were strippers, mate!" said Alex, pointing at the club behind me. "They strip – you watch. That's how it works."

"Right," I said.

"You're not supposed to talk to them. 'Engage them in conversation', as you'd say. It's a simple enough arrangement, and it doesn't need you to fuck with it."

"I'm not fucking with it!"

"Oh really?"

"Really!"

"Then how come we're out here!"

I replayed the previous few minutes in my head to see if I'd missed anything.

"Because you walked out of the club?"

"Before they threw us out!"

"Nobody was going to throw us out!"

"What kind of world do you live in?" asked Alex, moving closer, his eyes narrowing. When I failed to answer, he threw his hands in the air, turned, and carried on walking.

"Let me tell you about my world, Alex," I said, a few paces behind. "I live in a world where women are actual people. Where it's not just ok to talk to them but where it's considered rude if you don't! Especially when they can hear every bloody word!"

"Oh dream on!"

"You know that blonde we were watching? She was a really nice person. She probably didn't appreciate some jerk telling her that her dance wasn't worth the money." Alex stuck his middle finger up in the air, and started to walk faster.

"And you know what else, Alex? I've just realised that whilst talking to women can get you into all sorts of trouble, and maybe it's best not to utter every thought that enters your head, not talking to women – especially those that are having your children – is just storing up a world of pain!"

"Go fuck yourself!"

I stopped walking. "Ok then, try this," I said, shouting after him. "I live in a world where doctors are wondering whether it would be better to cut Tina open because they're not sure your baby – or Tina, come to that – will make it otherwise. That's the world I live in!"

Alex stopped, turned, and walked back to me.

"Is any of that true?" he asked.

"Yes," I said. "It is. Sorry."

"You bastard."

"Yeah," I agreed, my voice cracking slightly. "Yeah, I suppose I am."

"Why didn't you tell me this earlier?"

"Because you didn't want to know. At least, you told me you didn't."

"Ok," said Alex. "I can see that."

Alex spent the entire journey on the phone to Tina. He didn't say much, just listened, and occasionally mumbled, "Ok, but what does that mean?" Then he'd rub his forehead with his other hand and look slightly paler.

We pulled up outside his hotel. I stayed in the taxi and ten minutes later, once Alex had checked out of his room, and was back in the cab. We sat in silence as we headed towards Cannon Street.

It was only after we'd arrived and Alex had got out, that he turned back as if it was an afterthought. I moved across the seat and wound down the window.

"Can I leave you to sort this out?" he asked, gesturing at the cab driver.

"Yeah, yeah. Of course. You go."

"Right," said Alex. "Cheers." I watched as he walked into the station.

"Where next, mate?" asked the cabbie. I was about to say Fenchurch Street, but one look at the meter was all I needed to remind myself that I didn't have the kind of money for luxuries like taxis. Not any more.

"Nowhere," I said. "Here's just fine," and I passed a twenty pound note through the window.

As my train trundled homewards, stopping at every station it could find on the way, I listened hard for the voices that had kept me awake the previous night. But they'd gone.

And boy, was I tired.

CHAPTER NINETEEN
SUNDAY 15TH MARCH, 1999

It wasn't the most promising of starts. Scruffy, torn jeans. Old muddy trainers. A stained brown anorak that came down to her calves. And hair that, much like its owner, appeared never to have done a great deal of anything.

"Pippa?" I asked the girl.

"Yeah?" she replied. I wanted to ask her again, just to be sure.

"Won't you... come in?" She picked up the carrier bag at her feet, shuffled past me and proceeded up the stairs. I closed the front door, took a breath and followed her inside.

I found Pippa in the lounge, still wearing her anorak, sitting on my sofa like a five-foot bag of spuds.

"So," I said, "can I get you some tea?"

"No thanks," said Pippa, making no attempt at eye contact as she wrapped a wayward strand of hair round a finger.

"So you'd like to be a model?" I asked cautiously, as I sat myself in the chair opposite.

"Not really," said Pippa after a second or two.

"Ok," I said slowly. "So why are you here?"

"Well," said Pippa, brushing aside more hair that had fallen in front of her face, "last year I worked for Gap, yeah? But they made me work evenings and weekends and I missed all the good bands."

"Ok," I said.

"Whereas," she continued, "I figure if I do this modelling thing I could more or less work when I like, yeah? And you pay better."

"Right," I said. I pursed my lips and wondered what to do next. Whilst I was prepared to pay several times more than most shops pay their sales assistants, I needed someone who was at least familiar with the business end of a hair brush. Pippa continued to swat more unruly locks out of her face. But as I opened my mouth to say something, her eyes met mine, and I saw the steely look of determination within them.

"Why don't we take a look at what you brought with you?" I said.

"Wait a minute," said Alex. "Is this the bird whose aunt died?"

"No," I said with a sigh.

"So what happened to the dead aunt bird?"

"It was her great aunt, and that was," I took a deep, melancholy breath, "weeks ago."

"Ok, but what happened to her?"

"Do you want to know about yesterday's shoot or not?"

"Not particularly," said Alex.

"Let's forget it then."

"Fine by me," replied Alex with a shrug. We sat in silence and stared at the sludge-green wall in front of us, listening to the murmur of activity in the background, the occasional cry of an infant, and the frustrated sounds of someone whose job it was to shout names above the competing din. Alex shuffled in his seat and cursed the furniture under his breath. Eventually a heavily pregnant woman trudged past, dragging behind her a screaming toddler, and I did my best to hide a smirk as, out of the corner of my eye, I watched Alex cross his arms and let out an impatient huff.

"Ok," he said. "Tell me about yesterday."

"I don't do girly," said Pippa, turning the carrier bag upside down and emptying the contents over the bed. "A girl at college lent me this stuff." I picked through the assortment of tops and mini-skirts whilst Pippa, still wearing the anorak, shifted her weight from one leg to the other.

"Have you tried any of these on?" I asked.

"No!" said Pippa indignantly. I shook my head in despair. Actually, it wasn't a bad selection. A couple of little dresses, a short skirt or two, a fairly interesting halter neck top, two pairs of strappy heels, assorted bras, knickers, and suspender belts – all matching, a packet of stockings... and a hair brush. Someone, somewhere, had put some thought into this bag.

"Well, why don't we try you in this dress, and these shoes? What are you wearing in the way of underwear?"

"Just my boyfriend's boxer shorts," said Pippa. I looked back down at the bed. "Here," I said. "These'll do. The bathroom's through there. I'll be downstairs setting up the studio. Come down when you're ready." I left her to it.

"Wait a minute. So this is a new girl?" asked Alex.

"I met her yesterday – yes."

"And she decided to model because you pay... how much?"

"Twenty quid an hour."

"She's got a point." Said Alex. "Stand there. Get ya tits out. Earn twenty quid. It's not rocket science is it? I'd do it. If I was a bird." He arched his back, though whether this was in an effort to get comfortable, or a demonstration of his modelling prowess, I couldn't tell.

"They don't 'get their tits out'. And there's more to modelling than 'standing there'. For one thing, they have to be able to smile – something you find challenging at the best of times – and for another, they have to be able to take direction. And I'm fast realising that not every girl can do that. In fact, up till now I've been really lucky." In the distance someone yelled out "Hayward? Mrs Hayward?" before she was drowned out by the sounds of a child screaming.

"Mate," continued Alex, oblivious to the noise, "you talk like you've snapped thousands of models, and we both know you've only had two."

"Five," I said.

"Five?" Alex frowned.

"Six if you include Isabella," I clarified.

"And one of those was duff?" asked Alex

It wasn't the most promising of starts. Blonde hair, white stiletto heels, an enormous bust that was fighting to get out of her top – all of that was good – but the look on Kayleigh's face suggested she might be chewing on a wasp.

"Kayleigh?" I asked.

"Yeah?" she snarled. I took a step backwards.

"And Kayleigh's boyfriend?" I asked, addressing the guy standing behind her. He gave a barely noticeable jerk of his head in what I assumed was a greeting of some sort. "Well, come in!" I said, and stepped to one side. Kayleigh marched past me, looked me up and down, and sneered. Then her boyfriend followed like an obedient puppy, the toxic odour of his hair gel and aftershave following in much the same manner.

"So," I said, once we were seated in the lounge, "you said in your email that you've done some modelling before."

"Yeah," growled Kayleigh.

"For the *Sunday Sport*?" I prompted

"Gary sent some pictures in." Her boyfriend gave me the subtle head nod again. Of course, I thought, of course you're called Gary.

"So was it a competition or something?"

"No!" said Kayleigh. She seemed annoyed at the suggestion.

"Oh, right. Well that's..."

"They sent a man with a camera to our 'ouse," said Gary.

"Really?" I said. "That must have been –"

"He only stayed ten minutes!" said Kayleigh, glaring at me as if it were my fault that her modelling career had failed to clock up a quarter of an hour.

"Oh. Well –"

"So are you going to take some photos?" she asked.

"Er, yes," I said, clearing my throat. "I'd like to."

"Today?"

"If that's ok?"

"And you're going to pay me, right?"

"Of course," I said, regretting it immediately. Truth was, nothing made me want to photograph this girl, let alone give her money for it.

"Right then," said Kayleigh. And then she did it again. The sneer.

"Well – shall we have a look at what you brought with you?"

"What d'you mean?" Only then did I notice that she didn't have any bags with her.

"Did you bring any other clothes?"

"No!" she said, as though the suggestion was preposterous. "What's wrong with what I have on?"

"Stop, stop," said Alex, still wriggling around in the moulded plastic chair. "Why d'you care what clothes she brought with her? Just tell her to get her tits out!" He put a hand behind his back, and a second or two later pulled out a fluffy toy duck. He stared at it for a moment as if it might apologise for being there, then put it on the chair next to him.

"How many times do I have to tell you? I don't do topless! Or nude! Just glamour." I said.

"But you said she had an enormous bust."

"And I'm fast learning that doesn't mean anything."

"Of course it does," said Alex. "Tits are everything." I looked at my friend, and realised there was every chance that those would be the words they'd put on his gravestone. "I can't believe you paid a girl *not* to see her tits."

"That's what I do," I said with half-hearted jazz-hands. "Not that I'll ever sell the photos."

"Why not?"

"She was useless! Kayleigh was unpleasant, stupid, rude, completely ignored my email about bringing a selection of clothes, and couldn't smile for toffee! The only way I got her face to crack was to get her to look at gormless Gary – so I've got the occasional picture of her smiling, weakly, at someone off camera. The rest of the time she looked as if she wanted to push a broken bottle into my face. No wonder the *Sunday Sport* guy only stayed ten minutes!" I shook my head.

"So aside from this Kylie..."

"Kayleigh."

"...Dead Aunt Bird, that girl who wouldn't sign the model restraint form..."

"Release. It's a model release."

"the French girl..."

"Italian," I said.

"And Jaffa..."

"Pippa."

"Whatever. Who was the other bird?"

"Becky!" I said, opening the door and looking into familiar hazel eyes. "Nice to see you again."

Becky smiled.

"Hello," she said.

"And Becky's friend," I said to the taller girl standing next to her.

"Partner," said the girl, eyeing me with suspicion.

"Oh. Right. Well, come on in! Here, let me help you with that." I took the larger of Becky's bags.

"Thanks," said Becky, shooting me a big cheeky smile. Her partner said nothing, just continued to glare as she walked past.

"Wait a minute," said Alex, raising a hand, realisation dawning on him like a drunk who's figured out there may be a relationship between the rails he's been walking along and the sound of an express train in the distance. "They were... lezzers?!"

"So," I said, once we were seated in the lounge, "are you both modelling today?"

"I definitely am!" said Becky, still smiling. I glanced at Becky's partner, possibilities of a two girl shoot dancing around in my mind.

"Yeah, I don't think so," she said, with a toss of her head. "It'll be a cold day in hell before you manage to get me in front of your camera!"

"Bitch," muttered Alex, folding his arms across his chest.

I turned back to Becky. "So," I said, "it was nice to hear from you after all this time." Her partner let out a snort, and turned to look out of the window.

"Well, I kept your card behind the bar, and it got me thinking. Jane's always telling me what a nice figure I have." Becky put a hand on her friend's leg.

"Yeah," said Jane, removing Becky's hand, "but I didn't mean you should start getting your kit off for strange men!"

"We talked about this," said Becky, lowering her voice slightly. "Besides, I'm sure Jason's not strange. Not that much anyway!" She shot me the cheeky smile again.

"Hold on," said Alex again, the sound of the express train ringing in his ears. "So this is..."

"Becky. From the Doggetts."

"The barmaid?! And she's a lezzer?"

"She's a lesbian, yes – what's wrong with that?" I said. Alex closed his mouth, sat back and stared at the wall opposite.

"Bollocks," he said. "Can't ever go in that pub again."

My head reeled. "Why?"

"What would be the point? If she's a lezzer?"

"For the beer, maybe?" Alex considered this for a moment.

"Just get on with the story," he said.

"How long have you been doing this?" asked Jane, Becky's girlfriend.

"Since last August," I replied.

"Not that long then."

"No, I guess not," I said.

"And this is how you make your living?" she asked, a Kayleigh-style sneer sneaking in.

"I'm trying to," I said.

"Actually – it wasn't just your card," continued Becky. "I did a little modelling for a fashion designer friend of ours. I know it's probably not the same thing but I enjoyed it, and –"

"Did she get her tits out!?" asked Alex in a manner that suggested he might start gnawing his arm off if I didn't tell him something salacious soon.

"It's *glamour* Alex! *Glamour!*"

"It's a waste of time is what it is!" said Alex, far too loudly. I looked down the corridor to see how much attention we'd drawn, but the bustle of patients and nurses continued uninterrupted. "What about Jaffa?"

"Pippa," I said.

"Yeah, yeah. Did *she* get her tits out?"

I turned to face my friend. "You don't want to know about anything other than the tits, do you?"

"Not really, no," said Alex.

I'd have sworn that it was a different girl that came down the stairs. The short dress that I'd picked out for her didn't just fit, it looked as if it had been made with her in mind. And whilst she couldn't walk in heels without hanging onto something, it was hard to believe that her delicate little feet and smooth slim legs had ever been anywhere near a dirty pair of jeans or a muddy pair of trainers. Even the unruly mass of curls had been tamed into gushing luxurious brown locks that framed coy, angelic features.

"Wow," I said.

"Is it alright?" asked Pippa, checking the length of the dress like she couldn't quite believe that someone had intended it to finish so high against her thigh.

"It looks – you look – great," I said. Pippa glanced up at me and gave me an uncertain nod. "Why don't you go over there and sit on the sofa?" She tottered across the room and perched herself on the edge of the sofa, legs to one side, knees glued together. I picked up my camera, cocked my head slightly, and looked at the nervous girl before me. "Let's make you more comfortable," I said eventually. "Lose the shoes."

I tried a series of harmless poses, first sitting on the sofa with her legs tucked underneath her, then kneeling, then with her hands on her hips, then side on, then lying back. And with each pop of the flash Pippa's confidence grew until the frown dissolved into a coy, playful smile.

"Lie back Pippa. Play with your hair. That's excellent. Just look away for a moment – great – now back to me. That's good. Yep, that's good. That's... really good."

She was, too. Really, really good.

"Try kneeling again. Great, ok. Shall we try a few without the dress?"

Pippa froze.

"Really?" she said.

"Is that a problem?"

Pippa mused over this for a second or two, then crossed her arms, reached down to gather the bottom of her dress, and a moment later it was off. And she wasn't wearing a bra.

"Finally!" said Alex. "What were they like?"

"They were breasts Alex. They were like any other breasts in the whole wide world. But I didn't see them for long because I told her to go back upstairs and put a bra on!"

"Jesus mate – I never thought you were such a prude. The girls obviously aren't!"

"It's got nothing to do with whether I'm a prude or not. *Teaze* magazine doesn't print nudity. And that's my market!"

"But who the hell buys that magazine? Why can't you shoot for *Fiesta*, or *Mayfair*, something we can both be proud of?"

I closed my eyes and leaned back until my head met the cold hard wall behind me. "Why d'you want to talk about any of this stuff? The only time you ever mention the photography is to tell me that I should stop doing it and get a 'proper job'."

"Yeah, well, you should," said Alex.

"And I'm not going to – so why don't we talk about something else?"

"No. Carry on."

"Why?"

"Because it stops me thinking about other stuff."

I turned and looked at the side of my friend's head. "Is that why you wanted me here? So that you wouldn't have to think about 'other stuff'?"

"Yeah. Suppose so."

"Shouldn't you be in with Tina now whilst she's having her check up?" I asked, jerking a thumb in the direction of the nurses and the other hospital hubbub.

"I wouldn't be here at all if I had a choice. I only agreed to it because she said you could come too."

"Unbelievable."

"Where are you finding these girls anyway?" asked Alex. "They can't be girls you've approached in pubs because you haven't done that since the strip club." I shook my head in dismay. God forbid we should talk about the important stuff.

"Internet bulletin boards," I said eventually.

"You mean, like chat rooms?"

"Sort of. I found one for professional photographers and models."

"You're not a professional."

"Let's not have that conversation again, shall we?"

"Seriously. To be a professional you've got to sell something."

"And if you must know I'm sending some pictures to *Teaze* next week!"

"Really?" asked Alex, the whiney sarcastic tone of disbelief a little too prominent for my liking.

"Really!"

"And you reckon they'll buy them?"

"I can't see any reason why not!"

Alex opened his mouth, presumably to realign my expectations, when a nurse with the most vivid, punky, poppy-red hair, and an oddly familiar smile, sashayed purposely down the corridor and-

Ria?

She stopped dead in front of my friend. "Mr Cooke, I presume?" Ria asked, head cocked to one side, hands perched high on slender, curvaceous hips. She glanced at me. "Hello Jason," she said, with a smile and a wink. "Nice to see you again." She looked back at Alex and raised an eyebrow.

Alex sighed. "Yeah," he said, "that's me."

"Your wife wondered if you'd like to come in for a moment and talk to the doctor." Alex said nothing. I nudged him in the ribs. He let out another tortured sigh.

"Ok!" said my friend, and started down the corridor on his own. Ria flashed me another smile, which I returned with one of my own, a half-hearted wave, and an ache, and a flutter, from somewhere deep inside my chest. Then she turned and galloped after Alex, just as she'd galloped after her snot-ridden rugby player boyfriend, all those months ago.

Ria. The dance teacher.

And that was the first time I realised; I'd have happily traded my camera, my savings, and every photo shoot past and future, just to stop her from running away.

"I'd like to get you back again, if you're interested."

"Yeah, ok," said Pippa, stuffing her borrowed clothes back into the carrier bag. "How long for?"

"Probably do a couple of hours if that's ok. Maybe three. I'm hoping to get published in *Teaze* magazine."

"Oh right," she said. "I've never heard of that one. But my boyfriend probably has a couple of issues shoved under the mattress." She brushed a few stray strands of unruly hair out of her face. Already she was transforming back to her natural state, like Cinderella after the stroke of midnight.

"How about the same time next week?" I asked as we walked down the stairs.

"Yeah. Should be ok. Depends whether there are any good bands playing the night before, but I'll let you know," she said. "Shall I bring the same clothes with me?"

"Unless you can get hold of anything else."

"Ok," said Pippa as we got to the front door. "I'll see what I can do." I opened the door, and to my surprise the postman was standing there clutching a pile of letters in one hand. "My friend Jess has a basque, I think," continued Pippa. "Her tits are a bit bigger than mine but, you know, it might be ok." The postman looked at me, then at Pippa. I closed my eyes and waited for the ground to open up.

"That sounds great."

"Ok then," she said. We both looked at the postman who, open mouthed, thrust the post at Pippa.

"I don't live here," she said.

"Thanks," I said, taking the post. He nodded and walked back down the path. "See you next week," I said to Pippa.

"Yeah, ok," she said, brushing hair out of her face. And then she smiled.

I closed the door and flicked through the envelopes in my hand, separating my post from my neighbour's. One envelope caught my eye. I tore it open and pulled out the contents. My bank statement. I glanced at the figure in the bottom right hand corner and my heart sank. It was official. My savings had finally run out.

Chapter Twenty
Sunday 21st March, 1999

A week later, almost to the hour, five hundred and forty three images heaved their way from my camera onto my computer's hard drive. Five hundred and forty three images of Pippa from our second shoot. Five hundred and forty three chances of finally selling some pictures.

The computer chirruped. I grabbed the mouse and opened the first image. There was Pippa. Sitting on the sofa, holding her Student Union card in front of her.

I opened another image – Pippa on the bed in a short skirt and vest top. Hips off to the side. Big smile at the camera. Arms crossed like she was about to pull the top over her head. It was good. Really good. I checked a couple more in the same set. They were also good. Better than good!

I skipped a dozen or so files and opened another, and my racing heart stopped. There she was, sitting in my office chair, surrounded by all my computer equipment, chewing provocatively on the arm of a pair of glasses. She looked every bit the sexy secretary despite the fact that, other than a basque and a pair of black high heels, she wasn't wearing anything.

But I was torturing myself – I needed to see the last set. I scrolled all the way to the bottom and opened the last dozen or so pictures. And oh my.

My, oh my.

Say what you like about posh underwear, stockings and suspenders, uniforms, any of those things – in my opinion the fastest way to take an ordinary girl and make her look fabulous, or a fabulous girl and make her look jaw dropping, is simply to put her in a white t-shirt and stand her under a shower. The running mascara, the wet hair, the semi translucent material sticking to every curve... I covered my mouth, and to my astonishment found myself blinking back tears. I'd done it – I'd finally done it. I had a set of pictures – four sets, five if you included the few I'd taken of her whilst she was drying her hair – that I could sell. Nothing – nothing – stood in the way of me selling these pictures. My days as an out-of-work software developer were about to end. I would finally be able to put the word 'professional' in front of 'photographer' when talking about myself.

I took the pack of writeable CDs from the shelf, popped one in the drive and started copying the pictures to it. And when it was done, I put it in a case, slipped it into an envelope, along with the model release and the covering letter that I'd written that morning, grabbed my coat, and headed up the road to the post-box.

Days passed.

After a week of nothing – a week of waiting for the phone to ring – waiting for *Teaze* to call me and tell me whether they'd accepted my pictures -, I couldn't bear it any longer, and called them.

The staff at *Teaze* magazine were, it seemed, a little on the shambolic side. Nobody ever arrived before midday, and from about midday through to approximately three in the afternoon anyone who could possibly help me had always 'popped out for lunch'. Despite the late lunch, by four o'clock they'd all gone home for the day and once again I was invited to call back or leave a message.

I did both.

I even left my mobile number.

Up until that week in March 1999, the chances of me having my mobile phone with me were remote. Switched on – doubly so. So when it actually rang I almost lost control of the car.

"Hello?" I yelled into the handset, as I attempted to steer, change gear, and wedge the phone between my shoulder and ear. "Hello?"

"Could I... to... Smith?" crackled a voice at the other end.

"Yes, hello! Speaking!" At which point the phone slipped and fell into the foot-well. "Hang on! Hang on!" I yelled. I hit my hazard warning lights and pulled over onto the hard shoulder. I retrieved the phone from the floor. "Hello?" I said.

"... Jason? It's Clare Min... From Silvermoon Publications. You've... trying to get hold of me?"

"Yes! Hello!" I said. "Thanks for calling back."

"I'm sorry... didn't quite catch that," said Clare. I looked at the small green LCD screen. One tiny little bar out of a possible five. I got out of the car, walked round to the passenger side and onto the grass verge at the side of the road. "Can you hear me now?" I asked, pressing the phone as hard as I could against one ear whilst I stuck a finger in the other.

"Just about," said Clare. "How can I help?"

"Ok, well, I sent some pictures in for your consideration, and I was just wondering whether you'd received them? And whether you thought they were, you know, the sort of thing you could use? In the magazine."

"Hang on," said Clare, "… me just check for … When did you send them?"

"A week ago. Ten days actually." A juggernaut the size of Wales thundered past, making the ground shake beneath my feet. I stepped a little further into the bushes and brambles.

"…should be here," continued Clare. "Bear with me. Yes. I have it," she said. "Your CD. I'm sending it back to you."

"You're sending it back?"

"Sorry?" said Clare. "You went a bit crackly there."

"I said, you're sending it back?"

"I'm afraid so. Sorry," said Clare. "It's just that we can't accept submissions on a CD."

"Then how do I send the pictures to you?"

"Can you send … original…"

"Sorry? Say again."

"… original transparencies," said Clare. "Thirty five mil' transparencies are fine. We'll also accept negatives. Or prints, at a push."

"No, you don't understand," I said, raising my voice. "I shoot onto digital."

"…igital?" asked Clare.

"Yes, digital. I have a digital camera. There is no film. That's why the pictures were on CD."

"Sorry, what was that again?" asked Clare.

"I was saying –"

"Hello?" said Clare.

"Yes – I'm still here."

"Ee.. o.. ru..." she said. And then nothing. I looked at the small screen. It was completely blank. After all that, the damn battery had died.

They didn't accept CDs? In this age of mobile phones, and the internet, and a million other technical wonders, *Teaze* magazine couldn't cope with digital photographs?

My head began to spin. First, I hadn't known about model releases. Then my model had refused to sign one. Then, having found a model who would sign one, I discovered I there wasn't a market for my pictures. Just as I'd found a market I'd lost my second model. And now, when I finally had the girl, proof of her ID, and a potential market, *Teaze* magazine – purveyors of non-celebrity, non-nude, quality glamour photography, for men – only accepted pictures as transparencies. Or negatives. Or prints. At a push!

It was as if I'd fought the dragon, cut my way through the thorns, avoided the giant, and climbed the tower, only to have someone pop their head out of a window on the sixteenth floor and say "Coo-ee, Mister Handsome Prince? You do know the Princess was rescued long ago, don't you?" Then they'd stuck a blade in me and yelled "Better luck next time!" as they watched me fall into the lava-filled moat below.

I stood for a moment, cradling the phone in my trembling hands like it was a blood-soaked dagger I'd pulled from the gaping hole in my chest and, in a moment of rage and frustration that had been bubbling under the surface for weeks – no, months – I brought my arm above my head, lifted one leg, and prepared to throw the phone onto the carriageway and into the path of the next gigantic monster truck. To hell with you, *Teaze* magazine, and your outdated production processes! To hell with you, 'technology', and your bloody empty promises! And to hell with you, Jason Smith, and your stupid idiotic ideas!

Which is when I lost my footing, and fell into the brambles.

When I finally found Alex he was beating up a vending machine several corridors away from the maternity wing. He turned and looked at me.

"What are you doing here?" he asked.

"You asked me to come."

Alex frowned. "No I didn't."

"Yes you did."

"I think I'd know."

"You wanted me to come with you for…" I searched for the appropriate diplomatic phrase, "moral support."

"That was last time," he said.

"I thought it was a standing arrangement?"

"No," said Alex. I ground my teeth.

"Then why did you tell me there was another check-up?"

Alex shrugged. "Dunno. Thought you might be interested." I raised my arms in the air, ready to vent my frustration at having driven round the M25 to be with my best friend in his moment of need, only to discover he wasn't the least bit interested, but what was the point? I let my arms fall down by my sides.

"Fine," I said with a sigh. "Ok, well –"

"What happened to your face?" asked Alex, still frowning. I touched it, then examined my fingers. I was still bleeding.

"I fell over."

"Into what? Your jacket's ripped too."

"It doesn't matter. Look, good luck with everything," I said, waving in the general direction of the rest of the hospital. I turned.

"Where are you going?" asked Alex.

"Home!"

"You're here now. You might as well stay."

"For what?" I asked. "Are the nurses putting on a cabaret? Are they serving interesting knick-knacks in the hospital canteen?"

Alex's frown deepened. "You alright?"

"Just dandy."

"Ok." He gave the vending machine another kick and a can of Coke appeared at the bottom. He retrieved it, opened it, and started pouring the contents down his throat. I plunged my hands into my pockets and bit my bottom lip.

"Fucking *Teaze* don't want my pictures," I said after a moment. Alex paused for breath.

"Because they're shit?" he asked.

"No, Alex! They haven't even looked at them! Turns out that they don't accept digital photos!"

Alex looked at me for a second as though he was considering his response, then he let out a long, deep foghorn of a belch. A little girl who was skipping to the machine turned and ran back to her mother.

"Why not?" he asked.

"Do you actually care?"

"Not really," he admitted. He walked past me and sat down on a plastic chair.

"How's Tina?" I asked, taking the seat next to him.

"Alright, I guess," said Alex.

"So are they going to, you know, do a caesarean?"

Alex frowned. "No!" he said, as though that was the most preposterous suggestion he'd ever heard.

"Oh." I scratched my head. "When was that decided?"

Alex shrugged. "It was only ever a possibility. The baby seems to be doing ok now."

"You didn't tell me!"

"Jeez, mate – I can't win."

I shook my head. "If you don't need me here why aren't you in there with Tina?"

"I'm not the one having the baby," said Alex.

I leaned my head back against the wall and looked up at the ceiling. I was beginning to suspect that the world was seriously fucked up, but I was the only one who'd noticed.

"So what are you going to do now?" asked Alex, still drinking his Coke, though slowing to a steady sip.

"I have no idea," I said, leaning forward to rest my elbows on my knees. "Get a job, I guess." I waited for Alex to tell me that it was about time, but he said nothing. "My savings have run out," I said, by way of an explanation. Alex just stared ahead. I sighed. "Digital cameras are cheap and easy to use, but if I had to start using film then, well, I'd probably be out of my depth." Alex shot me a sideways glance, and I grimaced. He thought I'd been out of my depth from day one. I looked at the floor, ready for him to tell me so. Instead he drained the can, crushed it, and tossed it in the bin next to him. I massaged my eyes with my fingers. "If only life wasn't so bloody..." I sighed again, "inevitable." I wanted to say more, but if anybody knew about inevitability it was Alex. I felt the crushing condemnation of my friend's silence. "You still got that number?"

"What number?" asked Alex, staring straight ahead.

"Of that guy. Willis?"

"Wilson. I'll dig it out for you," said Alex.

"Thanks," I said, and went back to staring at the floor.

At that moment a shapely pair of legs in sensible nurses' shoes stepped into my field of vision.

"Mr Cooke!" said the legs. We both looked up – me into beautiful, familiar almond-shaped eyes, Alex into the face of his oppressor. "Hiding out in the corridors with Jason again?" asked Ria, with a hint of a smile, and one eyebrow raised higher than the other. "You're going to have to try much harder if you want to avoid me. Come on, your wife sent me out to find you. There's no escaping the inevitable." Alex swore under his breath, shook his head, got to his feet and set off in the direction of the examination rooms.

Ria put a hand on a hip as she watched him, then she turned to me, and winked. I smiled back. Boyfriend or no boyfriend, I just couldn't help myself.

"He's a one, your friend."

"Yes," I said. "He certainly is."

Then once again Ria turned and walked away, clicking her fingers and swaying her hips as she went. It was hypnotic. And as I watched I realised that not only was I still smiling, but for a heartbeat or two I'd forgotten all about *Teaze* magazine, my lack of income, and anything other than how this beautiful dance instructor kept swaying into my life, only to disappear moments later. And just as I thought that, Ria turned the corner, and was gone. Possibly forever. And I went back to examining the floor.

About five seconds later I heard Ria yelling Alex's name, and when I looked up to see what the commotion was about he was standing right in front of me.

"Mate," he said, "for a bright bloke, you can be a real bonehead."

"What?" I said.

"How long is it since you left work?"

"I dunno," I said. "Eight months, I guess."

"Right. And in all that time you never thought to check where you could sell your work? And whether they'd accepted digital?"

"Well, I..."

"Mr Cooke," said Ria, "your wife is waiting –"

"She can wait," said Alex, raising a hand without taking his eyes off me. Ria's mouth snapped closed in surprise and she took a step back. "Just like you never thought to find out about the model restraint form?" he continued.

"Release form."

"Whatever. Eight months, mate. What have you been doing with yourself?"

"Oh come on, I've –"

"Shut up, I'm talking. You're listening. If you were serious about this you would have worked harder. You would have done more research. You would have found someone who makes a living taking mucky photos and asked them how they do it!" I winced at the phrase 'mucky photos', afraid of what Alex might say next. Just then another nurse – small and mouse-like – came round the corner and approached us.

"Is that Mr Cooke?" she asked.

"I'm just bringing him," said Ria.

"It's just –"

"We'll be there in a moment!" said Ria, more firmly this time. The small nurse scurried off. "Sorry about that," said Ria, securing a lock of vibrant red hair that had come loose from its mooring. "Do continue." Alex turned back to face me, and he shook his head.

"Jesus, mate," he said. "You had eight months to make this work. Instead you pissed it up the wall, with me, in every pub in town. You talk like it's not your fault, when it's completely your fault!"

There was nothing to say; I just lowered my head in shame. Alex watched me in my misery. Then after a moment he reached inside his back pocket and pulled out his wallet.

"You got a pen?" he asked.

"No," I answered.

"I have," said Ria, taking a step forward, eagerly producing a biro from her breast pocket. Alex took the pen and removed something from his wallet.

"Can I use your back?" he said to Ria.

"Oh. Yes. Of course," she said turning round. Only then did I see what he was up to.

"You keep a blank cheque in your wallet?" I asked.

"The local offy doesn't accept cards – I keep a cheque in my wallet in case I run out of cash. Here," he said, and he thrust the cheque at me.

"What's this for?"

"You, you dipstick."

"Yes, I can see that, but why are you giving me a thousand pounds?"

"Second chance," said Alex. "Do you think you could make this gig work if you had more time?"

"I don't know," I said.

"Right," said Alex. I could tell that wasn't the answer he was hoping for. "Well, let's find out. That'll keep you going for a couple of weeks or more. In that time do some fucking research. Phone some people. Get off your arse and do something. Just make this work, and stop whingeing. Is that clear?"

"Ok," I said. "But..."

"What?"

"What about all those times you told me to forget about the..." I glanced at Ria, who was hanging on every word, "to forget about photography and get a proper job? What about that?" Ria looked at Alex. He looked at me and frowned. Then he shrugged.

"Here's the deal," he said, his bottom lip curling. "If you haven't made it work by the time this money runs out you have to call Wilson. Got it?" Ria looked at me.

"Right, ok," I said. "So – this is a loan?" Again Alex frowned.

"Don't know."

"Right," I said. "Ok."

"Good." Alex nodded, then turned and marched back to the examination room, leaving me and Ria in the corridor. After a moment she turned to look at me.

"Well," she said, "that was interesting."

"Yeah," I agreed.

"Men are amazing!"

"We have our moments," I said. She narrowed her eyes.

"Did you know that you're bleeding?" I touched my face again and looked at the bright red spots on my fingers, then dug deep in my pockets for a tissue. Ria looked around, like she was checking for something, then back at me.

"Come on, Mr Photographer," she said, extending a hand. "Let's get you patched up."

The phone rang. I ignored it. Downstairs, in the lounge, the answering machine kicked in, and I could just make out my pre-recorded self instructing the caller to leave a message. There was a bleep, but no second voice. I shrugged and turned my attention back to the image on the screen. A stunning statuesque woman, dressed in nothing but a wide brimmed hat, a basque and a pair of dangerously high heels, stood in the doorway of a stately home. One hand perched high on her hip, the other holding the leads of a pair of Rottweilers, she towered over the camera, which lay on the gravel in front of her fearsome beasts. A second or two later the phone rang again. I picked up the extension in the study.

"What!?"

"You bastard! You are there!" said Alex.

"Well, obviously!"

"What you doin'?" he asked.

"Working!"

"Were you looking at porn?"

"No. Yes..." I shook my head. "These days that is working!" I sat back in the chair. There was a familiar background noise at Alex's end of the phone. I glanced at the clock on the wall. "Are you in a pub?"

"Yep."

"At eleven thirty? On Monday morning?"

"Wanna join me – make an afternoon of it?"

"Can't," I said bluntly.

"Why?" asked Alex.

I sighed. "Because you told me not to!"

"When did I say that?"

"Last week! You said I should stop pissing my time against walls... or something."

"I said that?"

"Yes!"

"Bollocks," belched Alex. "You need beer. Men need beer. Beer is..." I could hear him trying to think of an adjective at the other end of the phone. "Good," he said, eventually.

"Shouldn't you be at work?" I asked, turning my attention back to the website. The images were stunning. Aside from a love of the dramatic, Dave Fells clearly enjoyed public locations. Two ladies in roller skates – and not a lot else – kissing across the table of a small café. An African lady standing in a launderette, a plastic basket of frilly undies perched on one hip. A tall slender redhead with long pink nails, bending over the engine of her broken down car, the Tower of London visible behind her, as she waited for someone to rescue her and bring her some clothes.

"Work work work..." burbled Alex.

It was a little intimidating. Clearly these were Mr Fells' best pictures, the cream of an entire career as a successful glamour photographer, but it was difficult to see how I would ever be in the same league. I shook my head and took a breath – it was time to find out. I clicked around the site to see if I could find any contact info – and there it was.

"Are you listening to me?" asked Alex

"Yeah, yeah," I said. "Look Alex, I'll call you later. I need to make a phone call." I hung up.

It was raining as I came out, not hard, but enough to be unpleasant. And although I wasn't the only person to exit Wapping tube station, I felt as if I'd arrived in some post-apocalyptic ghost town of dark brick dockyard warehouses. I shuddered, consulted my A to Z, found my bearings, and strode off down Wapping Lane to find Dave Fells.

The building was easy enough to find, though the entrance took significantly longer. Eventually I found a door tucked round the back, and next to it an intercom with an array of a dozen or so buttons. I pressed the one marked 'Fells'. After a second or two the door buzzed. I let myself in.

I climbed four or five flights of concrete stairs until I got to the top. A large door was propped open with a fire extinguisher. I knocked, and peered inside.

"Hello?" I said, before venturing in a little further. The room was huge. Along one side dirty windows looked out onto the street below, the small grimy frames creating that authentic 'Victorian prison' look. Less prison-like, however, were the whitewashed walls, and filling the enormous space between them were huge rolls of paper, industrial-sized lights, and reflective umbrellas. All on stands. Then scattered amongst the professional paraphernalia were more mundane items: two calor gas heaters, an old leather sofa, a matching armchair, drawer units piled high with large padded envelopes, magazines, overflowing ashtrays, and an electric guitar.

"Yeah, but he's not exactly Hugh Heffner, is he?" said a male voice from around the corner created by the stair-well. The owner of the voice walked into view, a cordless phone wedged between his shoulder and ear whilst he used his hands to light a cigarette. He was taller and older than I'd expected, skinny to the point of being undernour-ished, but the ripped jeans and faded Iron Maiden t-shirt were somehow exactly what I'd envisaged. He saw me and beckoned me to come over. "Yeah, but John, with all due respect, mate," he said, wandering over to the sofa, "that is total bollocks, and once again you happen to be talking out of your arse." He picked up a package. "Yeah well, see what you can do, yeah? Ok mate. Yeah. Later." He tossed the phone on the sofa. "Sorry about that," he said, thrust-ing the package towards me. "There's one to come back." I hesitated. "You're not the courier?"

"No," I said. "Sorry."

"Oh."

"Jason Smith," I said, extending a hand. "We spoke on the phone?" There was a pause.

"Yeah?" asked Dave. I swallowed slightly, my hand still outstretched.

"I called you this morning? Wondered if you could spare me five minutes?"

"Right. Yeah, yeah," said Dave. He grabbed my hand and shook it enthusiastically. "Right, yeah. You're the guy who phoned."

"That's right," I said, "that's me!"

"Cool, yeah. Yeah, I remember. You work for Northern & Shell?"

"Er, no."

He let go of my hand. "Oh. Yeah well, probably just as well – they're all tossers over there."

"Right," I said.

"But we spoke yesterday, yeah?" he asked, taking a drag on his cigarette.

"Erm, no. This morning. Midday. Ish."

"Yeah? Cool. And you want to know what exactly?"

I swallowed again. "Well, about you, really. You know, the photography, how you got into it, and erm, how it's… working out for you, and how you, how you manage… to make a living…" My voice trailed off. I was beginning to wonder if I should make my excuses and leave.

"You're the *Teaze* guy!" he said enthusiastically. "You're the guy who wanted to know why *Teaze* wouldn't buy your pictures!"

"Yeah! Yes – yes, that's right," I admitted. He took another long drag on his cigarette.

"Yeah, well," he said, exhaling. "I'm not sure what I can tell you that I didn't say yesterday."

"This morning – and you didn't tell me anything, you just told me to 'pop by'."

"Yeah?" asked Dave. "I did?"

"And to bring a copy of the pictures with me."

"Yeah! I did. Yeah, yeah, it's all coming back to me."

I reached into my shoulder bag and took out an envelope. "Would you like to see them?" I asked.

"Yeah, sure," said Dave. He took the envelope and wandered further into the room. "Who at *Teaze* did you see?"

"Someone called Clare," I replied.

"Oh yeah? Yeah, Clare. She's a good girl," said Dave. "Amazing rack," he added wistfully.

"I wouldn't know. I spoke to her on the phone."

"Yeah? Why didn't you pay 'em a visit? They're only up the road."

"Oh, I live near Southend –"

"Yeah? Southend. Right. Gotcha."

"You think I should have visited them in person?"

"Wouldn't have done any harm," said Dave. He walked over to a white table, picked up the ashtray, and with the other arm swept the mountain of magazines and packages onto the floor. "Clare's great," he continued. "The rest of 'em are tossers." He flicked a switch under the corner of the table and the white Perspex surface flickered into illumination.

"Oh, sorry, I should have..." Dave slipped the contents out of the envelope."

"Oh. Yeah. Right. I see. What are these? Prints?"

"Yeah – yes! – Sort of. I printed them onto photographic paper."

"Yeah? Cool," said Dave, holding one up and peering at it closely. "You need a special printer for that?"

"No, just a normal printer."

"So where are the trannies?" he asked, leafing through the other pictures.

"Trannies? Oh – transparencies. No, I er, I shoot on digital."

"Yeah? Cool. I've got a digital – use it instead of a Polaroid these days. Not a bad toy. Clare said they'd take digital?"

"No."

"Right, yeah. Didn't think so. None of the mags do. Not yet, anyway. The tossers are still in the flippin' stone age. Save me a flamin' fortune if they did."

"So no one accepts digital?"

"None that I know of," breezed Dave, sliding the photos back into the envelope. "Mind you, it's been a while since I asked, yeah? I mean, one of these days I'll rock up and they'll say 'Sorry Dave, we don't accept trannies any more. Di'n't we tell ya? You got any digis?' The tossers."

The phone went. Dave took two large bounds towards the couch and picked up the receiver.

"'ello? John! So? Yeah? Yeah. Yeah? Yeah. Bollocks. Bollocks!" He dropped my envelope on the coffee table in front of the couch and walked away into a kitchen area. I looked around me at the piles of packages, and took advantage of Dave's turned back to peek into one of them. As I suspected, it contained sheets of large square transparencies. I stood up, put my hands in my jacket pockets and let out a sigh. No one accepts digital. Well, what did I expect? Clare had told me as much.

"Alright, well fuck you mate," said Dave. "Catch ya later, yeah? Ok." He dropped his head for a moment and then, throwing his arms in the air, shouted "Bollocks!" He dropped his arms to his sides again. "You fancy a brew?"

Dave Fells had been a glamour photographer for twenty years. Prior to that, he was a roadie for various heavy metal bands. He'd always had a passion for photography and when he wasn't photographing the bands, he turned his attention to the groupies.

"I sent a few sets into a magazine," said Dave as he lay back on the couch and lit another cigarette. "Pretty soon I was making more money out of photographing girls than I was lugging speakers." I looked at him from the armchair. Somehow I couldn't imagine Dave ever lugging anything heavier than his own body weight, which ruled out anything bigger than his camera and a flash gun. "Those were the good old days, yeah?" said Dave, blowing smoke rings.

"How so?" I asked.

"Not many of us doing it. Porn was still a dirty word, yeah? Only two or three real players in the market. Internet didn't exist. Nowadays any John with a camera thinks they can make the big time." I watched as the cogs turned in his mind. "No offence, yeah?" he said, jerking a look at me. I waved it away.

"Business not so good then?" I asked.

"Jesus, no! I mean, yeah, I'm still making a living, but not like I used to, yeah? If you want my advice, forget it."

"Really?" I asked, my heart sinking further.

"Not that there's anything wrong with your pictures," said Dave, swinging his legs round and sitting up. He grabbed the envelope from the coffee table, slid out my pictures, and flicked through them again. "They're good."

"Really?" I asked. "You think so?"

"Yeah, yeah – but that's the sad thing," he said.

"Sad?"

"Even if they were trannies *Teaze* probably wouldn't take them." I felt my pride pop like a bubble, and my bottom lip quiver.

"But... why?"

"They're going out of business," said Dave, plopping them back on the table.

"Out of business?"

"Well not the whole company," he continued, "But definitely that title. Haven't you noticed? These days they just re-print the softer images from sets that have already appeared in their regular top-shelf mags. Saves on production costs. Bloody internet again, yeah? Truth is there isn't a market for your old fashioned 'glamour'. Not now. Now when Joe public can get it all for free on his computer."

Out of business? I put a hand to my forehead to stop my head from spinning. It was like the Universe was already planning my next disaster before I'd even managed to recover from the current one!

"Anyway," continued Dave, unaware of my turmoil, "if you shoot onto digital then you must be selling your pictures to the internet, yeah?"

"I don't understand," I said. "What, you mean..."

"All those porn sites?" said Dave. "They've got to get their images from somewhere."

"Hang on, so..." but that's as far as I got. My brain was too busy experiencing the mental equivalent of noticing a small sign that says 'pull' on a door that I'd spent many months pushing against. All the time I'd spent trying to flog my work to magazines – magazines that I'd stopped buying years ago because an entire world of porn was available on the internet – and it had simply never occurred to me that the websites I frequented bought their images… from a guy like me.

"Shit!" said Dave, looking at his watch. "Shit, sorry man but I've got to go... yeah?"

"Oh, right," I said, standing up and extending my hand. Dave shook it. "Thanks for your time, I appreciate it."

"Hey, you're welcome," said Dave. "Sorry I couldn't be more help, yeah?"

"No – you've been great. Thanks."

"Well, you know, whatever, yeah?" said Dave.

"Yeah," I said in response, but I wasn't listening. All I could hear was Alex's voice in my head. He was right. For a bright bloke I could be a real bonehead. I took my mobile phone from my pocket and dialled his number.

"Sssho we've establisshhed you're a bonehead," slurred Alex.

"Yes, but that's not the point, is it!" I said.

"No," he said. "I mean, yes! It is! It is very much the point. You are a bonehead of the highest order, my friend, and that..." Alex waved a finger in front of me. "That deserves some sort of... badge!"

"Badge?"

"Yes! Like an award. It could say 'I am a real bonehead'." He nodded sagely, then tried to locate the pint in front of him. I shook my head.

"Ok, I'll get a badge," I said, "but in the meantime, what about the website thing?"

"Website thing?" said Alex. "What website thing?"

"About selling my work to websites!"

"I think," said Alex, "that you..." He looked at me, his eyes rolling slightly whilst he tried to focus.

"Yes?" I prompted.

"What was the question again?"

"How many have you had?"

"That wasn't the question."

"Maybe it's time we called it a day."

"Called what a day?"

"Alex, you've been drinking since eleven o'clock this morning."

"You say that," said Alex, waving his finger again, "like it's a bad thing." I grabbed his hand and slapped it back on the table.

"Should you even be drinking?" I asked. "What if Tina goes into labour?"

"She's the one having the baby. I can drink as much as I like."

"But she's probably relying on you to get her to the hospital!"

"She's not due for another three weeks," said Alex, now waving his half-filled pint in the air.

"What if the baby's early?"

"No son of mine would ever be early."

"What if it's a daughter?"

Alex paused for a moment whilst he considered the likelihood of this scenario. "Are you trying to get out of the next round?" he asked. I sighed. Again. "Then I guess there's nothing for it." He stood up, and half staggered, half fell backwards into a group of drinkers behind him. I intervened.

"Sorry about that," I said, addressing the group. "Mate, why don't you sit down?" I smiled at the people around me whilst Alex tried, and failed, to locate the stool with his bottom.

"Here, let me help," I said, dragging him off the floor and manhandling him into a sitting position. He nodded gratefully. Was another round a wise idea? If the tables were turned, would I want my best friend to get me another beer, or would I want him to put me on a train and send me home to my wife? My heavily pregnant wife? Who's relying on me to get her to the hospital?

I looked at my friend. The damage had already been done. If Tina did go into labour early, there was no way that Alex would be in any condition to help her. So what harm could another pint do? Really?

Chapter Twenty-One
Tuesday 6th April, 1999

Tina slapped both hands on the dashboard, dug her nails into the plastic, and started making a sound that could only be replicated by putting a chipmunk in a deep fat fryer. I glanced nervously in her direction. From all the puffing and wheezing and growling it was clear that something wasn't right. Worse still, I got the distinct impression that she blamed me entirely.

"Drive... faster," she snarled. I snapped my head back into the eyes forward position and put my foot down a little more. Then I grabbed the mobile phone from my lap and pressed the green button to redial Alex's number. I wedged the phone between my shoulder and my ear and prayed to whatever deity might be listening that Alex would answer.

Voicemail.

"Hey – mate – me again – just driving Tina to the hospital." I shot another glance at my passenger. "Really hope you're getting these messages – give me a call – Now!"

I'd been having a nice dream about working and living in an open-plan converted Wapping warehouse, – surrounded by soft boxes, reflectors and floodlights, my days an endless stream of photo shoots and beautiful ladies, one of whom might turn out to be... when, in the dream, my cordless telephone started to ring. As well as my mobile. And my camera. And the kettle.

I'd crawled out of my bed and half stomped, half staggered across the hall to my study. If unplugging the phone hadn't involved crawling under my desk amongst the cables and dust then that's what I would have done. Instead, I answered it and intended to give the caller a piece of my mind. Did they know what time it was? No? Neither did I! But whatever time it was I didn't appreciate being woken from possibly the best dream ever. And if they could just see their way to never calling here again…

The brief facts, conveyed to me by the hysterical screaming pregnant woman at the other end of the phone, were these: Tina was having contractions. She couldn't raise Alex on his mobile. She'd phoned the hospital. They'd told her to make her way in as soon as possible. And of all the people in the known universe, with a car, I was apparently the closest and the only one likely to be home. Or something like that. It was hard to pay attention when the only thought running through my mind was that if I'd sent Alex home when I'd had the chance, none of this would have had to involve me.

We pulled up outside the hospital and parked in one of the two spaces reserved for dropping off. I'd half hoped that Tina would get out of the car, thank me for the lift, maybe give me some petrol money and toddle off to give birth, but as she was still attempting to beat the Guinness World Record for rapid breathing I fetched her bags, then opened the passenger door and offered my hand.

"You're not serious!" barked Tina. "Do I look like I'm in any condition to walk?"

"I don't see what other option there is! I've got your bags, all you need to do –"

"Jason, I'm about to give birth!"

"Well, I can't bloody carry you!"

"Don't swear at me!"

"'Bloody' isn't swearing!"

"Jason –" but my attention was elsewhere. There, just by the entrance, completely unattended, was a wheelchair. Just sitting there. And not some pre-war NHS contraption either, but a gleaming padded wheelchair, complete with blanket.

"Wait here," I said. Two minutes later I had both bags slung over my shoulders and was wheeling Tina through the automatic doors – and God help anybody who happened to get in our way.

For a fleeting moment it felt like I was winning. Who would have thought that those afternoons accompanying Alex to this hospital would pay off? I knew exactly where the Maternity Ward was – all I had to do was hand Tina over to someone vaguely medical and I was free! The end was in sight. I barely noticed the pain in my shoulders from Tina's bags, or the throbbing in my arms as I wheeled her huge bulk ever onwards. I even managed to block out her grunting and whines as another contraction kicked in. And together we tore down the corridor towards the stairs.

Stairs?

In all my visits to St Anne's Hospital it had never occurred to me that it might be odd to put a department frequented by heavily pregnant women on the first floor! And, more to the point, that the lift wouldn't be right next to the fucking stairs where you'd expect it to be!

"Where's the lift?!" I asked the back of Tina's head. But no answer was forthcoming. I looked down at my normally vocal passenger who was gripping the arms of the chair like she might explode at any moment. "Tina?" She lifted her pillar-box red face, looked at me through eyes that were almost on stalks, and said nothing.

Which was when I saw an angel. My angel. Strolling towards us, clicking her fingers and swaying her hips to the rhythm in her head. I've never been more relieved to see anybody in my entire life.

She caught my eye, smiled, and then, seeing the desperation on my face and my ticking time bomb of a passenger, broke into a half run.

"Good afternoon, Mrs Cooke," Ria said as she came towards us, "and how are we today?" Tina shot her a look. "I'm having a baby – how the hell do you think I feel!" Ria nodded an acknowledgement. "Hello Jason," she said, flashing me another smile. "You look like you could do with some help."

"Yes! Please!" I blabbered.

"Here, let me," she said, slipping between me and the chair with a wink and a smile. "Mind yourself now." She placed a foot on the back wheel and spun the chair through one hundred and eighty degrees before heading back up the corridor. "Keep up now," said Ria over her shoulder. I stood for a moment in awe, then galloped off in pursuit.

Ria steered round obstacles, both moving and stationary, like the chair was on rails. And as I followed her round the corner I was just in time to see her take a short run, then lift herself off the ground to glide down the corridor behind her oblivious passenger. She looked over her shoulder, and winked – and just for a second or two time seemed to slow, allowing me to savour the moment, to drink in the majestic playfulness of her pose, to be seduced by the slender curves beneath her uniform.

Rubber-soled shoes touched the ground again, and as they did Ria brought the wheelchair to a skidding halt in front of a pair of lift doors.

"Nice wheels," she said as I caught up with her.

"Oh, I found it outside," I said, trying to ignore the traumatised look on Tina's face.

"Really?" said Ria, brushing a lock of flaming red hair out of her face. The lift doors opened and we got in. "And did you happen to notice the old boy standing on the corner? Having a cigarette?" She selected the first floor and the lift doors closed on us.

"Sorry?" I asked.

"Dressed in his pyjamas and a dressing gown?"

"No..." I said.

"Mr Morley," said Ria, nodding. "It's his wheelchair."

"Oh, crap," I said, squeezing my eyes closed.

"Don't worry," said Ria, waving my concern away. "I'll take it back later. What about Mr Cooke? Is he on his way?" The lift doors opened. I reached into my pocket and took out my mobile phone.

"Oh! Er, yes. Yes! I'm sure he won't be too long." I clutched the phone to my ear. He'd better bloody not, because if Tina didn't kill him I definitely would. Voicemail again. I hung up.

"You can't go any further, I'm afraid," said Ria, coming to a halt by a set of doors and a reception desk. Through a window a large lady glanced up at us, then back at her computer. "Beyond this point it's mothers-to-be and family only."

"Oh, right," I said.

"We can take those bags," said Ria. "I'm sure Mrs Cooke won't mind holding them for a moment." Tina winced, but Ria ignored her and piled the two bags on her lap.

"Halex," said Tina.

"Right, well, I'll be off then. Hope everything goes alright," I said to Tina.

"Halex!" she said again.

"Sorry?"

Tina puffed some more. "Alex!"

"Yes, I'm sure he's on his way," I reassured her.

"Go... get... Alex!"

"I think, Jason," said Ria, getting behind the wheelchair and backing towards the door, "Mrs Cooke would like you to find the father-to-be." The door buzzed and Ria kicked it open with her foot. "If that wouldn't be too much trouble." I looked at Tina, then back at Ria.

"Ok," I said. "No, no trouble at all. I'll go and get him!"

"Ok then," said Ria. Tina stared at me, her eyes ready to pop out of her head.

"Right then," I said. "I'll... Right."

"You can't park here, mate."

"Yeah – I'm just moving it."

"You're lucky I haven't clamped ya."

"Ok, thanks – I'm moving it now."

"I'm just saying, is all."

"Ok. Thanks. Don't let me keep you." I got in the car and sat there for a second, the panic beginning to rise in my throat again. I took out my phone and redialled. It rang. And rang. "Answer, goddamn it!" And then-

The parking attendant tapped on the glass. I waved a hand at him frantically as I pressed the phone to my ear. It wasn't ringing any more, but I couldn't hear anyone. Just the sound of... What was that?

"Mate, I'm going to have to call security if –" I slapped my free hand to my other ear to block out the parking attendant, and concentrated. The sound came into focus. The sound of an announcer calling out station names against the background noise of a train. I hung up the call, dropped the phone into my lap, and turned the ignition.

Thirty minutes later, having driven round aimlessly, and eventually resorted to asking someone, I found the nearest station – less than a mile from the hospital – and there was Alex, standing at the taxi rank. I pulled up. Alex opened the door and slid into the passenger seat.

"Queens Han – Hanne – zzz hos... hospital," he said, without even looking at me. I frowned.

"Hi," I said. Alex turned, looked at me, and almost leapt out of his skin.

"Mate?!"

"What?"

"Isshh thish... is thish your car?"

"Of course it is!" I said with a frown. Alex looked around; he even opened the glove compartment.

"You're right!" declared Alex. "But... you don't have..." He held a partially clenched hand in front of his mouth. "Calling all cars," he burbled. I sighed.

"How many have you had?" I asked.

"Not that many," said Alex defensively.

"What time did you start drinking?"

"What day is it today?"

"Tuesday!"

Alex frowned. "Already?" he asked.

"Have you been home since I saw you last?" Alex shook his head, slowly and deliberately, like he was thinking very carefully about the movement. "Then where the hell did you sleep last night?"

He shrugged. "The office."

"You slept at your desk!?" I shook my head, put the car into gear, and pulled out.

Alex didn't say another word. Once we got to the hospital he merely trailed after me like an institutionalised convict following his jailer. I led him to the reception desk where I'd left Ria and Tina, and handed him over to the staff there.

"Right then," I said, slapping him on the shoulder. "Best of luck, mate." Alex lifted his head slightly and looked at me through bloodshot eyes. Somehow in the past thirty minutes he'd aged as many years. The door buzzed, and Alex walked through, letting it swing closed behind him.

I let out a long weary sigh, passed my fingers through my hair, scratched at my scalp and rubbed my aching tired eyes with my palms. I walked over to the water cooler, poured myself a plastic cup of water, and took a moment to quench my thirst.

Just as I started to pour myself a second cup the door behind me buzzed again and there was Alex, being guided back into the waiting area by a slightly ruffled-looking Ria.

"Hello, Jason," said Ria, straightening her punky hair with one hand and holding Alex's shoulder with the other. "I see you found our Mr Cooke. I wonder, would you mind staying out here with him for a little while?" She shot a sideways glance at Alex. "Just until he's sobered up."

"Cheese and tomato," I said, returning to the waiting area armed with refreshments. "They didn't have anything with bacon in it. And I got you another can of Coke."

Alex took the drink. "What about ham?" he asked.

"No ham, no bacon, no pig-based sandwich products of any description."

"Chicken?"

"Just eat it!" He took the sandwich. I sat down next to him and started tucking into my own sad excuse for an evening meal. "How's Tina doing?" I asked.

"Dunno," said Alex after a mouthful or two. I turned to my friend and watched as he devoured the food, seemingly oblivious to my annoyance.

"Did you even ask?"

"They'll come and get me if they need me," he said.

I shook my head.

"You can leave if you want," said Alex without even a sideways glance.

I let out a single humourless laugh. "Your wife would never forgive me." Alex said nothing. Just continued to stuff the sandwich into his mouth like it was the first solid food he had eaten in over twenty-four hours – which it probably was. He picked up the can from the chair next to him, popped the lid, and poured the contents down his throat. I looked down at the partially-eaten food in my hands and put it to one side.

"So? That photographer guy," said Alex.

"What about him?" I asked.

Alex shrugged. "Was he right?"

I frowned. "About what?"

"'Bout selling your stuff to porn sites?"

My frown deepened. "How can you possibly remember that? You never remember anything I tell you – particularly after a few beers – and last night you could barely stand up!"

Alex shrugged again. "So can you?"

"When exactly would I have had the time to find out?! I left you shortly before the pubs closed and was rudely awoken by your wife around midday! And since then I've spent the entire day ferrying one or other of you to this hospital!"

"Yeah, but," said Alex, finishing the can of drink and throwing it across the waiting area into the bin opposite, "an idea like that. You would have gone on the internet the moment you got home. Doesn't matter what time of the morning it was." I tucked one arm under the other and gnawed at a thumbnail whilst I considered my reply. It annoyed me that Alex knew me so well.

"So?" said Alex.

"Yes – I can sell my work to websites. In fact, there's an entire industry out there doing just that." I shuffled around in my seat. "There are these other websites – they call themselves 'content providers' – that act as middlemen between photographers and people who build porn sites. They're like porn wholesalers."

"The porn websites buy their stuff from other websites?" asked Alex.

"Yep."

"That's weird." I went back to chewing on my fingers.

"So? Are you gonna do that?" asked Alex after a long pause.

"Dunno," I said. "Probably not."

"Why?"

"Because they pay next to nothing, ok?!" I blurted out. I took a deep breath. "The going rate appears to be fifteen to twenty dollars per set," I said as calmly as I could.

"Dollars?" asked Alex.

"All the content providers work in dollars." I let out a long sigh. "And they all take fifty percent in commission. So if they sell a set of my photos for twenty dollars, they'll send me a cheque for ten, which, after my bank has converted it to sterling and charged me for the privilege, leaves me with a fiver. Maybe." I could see Alex's frown shift from one of grumpy disinterest to one of dawning realisation.

"How much do you pay the models?" he asked. I rolled my eyes and let out another sigh.

"Twenty quid an hour."

"And how many –"

"Mate, I've already done the sums! I'd have to sell two hundred sets per month, at the very least, to make anything approaching a living. Which might be possible were I Dave Fells with a lifetime of amazing photographs just lying around waiting to be uploaded – but I'm not."

Alex's frown didn't change. "How many sets have you got?" he asked.

"Maybe a dozen." Alex nodded. "So unless you have another blank cheque in your wallet – and a considerable amount of spare cash – my career in glamour photography," I paused to take a breath, "is over."

It was the first time I'd admitted it to myself. I let out another long sigh and slumped forward, my arms resting on my knees.

"So that's it then," said Alex.

"You told me months ago to forget it," I said, running my fingers through my hair. "I should have listened to you."

"Yeah, but I was kinda hoping you'd prove me wrong," admitted Alex. I turned to look at my friend, and managed to summon a sad half-smile.

"Cheers," I said. "So was I. But like all my ideas, it was completely crud!" Alex curled his lip and shook his head slightly.

"Don't beat yourself up," he said, slapping me on the shoulder. "Few people get to have their dream job."

"Yeah, but it wasn't even 'my dream job'!"

"Of course it was," said Alex.

I sat up. "No – Alex, don't get me wrong, it's a lot of fun – the shoots and everything. It definitely knocks writing computer code into a cocked hat. But I wasn't trying to become the next David Bailey, or satisfy my inner muse, or find 'my calling'. I just wanted to pay the bills, and work in a profession where… you know… I might meet… well, the point was to find 'her'."

Alex looked at me. "Who?"

"Her!"

"Who's 'her'?"

"The woman in the photograph! My woman! My perfect woman!" Alex blinked, and in the time it took to do so his sympathy evaporated.

"This whole thing was so you could get laid?" he asked.

"No – not laid, Alex – increase my chances of –"

"Of getting your end away! Mate, if all you wanted was a shag, there were smarter things to do with that grand I gave you!"

"You just don't get it, do you?"

"I get that you're an idiot!"

"I'm the idiot?!"

"That's what I said."

"Says the man stinking of booze and doing everything he can to ignore the fact that his wife is giving birth on the other side of the wall!"

"I'm not ignoring it," said Alex, folding his arms.

"Really? Because I'm pretty sure if I wasn't here to stop you, you'd be propping up the bar of the nearest pub!"

"You don't know that," he growled.

"I know you've been drunk for the past forty-eight hours!"

"I'm not drunk."

"You didn't even recognise me when I picked you up from the station!"

"That was hours ago!"

"Oh! And you're sober now?"

"Yes."

"Then why are you still sitting here talking to me when you should be next door with Tina?"

"Fine!" said Alex, getting to his feet. I shifted in my seat ready to wrestle him to the ground if he took one step towards the lift, but instead he walked to the reception desk and a few seconds later the door buzzed to let him through to the maternity ward.

I stayed put, half expecting Alex to come back when he thought I'd gone, half hoping that Ria would bring him back so I could see her. But the door never buzzed, and I sat in the waiting area like it was my own private purgatory, not knowing whether I should stay or go, whether Alex and I were still friends, and who was the bigger idiot.

"Wake up, Mr Photographer," said a familiar voice as someone gently shook my shoulder. I opened my eyes to see Ria's smiling face, her lovely brown eyes full of kindness and compassion as she crouched over me.

"Oh, hi. What time is it?" I blinked a few times and then sat up.

"Three-ish," she replied, sliding into the seat next to me.

"Three am?"

"Yes."

I rubbed my eyes. "My God. It feels like I've been here forever. Has she had the baby?"

"Little while ago. I was just on my way home. But you're an uncle, Mr Photographer. You're Uncle Photographer." She poked me in the ribs with a slender finger.

"You don't know if, if Alex –"

"Mr Cooke's with his son," she said.

"It was a boy? Cool."

"Would you like to meet him?" asked Ria.

"Alex?"

She smiled. "The baby."

"Oh," I said. "Can I? Yes. Why not?"

Ria took me through the security door, past a nurses' station and along quiet corridors into a room that seemed to be a cross between a dedicated baby service area – with scales, tables, towels and tubes, charts and diagrams – and a lounge. Curled up on a sofa lay a dishevelled Tina, sound asleep, whilst in the neighbouring armchair sat an equally comatose Alex, his head right back, his mouth wide open. Between them stood a unit with dials and readouts and buttons and a clear plastic box about the size of a milk crate, and in it – doing his darndest to kick his way out of a blue mini-jumpsuit and sporting a matching woolly hat – was a miniature version of Alex. His crumpled grumpy little face betrayed a raging desire for a pair of engorged breasts and a satisfying beverage. Yearnings that I had no doubts would stay with him for the rest of his life.

"He's tiny," I whispered to Ria.

"Actually he's a pretty good size given that he's three weeks premature."

"Right. Yeah. Did that make things complicated?"

"Nah," she said, with a wiggle of her cute button nose. "All in a day's work."

"Yeah," I said. "I suppose so."

"Come on, Mr Photographer," she said, taking my arm, "let's leave this family to rest. You can walk me to my car."

"Right," I said with a tinge of disappointment. "Of course." I looked at Alex. I wanted to wake him. Let him know how proud I was. Ask him if we were alright. I looked around for something to write a note with, but there was nothing. So instead I picked up a small fluffy yellow duck – similar to the one Alex had sat on all those weeks earlier – and laid it gently in his lap.

"I don't know how you do it," I said as we got to the lift. "The hours, the stress – I'd be a basket case."

"You get used to it," she said. "Bit different from what you do, though." She gave me a wink, and that smile.

"Er, yeah," I said pressing the lift call button, "yeah." We exchanged more smiles. Then I shuffled on the spot, or admired my shoes, suddenly aware that my best friend's hospital dramas had been the only thing keeping this girl in my life, and that despite her rugby-playing boyfriend I really didn't want to let her go. Not this time. Possibly not ever.

"Must be fun," she said, the smile broadening. "Glamour photography."

"Erm, yes. Yes, it is. Fun."

Three, maybe four minutes. That's all I had – the time it would take us to get from here to the car park. And if I didn't come up with something, some plan, some devious strategy, to see Ria again, regularly, or even just the once, then she'd get in her car and disappear from my life – this time for good.

"I'll bet," said Ria. The lift doors opened and we stepped inside. As the doors closed again I got the uncomfortable feeling that I was missing something obvious, an answer to my dilemma, a way to see Ria. Which was when she turned to me and said, "So Mr Photographer, just how does a girl go about getting in front of your camera?"

Chapter Twenty-Two
Friday 9th April, 1999

Just over forty-eight hours after Baby Alex entered the
world, I sat on my bed and cradled my camera in my
hands. That had been the best shoot – ever. True, with
nowhere to sell my work my days as a glamour photographer
were officially over. And true, the girl had been completely
incapable of holding a pose or staying still for more than a
second. And though she'd brought some great outfits – one
outfit in particular – much of the time she'd either been
giggling, taking the mickey out of me, or just out-and-out
flirting. Despite this, of all the shoots I'd ever done, none
had shown as much potential.

Girlfriend potential.

I heard the sound of the toilet flush, and a few moments
later the bathroom door opened.

"You alright?" asked Ria as she brushed her gloriously
red hair.

"Yeah," I said, shaking myself back into the here and
now. "Yeah."

"So that was fun!"

"Good!" I said, adding a smile.

"More difficult than I imagined," said Ria. "Who would
have thought taking your clothes off could be hard work!"

"Right," I said. I didn't know what to add to that.

"So are you going to buy me a drink then?" asked Ria.

"What, now!? Today?" I asked, choking on the words.
"Why not?"

"Ok – yeah, sure! That would be – nice."

"Good," she said, grabbing the bag on the bed and dragging it towards her. "Just let me get my stuff together."

"Oh, wait," I said as she stuffed assorted underwear into the oversized handbag, "don't forget this." I took down the nurse's uniform that had been hanging on the back of the door and handed it to her.

"Oh, thanks!" said Ria, taking it from me with a smile. "Now that would have been hard to explain."

"Cheers," said Ria as I returned to the table with our drinks. "So, Mr Photographer, what happens next?"

'Next' wasn't a concept I'd even considered. I was still getting my head around 'now'. In the past few hours we'd gone from willing and unwilling participants on Alex's journey into fatherhood to photographer and model, and now circumstances suggested we were having what looked very much like a 'first date'. And other than being there as events unfolded, none of it had been down to me.

"Have I passed the audition? Are you going to turn me into a top glamour model? How long before the surgeons in the east wing are giving me knowing looks and pinning my picture in their lockers?" My mouthful of Guinness developed second thoughts about its journey to my stomach and decided instead to hang about in my throat. I coughed, and thumped my chest. "You ok?" asked Ria, reaching forward to touch my arm. "Should I call for a nurse?" I gave her a weak smile, and forced the Guinness down.

So it wasn't a date. We were still photographer and model. Which meant – given that my days of glamour photography had died hours before Baby Alex had been born

– that there wasn't a 'next'. Suddenly the shoot didn't seem as promising as I'd hoped, and my true motives for agreeing to photograph her less than pure.

"Ok, well, um. The thing is..." I glanced at the pub around us. Its tired peeling wallpaper. The faded carpet. The grimy tables. Even the bar staff had a weariness that I hadn't noticed before.

"What's wrong?" asked Ria, tipping her head to one side. "Has this something to do with that conversation you had with Mr Cooke?"

I lifted my head. "Conversation?"

"The one where he handed you the cheque!"

"Ah. Yes – I suppose it does."

"So? Did you follow his advice? Did you find another photographer?" I looked into her eyes. Those almond, oriental-shaped eyes. Her irises like miniature mugs of hot chocolate, flecked with caramel and dark chocolate shavings, all framed with long dark luxurious lashes. I really liked those eyes. Ria pulled a face, and stuck out her tongue.

I sighed. "I went to visit a photographer in East London."

"And?"

I shrugged. "He basically told me there was no way I'd ever sell my pictures."

Ria sat upright, the warmth evaporating from her face. "So all that we just did was a waste of time?" She adjusted her cardigan, pulling it around her.

"No! No, not at all," I said, scrabbling with my thoughts, trying to find a way to salvage the situation. "Not a total – I mean, you wanted... and I..." Ria's expression didn't change. I swallowed. "There is one thing, but I've kind of dismissed it."

"What?"

"I could try selling my pictures via content providers." Ria frowned. "They're like photo libraries. Providing images to websites. A bit like –"

"Greengrocers," said Ria.

"Green... grocers?" I asked, not entirely certain that I'd heard her correctly.

"Yes," said Ria, brightening, the rouge returning to her cheeks, the freckles on her nose becoming more obvious. "You're the farmer, your pictures are the carrots, and these content people are like greengrocers!"

"Well, I suppose –"

She put both arms on the table and leant forward. "It sounds like the perfect arrangement," she said. "So what's the problem?"

"Well, um, they don't pay very much. In fact, it's pretty pitiful." Ria didn't move. I took a breath. "It's only worthwhile if you have a large back catalogue of –"

"Carrots!"

"Erm. Yes. But the point is –"

"Or tomatoes."

"I suppose so. But you see –"

"Maybe some turnips, and leeks, and onions!" Ria smiled and batted her eyelids at me. Cute though she was, the conversation was depressing.

"Turnips?" I asked.

"Or whatever."

"Right, ok –" Ria went to add another vegetable to her comprehensive list but I raised a hand, "– it's still a truck load of veg!" Ria's mouth snapped closed. "Sorry," I said, bringing my hands to my face and rubbing my eyes.

"That's ok," said Ria. "I get it."

"You do?"

"You don't have many carrots."

"No. And unfortunately I can't afford to... *grow,* any more."

"Why not?" she asked, leaning forward some more until our noses were within inches of each other. I could have kissed her then – if the mood had been better.

"Because models cost money," I said after a moment. Ria thumped me in the arm.

"Ow! What was that for?!"

"Being a dummy!"

"What? How?"

"What you need," she said, her calm nurse persona taking control, "is a business partner."

"I do?" I said, rubbing my arm.

"Sure," she said. "You need to build up your stock without incurring losses."

I blinked. "And how am I going to do that?" I asked

"With me, dumbo!"

"With you?"

"Here's what I'm thinking: Me and you go into business. We create lots and lots of carrots. Then we send them to the greengrocer and split the profits fifty fifty. Ta daa!" She threw her arms in the air like a magician's assistant on opening night. I brought my hand to my chin and considered the idea for a millisecond or two, though I didn't need all that time to know it was a completely loony idea. Sure, Ria had eliminated my costs, but a partnership would effectively double the number of sets I – we – would need to sell to make any kind of living. If two hundred sets a month seemed unrealistic, four hundred was impossible. "Come on," said Ria, prodding me with a finger. "You know it makes sense." She stopped prodding. I looked at where her finger had been and then into her face, tracing the outline of her cheek with my eyes.

A joint venture would involve a great deal of time in Ria's company.

That was an extremely attractive prospect.

Despite the lunacy of the numbers involved, the opportunity to see her regularly was almost impossible to pass up.

I shook my head. No. I couldn't agree to a business proposition that I knew had no chance of success, just to be close to her. That would be against my Good Guy principles. It would also be torture.

"It's a nice idea," I said to Ria, "but..."

"But what?" She cocked her head on one side.

"I just don't see how we'd never be able to sell enough pictures."

"What do you mean, enough?"

"Enough. To make a living. It's just not possible."

Ria blinked. "But I'm not trying to make a living!" she said with a laugh. She looked at me, and then laughed again.

"Well, I am!" I said.

"Oh," said Ria, pulling a face. "Sorry. But haven't you got a day job or something?"

"This is the day job!" I exclaimed. "Or it was."

"Really? I thought you'd be an accountant, or something."

"An accountant! You think I'm an accountant!"

Ria reached forward to touch my arm. "Of course I don't think you're an accountant! You're a photographer – of glamorous ladies! That's very cool – that's the real you. But everyone needs a day job. Take Superman, for instance. Saving the world doesn't pay the electric! That's why he's a reporter for the *Daily Bugle*." She took her hand away and picked up her drink.

"Planet," I said.

"Sorry?"

"Superman's a reporter for the *Daily Planet.*"

She took a sip. "Whatever. He's a reporter, I'm a nurse – but it's not who we really are."

"You're not a nurse?"

"Only to pay the bills! Dance is where my heart is. People are rarely the person they pretend to be between the hours of nine to five." She took another sip of her drink, then placed it back on the table and ran a slender finger slowly round the rim. I watched, transfixed, until the finger stopped moving. I lifted my eyes to look into hers. "You, Mr Photographer, need a day job, then you and I can grow some carrots."

I took a breath. "It's just..." I said, but got no further. Those lovely brown eyes, that freckled nose and those soft pink lips. Barely an hour earlier I'd watched her undress whilst she teased and flirted with me. Two days earlier I'd marvelled at the wonder of new life whilst she stood so near I could have closed my hand around hers. The day before she'd slipped between me and a wheelchair, trying and failing not to brush against me. And a few days earlier she'd gently dabbed at my cuts and started to patch up more than my physical wounds. Why was I trying to talk myself out of this?

"Ok," I said. "Let's do it."

"They're just changing the barrel," said Alex, returning to our table. I said nothing. Just stared at my friend and hoped that he'd burst into flames or be struck by lightning.

"What?" he asked after a moment.

"'Gary'!?" I said.

Alex shrugged. "We had to call him something."

"Yes, but 'Gary'!"

"What's wrong with 'Gary'?"

"You know how I feel about the name Gary!"

Alex shifted in his seat, and continued to avoid eye contact. "Oh for fuck's sake," he said. "It's only a name."

"It's the worst name in the whole bloody universe!"

"Well pardon me if we didn't check with you first, mate!"

"Seriously! What were you thinking?"

"I wasn't thinking anything," said Alex. "Tina suggested it and I agreed."

I leant forward. "Why?"

"Because I did, ok?"

"Couldn't you have thought of another name?"

"Like what?"

"Like anything! John, Paul, George, Ringo, Eric, Sebastian –"

"Oh, shut up."

"– Bert, Stuart, Peter, Phillip, Eric –"

"You've said Eric."

"Any bloody name apart from flippin' Gary!"

Alex looked at me. "Look! I came home. Tina said we ought to name him Gary. I said 'fine'."

"You said 'fine'?"

"It was either that or stand there and have a long discussion about it!" He sighed, then pulled his tie loose and undid his top button. I shook my head and sat back in my chair.

"How come you're working today?" I asked.

"Why wouldn't I be?" asked Alex.

"Shouldn't you be on paternity leave?"

Alex looked over at the wall. "I said I'd take it later."

"Later?"

"Yeah. In a few weeks."

"You can do that?" I asked, my eyes narrowing.

"HR said it would be ok. We're busy, so it worked out well for everyone."

"But shouldn't you be – you know – helping, or something?" Alex let out an impatient huff.

"Tina's mum has moved in for a couple of days. They don't need me." He reached into his jacket pocket and pulled out his phone.

"Who are you calling?"

"Wilson. Find out where the hell he is." Then something caught Alex's eye. "Thank Christ – he's here." He raised a hand, and I turned to see a tall wiry man in a long dark raincoat striding towards us.

"How about the first week in May?" suggested Wilson, staring at his Psion organiser whilst sipping his second pint. Alex shot me a sideways look that plainly said, "Don't fuck this up." I swallowed hard. This was it. I was about to re-enter the world of full time employment. No more getting up at midday. No more going to bed at four in the morning. And no more glamour photography. At least, not on a full-time basis. Not as a means of supporting myself. Not that it ever had. Still, I'd always hoped. And now I was about to stamp on that hope, crush it into the ground and resign myself to the drudgery of the nine to five. It felt like a death sentence, and my stomach churned at the very thought.

And then I thought about Ria, her eyes, and our deal. "The dream was never the job," I'd said to Alex, "the dream was to find 'her'." This wasn't a death sentence. It was just a day job.

"Whatever works for you," I said.

"Hi," said Ria as I opened the door. "Ready to grow some carrots?"

Sunlight poured through the windows, filling the room with warmth and happiness. Ria knelt on the bed, hips swaying gently from side to side to the music in her head as she started to unbutton her top. I shifted position to get a better angle. The photographer inside me needed to move backwards to get her all in. I ignored him, and moved closer.

"So how come you don't have a girlfriend, Jason?" asked Ria as she flashed me a smouldering glance over a bare, freckled shoulder.

"Is it that obvious?" I asked, trying to keep up with the speed at which she changed pose.

"Well, you've never mentioned anyone. And if you did have a girlfriend it would be a very special lady who'd let you photograph other women." She arched her back and let the short sleeved shirt slide down her arms. Then she tossed the shirt to one side, wrapped her arms across her chest, and gave me the schoolgirl pouty look through her fringe. I fumbled with the camera. "And there's a distinct lack of anything more interesting than a toothbrush and a bar of soap in your bathroom," she continued, dropping forward onto her forearms and flicking her hips into the air so that the short plaid skirt barely covered her bottom. She arched an eyebrow. "Oh, and any girlfriend worth their salt would have thrown out that old t-shirt years ago," she said with a wink.

"Oh Jason, that's wonderful news!"

"It's just a job, Mum," I said, cradling the phone under one ear and turning back to the computer.

"Oh Jason, how can you say that after all this time? Still, at least all those months of job searching and interviews paid off – you must be so pleased!"

"Er, yes," I said, moving my mouse around the screen. "Yes. Delighted." I clicked the button labelled 'transfer selected', then tipped my head on one side whilst I studied the images on the screen.

"Jason?"

"Yes – still here – I couldn't be any..." I squeezed my eyes closed, "happier."

"Well, I don't mind telling you how worried we all were. I was only telling your father the other night... You're not typing, are you?"

"No," I said, "not typing." I clicked another button.

"So when do you start?"

"Couple of weeks," I said.

"Why the delay? What on earth are you going to do in the meantime?"

"Oh, I'll think of something," I said, basking in the glorious images of Ria all over my screen.

Ria pulled the t-shirt over her head and tossed it in the air. It landed over the kettle. Then she put her hands on her hips and gave me that wink. I took the picture, and gave a contented sigh.

"Tell me more about Liz." I sighed again, though far less contentedly this time. I'd spent much of the previous week fending off questions about previous relationships and ex-girlfriends, and yet here we were again. There was a fleeting moment when I considered deflecting all this Liz-talk by asking about her sneezy boyfriend, whether he'd got over his cold, and why he didn't seem to mind that his girlfriend had spent the last three Fridays in my company and in various states of undress. But the last thing I wanted to hear about was his rugged rugby-playing manliness. What a great salsa dancer he was. How he was probably a fireman when he wasn't scoring tries for England. I didn't even want to know his name. In fact the longer we went without mentioning him the easier it was to pretend he didn't exist at all.

"You don't want to know about Liz," I said, crouching down on the floor and looking up at her. Ria turned her back to me, placed both hands on the worktop, and did a salsa sway with her hips.

"But you can tell a lot about a person from their partners and ex-partners," she said.

"Liz wasn't really a partner," I said, lying on the floor to get a more dramatic angle.

"Oh please," said Ria, hooking her thumbs into the side of her knickers. "You were with her for three years. Tell me why you broke up again?"

"Three ties?"

"Of course three ties!" said Sian, dumping them into my arms on top of the half dozen shirts she'd just picked off the shelves.

"But why can't I just wear the same tie every day?" I asked, following her through the islands of suits and shirts.

"Don't be stupid, Jason," she said. "Come on, you need trousers."

"Thanks for offering to do this," I said as I watched Sian flick quickly through a rack of grey slacks.

"No problem," she said, without even looking up. "It was nice to hear from you – I was beginning to wonder if I ever would. Though I can't believe it's taken you nine months to get another job! What on earth have you been doing in the meantime?"

"Oh," I said, "nothing much."

I stood over Ria and looked down at her as she lay on the rug. She stared up at me, one arm resting above her head, the other draped across her chest. Then slowly she gave me a soft, coy smile. For a fleeting moment I wondered what she would do if I put the camera to one side, knelt astride her, and kissed those lips. I shook that dangerous thought out of my head, stepped to one side, and sat on the floor next to her.

"So," said Ria, rolling onto her side to face me. "Why did you break up with Liz again?" I sighed.

"I told you last week," I said.

"Actually, you didn't." Ria hooked a finger into the side of her thong and teased it down her thigh. I moved in for a close up. "Did she uncover your secret photography ambition?" She winked.

"You really want to know about the break up?" I whined.

"No – just what brought it about."

"Nothing. It just happened." She rolled onto her other side and faced the wall, and I shuffled backwards to get as much of her as possible into the frame. If only it were as easy to get her in my life.

"There must have been some sort of catalyst though?" asked Ria. "Something that upset the status quo?"

"No," I lied. "No catalyst."

The receptionist threw me one of her "he shouldn't be much longer" looks. I acknowledged it with an awkward smile, and returned to watching the steady stream of people walk through the rotating glass doors, and stand in front of the lifts. Sometimes they hedged their bets and stood between the lifts, glancing quickly from one to the other. Other times they took a gamble and stood confidently in front of a set of doors, radiating the aura of someone who is at one with the building, until the other doors opened and the illusion was shattered. It took me a moment to recognise Glynn Wilson as he walked out of the lift and strode in my direction.

"Jason," he said. "Sorry to keep you. Welcome aboard."

There's something wrong with me. I realise that now. I'm not wired properly. Other guys watch a woman undress, and their small minds empty with an inaudible flush, leaving nothing but the stench of dark, carnal thoughts, their only instinct to satisfy those desires. But my own lust is competing with a force far greater. Something gets switched on – like a generator – and great arcs of surging, blistering power reach out from my heart like tendrils of light, touching every part of me until my entire being is so supercharged I feel like I might explode.

Ria moved around in the foamy waters and, with all the grace of a ballerina, extended a long leg high into the air, pointing her foot skywards. I watched as the bubbles succumbed to the effects of gravity and moved along her flawless skin.

For the fourth week running my head was full of poetry. Other men might grunt and mutter words that they'd probably never say out loud, but I wanted Ria to bathe in the contents of my mind, feel what I felt, share in all the wild, crazy, dangerous ideas between my ears.

"What was wrong with Liz?" asked Ria, squeezing a soapy sponge against her thigh. I took a deep breath and prepared to defend myself against today's onslaught of questions.

"There wasn't anything wrong – we just weren't right for each other."

"How so?"

"Look – there are two types of girl in this universe. There are girls like Liz and then there are... others. I happen to prefer 'the others'."

"And these 'others' – do they have a collective name?" she asked.

"Let's say they're the Kylies."

"Aha. Kylie. And what are the Kylies like?"

"They're... different."

"In what way?"

"Sort of... you know."

"I don't think I do," she said, her eyes widening playfully.

"It doesn't matter," I said. Ria did her eyebrow raising thing. Then slowly she moved around in the bath, very deliberately covering her nakedness, whilst at the same time drawing my attention to it until I really couldn't think about anything else.

"So Jason," she asked, "would you say I'm a Liz, or a Kylie?" I swallowed.

"You're definitely a Kylie," I said.

Nine am. Monday morning.

It starts with the shuffle. The shuffle of skirts, suits, shirts and shoes. The shuffle of inevitability.

Then other noises join the din, until you can barely hear yourself think above the ring of phones, the hiss of air conditioning, the hum of computers, the rumble of photocopiers, the jarring ripple of hysterical laughter, and the hustle and bustle of a world made of plastic.

Plastic binders. Plastic cups. Plastic smiles.

A plastic world populated by secretaries and supervisors. Meetings and managers. Colleagues and co-workers. People you like. People you don't. All asking a never-ending series of meaningless questions.

Who's responsible?

What's our objective?

How many man hours?

When will it all end?

Y2K.

Then, not a moment too soon, five o'clock saves us.

The day job draws to a close.

And we can all go back to being Superman.

"How many carrots do we have now?" asked Ria as I handed her a mug. She took it with both hands, causing her towel to loosen significantly. I sat on the edge of the bed, and though my eyes were waiting for the towel to give up the job of preserving Ria's modesty, my mind was actually elsewhere, dominated by one thought. The same thought that I'd spent the past few weeks trying to suppress.

Kiss her.

"Well?" Ria smiled. Always that smile. I'd cross oceans for that smile. Kill for that smile. Do anything just to...

Kiss her.

"Let's see," I said. "Six consecutive weeks, four or five hours of shooting each week – less the time we spend just chatting, of course – and last week we didn't come back from the pub after lunch, so probably twenty five, maybe thirty sets?"

"Bags of carrots," corrected Ria. I wanted to smile, but it just wouldn't come.

"What's wrong?" she asked.

"Nothing," I lied, forcing the corners of my mouth upwards. Had it been six weeks? Six weeks of feeling like this – falling like this. Six weeks of completely failing to –

Kiss her.

"Ria –" I said.

"So who is Kylie really?" she asked.

"Sorry?"

"Well I seriously doubt that you've met the actual Kylie, so I suspect, Mr Secretive Photographer, that when you talk of 'Kylies' you really mean someone else. Who is she?"

I shook my head and picked up my mug. "Have you ever considered a career in psychology?"

"Yes, but it didn't come with a man-magnet uniform. So?"

"She's... nobody."

"Interesting choice of words!"

"Why?"

"To be a nobody, she has to be somebody!"

I thought about this for a moment. "No, that's not..." But Ria continued to look at me over the rim of her mug as she sipped at her tea. I shook my head. What the hell. If she wasn't going to let me talk about us at least it made a change not to be talking about Liz.

"There was this girl," I said.

"Oo, now we're getting somewhere." Ria was bristling with excitement. "Name, please."

"Melanie. Melanie Jackson."

"And what happened between you and Miss Jackson?" asked Ria.

"Nothing," I replied.

"Come on!"

"No, really – nothing ever happened. That was kind of the problem."

Ria watched me for a few seconds. "And when was the last time you saw Melanie?"

I put down my tea, and told her.

Chapter Twenty-Three
Saturday 13th December, 1997

"Stop a moment," said Liz.

"Why?"

"Just stop." I pulled the car into a space outside a hairdresser's. Liz span around in her seat to look through the back window.

"What is it?" I asked, making no attempt to follow her gaze.

"Christmas trees," she said, getting out of the car. I bit my lip and considered the ramifications of driving off and leaving her in the December drizzle – then I too got out of the car.

"You already have a tree," I said, turning the collar up on my jacket.

"It's not for me – it's for you," said Liz, wrapping her arms around herself for warmth.

"But I don't want a tree," I said, for about the millionth time that month.

"Yes you do," said Liz. "Come on." She set off towards the small garden centre on the street corner. I counted to ten, then followed.

"Why do I need a tree if you already have one?" I asked as I caught her up.

"What if I want to spend time at your place in the next few weeks? It'd be like living with a scrooge!" said Liz. "Honestly, you are such a misery sometimes! I can't understand why you don't love Christmas. I do."

"It's just not my favourite time of year."

"Jason," said Liz as we reached the entrance, "aside from beer and female pop stars beginning with the letter K, you don't have a favourite anything." She strode into the garden centre and set about finding something large and green to fill up my lounge. I stood my ground, glancing at my feet to make sure I hadn't stepped over the threshold into the winter wonderland that was Leigh Garden Supplies.

"Jason! Come on," said Liz. "I'm not doing this on my own." There was no getting out of it. Not now. Not ever. I glanced at my feet again, then at Liz, and felt a little more of my soul shrivel and die as I stepped into her world.

"What about this one?" I said, grabbing the smallest tree within arm's reach. Liz turned, looked it up and down and wrinkled her nose.

"Too short," she said.

"This one then?"

"That's a twig!"

"Ok, well, this one."

"Jason," said Liz, "you're not taking this seriously. You can't pick a tree from the entrance. It's a well known fact that garden centres put all the trees they can't get rid of right by the entrance."

"You just made that up!" I said. "Why would they do that?"

"For people like you!" said Liz. I wasn't even sure what a person like me was any more. I'd spent the previous three years on auto pilot, waiting for each moment to pass, and hoping the next would be different somehow.

"Right. Well, I'll check over here then," I said – but Liz was too busy rummaging through foliage to hear me.

I fought my way further into the garden centre, past another couple engrossed in the pointless exercise of choosing between one near identical tree and another. It was such a big deal too. Like they were picking out their first child to bring into this world. Will this one grow up big and tall? Will this one cope with the number of presents around its trunk or the cat playing with its baubles? "What about two trees, darling? Twins – they could keep each other company?"

I made my way to the back, amongst the shelves of poinsettia. With a bit of luck, if I stayed out of sight for five minutes Liz would find something to her liking, and then the whole –

It took my head a moment to recognise her, but my guts knew instantly. They clenched, unclenched, and clenched again, like they were trying to send Morse code to the rest of my body. My throat tightened. My mouth dried. And my heart – why wasn't my heart doing anything? Shouldn't it at least beat? Then suddenly that's all I could hear. The deafening beat of my heart.

Instinctively I glanced over my shoulder to see where Liz was, before –

"Jason?" she said. "Jason! I can't believe it!" Her face brightened in recognition. She took a step forward and, without thinking, I took half a step back. Long expressive eyebrows furrowed over eyes filled with confusion. Stunning green eyes that I hadn't looked into in ten years. Not since that evening in London. Not since she'd disappeared into the rainy city streets, and out of my life.

"Mel," I said, louder than I'd intended, and like it was a statement of fact rather than a greeting.

"Hi," she said, her confused expression evaporating into that same warm smile that I'd basked in all those years earlier.

"Fancy meeting you here," I said. "I mean... What were the chances... How are you? I mean..." Oh, for the love of God!

"I'm fine," she said, "just fine. How are you?"

She'd changed. Of course she had. She seemed taller, somehow. A little more grown up. Her hair was much, much shorter – and a different colour, a deep claret red that only emphasised the greenness of her eyes, but she was still Melanie Jackson – and more beautiful than I ever remembered. All those years ago, sitting on Alex's bed, staring at Linda Lusardi on his wall and wondering whether Melanie would ever be that beautiful, and here she was, proving that Linda Lusardi had been a mere pit stop on the road to physical perfection, one that she'd long since passed.

"Me?" I said, realising there was still a question to be answered. "Oh, yeah, great. Yeah great. Really really great. Couldn't be better, in fact. Just great. Yeah... You? What about you? Tell me about you."

"I'm fine," said Melanie again.

"Fine! That's great. I'm really pleased. It's good to know that you're fine." I swallowed, hard. "So... are you..." I took a breath, "shopping for a... er, plant?"

"Just looking around. Killing time whilst I wait for someone," said Melanie.

"Yeah," I said. "Me too."

"Really?" she asked.

"Well. Sort of," I said, praying she wouldn't ask for more details. I looked over my shoulder again to see if I could locate my girlfriend.

"So do you live round here?" asked Melanie.

"Yeah," I answered. "Just round the corner. Ten minutes away. By foot. Quicker if you're, er, driving... You're not –" I croaked. "You're not local, are you?" My God, what if she were local?

"No," said Mel, letting a gloved hand play with the leaves of a poinsettia. "No, just visiting."

"Oh," I said, failing to conceal my disappointment. "Well, that's... nice."

"Yes," she said idly. I watched as she caressed the plant. I'd never wanted to be a poinsettia so much until that moment – and then suddenly I felt sick to the stomach, like I was struggling to hold down my lunch. Ten years! Ten years I'd spent waiting for this moment, the moment when I might get her back, and my life could continue. I hadn't realised it at the time, of course. I'd just stumbled through my twenties as I'd always done, letting my life take whatever path it wanted and kidding myself that I'd always intended it to turn out this way, but standing here now, surrounded by Christmas foliage, I knew I'd been waiting for 'the moment'. And now that it was finally here what was I doing? Making fucking small talk!

"Mel..." I started. She held my gaze, waiting for me to finish the sentence.

"Yes?" she asked.

I closed my mouth. This wasn't going to work. I couldn't just blurt out questions. Why did you leave me that night? Was I the only one who thought it was magical? Where have you been for the last decade? They were important questions, of course they were, but I needed to start small. A run up question, if there was such a thing. Something innocent. Easy to ask. Easier to answer. Something like:

"Would you like to get a coffee? Sometime?"

Mel looked at the ground. "Oh, Jason..." she said, shuffling her feet. My so-called small question wasn't small enough.

"Well. It was just an idea," I stammered. "If it, you know, it doesn't –"

"How about now?" interrupted Mel. "I'm not doing anything now."

"Now?" I said, flushing.

"Why not?" said Melanie, her shy smile growing into the grin that had held my heart captive that rainy January night.

"But I thought you were waiting for someone?"

"I am," said Melanie. "Well, was. But they can wait for me for a change."

"Oh. Ok. The thing is..."

"I think there's a pub just over there. How about I buy you a drink? I probably owe you one." She smiled some more.

"Well, that's a great idea, it's just that..." I said.

"You don't want to?" asked Melanie.

"Of course I do. It's just that right now..."

"There you are!" said Liz.

Melanie looked at Liz, then back at me. I opened my mouth to say something, but instead turned to Liz, who looked at Melanie, and back at me. I took a deep breath, looked at Melanie, and then back at Liz.

"Liz," I said, "this is Melanie, Mel, a, er... school friend." Melanie flashed me a look, then she turned to Liz, and smiled. "Mel, this is my… this is Liz, my, my..." But the words shrivelled up and died in my throat, and once again I found myself looking down at the ground, hoping that this time it really would open up and finish me off.

"Fiancée," said Liz.

My head snapped back upwards, and with wide eyes I stared at my liar of a girlfriend who was reaching forwards to shake Melanie's hand. "Lovely to meet you."

"Yes," said Melanie, taking the proffered hand and responding with her trade-mark smile. "You too." Liz forced the corners of her mouth upwards, but devoid of any warmth all she could achieve was a thinly disguised snarl.

"And congratulations," said Melanie, retrieving her hand. "When's the big day?"

My eyes flicked from the girl masquerading as my wife-to-be to the woman I'd happily give up half of everything for, and back again. This had to stop. Now.

"We're not–" I started.

"We're still discussing that, aren't we Jason?" said Liz, plunging her ringless hands into her pockets. "But I expect it'll be sometime soon. Next year probably. Wouldn't you say, darling?" Her eyes locked with mine. Defiant. Daring me to call her on the fabrication she'd so effortlessly conjured out of nowhere. I said nothing. Instead we all stood for a moment, in a triangle, taking it in turns to glance at each other or the ground, before Melanie finally said:

"Well, it was nice to bump into you again Jason. Take care."

"Yes," I said, "you too." Our eyes met one last time, hers full of questions, mine trying to convey my complete lack of control over the situation. And then she turned to Liz.

"Nice to have met you, Liz," she said, before she walked out of the garden centre. I watched, helpless, aware that Liz was staring at me, aware that a gigantic void had opened up within me into which whole galaxies could fall and be lost forever. But only when Melanie had disappeared from sight could I bring myself to look at the woman who'd finally slain my last hope of happiness.

"I've bought a tree," she said.

"Right," I said. Liz nodded slightly, and walked back into the main part of the garden centre.

I didn't follow her. I just stood there. Amongst the fir trees, the plant pots, and the wreckage of my life.

Chapter Twenty-Four
Saturday 15th May, 1999

Ria put her empty mug on the bedside table.

"And that was a year and a half ago? Just before Christmas?" she asked.

"Yes."

"So you broke up with Liz –"

"A few days later."

She nodded, and secured her towel tightly around her chest. "So why don't you go and find Melanie?" she asked. "What's to stop you?" I wanted to tell her to leave the towel – that despite my confession about Melanie my feelings for her hadn't changed. But that would have assumed that my feelings were important, and I realised now, more than ever before, that we were nothing more than photographer and model. "Well?" she prompted.

"I wouldn't know where to start," I said, "and besides..."

"What?"

"When I think about her now I'm not so sure that she wasn't just that thing you said a couple of weeks back."

"What thing?"

"You know – a catalyst? She made me realise how much of my life had passed me by – made me realise that so long as I stayed with Liz I would never have what I wanted, but," I let out a long, deep sigh and stared at my fingers, "if Melanie

Jackson was all that I wanted then I don't think I'd have spent the last eighteen months searching... for someone else. She kind of represents – a moment."

"So what is it that you do want, Jason Smith?" she asked. I felt my skin goose bump. The last time anyone had asked me that I'd been sitting on the floor outside their bedroom, talking through the door and telling them I didn't know. But as my eyes met hers I knew I'd never been more sure of anything in my entire life. I knew exactly what I wanted. Yet the words I so desperately needed to say were stuck in my throat.

"Ria," I said with a croak, "I need to tell you something."

"Ok."

"It's not working."

Ria blinked. "What do you mean?" she asked, her eyes watering slightly.

"I've checked every day. We're not selling any pictures. The facts are, we just haven't got enough... carrots. And I don't think we ever will. I love photographing you – it's the high point of my week – but I can't keep pretending that I'm doing it for financial reasons – because I honestly never did."

Ria said nothing. Just gazed at me with those breathtaking eyes of hers, her mouth slightly open, her lips plump and pink.

"Jason," she said eventually, "you really are a complete berk. It was never about the money – or about being a glamour model. It was always about you." I blinked.

"But..." I stuttered. "But what about your boyfriend? The rugby player."

"Who?"

"The guy waiting for you." Ria frowned. "At the dance class. The guy with the cold." For a moment Ria's expression didn't change, the frown etched onto her face, and then, like the sun coming out from behind a cloud, the smile, *that* smile, reappeared, developed into a full-on grin, and was quickly followed by a laugh. The sort of laugh that happens when things that didn't make any sense before suddenly fall into place.

"Oh Jason," she said, cocking her head on one side "that's my brother!"

"Brother?" I said. "Right." I didn't know what else to say.

"Come over here," said Ria.

"Why?" I asked.

"Just... come here."

I leaned forward slightly, and when I was within arm's reach she grabbed my t-shirt and pulled me closer.

And then she kissed me.

The problem with life, as someone I knew once observed, is that whilst it would be nice if it were one long 'romantic comedy' it just doesn't work like that. There are no credits that roll, or curtains that fall, nothing to let you know that you've arrived at the big Happy Ever After scene. If you're not paying attention you can miss it entirely.

I didn't think about this at the time because, if you haven't already figured it out, we were too busy making love to think about much more than each other – two bodies finding each other for the first time, after such a long time, lost in the here and now – and that's most definitely the way it should be. But later – much, much later – as Ria lay – naked – in my arms, I marvelled at the poetry of it all. How all the little moments in the previous eighteen months, both the accidental and the engineered, had led me to this moment – 'the moment'.

The moment when my life changed.
The moment when everything would get better.
And all because of her.

The End
(for now)

ACKNOWLEDGEMENTS

"Why don't you go and do some writing?" That's what my wife Kate had said to me. And when I returned half an hour or so later with a daft paragraph or two about how I always hoped Kylie Minogue might break down outside my flat, she roared with laughter and told me I'd just written an excellent first chapter. First chapter? I was just killing time.

Ten years later, and this is what that original scene evolved into. And during that decade so many people have come along and shared this journey that I really ought to start thanking people, or there's a significant risk you might think I did it all by myself.

So in no particular order I'd really like to thank:

Peta Nightingale – for taking a chance on me (and Jason), and for all your advice, work, and wisdom. Here's to the next book and a long and fruitful partnership.

Jules – for your endless wisdom, friendship, removing all the 'poncy' bits (though you missed this), and making the really important stuff in my life 'happen'. I couldn't have done this without you.

Della – for your love, support, feedback, and advice. For reading this book, several times – usually when you should have been doing something else.

My dear friend Wendy – for your endless passion and encouragement.

Lucy Luck, Juliet Mushens, Becky Bagnell, and also Robert Grant, for your sometimes brutal - but totally invaluable - honesty.

Alison the 'proof fairy' for beating my words into shape.

Pat Rutland for inadvertently sending me to Alison and for all your support and nagging (in equal measure).

Connor McGurl – for your invaluable Star Wars knowledge, but also your mum Kath McGurl for giving you your moment to shine.

All my Facebook & Twitter pals & followers for helping spread the word and your 'office banter'.

And to you, dear reader, for taking a chance on this book and reading this far. Drop me a line so I can tell you how incredibly awesome you are!

Thank you all.

NEED A *REAL* *GUIDE* TO
GETTING THE GIRL (OR GUY)?

Like most things in life, dating isn't quite as straightforward as it would first appear. After many, many years of making every dating mistake there is to make, Peter Jones finally cracked it.

There's love in his life.

And it wasn't an accident.

If you've ever found dating a challenge, if you've found dating websites to be less than fulfilling, if the thought of a 'first date' terrifies you... here are two books that will guide you through the potential pit falls, help you avoid the liars and lotharios, and show you how to meet and date people you actually like the look of.

How To Start Dating And Stop Waiting

Includes:

- The Nine Golden Rules of Dating – break them at your peril!
- Flash Bang Wallop What a Picture – why it might be vitally important to borrow your friend's dog.
- First Contact – what to say in your opening message... and what to do when they reply!
- Forget 'First Dates'! Finally there's a smarter, easier, stress-free way to meet someone for the first time

From Invisible To Irresistible

Includes:

- Changing Your Mind - How you can think yourself more attractive.
- Changing Your Image - Why it might be a good idea to cut off your hair (or grow it back).
- Changing Your Environment - Why it's vitally important to have the right sofa.

Both books are available, now,
from all good bookstores. Visit
howtostartdatingandstopwaiting.com
for more details

46536487R00206

Made in the USA
Charleston, SC
21 September 2015